THE
DEVOURING
GRAY

to point nor
"Like a
"The very

mount to
plore, to
Mateo

CHRISTINE LYNN HERMAN

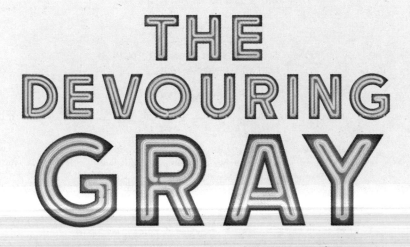

THE DEVOURING GRAY

TITAN BOOKS

THE DEVOURING GRAY
Print edition ISBN: 9781789090253
E-book edition ISBN: 9781789090260

Published by Titan Books
A division of Titan Publishing Group Ltd
144 Southwark Street, London SE1 0UP
www.titanbooks.com

First edition: April 2019

10 9 8 7 6 5 4 3 2

Names, places and incidents are either products of the author's imagination
or used fictitiously. Any resemblance to actual persons, living or dead
(except for satirical purposes), is entirely coincidental.

A CIP catalogue record for this title is available from the British Library.

Typeset in Bembo by Palimpsest Book Production Ltd, Falkirk, Stirlingshire.

Printed and bound by CPI Group (UK) Ltd, Croydon, CR0 4YY.

For my siblings:

Joanna, who helped me find Violet's voice
Louis, who made me cut every scene I didn't love
and Andrea, who read all the books
that came before this one—

Thank you for teaching me how to tell stories.

PART ONE

THE FIVE
OF BONES

ONE

AFTER THEY FOUND THE third body that year, Justin Hawthorne knelt in his backyard and prepared to hear his future.

His sister, May, dealt the Deck of Omens facedown on the grass between them. The all-seeing eyes on the backs of the five cards stared emptily at the canopy of leaves above. Justin's skin prickled as he studied their irises—white like the eyes of the dead.

He hadn't seen the latest body, but the remains of the corpses spat out by the Gray always looked the same. Eyes bleached the color of milk. The rib cage inverted, bones slicing through bloated skin like antlers rising from the body's back.

"I don't have to ask the cards." May's voice didn't lend itself well to gentleness, but she was trying. Justin hadn't asked for a reading since he failed his ritual. She knew how much it had cost him to ask now.

Because it should've been him commanding the Deck

of Omens. Him wielding his family's abilities and protecting their town.

Yet he was helpless. A rotten branch on a healthy tree.

The Gray had grown bolder this year, luring victim after victim into its world, where the Beast hungrily awaited its prey. Justin had believed, foolishly, that he would be able to stop it when he came into his powers.

But he had no powers. And now another man was dead.

Justin wouldn't sit idly by as others died. Powers or not, he was still a Hawthorne. He would find a way to keep Four Paths safe.

His fate lay in the cards.

"Show me," he said, gripping May's hands.

May shut her eyes. A moment later, he felt her familiar presence in his mind—sharp, clear tendrils of intention snaking through his thoughts. He knew May was feeling more than seeing, letting his past and present inform the patterns she could predict in his future.

She pulled away after a few seconds, exhaling softly, her eyes fluttering open.

"They're ready," she said hoarsely, turning the cards over so the all-seeing eyes gazed at ground instead of sky. Justin had barely glanced at the individual cards when his sister hissed with displeasure.

"What...?" A slice of fragmented sunlight turned the glass medallion around May's neck from dull red to flaming crimson as she leaned forward, like a wound opening across her pale throat.

May had read his future dozens of times over the years, for fun, for practice. He had never seen her look so shaken.

His gaze darted to the spread of cards between them. The Eight of Branches was centered, of course. Justin's card, painted with the familiar art of a young boy perched on a tree stump, a bundle of sticks in his arms. He hadn't noticed until he was older that there were roots wrapped around the boy's legs, tethering him to his seat.

It only took him a second to understand May's distress. Her card, the Seven of Branches, always sat at his left. But this time, it wasn't in the reading at all. Instead, a card he'd never seen before was nestled beside his. The art was sharp and vivid: a figure standing in the Gray, ringed by trees. Its right hand was shrouded in shadow.

Its left hand had been stripped down to the skeleton.

The "Founders' Lullaby" rang through Justin's mind. *Branches and stones, daggers and—*

"Bones," May said flatly, pressing the edge of her polished fingernail against the wood. Her hand was trembling. "It shouldn't—I must've…" But she trailed off. Even a panicked May would never admit that her mastery of the Deck of Omens was lacking.

"We both know you don't make mistakes." Justin couldn't tear his eyes from the card. "So tell me what it means."

"Fine." May snatched her fingers away. "You'll find a way to help the town. But the process is muddled. Here you've got the Knotted Root, a series of choices with no good outcomes. Pair that with the Shield and it looks like you'll be trying to mediate, as usual. Probably the Three of Daggers's fault, because Isaac is always screwing up somehow—"

"You can't pretend it's not there." The card between them almost seemed to glow, even in the shade. Flesh and bone entwined, a braided line between the living and the dead. "May. Tell me."

May bundled the cards together with a single practiced flick of her wrists. She shuffled them into the rest of the deck as she gazed over Justin's shoulder. Her light blue eyes were still locked on the trees behind him when she spoke again.

"It's the Saunders family." May rose to her feet. "They're coming back, and I'm telling Mom, and you're not telling anyone. Not even Isaac."

"Wait!" Justin scrambled after her, but May was fast when she wanted to be. Her fingers were already wrapped around the handle of the back door. "What does any of this have to do with me helping Four Paths?"

May's pink headband was askew. For his sister, that was disheveled, but she didn't even seem to notice. "I'm not completely sure I understand," she said. "But you'll have a chance to make a real change in Four Paths once they're here."

This time, Justin let her go.

He stayed in the courtyard for a long while, staring at the hawthorn tree that rose behind him, its gnarled branches stretching across the gabled roofs of his family home like grasping fingers.

For the first time in his life, there would be a real member of every founding family in Four Paths.

He would be a part of that. He would have a chance to change things, to help.

Justin believed this. He had to.

The Deck of Omens had told him so, and unlike the Hawthornes who used it, the Deck of Omens couldn't lie.

TWO WEEKS LATER

It was a single strand of turquoise hair that made Violet Saunders come undone. She was fiddling with her sheet music binder when she caught sight of it, sprouting like a seedling from the space between her seat and the cup holder.

Violet's hands froze on the binder, clammy sweat collecting on the navy-blue plastic. She couldn't concentrate on the highway rolling past the Porsche's windows, or her fingerings for Schumann's Abegg Variations, op. 1. Her enthusiasm for the piano piece was gone.

One by one, her fingers unpeeled themselves from the binder's edge. Her left hand was creeping toward the hair like a pale, veiny tarantula when her mother silenced her Bluetooth headset.

"You okay?" she asked Violet. "You look queasy."

Violet jerked back her hand. She cranked down the Schumann blasting through her earbuds, trying to hide her surprise—it was the first time her mother had spoken to her in over an hour. "I'm just a little carsick."

Juniper Saunders considered this, tilting her head. The headset on her ear blinked, casting blue light onto her cartilage-piercing scars. They were the last lingering reminder of a version of Violet's mother that was long extinct. "Let me know if you need to vomit," she said. "I'll pull over."

Being the target of Juniper's concern made Violet's stomach clench. Her mother hadn't said a thing when Violet quit her piano lessons. But then, she'd barely seemed to notice when Violet painted her bedroom dark red the morning of an open house, either; or after the funeral, when she'd hacked off every bit of hair below her collarbones in a sloppy bob. Yet somehow, Juniper had noticed her distress in the middle of a conference call.

It made no sense, but then, Violet's mother had never made any sense to her at all.

"It's not that bad." Violet raked a nail across the edge of the binder. "The carsickness situation, I mean. I am decidedly pre-puke."

Juniper's headset blinked again. "Do you mind if I get back to this conference call, then? The London office is having a meltdown, and they need me to talk the developers down before things go nuclear."

"Of course," said Violet. "I can't be responsible for that kind of damage."

"I suggest curbing the attitude once we get to Four Paths."

Violet slid the volume up until Schumann blasted through her earbuds again. She knew every phrase, every pause, every fingering—the recording was her playing, after all. "I guess that means I'll have to get it all out in the car."

Juniper rolled her eyes and started talking again, something about a bug in the software her company was developing. Violet tuned her out and sank down in her seat.

Four Paths. The place her mother had grown up, not that she ever talked about it. Juniper never talked about anything—why she'd been so insistent Violet and her sister have her last name, not their father's; why she'd left town after high school and never come back. Not even when her parents died. Not even when her sister, an aunt Violet had never met, started to get sick.

The thought of sisters made Violet sink farther. There was no way they'd be driving back to Four Paths right now if her family hadn't had a nuclear meltdown of its own.

A giant cargo truck roared up on the right side of the Porsche. Violet's heartbeat rammed against the back of her throat as the truck's massive container blocked her field of vision. She'd been out on the road countless times in the five months since Rosie's accident, but trucks like this one still left a cocktail of nausea and fury brewing in her stomach.

She forced her gaze away from the offending vehicle, but then, of course, the hair was still there. Mocking her. Violet stopped her practice recording, put the music binder on her lap, and snatched the strand of turquoise out of its hiding spot.

It was heavier than Violet had expected. As she lifted the hair up, she realized this was because it had been tangled up with the clasp of a thin silver bracelet, which had been wedged between the cup holder and the edge of the car seat. Violet's fingers moved over the filigree rose attached to the bracelet as Juniper continued barking orders into her headset.

The funny thing about grief was that once Violet got past the first few weeks, where she relearned how to sleep and eat and breathe, it was almost harder to function. There were protocols for handling funeral arrangements and overly caring neighbors and therapy. But nothing in all the empty platitudes and well-meaning advice told her what to do when you found your dead sister's jewelry in a car, months after the rest of her things had been boxed away.

It wasn't even a piece of jewelry Rosie had liked. In fact, Violet had a distinct memory of the way her sister's lip had curled when she'd opened up the box at her sixteenth birthday party. It was a gift from a great-aunt on her father's side of the family who hadn't seen Rosie and Violet since they were little, who only had a cursory understanding of what teenagers were and how they functioned.

"A rose? Really?" Rosie had said later, when they were in her room, examining the heap of clothes and odd art projects Rosie had received from her friends. "How basic. I mean, I'll wear it to be polite, but it's like one of those necklaces girls wear that have their names on them. Like a dog tag."

Violet agreed with her like she always did, deriding the gift, but she remembered thinking at the time that even though the bracelet wasn't really Rosie's style, at least their great-aunt had tried to connect to them. Juniper hadn't kept in contact with any of their dad's family after he died, and Violet relished every clue about them she could get.

Now she stared at the filigree rose, slightly tarnished from its time in cup holder purgatory.

Oh, what the hell. Violet opened the clasp and tucked the hair into her binder. Then she fastened the bracelet around her wrist, turning the rose until it covered the purple veins that threaded up toward her palm.

It was a cheesy thing to do. Rosie probably would've hated it. But as they turned off the highway, Violet felt a little less alone.

The Porsche turned onto a series of increasingly empty side roads, the landscape changing from the busy highway to well-tended farmlands. The farms bled into foliage, and soon the car was surrounded by trees crowding together at the edge of the asphalt, their branches backlit by the early afternoon sunlight. Violet stared out the windshield at a landscape swathed in deep, green-tinted shadows as the music in her ears switched from Schumann to Bach to Chopin.

Something in the trees drew Violet's attention. The definition of the trunks, the vibrancy of the leaves, pulled her focus so thoroughly away from the road and the sky that the branches might as well have been waving in front of the Porsche.

Finally, they turned off onto a winding, badly paved pathway. A sign dangled from an overhanging branch on rusted chains, welcoming them to Four Paths, New York, in scorched black letters.

"They've still got the sign." A half chuckle escaped Juniper's lips. "You'd think they would've replaced it with something a little more professional by now."

Violet tugged her ear buds out. "This has been here since you were in high school?"

"It's been here for as long as I can remember."

This was the first piece of information Juniper had ever voluntarily offered about Four Paths. Violet's throat swelled with a lifetime of unanswered questions as the Porsche rambled past a series of worn-down houses. Reddish-brown bells hung beside every front door, sometimes one or two, sometimes close to a dozen. The wind tossed the bells back and forth, but Violet heard no sound, even when she rolled down her window.

She peered at them, trying to get a closer look, but the car moved on into what had to be the main part of town, if only because the ramshackle houses had turned into ramshackle buildings.

There was no such thing as a chain store here, only a small collection of shops ripped out of a black-and-white photograph. Violet identified the building on the corner as a general store from the peeling gold letters emblazoned across its front. There was a secondhand clothing shop, a dive bar, a grocery store, a public library with a sloping gabled roof. People loitered in front of a fifties-style diner, tossing cigarette butts onto the pavement. Their heads snapped to attention as the Porsche rolled past them.

Although they'd only left Westchester County five hours ago, Violet felt as if she had been beamed onto an alien planet.

Juniper pointed out the town hall, which was gorgeous and imposing and utterly out of place among its shabbier brethren. The forest spread out wide behind it; stray branches snaked across either side of the roof, reaching for one another. Back in Ossining, Violet's hometown, every tree had felt like an interloper, sprouting stubbornly from loose gravel or growing in fenced-in little boxes on the street. But here, it was the buildings that didn't belong; they merely interrupted the woods.

The only place the trees were absent was a small field behind the town hall. A lone building stood between the meadow and the trees, some distance back from the main road. There was a symbol she didn't recognize on the door: a circle with four lines extending through it, not quite touching in the center, like a target.

"Is that a church?" asked Violet, examining the way the scalloped marble embedded into the front of the building arched up into a point at the top.

Juniper shook her head. "Four Paths doesn't have churches. It's a mausoleum. Around here, everyone is cremated and buried underground. This serves as a memorial for everyone."

"Creepy," Violet muttered.

Juniper shrugged. "It's efficient."

But Violet couldn't shake her unease at the thought of a town with no church and no graveyard.

After the field, there was another small street of stores; then Main Street receded to houses once more.

"Wait." Violet turned around to stare. The town hall disappeared behind a waving branch. "That's it?"

"That's it."

They were in the thick of the woods now, the car barreling through a tunnel of greenery. Violet tried to take a picture on her phone, but the branches kept coming out blurry.

The Porsche broke through the line of trees. Violet squinted against the sudden assault of sunlight streaming through the windshield. She was still blinking away dark spots when the building before them came into view.

"This is our house?" she asked, and maybe her mother said something, and maybe she didn't. Violet was too focused on the house to care.

It looked the way things do in dreams, ragged and unpredictable and slightly askew. Walls of reddish-brown stone rose above the trees before dividing into three spires, each adorned with a point of corroding iron.

Violet wasn't even sure if the car was parked as she grasped for the door handle and tumbled out onto the driveway. There had been a garden surrounding the house once, but it was hopelessly overgrown now. Violet reached the end of the driveway and clambered up the moss-encrusted stairs to the front porch.

"I'm amazed the place is still standing," said Juniper. "It's structurally unsound, you know."

"It's perfect." Violet stared at the honest-to-goodness brass knocker hanging on the door. Her wonder abated as she considered how much Rosie would've loved this place. It was exactly the kind of house they'd dreamed of moving into. A creaky old manor where Rosie would paint murals on the walls and Violet would play piano all day, and the neighborhood kids would think they were witches. Violet tried to shake those thoughts away as she thumped the knocker against the door. But they stayed anyway, like the grief always did, like a thin film across her skin that left her cocooned in her own body.

The door swung open, revealing a white woman at least a head shorter than Violet, with frizzy hair and a dress knitted from crimson yarn. In her face Violet saw a funhouse-mirror version of her mother; a Juniper who let her gray streaks grow out, who would rather go barefoot than wear heels.

"Daria," said Juniper. "It's us."

The woman—Aunt Daria—tilted her head. "Solicitors don't get inside privileges."

She slammed the door shut with an impressive amount of vigor for someone so small. Violet jolted back from the knocker, startled. When her mother told her Daria was sick, she'd pictured someone bedridden and frail. Not this.

"Daria!" Juniper yanked on the doorknob, to no avail. "This isn't funny. Open up!"

"Is she all right?" said Violet softly, staring at a bit of red yarn stuck in the door hinges. There had been no spark of recognition in Daria's eyes. Not even for her own sister.

Juniper turned, her hand still clenched around the doorknob. A bit of hair had sprung free from her bun and frizzed across her forehead.

"No, she's not." Her voice was sharp, coiled. "She has early-onset dementia. The doctors wanted to put her in a home. That's why we're here."

The silver rose pressed on Violet's wrist, cool and heavy against her rising pulse. "You didn't think to explain that before we got here?"

Juniper frowned. "I told you she was sick."

The vague puzzlement on her mother's face was the same expression she'd worn at Rosie's funeral. Juniper had handled the entire thing with careful, practiced ease; she'd even picked the coffin out on her lunch break at work, where she had neglected to take a single day off. Her mother sat through the services, her face slack with polite disinterest that didn't go away even when they were standing beside the grave. Violet had fought the urge to push her into the ground along with the coffin, but ultimately, common sense had won. Besides, Rosie deserved better company.

As Violet stared at her now, she saw that trying to make Juniper realize she was hurt would be a waste of time. If Rosie's death five months ago couldn't make her pay attention to the daughter she had left, nothing ever would.

"Unbelievable," Juniper muttered. She'd already moved her focus away from Violet, her heels clicking as she paced from pillar to pillar. "We came all this way... can't just make us sit out here..."

"Can too!" called a hoarse voice, slightly muffled behind one of the house's side windows.

Violet leaned off the edge of the porch. Daria's wrinkled face was pressed against the glass. Which gave her an idea.

She was down the rotting steps in seconds, the slight heels on her boots sinking into the grass as she stomped through the garden.

"What are you doing?" Juniper called after her.

Violet ignored her mother and hurried to the backyard, where the grass sloped down into a tree-lined hill. From this vantage point, the topmost spire of the house impaled the sinking sun on its iron point.

The back door was much less ostentatious than the front. Violet wondered if it had been some kind of servants' entrance. Although the doorknob didn't give when she turned it, the dirty windowpane was already spiderwebbed with cracks. Violet gazed back out at the yard, considering it for a moment.

She'd only seen it for the first time minutes ago, yet she couldn't deny that she felt a strange sort of kinship with the place.

Her whole life, it had only been her and Rosie and Juniper, her father a hazy half memory, pieced together from a few short anecdotes and precious pictures, the Saunders family nothing but a mystery.

This house was proof that there was more to her family than that.

Violet tore her eyes from the trees and checked the most common hiding places she could think of, until she unearthed a spare key under a planter full of dead flowers.

The key was rusted and filthy, but it fit the lock. A few seconds later, she was striding through the ground floor of her new home. It was a musty place, full of dark, echoing rooms that looked virtually unused. A row of taxidermies lined the walls of the main hallway. Violet shuddered as her hand accidentally brushed against a passel of mounted birds.

She caught sight of crinkled red yarn and frizzy hair sticking out from behind a couch in what was probably the living room. Violet sighed and walked on until she reached the sun-drenched foyer.

When she swung the front door open, her mother was leaning against the porch railing, scowling.

"Thank god." Juniper hurried inside. "I swear, this place has always hated me."

Violet trailed after Juniper, stopping when her mother paused at the half-open door to the living room. Daria was visible now, her knees drawn up to her chest, the dress spilling across her front like a woolly bloodstain. Her hands were embedded in her wiry hair. Saunders hair—Violet had heard her mother call it that multiple times, always sounding annoyed, like their distant Scottish ancestors were to blame for all their problems.

Juniper placed a hand on Violet's shoulder. Violet

stiffened—she couldn't remember the last time her mother had touched her. Even before Rosie's accident, there had always been several inches of deliberate space between them. "I'll handle my sister. You can start unloading the U-Haul."

There was something soft in her mother's voice, almost apologetic. It was worse than polite disinterest, the same way her talking to Violet in the car was worse than ignoring her. Because it meant Juniper could care about her if she wanted to.

Violet shrugged out of her mother's grip. "Fine."

She pretended to walk to the front door but turned back after a few paces, watching her mother kneel beside Daria. Indistinct words echoed through the foyer. Although Violet couldn't make them out, she heard the underlying notes of rage and regret.

Daria braced her hand against Juniper's shoulder—to support herself or push her sister away, Violet didn't know. They rose together, a four-legged beast backlit by the sun streaming through the picture windows. Their figures blurred into shadowed, indistinct silhouettes, and, as Violet squinted into the hazy light, she could've sworn she saw a flash of turquoise hair behind their heads.

TWO

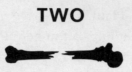

R IGHT WHEN JUSTIN'S HEART was about to impale itself on his rib cage, he heard three sharp blasts of sound from the side of the track.

"That's enough!" Coach Lowell barked, lowering his whistle.

Justin sagged with relief as his pace slowed from a sprint into a steady jog. He normally looked forward to practice, but preseason conditioning had melted him into an exhausted, sweaty puddle on the track behind Four Paths High School. The rest of the cross-country team straggled behind him, panting and swearing softly as they staggered into a cool-down lap. Next week, he'd start his senior year of high school—his last year with this team.

"Time?" he called out, doubling back, slowing from a jog to a walk. Trees crowded at the edge of the athletic field, their roots rippling like veins beneath the puckering asphalt. Kids often wiped out on that section of the track during meets, but they were never locals.

Justin had grown up in those woods. But now, having those tree trunks so close to him, those branches crowding above his head, he felt a spark of unease kindle in his chest.

He couldn't shake the feeling they were reaching for him.

Coach Lowell frowned down at the stopwatch in his meaty hand. "Hawthorne," he said brusquely. "Come here."

Four Paths High School was too small and underfunded for a real athletics program, but the cross-country team went to meets, and sometimes they even won races. Mostly Justin was the one winning races. But judging from the scowl on Coach Lowell's face, he didn't think he was being summoned for a congratulations.

"Look at this." Coach Lowell thrust the time sheet in Justin's face. Justin gaped at the time beside his name.

He hadn't run a lap that slowly since freshman year—hell, he hadn't run a lap that slowly since middle school.

"What's going on?" asked Coach Lowell sharply. His dark brown face was furrowed with annoyance. "Gonzales almost had you on the third leg there."

Justin bristled. "I could lap Cal Gonzales in my sleep."

"The team looks to you to set an example, Hawthorne. If you're not focused, they're not focused."

Justin dug the toe of his sneaker into the fading asphalt. Coach was right. He was off.

It just seemed so petty to be concerned about his running performance when a man was dead. He couldn't stop wondering how this latest death, this latest man, had felt in the moments before the Gray swallowed him whole.

The man had a name. Hap Whitley. The obituary said he'd worked with his father at the auto repair shop. Justin had spent fifteen minutes studying the picture they'd pulled for the *Four Paths Gazette*: the backward baseball cap pulled low over loose curls, the slight squint, the shy grin.

It had been two weeks, and he still couldn't stop picturing what the man in that photo must've looked like, before they'd had him cremated and tucked away in the mausoleum.

The Saunders family had arrived today, just as his sister had predicted. Half the town had seen their shiny car on its way to the Saunders manor's driveway. Justin had been expecting this. But he hadn't been expecting his mother to call Justin and May into her office and order them to keep their distance from the new founders.

"They don't know how this town works," she'd said. "They're most likely a dead branch of the bloodline. Don't burden them with their heritage."

Although Augusta Hawthorne had been talking to both of them, her eyes had stayed fixed on Justin throughout the conversation. He thought about the thin wooden card lying between him and May, the entwined fingers of flesh and bone, the smell of mushrooms rotting beneath the hawthorn tree.

So yes, he'd been distracted. But it had been his mistake to show it to Coach Lowell.

Justin had no powers, but he had a knack for putting people at ease. He mirrored Coach Lowell's slouchy posture, the arm that swung idly at his side.

"It won't happen again." Justin gave each word

22

conviction, let them ring across the track.

Coach Lowell relaxed almost immediately. He trusted Justin, or at least, he trusted the Hawthornes.

"I know it won't." He clapped Justin on the shoulder, gave him an easy smile. "Just want to make sure you're ready for Long Lake. Scouts will be there—and even local schools give scholarships."

Scouts. College scouts.

Justin nodded weakly, pretending that his thumping heart, his uneven breaths, were just a side effect of track practice. The rest of the team wove around him as they walked toward the locker rooms, talking animatedly among themselves about the start of cross-country season.

He knew all of them, of course, from school and parties and practice. But it didn't matter that he and Cal had been racing each other since they were kids, or that he'd dated Seo-Jin Park and Britta Morey and Marissa Czechowicz. There was an acute distance between them. When Justin was younger, he'd relished the way they treated him. Their exaggerated laughter at his jokes, the stares, all were part of the respect his family commanded. It was a mark of how much good they'd done.

But since the first body had been found that year, the stares had turned from friendly to expectant. The Gray claimed a new victim every few years in Four Paths, usually around the equinox, but never this many in such a short period of time. And Justin was slowly realizing there were consequences to being one of the people Four Paths looked to at the first sign of trouble.

Especially when there was nothing he could do about it. His mother had kept his lack of powers a secret for almost a year, but it wouldn't last forever. The truth would come out eventually, and when it did, the town's respect would turn to disgust.

Which was why his mother had cornered him after dinner a few weeks ago and handed him a packet full of athletic scholarship applications.

At first, Justin hadn't understood what she was proposing. Only one branch of a founding family could inherit powers at a time, so when the founder children who'd completed their rituals graduated from high school, they didn't leave. Especially now, with the town on edge, with the remaining founders dwindling. Online courses and community college were a small price to pay for keeping the town safe.

But the Hawthornes weren't just any founder family. They were the ones in charge. His mother had explained that day that Four Paths had to see them as the perfect leaders. And Justin's lack of powers could ruin their reputation.

Augusta Hawthorne had told him to leave Four Paths before the town could learn the truth. She would pay his college tuition to a state school—if he promised to never come back.

He hadn't decided whether or not he would listen.

Maybe the future May had seen would let him stay.

Maybe he was just deluding himself.

Justin usually went home after practice, but he'd agreed to take a dishwashing shift at the Diner. Augusta

Hawthorne's position as the sheriff meant Justin didn't strictly need to work. But Four Paths noticed when he did, and he had done his best to build a reputation as the founding family member who was committed to serving people, not just protecting them.

The sun sank toward the trees as he pulled into the deserted lot behind the Diner. He slung his staff apron over his shoulder and left the truck behind, waving hello to the pair of cops chain-smoking outside the restaurant.

"Your mother have you on patrol tonight?" Officer Anders asked him.

Justin shook his head. "Tomorrow."

"Ah. Keep an eye out. Three this year is too many—we don't want four." The officer's free hand closed lovingly over the holster at his waist, as if that would protect him. The forest rose behind the Diner, oak trees dwarfing the building beneath them.

A gun would do you no good if you slipped into the Gray, but half his mother's staff carried them anyway. They were security blankets for people without founder blood, just like the stone pendants around their necks and the sentinels above their doorways.

"I'll be careful," Justin said, although he could've done his patrol routes drunk and naked if he wanted to. Augusta Hawthorne hadn't let him near any real danger since he'd failed his ritual. Nowadays, he only patrolled to keep up appearances.

Justin's medallion dug into his wrist—a disc of crimson glass, a symbol that was supposed to signify that, since he'd come into his powers, he didn't need the protection of the stone pendants the rest of the town wore. His medallion was a lie, but he wore it for Officer Anders, for everyone else who believed he was still a real founder. Justin said goodbye and walked into the Diner, fighting back shame.

Everything in the restaurant always looked like it was about to break. A barely functional jukebox sagged against the wall, piping out a faint, warped recording of a Beach Boys song. Bits of yellow foam oozed from the plushy blue booths, flickering in the sickly glow of the fluorescent light. Justin ran a hand across one of the tables as he passed, tables that would never look clean no matter how many times someone wiped them down.

"Oh, good." Isaac Sullivan was reading behind the cash register. "You can take over during the dinner rush."

The best word Justin had for how Isaac presented himself was *deliberate*. His half-shaved head and dark, tumbling curls. The flannel shirt buttoned tightly around his throat. The twin medallions tied around his wrists that gleamed red against his pale skin—the one he'd earned, and the one he'd taken from his brother.

"Everyone will watch us founder kids no matter what," he'd say. "Might as well give them something interesting to stare at."

It was part of why they were best friends. Isaac understood how it felt to constantly be seen.

Justin tied his apron around his neck. "I'm not working the counter. I'm on dish duty."

"I'll take dish duty," said Isaac, snatching up his book and backing away from the counter. "You handle the customers."

Although they'd been working at the Diner for months now, Justin couldn't resist a snicker as the message on Isaac's apron came into view.

Welcome to the Diner! read the curlicue script. *I'm your friendly server. There's nothing I won't do to make a customer satisfied!*

"Really?" said Isaac. "You're wearing an apron, too."

"Yeah, but it pisses you off more."

Isaac's jaw twitched. Justin had learned years ago what the hard-edged expression on his face meant: trouble.

"Not anymore," he said, touching his fingertips to the front of the apron. The air in front of the embroidery blurred and shimmered as the stitches singed themselves beyond repair, leaving behind a blackened, ashy hole.

Justin cursed himself silently. Baiting Isaac was a foolish move—especially at work.

Isaac had gotten the job at the Diner after an incident at the grocery store led to an impressive amount of property damage. Everyone in town knew it was only his founder kid status and the Hawthornes' influence that kept him there. Even the book in Isaac's hand would've made a better waiter than he did.

"Oh, you're here. We need you out back before the dinner rush starts." Pete Burnham strode out from the kitchen doors. His family owned the restaurant, but he was the only one who actually kept it running. Then Pete caught sight of Isaac's apron. "Not again," he said, sliding a hand across his bald head. "You know Ma Burnham embroiders those aprons by hand?"

27

Isaac looked decidedly unimpressed by this revelation. "So buy her a sewing machine. Or tell her to get a better hobby."

"Don't disrespect Ma."

"You've got a weird thing about your ma. Has anyone ever told you that?"

"I don't have to take this from you, Sullivan."

The air around Isaac started to churn and shimmer, like a heat wave rising over asphalt. Across the Diner, Pete stepped back, toward the kitchen doors.

Justin readied himself to intervene. Isaac usually listened to reason, or at least he did when the reasoning came from him. But before he could speak, the door to the restaurant creaked open, revealing a white girl Justin had never seen before.

She was all sharp angles and knobby limbs, dark eyes and shoulder-length hair that shone jet-black. The rips in her high-waisted jeans showed off half her thighs.

There was something almost feral about the way she was assessing the Diner. It made him uneasy. She barely spared a glance toward Isaac's apron or Pete's obvious distress as she marched up to the counter.

"I assume one of you works here?" she said in their general direction.

Pete sprang into action, jumping behind the counter and shooting her his best customer-service grin. "Pete Burnham," he said. "Manager of this fine establishment."

"Lovely," said the girl. She was one of the Saunderses. She had to be. New people didn't just show up in Four

Paths without a reason. "Then you can tell me if the Diner does takeout."

Pete nodded wildly, like a bobblehead. "Of course," he said. "You made an excellent choice. We've got the best food in town."

"You don't have much competition," the girl noted dryly.

"Yes, well," said Pete. "Quality over quantity."

She ordered off the menu behind the counter, which Justin had never actually seen anyone look at before. Pete bolted into the kitchen—probably happy to get away from Isaac—promising to stand over the chef until the food was done.

The girl stayed by the cash register, tapping her fingernails absently against the glass. Her collarbones protruded sharply beneath the straps of her tank top. A tangle of crystals hung around her neck, glimmering dully in the fluorescent lighting.

If this girl was a Saunders, she could be the person on the card.

Talking to her could be the first step in preventing the next death.

Justin remembered his mother's orders to keep his distance. But no crimson founders' medallion was tangled in her necklaces or tied at her wrist. If Augusta got on his case about talking to her, he could just say it had been an honest mistake—he hadn't known who she was.

He glanced over at Isaac, who had slid into the nearest booth and opened his book. Isaac scanned the pages with an intensity that, while fake, indicated his complete lack of interest in the current situation. Which was strange, considering Four Paths hadn't had a single newcomer since they were in second grade.

But it meant Justin was on his own, at least as far as talking to strangers was concerned.

"I'm Justin Hawthorne," he said to her, trying to echo her snappy tone. The words sounded strange and forced coming out of his mouth, but he smiled anyway.

"Violet Saunders," she said reluctantly, after enough time had gone by for her to realize he was, in fact, talking to her. "Are you about to extol the wonders of the cuisine here, too?"

"Pete runs the place," said Justin, who wasn't quite sure what *extol* meant. "He has to say that."

"So you're saying the food here isn't actually good?"

"No! No, the food's fine."

"Well, there's something on the menu called a garbage plate," said Violet. "So that doesn't exactly inspire confidence."

"It's an upstate thing!" said Justin, flustered. "It's fine."

"Fine, or good? There's a difference."

Justin frowned, unsure what he was supposed to say. Isaac smirked behind his book.

"Good, I guess." It was the truth, although it was also true that if the Burnhams thought he was insulting the Diner, they'd take him out to the parking lot and slug him, Hawthorne or not. And Justin liked his nose better when it wasn't broken. "You're new here, right?"

It was a basic thing to say. But he didn't know what to tell her. She'd displayed no sign of recognizing his last name, so she definitely didn't know about the founders. Which meant his mother had been right, and he had no idea how she was supposed to help him if she knew nothing about the Gray, or her family's powers.

"Is this town really small enough that you can tell instantly?" Violet moved her hand away from the counter. "Or do I just look like I don't belong here?"

Her arms shuttered across her tank top. That simple gesture, the way her body caved inward, made him think of Harper Carlisle.

Thoughts of Harper were always followed by guilt. Justin shoved her image back down into the recesses of his brain, but it was too late to stem the shame that rose in his throat.

"Are you just going to stare?" Violet said sharply.

Justin realized with a stab of horror that his easy smile was gone. Harper did that to him—made him forget how to be a Hawthorne. Made him slip.

"I wasn't—" he started, but Pete emerged from the kitchen, holding a giant paper bag.

"Here you are," he said.

"Thank you." Violet grabbed the bag of food and paid faster than Justin had thought possible. She started toward the exit, then paused. Justin felt a brief flash of hope, but her eyes darted over to Isaac instead, who had arranged his book very carefully over his face. "You won't like the way that ends."

The Beach Boys warbled behind her as she strode out the door.

Isaac lowered the book. "That went well. I bet when you get home, you'll find her waiting in your bed."

"Hey, I'm already down. No need to kick." Justin leaned over the booth. "And why didn't you talk to her? She's a new founder. Seems like you'd care."

"Didn't you get the sheriff's lecture?" said Isaac. "Dead bloodline, no powers, leave them alone?"

Maybe Justin should've been surprised that she'd talked to everyone else, but he wasn't. Augusta was always thorough. "You listen to my mother less than I do."

Isaac shrugged. "Maybe I think she's right."

That wasn't it. Justin knew Isaac better than anyone— well, anyone who was still alive. The slight deepening in his voice meant he was lying. But there was no point in pushing, not with Pete hovering at the front of the restaurant.

His eyes caught on the book Violet had commented on. *Brave New World.* Isaac loved books with the kind of sharp, pretentious titles that made Justin feel foolish.

"You've read that one before, right?" he asked.

Isaac nodded.

"What happens at the end?"

Isaac snorted, flipped the novel shut. "The last hope for humanity's soul kills himself."

Justin shook his head. "Shit, man. Why would anyone want to read about that?"

"And you wonder why she didn't want to talk to you."

"Sullivan!" called Pete from the front of the restaurant. Justin could tell he hadn't forgotten Isaac's comment

32

about his ma earlier. "Are you planning on working at all this shift?"

Isaac took an exaggerated look around the empty restaurant. "I'm keeping all the customers satisfied."

Pete frowned. "Just get a new apron and do your damn job. And yes, I will be docking the cost of that uniform from your paycheck."

Isaac slammed his book on the table, and for a second Justin was nervous again. But then he was walking to the back of the restaurant, and the air around him almost looked normal. With Isaac, almost normal was as good as it got.

"He's not usually such an asshole," said Pete, after Isaac had disappeared through the swinging doors.

"He always gets like this in the weeks before the anniversary."

"Ah. Right, then." Pete was suddenly preoccupied with the cash register. "I'll go easy on him."

The door to the kitchen banged open, revealing Isaac once more. He'd fetched a new apron.

"If I have to work, so do you," he said. "Stop complaining about me and go wash some dishes."

Justin glanced back toward the front door of the restaurant as it swung open, revealing the start of the dinner rush.

"Actually, you can wash dishes," he said. "I'll take over server duty."

The corner of Isaac's mouth twitched. "I guess, if that makes it easier for you."

He vanished back into the kitchen, but not before Justin

caught the unspoken gratitude in Isaac's eyes. As he walked to the front of the restaurant, he felt the burn of his calves, already stiff and sore from post-practice fatigue. A full shift of running around with plates in both hands would leave him curled up in a ball by the end of the evening.

But he made himself stand tall, walk normally, keep his smile straight. Because Isaac needed him, and Four Paths had expectations for him, and he'd be damned if he let anyone know how much he'd already disappointed them.

Dinner was uncomfortable. Instead of eating with Violet and Juniper, Daria spooned herself a bowl of some leftover stew and sequestered herself in her bedroom. Her cat, Orpheus, a haughty-looking thing with yellow eyes and a bit of red yarn tied around one ear, stayed and hissed at them until Violet caved and tossed him some chicken.

Violet wondered what it would be like to live alone for years, only to have your peaceful existence interrupted by people who claimed to be your family. It sounded frightening.

"Does it hurt you?" she asked her mother. "To see her like this?"

Juniper's mouth twisted. "What do you think? She barely remembers me." She rose from the table, gesturing at Violet's scraps. "Here. I'll throw that out."

Violet suppressed the urge to remind her mother that at least she still had a sister. She handed over her plate in silence, remembering the two white boys in the restaurant as she swallowed her final mouthful of chicken parmesan.

Justin, blond, pretty, predictably confident. And the reader, who had been so purposely aloof. There had been something expectant about the way they'd looked at her.

Well, whatever they wanted, she wasn't going to give it to them. She'd never been much for boyfriends, or girlfriends, for that matter. There had been crushes; she'd even come out to Rosie as bisexual a few years ago, she just hadn't felt ready to date anyone yet. Her sister and the piano were all she'd needed, and her few distant friends had faded away after Rosie died, unsure of how to handle her grief. Starting at a new high school next week would've bothered her more if she'd had anyone from Ossining to miss.

Violet realized with a quiet rush that it had been almost a full day since she'd played. Unloading the U-Haul had been a slow, laborious process, and by the time Violet left to grab dinner, she had barely managed to drag the relevant boxes to her new bedroom. The rest waited downstairs, flanking her like a row of cardboard sentinels as she strode through the foyer and into the room on the left, where she'd spotted the piano.

Violet did not share the Saunders family's apparent fondness for taxidermy. She averted her eyes from the glassy gazes of three mounted deer heads as she unfolded the top of the piano. A perfect set of ivory keys gaped at her like a smiling mouth—at last, something familiar.

She stretched her hands across the keys, relief and exhilaration spreading through her. As long as she could play, she was home. It had been that way ever since her first piano lesson at age four, when she had to be dragged out of her piano teacher's house, kicking and begging to plink away at the keys for just one second longer.

She played an experimental scale. To her great surprise, the instrument was in tune—perhaps Daria played. The acoustics in the room were lovely, and soon Violet was running through Bach's Prelude & Fugue no. 6 in D Minor.

After Rosie's funeral, her playing had become wildly inconsistent. Sometimes she had good days, but usually the music swam, unreachable, inside her head. She'd quit her piano lessons, but she practiced her audition program a few times a week anyway, trying to convince herself that things could still go back to normal. But it only took a few minutes of playing now for the sharp clarity that practicing her program had always brought her to fall away.

She wasn't going to music school. Not anymore.

Her hands drifted across the keys, spiraling away from her program and improvising new phrases. Violet closed her eyes and let the melody go wherever it wanted.

After a time, Violet became dimly aware of a new noise penetrating her bubble of music. Distracted, she lifted her hands from the keys. It was strangely hard to tear her fingers away from the piano.

She opened her eyes.

The room was pitch-black.

Violet blinked, confused, as the noise rang out once more, a hollow, tinny sound. A pair of glowing eyes appeared in the darkness, and Violet scrabbled backward on the piano bench, grasping for her phone. She'd drawn in a breath to shriek when a familiar bit of red yarn emerged from beneath the bench.

"Oh." She let out a tumble of pent-up air. "It's just you."

The cat gave his odd mewl again, which sounded like a miniature chainsaw, and pressed himself against the piano bench. Then he bit her on the ankle.

Violet cursed at him and drew her legs onto the piano bench. She finally found her phone on the music stand. But as the screen flickered to life, she froze.

It felt like Violet had only been playing the piano for ten minutes, maybe twenty, but her phone said she'd been sitting in the music room for almost four hours. She'd gotten carried away with her playing before, but never like this.

Violet rose from the bench and hurried to the door.

That discomfort still lingered when she reached her bedroom. It was much bigger than her room in Ossining, the walls reddish-brown stone, the bed a large four-poster thing that looked like something out of a museum. Also, there was more creepy taxidermy. Violet carted out a crow and a deer head and dumped them in the room next door, fighting a strange urge to apologize to them.

She swung open the door to her bedroom, and her eyes lit on the pyramid of boxes stacked beside the far wall, each marked ROSIE in big black letters.

The night before Juniper packed up Rosie's bedroom for the move, Violet set foot inside it for the first time since the accident. She combed through the bookshelves, the dresser, the closet, and exorcised her sister's secrets: the half-drunk whiskey bottle beneath the mattress, the lingerie stuffed in her T-shirt drawer, the love notes from Elise tucked into her jacket. She spent an hour turning Rosie from the person she had been into the person her mother had wanted her to be, and when she was done, she'd curled up in her own bed, a hollow, ashy taste in her mouth.

The boxes were the result of that packing, a colorful but tasteful portrait of a girl who'd been artistic, but charmingly so, more Monet than Van Gogh. Violet turned her eyes away from the boxes to the painting that hung above them.

It was one of Rosie's portfolio pieces, an abstract meant to represent Violet, bits of paint all blurred and pushed together in dizzying patterns that spun and whirled if you looked at them from the right angles. She'd done four canvases, one for each member of the Saunders family, even though their father was long dead, and they'd gotten her into her top three art schools. Soul paintings, she'd called them, and although Violet had teased Rosie about her New Age proclivities, she couldn't deny the name felt right.

Maybe the rest of Rosie's things were a lie, but Violet's soul painting wasn't. Violet stepped toward it, her discomfort fading away as she stared at the familiar canvas.

She touched her fingertips to it, then drew the curtains across her bedroom window. The black outlines of the trees gleamed in the moonlight, zigzagging along the side of the house like a row of broken teeth.

THREE

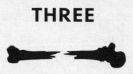

ARPER CARLISLE MOVED THROUGH a fluid series of parries and ripostes, her bare toes pressing into the dirt as she upped the pace of her footwork. She pictured the monster in the Gray—thin, skeletal, faceless—and lunged. The yellowing lace of her nightgown bunched around her knees as she drove her blade through the imaginary creature's chest.

She didn't know what the Beast looked like. No one alive did.

Harper knew what it sounded like, though. Hardly a day went by where she wasn't haunted by the memory of its hollow, tinny voice inside her head.

It was almost dawn now, but she'd been up since three, practicing her swordplay behind her family's cottage. Stone animals nestled in the dying grass around her, a reddish-brown audience. These statues were the closest thing the Carlisles had to family heirlooms. Some were sentinels, carved from the rock excavated from the family lake and serving as crude vessels for the Carlisles' eyes and ears—but others, like the deer, had been real animals once, before a Carlisle turned them to stone guardians that could bend to their will with a mere touch.

It had been a long time since Four Paths had seen a Carlisle that powerful.

"I win," Harper said softly, just as the phone she'd nestled between the dormant deer guardian's ears began to sound with her morning alarm. She kept the sword with her as she headed back inside, even though she had to use her residual limb to jimmy the doorknob open. Losing her left hand had changed the way she fought, altered her balance and footwork, the way she lunged across the grass. But it hadn't changed how confident Harper felt when she was holding a sword.

It was far less daunting to think about the first day of school with a blade in her hand.

Harper wiped her feet off and moved soundlessly through her house, stopping only to reluctantly slot the sword back into its place of honor above the mantel. Maybe waking up this early to practice was excessive, but there were eight members of her family. All were nosy, including the baby. And none of them knew she'd kept training after the accident.

Harper was willing to take drastic measures to keep it that way. It wasn't like she'd slept much since the day she'd lost her left hand.

The day she'd slipped into the Gray.

Three years later, and Harper still dreamed of the lake

40

closing over her head. Of resurfacing somewhere new, where her breath couldn't fill her lungs and her arm crumbled into stone on the riverbank. It was a forest, or at least it looked like one, but the trees were skeletal and twisted, bowed beneath an unmoving sky that shone like splintered steel.

There was no color in the Gray. No color except the sharp crimson shine of her blood.

Harper shook the memories away, shuddering, and went on with her morning.

By the time her parents' alarm went off at six, Harper had dressed, given up on her waist-length dark curls, and perfected her eyeliner. She spent the next half hour wrangling Brett and Nora out of bed and getting them ready for school, all while trying not to trip over the cord of Mitzi's hair straightener.

"A little help here?" She glanced toward the vanity table, where Mitzi was weaving her founders' medallion into her auburn hair.

"Go wake Seth up." Mitzi tilted her head, admiring the way the glass shone. "I'm busy."

"Busy staring at yourself?" Harper couldn't stop the bite of jealousy in her voice. She'd never earned her medallion, and so she had to content herself with her simple stone pendant.

Mitzi's reflection in the smudged mirror was an odd mixture of smugness and pity. "Can you blame me?"

"It's okay!" said Nora, who was busily pulling on two completely different shoes. "I can do it myself."

"You know those don't match, right?" said Harper, grinning at her little sister. Nora's boundless energy had driven many babysitters to quit, but Harper loved it.

Nora pouted at her. "I like how they look."

The door to their room swung open before Harper could respond. Silhouetted in the reinforced wooden frame was Harper's father, Maurice Carlisle, baby Olly fussing in his arms.

"Come to breakfast, kids," he told Brett and Nora. "I'm making pancakes."

Brett and Nora bolted for the door, and as he stepped aside to let them by, a smile carved its way through his craggy features. "I can take it from here."

Harper's father usually took charge in the mornings, since Harper's mother, Laurel Carlisle, was often busy with her job as an attorney in the next town over. But Harper didn't mind. Her parents did not treat their children equally—Laurel favored Mitzi, while Maurice had always favored her. She was glad he was the one who spent more time at home.

The rest of the morning was a blur of walking Brett and Nora out to the bus, and Seth, Mitzi, and Harper piling into Seth's broken-down car and sputtering off to Four Paths High School. Seth jolted the car to a stop in the middle of two parking spots, then made a beeline for the slackers who hung out behind the school every morning, smoking cigarettes and talking a big game about their joint-rolling skills. Mitzi vanished a moment later, her red hair whipping behind her.

Harper was slower, her messenger bag heavy on her shoulder. Ahead of her, the crowd split in two, automatically moving away from the bench where the Hawthorne siblings were holding court. Justin's broad shoulders rose easily above the crowd, straining at the thin blue fabric of his T-shirt as he turned to laugh at something May had said. The morning light turned his blond hair into ripples of molten gold, and the medallion at his wrist shone bloodred.

Founder descendants were revered in Four Paths, but the town's love for Justin far surpassed familial respect. He had a warm greeting for everyone, even clapping a chosen few on the shoulder. People looked dazed when they wandered away from him, like they'd been staring into the sun.

But all his carefully arranged smile did was stoke Harper's rage, like a whetstone sharpening the edge of a sword.

After her accident, she had been convinced she was a disappointment. But her father had told her to use the word *survivor* instead—and she'd listened. There was no point in being angry at herself for failing her ritual. That anger belonged somewhere else: with the Hawthornes, who had decided she was nothing after she returned from the Gray without her powers.

And with Justin Hawthorne, who had cast aside a lifelong friendship when he sided with his mother instead of sticking up for her.

"Coward," she muttered as she cut through the crowd.

Harper was the first to arrive in her senior homeroom. She took the same seat she'd had since ninth grade as her classmates drifted in, most deigning to enter the classroom only after the second bell had rung.

There were only fifty-seven seniors at Four Paths High School. They had all known Harper her entire life, and although she felt their eyes on her, they didn't say hello. Lia Raynes and Suzette Langham gossiped as they sat in front of her; they were best friends recently turned girlfriends, already shoo-ins to be voted class couple for the senior yearbook. Danny Moore took the seat on her right, while Seo-Jin Park and Cal Gonzales slid in beside him, talking animatedly about the track team.

Harper was used to being avoided. After the accident, she'd learned quickly that no one knew how to talk to her anymore. At first, she'd thought it was because of her hand. She'd chosen not to wear a prosthetic on the bottom half of her left arm; her family couldn't afford a myoelectric prosthesis, and she didn't want a cosmetic one. Everyone knew what had happened to her; they would stare anyway.

But by now, she knew the stares and the awkward conversations weren't really about her arm at all.

Nobody in Four Paths had ever survived the Gray for longer than a few hours. Harper had made it four days.

She'd heard the rumors that the Gray had left her forever altered, that she'd only been released because she'd been allowed out by the Beast, that she was a founder turned spy, a monster lurking in a teenage girl's skin.

They were nothing more than stories. But Harper had

learned by now that some people would always prefer a story to the truth.

She was fiddling with her pencil case when Justin appeared in the doorway. Half the class called out greetings as he walked through the room, flanked, as always, by Isaac Sullivan—his flannel-clad shadow.

Isaac had never warmed up to her, despite a lifetime of being shoved together in the way all founder kids were. But the dislike was mutual. After Harper had been forced away from Justin's side, Isaac Sullivan had taken her place. And although Harper knew she shouldn't resent Isaac for being living evidence of how easy it had been for Justin to replace her, she did it anyway.

So it gave her a small rush of petty satisfaction to notice the way people grimaced when Isaac walked by. People watched Justin because he'd earned their respect. They watched Isaac because he'd earned their fear.

Three years ago, she would've been with them, breezing in late, laughing at Justin's bad jokes as they slid into the back row of the classroom. Harper wondered if it was hard for Justin to act like he'd never known her. It probably wasn't. Not the way it was for her. After all, he was the one who'd acted like she didn't exist as soon as she wasn't useful anymore. Which meant they'd never been anything at all.

Harper pushed down her fury as a wave of murmurs swept through the classroom. She followed her classmates' stares to a white girl standing uncomfortably in the doorway, scanning the room for an empty seat. Harper didn't have to look to know the only desk left was the one in front of Isaac Sullivan. Even the most oblivious kid at Four Paths High knew better than to sit there. But the new girl didn't have a choice.

She walked across the classroom, her gaze raised above the students' watching eyes. That kind of scrutiny would've made Harper's skin crawl, but the girl didn't flinch. A new student at Four Paths High was almost unheard of. The last person to move in had been Britta Morey, in second grade, and people still treated her like an outsider.

Mrs. Langham—Suzette's mother, and also their homeroom teacher—cleared her throat as the new girl found her seat.

"Welcome back, everyone," she said, with a pointed glance at the girl as she dropped her backpack on the floor. "I know you're all excited to be returning for another year at Four Paths High."

The class stared back at her. Isaac's desk began to vibrate at the back of the room, his foot tapping rapidly against the floor. Mrs. Langham ignored him.

"Let's try that again, shall we?" she said. "Are you excited to be returning for your final year at Four Paths High?"

This time, the room broke out into half-hearted clapping. Even Harper couldn't suppress a grin. A year from now, she'd be done with this place forever, starting her freshman year at whatever state school gave the best financial aid— SUNY Binghamton or Geneseo, if she was lucky.

Harper knew a significant chunk of her graduating class would stay in Four Paths forever. She couldn't imagine a worse fate. All Harper wanted was an escape—

from her ever-growing pack of siblings, from the Hawthorne family's cold disdain, from a place where she would never be able to overcome her mistakes.

"Seniors," continued Mrs. Langham, "please be extra welcoming to our new student, Violet Saunders."

Saunders.

Harper's pulse quickened as the murmurs started up again, louder this time. The new girl stared resolutely at her desk as the few people who hadn't been looking at her turned their focus toward her.

Harper wondered why the Saunders family was back. Why anyone would ever return to this town, even someone with founder blood, was beyond her. It was surely making the Hawthornes uneasy, though, having all four families in play. Harper's father had told her about when he was a kid, when Mayor Saunders had trusted each family to patrol their own territory. But that was before the Saunders family began to dwindle. Before the Sullivans fled. Now it was mostly just the Hawthornes and the Carlisles going on patrols, and Sheriff Hawthorne acting like everyone else mattered less than she did.

Mrs. Langham sorted through schedules at the front of the room, calling up the students one by one. Her voice was undercut by the sound of Isaac's desk banging into the floor. As always, he was blatantly inattentive, his book splayed across the desk as it vibrated in time with his breathing. It knocked against the back of Violet Saunders's chair, until finally she turned, nostrils flaring, and gripped the edge of Isaac's desk.

"Hey, *Brave New World*." Her voice was melodic but strong, a voice that made people pay attention. Harper would've killed for a voice like that. "Would you mind stopping before you put a permanent dent in my back?"

Isaac's deep voice rang with false innocence. "Stopping what?"

"Banging your desk into my chair," Violet said, perfectly deadpan. "Some of us arc trying to pay attention, and it's distracting as fuck."

Her words sucked the air out of the classroom. No one talked to founder kids like that, especially not to Isaac Sullivan. Not after the rumors about his ritual day, the whispers that he was the reason his whole family had left town.

Isaac's desk went still, and the air in front of his hands began to shimmer. Harper braced herself as the new girl's eyes widened. Lia and Suzette were holding hands; Cal and Seo-Jin had already half risen from their seats.

And then Justin Hawthorne leaned through the refracting light until his hand was resting on Isaac's arm. Neither of them spoke, but Isaac's head turned sharply to face him. Their gazes stayed locked together, solemn and impassive, as the world faded back to normal.

"I guess I didn't realize," Isaac said.

Justin's head inclined in a sharp nod before he retreated to his seat. The tension in the room went with it.

"Thanks," said Violet, but she was looking at Justin when she said it.

Harper could see it now. How Justin would ensnare

Violet the same way he'd ensnared Harper, when they were kids, before she'd disappointed everyone.

And the only thing Harper could do about that was something she should've done the second she realized he'd abandoned her.

She could let Justin Hawthorne go.

Harper turned back toward the front of her classroom. She wondered how long it would take before Violet was sitting in the back of the room on purpose, in the spot that should've been hers.

She wondered if she would ever truly be able to stop herself from caring.

Violet arrived home from her first day of school to unfamiliar cars parked in front of her new house. Her first day at Four Paths High School had been the complete opposite of her high school in Ossining—her classes were tiny to the point where Violet recognized most of her grade by the end of the day. Her muscles ached from the effort of biking, but taking the Porsche to school was out of the question. Rosie had been driving when her car was T-boned by a semitruck. Violet hadn't touched a steering wheel since.

She yanked her bike over the rough gravel of the driveway, frowning at the vehicles. A flurry of exterminators and cleaners had swept through the mansion since they'd moved in, but this many at one time seemed excessive.

As she dragged the bike through the garden, a series of deep, throaty barks rang out from behind the porch. Two gigantic mastiffs, one black, one mottled brown, padded forward. They were chained to the rotting wood of the railing.

The look in their eyes reminded her of the boy who'd been reading in the Diner, who'd been so hostile to her in homeroom—a quiet, menacing confidence that could only come from creatures too dangerous to be frightened. Violet had seen the boy and his friend—Isaac and Justin, those were their names—engaged in some kind of intense meeting in the courtyard after school, along with a blond girl who looked so much like Justin that she had to be his sister.

There was something eerie about the way everyone automatically deferred to them; how the other students had practically lunged out of their seats to say hello when the boys had walked into her homeroom. In Westchester, the popular kids had been standard-issue athletes and student body presidents who were headed straight for the Ivy League. This trio was something different.

They weren't the kings and queens of Four Paths High School—they were its gods.

"Good boys." Violet leaned her bike against the opposite side of the porch. "Nice, giant, possibly people-eating dogs."

She pushed through the front door, wondering who would want to own an animal that could probably bite off a limb if you made it angry.

Inside was sloppy, chortling laughter and faint, twangy music. Violet followed the noise to the living room, where maybe twenty adults stood in small clumps, drinks in their hands, heads bobbing to the country music playing on Juniper's high-end speakers.

The scene was bizarre. Her mother hated parties. And besides, they hadn't even been in Four Paths a week. How had she possibly rounded up this many old friends?

Violet made the executive decision to hide in her room until the party was over. But before she could flee, her name was squealed at a pitch only the mastiffs outside should've been able to hear.

"Violet Saunders!" A black woman Violet recognized from homeroom tugged her into the room, her dark braids twisted atop her head. "So good to see you again."

Violet resisted the powerful urge to run. "Thanks," she said. "Good to see you too, Mrs., uh…"

"Mrs. Langham, honey."

Another woman sidled up to them, this one pale-skinned and freckled. Two chunky stone bracelets adorned her wrists. "And I'm Ma Burnham. Or at least, Ma to everyone under twenty-five."

Violet shook Ma Burnham's hand. The woman's beady gaze was narrow, assessing. "You're Juniper's daughter?"

Violet nodded. "Yes."

"You look like her."

It was the first time Violet had ever heard that. Rosie and Juniper were the ones who looked alike—frizzy hair, round faces, wide smiles with slightly crooked incisors. Violet had her father's thick, straight hair and an inability to step outdoors without getting sunburned —something Rosie, who loved to tan in the backyard while sketching, had never worried about.

But Rosie was gone now. She and Juniper were the only ones left.

"I guess," she said hoarsely. "So, you were friends of my mom's?"

Mrs. Langham chuckled and nodded. "As friendly as someone like her would be with the likes of us, sure."

"What do you mean?" Violet asked.

The women exchanged quiet, knowing glances as they sipped from their wine glasses.

"None of you founders were ever really friends with us." There was a bitterness in Mrs. Langham's voice that Violet hadn't noticed before. Now it was all she could hear. "You've always had other things to worry about."

"Founders?" Violet echoed.

"Now, Clara." Ma Burnham placed a warning hand on Mrs. Langham's arm. "You have to understand, Violet, she doesn't intend to speak badly of your mama. You can't blame her for leaving us, really, especially after all that nasty business with Stephen..."

Another name Violet didn't recognize. But before she could ask about that, too, a low, cool voice cut both women off.

"Gossiping, I see." The white woman who'd joined them was a behemoth of a person, muscular but regal, a queen and a bodyguard all wrapped up into one. "Don't you ladies think you've told her enough nonsense for one evening?"

Mrs. Langham and Mrs. Burnham melted away, gabbling hasty goodbyes before Violet could ask them any more questions. Which, Violet sensed, was the last thing they wanted her to do.

"Augusta Hawthorne," the woman said, holding out a gloved hand roughly the size of Violet's head.

Violet shook it, expecting her fingers to be crushed, but the soft, cracked leather and the grip beneath it were surprisingly delicate. "Violet Saunders. I think I've met your son."

She would've noticed this woman's resemblance to Justin even if she hadn't revealed her last name. They had the same handsome, angular features, the same pinkish skin and thin blond hair, the same way of standing, as if they expected everyone else in the room to turn toward them. And maybe everyone did—at the very least, the party's collective gaze seemed to be boring into Violet's artificially distressed T-shirt.

"Ah. Justin." Something unreadable flickered across the woman's face. "He tends to make an impression."

"I guess."

"I'm here to introduce myself." Augusta flipped open her wallet. A silver shield glimmered inside with a circle of red glass embedded in the center—a badge. "As the sheriff of a small town, I like to tell everyone personally to contact me if there's ever a problem."

"That's admirable." There was something in the woman's voice that made Violet wonder what kind of problem she was referring to.

But Juniper appeared at her side before the thought could fully blossom. "There you are," her mother said to

Augusta, sharp, obvious recognition splashed across her features. "I'm assuming this get-together was your idea?"

So Juniper hadn't planned this impromptu party. Violet felt a rush of satisfaction that her gut had been right—her mother *didn't* like people that much.

Augusta inclined her head. "It seemed the thing to do. I mentioned the idea to a few others, and they were all quite interested in catching up."

"Interested in nosing around my house, you mean," said Juniper. "If you wanted to catch up, you had thirty years to call."

"And you had thirty years to visit."

Juniper's gaze went as cold and glassy as the eyes of the deer head on the wall.

"I heard you wound up in law enforcement." Her voice held the same quiet viciousness Violet had heard her use on the phone with unruly investors. "You must love that."

"And I hear you went into... what was it, finance?"

"Software development."

"Fascinating."

Those other women's knowledge of Juniper had come from rumors rather than experience. But Augusta Hawthorne was different. There was a kind of tainted familiarity here that made Violet realize her mother hadn't just left a town behind—she'd left a life. Daria was one of her casualties. The sheriff, it seemed, was another.

"I hope you don't mind if I leave you here," Augusta said. "I've got to check on the dogs. They have a tendency to misbehave in unfamiliar places."

So the mastiffs belonged to her. Violet wasn't surprised.

"Of course," said Juniper.

As Augusta walked away, Violet turned toward her mother. "Who was she?"

Juniper tugged uncomfortably on the lapel of her blazer. "My best friend."

Violet took a deep breath. "And who was Stephen?"

Juniper went still. The country music seemed fainter somehow. Violet was suddenly conscious of how the dead in this room outnumbered the living: the deer head on the wall, the stuffed foxes in the corner, the nest of pinned-down birds rising between two couches.

She knew before Juniper spoke that her mother would lie.

"Maybe someone else in town?" said Juniper carefully. "It's been a long time. I can't remember everyone."

"I don't believe you."

Violet had never seen her mother look so lost, or sound so shaken.

"I'm not doing this here."

Violet gestured toward the doorway. "Good. This party sucks anyway."

The hallway was quieter. Juniper's eyes darted down the corridors of reddish stone, her body relaxing only when she seemed certain they were alone at the foot of the staircase. "I suppose it was wishful thinking to hope this town had moved on."

"Moved on from what?"

Her mother's hand clutched her wineglass for dear life.

"From Stephen," she said. "My little brother."

The words sent a jolt down Violet's spine. She wasn't sure what she'd been expecting, but it wasn't this. "You have a brother?"

Every word Juniper said was clipped and careful, the same way they'd been at Rosie's funeral. "Had. He died a few months before I finished high school."

"You never told me." Violet couldn't keep the accusation out of her voice. "Is this why you left town?"

Juniper took a deep, shuddering breath. "Yes. Stephen is why I left."

"Gossiping?" Daria crouched on the second-floor landing like a spider, her eyes gleaming brownish-yellow in the light of the dusty chandelier above their heads.

"I can't talk about this in front of Daria." Juniper's voice slipped, revealing the slightest tinge of panic. "It'll just upset her."

"Looks like you're the upset one to me," said Daria.

"So if Stephen was your brother—"

"Another time." Juniper's voice was firm and steady again. She hurried back to the living room, downing her entire glass of wine on the way.

Violet didn't chase her. She didn't feel stable enough to move just yet. She was too overwhelmed, filled to the brim with a new, awful understanding of her mother.

"Stay out of the woods, little bone," Daria said reproachfully from the top of the stairs. "I can see those branches reaching for you."

But Violet could barely hear her.

Juniper's brother had died, so she had run away. And she'd kept running, cutting Violet off from her father's family after he died, then yanking them away from Ossining after they'd lost Rosie. She didn't care who she left behind. She didn't care about the damage she did along the way.

Violet stumbled to her room, her head throbbing. She curled up on her bed and cried all the tears Juniper wouldn't, for the father and sister she had lost and the uncle she would never know. When she was done, the noise from downstairs had faded away.

She wiped her face with her comforter, then padded resolutely to the music room.

Violet needed the piano. It was the only thing that could possibly clear the dullness from her mind, ease the aching in her chest.

This time, she didn't even try to play her audition program. Her fingers flew freely across the keys, the pain she couldn't verbalize emerging in the chords that echoed off the cavernous walls of the music room. This was her life without Rosie, these great bursts of sound with no audience. And Violet knew in that moment that she would do anything—anything—to have her sister back for just one more moment.

She closed her eyes, trying to push the longing away, push the pain out. When she opened them, the piano was gone.

In its place was a sky full of still, gray clouds that shone like blunted steel.

FOUR

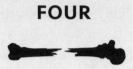

VIOLET LAY FACEUP ON the ground, her arms and legs splayed out like a discarded toy.

Above her was an endless expanse of dark, ashy trunks and naked branches that spiraled toward an unmoving sky. Everything was colorless and completely still. The world felt two-dimensional, like the set of a play, a forest of cardboard and painted plywood.

Pain shot through Violet's spine as she sat up—every part of her was sore; her bare feet, her callused palms. Her arms were caked with dirt from the tips of her fingers to her elbows.

She didn't know where she was. Why she hurt. How she'd gotten here.

Fear flooded through Violet's chest as she struggled to her feet, but it didn't overwhelm her.

Until she saw the body.

The limbs were grotesquely twisted, splinters of bone poking through at the joints. The skin was bloated and gray. A perfect semicircle of puncture marks glistened on its torso—a bite mark, maybe, although Violet couldn't picture an animal with jaws that wide. Something clear and oily oozed through where the skin had broken.

The only sign that it had been a person at all was a silver shield pinned to its chest.

Violet met the corpse's sightless eyes, bleached completely white, and realized its tongue was bitten in two.

She sucked in the biggest breath she could and screamed—or at least, she tried to.

The noise ripped itself out of Violet's throat, but there was no cry of raw terror, just her wheezing silently in the woods—and then the scream rang out, seconds too late, high and shrill and horrified.

Violet did the only thing that made sense anymore. She bolted.

She ran until the trees and the ground and the static sky all blurred together, her breath heaving in her lungs, her footsteps ringing out a second too late across the forest floor. When she couldn't take another step, she doubled over and emptied her stomach.

And when she stood up, shaking, the last thing she was prepared for was her sister standing in front of the nearest tree.

Violet's mouth opened, but nothing came out.

Rosie wore the outfit she had died in—ripped jeans, a paint-splattered tank top, and a crimson bomber jacket that clashed horribly with her blue hair. She was the only thing in this strange gray world with any color at all, resplendent in the weak light of the off-white sky.

"Rosie?" Violet whispered, woozy with joy and shock. "Where am I? What is this?" But as she started toward her sister, Rosie's body flickered around the edges, then went transparent enough for Violet to see the outline of the misshapen branches behind her.

She wasn't real.

And the crushing knowledge that of course Rosie wasn't really here, she couldn't be here, hurt her more than the sight of the body had.

Rosie took a step back, the branches weaving and pulsating above her head. Violet had spent her life trailing after her sister. She wanted to follow her.

But there was something that made Violet pause. The way Rosie was standing—her legs and arms crooked just slightly wrong, as if she were trying to be a person, but didn't know how.

A tinny, hollow sound whistled through the forest, almost like a voice.

It was coming from the trees.

The branches behind Rosie were reaching forward. Reaching for her, every twig pulsating with unnatural life. Violet backed away, panic rising in her throat again. A branch brushed against her arm, and the motion shocked something in her, the *wrongness* of it all, this dull, devouring gray.

She would not let this be the place she died.

She turned again, ready to run, but she'd scarcely taken

a step when a great cacophony of sound erupted, the rich, eerie pealing of a thousand bells. And as Violet jolted backward, shocked at the sudden burst of noise, color rushed into the world in a swirl of brown and green and blue.

All around her were lush, healthy chestnut oaks, their branches weighed down by leaves tinged orange around the edges. Above her head, the three familiar spires of the Saunders house rose over the trees, backlit by the thin, rosy light of dawn.

The first thing Violet did was cry, really cry, great sobs of relief as her lungs flooded with proper breath.

Maybe she had sleepwalked, and all of this had just been a nightmare. The body, the trees, Rosie—it couldn't have been real.

But when Violet looked at her left hand, a single gray twig was still clenched between her fingers.

The Hawthorne mastiffs began to bark at dawn.

Henry and Brutus were too well trained to make a sound unless there was trouble. And Justin's mother had been out on patrol the night before.

Justin took the stairs two at a time, his backpack forgotten on his bed, and reached the front door just as Augusta Hawthorne swung it open.

Her cheek was bruised, her knuckles scraped raw. The founders' medallion pinned to her sheriff's badge was caked with dirt.

But the thing that truly frightened him was the panic

flitting behind her neutral expression. Because his mother didn't show fear the same way May didn't admit to making mistakes.

"What happened?" Justin's voice was hoarse. Behind them, the dogs let out a series of mournful howls.

His mother's face tightened. "Reading room. Now. I'm getting your sister."

She disappeared before he could say anything else. Or mention that it was a school day, although the thought of attending school had vanished the moment she walked in the door.

There was only one reason Augusta Hawthorne was summoning her children to the reading room.

She wanted to see the future.

May and Augusta were waiting for him at the scarred wooden table—the only piece of furniture in the reading room, older than everything on the Hawthorne grounds except the tree that had given them their name. Justin slid into his usual seat across from the window, where the indistinct shapes of branches pressed against the side of the house.

"Are you ready?" said Augusta. Above her head was a portrait of Hetty Hawthorne, one of the founding members of Four Paths and the matriarch of their bloodline. Her face was a testament to the consistency of the Hawthorne gene pool—a blunt, blond, severe attractiveness pulled together by a smile that was just a well-disguised smirk. Hetty had painted it herself, just like she'd painted the Deck of Omens a century and a half ago. Justin was fairly certain he'd once seen the portrait tuck a loose strand of hair behind its ear.

"I can read your cards, but I'd prefer an explanation first. It will make my process easier." The only clue that May was anxious was the slight tremors in her fingers as her hands folded around the Deck of Omens. Not every Hawthorne could read the future, but their power was tied into predicting and influencing the roots and branches that knotted the town together, the same way the Carlisles worked with stone and the Sullivans could hurt or heal with a single touch. Each family protected Four Paths in a different way.

Or at least, they were supposed to. Lately, Justin wasn't sure they were protecting Four Paths at all.

Augusta sighed but nodded in acquiescence. "Early this morning, I was alerted that there had been a disturbance at the border. I was skeptical, but I investigated the matter personally. The deputy was correct; however, we were unprepared for the consequences."

"Consequences?" Justin couldn't stop the question.

There it was again; that flicker of fear across his mother's face, even though her words were perfectly steady. "Deputy Anders is dead."

The reading room went blurry and Justin's insides froze as he fought a sudden, overwhelming wave of guilt.

Just last week, Anders had warned him to be careful. He thought of the man's broad shoulders, his wispy mustache, the holster at his hip.

The gun never had a chance of saving him. But if

Justin had powers, maybe he would've.

Justin's ritual day was still frozen into his memory. How his palm had burned as he sliced the knife across it, then pressed it to the heart of the hawthorn tree, blood dripping down the bark.

How he'd waited. How each excruciating second had passed as he hoped desperately for something to happen, while May and his mother shifted uneasily behind him.

But when Justin finally felt the tree spring to life, heard its deep, glorious heartbeat, it did not bend in submission the way he'd believed it would. Instead a great dullness had spread through him. The air had split and the Gray had rushed around him—the static sky, the dark, pulsating trees—and he had felt so helpless, so small.

A choking panic had seized him, and he'd dropped to his knees, a tinny, hollow voice hissing in his ears. He hadn't understood the words, but being close enough to hear the Beast's voice meant he was already dead.

Yet he'd been too petrified to fight back.

That was what the Beast did to people who didn't have powers—it made them see and hear whatever it wanted. It made them believe, long before it killed them, that they were better off dead.

It was May who had saved him. May who'd pulled him back to Four Paths before the monster in the Gray devoured him, just as it had devoured every other Hawthorne who was unworthy of power.

So Justin had lived, more or less.

And now, because he was powerless to protect the town

as the Gray grew stronger, four innocent people were dead.

Across the table, May's voice had gone as soft and quiet as footsteps over grass. "I'm so sorry."

Augusta shrugged. "Don't apologize to me, May. I'm not the dead one." There was a moment of sharp, stunned silence, like the aftermath of a slap—or a scream. "Now, if you could continue with the reading?"

May cleared her throat, sniffling. "Of course, Mother. Please, ask us your question."

"Who or what is causing this strengthening of the Gray?" asked Augusta carefully. "And how do we eliminate them?"

People weren't supposed to ask two questions, but Augusta always did. As soon as she was done speaking, May began to shuffle the cards. They vanished one by one as May's power took hold, until only four remained.

She laid them out on the table, each all-seeing eye facing a different direction. Augusta never took her gloves off, so May was forced to close her hand around her mother's wrist—skin-on-skin contact was part of the reading. Augusta's other glove slid into Justin's hand; a second later, May's slightly clammy palm rested against his. They sat like that for nearly thirty seconds before May broke the circle.

"They're ready." She flipped each card over. The shadows of her fingers darted across the table like lines of ink seeping into the wood—and then they froze, hovering over the final card.

It was another Saunders card. The Eight of Bones this

time. Two skulls nestled nose to nose; one hopelessly cracked, one smooth and whole.

"Isn't that interesting," Augusta said, her voice dangerously soft. "Tell us what you see, May."

When May spoke, there was a slight tremor in her voice. "There is something fundamentally wrong in Four Paths." She pointed to the first card—the Scales of Balance. Hetty Hawthorne had painted a great wooden frame with two cups hanging from each end. A man and a woman sat inside each one, legs crossed, eyes closed. "You asked how we can stop the Gray from growing stronger. This is part of your answer. It means there's been an unbalancing in this town—something big."

"Understood," said Augusta. "Does it say if we'll be able to fix that?"

"We might," said May, frowning. "Whether we succeed or not depends on the Eight of Bones. Either they will be what helps us return to normal, or they will change everything. Permanently."

Augusta tapped her chin. "So the Eight of Bones is what caused this. A Saunders card."

"You'd think so," said May. "But the last part of the reading is more troubling. You asked the question, so this"—she indicated the Six of Branches—"didn't seem like such a shock at first, since it's your card."

The art on the card was a sapling struck by lightning, badly damaged. Two serpents twined around the trunk. Justin could never tell if they were trying to keep the

66

tree together or pull it further apart.

"Readings often tell us the version of events that will directly impact whoever asks the question, so it's normal for a person's card to show up. But your card isn't here because you asked the question. When paired with the Skeleton, it actually…" May hesitated, and Justin realized in a sudden moment of clarity that his sister hadn't been stalling because of the Eight of Bones.

This was the part of his mother's reading she didn't want to talk about.

"You won't like this," May said.

Across the table, Augusta raised an eyebrow. "Enlighten me. And I'll decide on my own if I like it or not."

"All right, then," said May. Justin heard the tremor in the back of her throat. He reached under the table and squeezed her free hand. She squeezed back, her palm coated in sweat. "The Skeleton signifies a big change. A reckoning, if you will. And when it's paired with your card… well, Mother, it answers your second question. This danger to the town has something to do with you."

Across the table, Augusta's face drained of color. "That's preposterous. All I've ever done is put this town first. My children should know that more than anyone."

May's fingernails dug into Justin's hand. "The cards don't lie."

"Then you read them wrong." Augusta slammed her hands on the table. May jolted backward, a slight whimper escaping her lips. "Do it again."

"There is no other way to read them." May was almost

whispering now. "I know this isn't what you wanted to hear. But you asked two questions. This is how the cards have answered them."

Augusta's voice dropped into a coiled, vicious whisper. "A good man is dead, May. How can I possibly know that didn't affect your ability to do the reading?"

Tears pooled in May's eyes.

Justin felt a white-hot bolt of fury toward his mother. May had idolized Augusta her entire life. Punishing her for her honesty was cruel.

"I guess you'll have to trust her," he said. "Which I know is hard and all, since we're the only people in Four Paths you can't use your powers to manipulate."

Augusta let out a snarl of frustration as she stood, her head nearly brushing the ceiling of the reading room. Justin braced himself for a verbal assault, but her words, when they came, were quiet. "The Saunders family used to run this town. We have done a better job of protecting it than they ever did. I intend to keep it that way."

Her exit was accompanied by the howls of the mastiffs waiting for their mistress to return.

Justin stared at the Eight of Bones, realizing for the first time that there were bits of flesh still clinging to the cracked skull. He wondered what had driven Hetty Hawthorne to paint such gruesome, vivid images. Then he turned to May, who had wrapped her arms around her knees.

"We've known Deputy Anders our whole lives." The vein in her forehead bulged out against her skin, like a root snaking across her skull. "Now he's just… gone."

"Yeah, and that's why Mom's angry. It's not really about you."

May ducked her head. "I know."

"You did the right thing. Telling her the truth." Justin wasn't sure he meant that. But May needed to hear it.

"Did I?" The dim lights of the reading room enhanced May's features until she looked the way she sounded: delicate and thin, like a crystal bowl balancing on the edge of a mantelpiece. "All I do is give bad news, Justin. People die or hurt each other or disappear."

"You know there's more to it than that," said Justin. "The cards are tricky. They don't always tell you everything."

"They tell me enough." May stared resolutely forward. "Sometimes I hate it. The knowing, the responsibility." And then she spoke the words Justin knew she'd been holding in since her own ritual, three months earlier: "You wouldn't understand."

The second his sister touched the tree that day, its branches had sprung to life. The hawthorn's gnarled trunk bent low. And Justin had watched, choking back tears, as the forest in front of them began to kneel as well, until he could see the lake behind the Carlisle cottage glittering through its bowed branches.

If Justin's ritual had been the worst day of his life, May's was a close second.

"Guess not," Justin said dully. "Tell me again how hard it is to be powerful."

"I'm sorry. I didn't mean—"

"I know," said Justin, and then, because his lack of powers was the last thing he wanted to talk about, he added, "The Saunders family. May, if there's any chance they could help us keep things from getting any worse—"

May's face went solemn. "I know." She paused. "But Mother said to stay away from them. And Mother always has her reasons."

Justin thought of the fear on Augusta's face. What she'd said. How she'd stared at the Eight of Bones with a mixture of dread and resignation, as if she'd known, all along, that the Saunders family was undeniably intertwined with their futures.

As if she would do anything to convince herself otherwise.

Which meant that, if there was any chance of Violet Saunders being a useful ally to the Hawthornes, Justin would have to seek her out himself.

FIVE

HARPER HAD BEEN MOVING through the strength-
building exercises she'd adapted for her training
when she heard it—a snatch of song, a low, deep voice
drifting through the trees.

She knew that voice, that tune. Her father hummed it
in his workshop while he carved stone excavated from
the lake into sentinels.

Once, every house in town had boasted protective
guardians on their doorsteps: statues that moved at their
master's command. The Carlisles had been in charge of
protecting the rest of Four Paths with these guardians
every fall and spring equinox, the nights of the year when
the Gray was strongest and the founders were the weakest.
When the line between reality and nightmare blurred.

But Harper's grandmother had been the last Carlisle
who could control a guardian. So the sentinels Maurice
Carlisle carved in his workshop hung above the town's
doorways instead. They were weak replacements—only

able to sound an alarm when danger came, not come to life and stop it.

The family was a shade of what they could've been, what they once were.

"Little children, led astray, wandered through the woods one day..." Footsteps stomped across the nearby underbrush. Harper's father was a Carlisle through and through, solid and steady, and he did nothing quietly, not even walking.

Harper's first instinct was to panic. She'd hidden her training for a reason; she didn't need her father's pity. A burning sensation surged through her left arm, sharp and sudden—although she knew her left hand was gone, she still felt phantom pain in it sometimes, especially when she was stressed or frightened. Harper shuddered, grabbed her blade, and dove behind the nearest tree.

Her father's voice was closer now. *"Stumbled right into the Gray, never to return..."*

Her pulse increased as he appeared at the edge of the clearing. She shifted closer to the tree, the burning in her arm growing more intense—and gasped as she lost her balance, her blade clattering to her feet.

The noise cut through the quiet of the night like a gunshot, stopping her father's song midline.

"Who's there?" Maurice Carlisle slid a hand into his pocket. The sharp silver edge of a dagger winked in his fist when it emerged.

There was a hardness in his expression Harper had never seen before. She hurried out from behind the tree, unease swelling in her chest. "Dad. It's just me."

Maurice's face softened into puzzlement. The knife returned to his pocket so fast she wondered if she'd imagined it. "Harper. Why are you out here in the middle of the night?"

Harper swallowed, hard. She was overly conscious of her mother's nightdress, her bare feet, the blade lying in the grass behind her. Her father's bemusement always made her feel like a little girl again. "I could ask you the same question."

Maurice chuckled. "I'm just coming back from patrol. A little jumpy."

But there was a calendar of patrol times propped up on the kitchen counter. Harper knew it by heart—it hadn't changed in months. "You patrol on Wednesdays and Saturdays," she said, folding her good arm across the residual limb below her left elbow. "And we don't go on the equinox schedule for another week and a half."

"I suppose we don't." A stripe of moonlight cut across the bridge of her father's nose. "And you weren't just coming out here for a witching-hour stroll with one of the family swords."

"No." Harper's father had taught her never to back down from a fight where the stakes were equal. And it was clear they both had something to hide. "I wasn't."

There was something assessing in Maurice Carlisle's gaze. He shifted back and forth for a moment, his jaw working to one side. "Have you been training?"

He didn't sound pitying, like she'd feared. He sounded almost... impressed.

So Harper nodded.

And she was rewarded by a grin—a real grin. "I should've known you'd never stop. You always loved blade-work."

Harper jutted out her chin. "I still do."

Maurice looked at her thoughtfully. "Yet you don't have anything to fight."

Harper had a brief, unbidden vision of holding a blade to Justin Hawthorne's throat. "Not yet."

"Listen." Her father stepped toward her until his graying curls blocked out the moon, leaving him little more than a silhouette. The assessing tone in his voice was gone—whatever decision he'd been contemplating had been made. "Do you really want to know where I was tonight?"

She merely hadn't wanted to be caught. But now it was too late for that, and it felt as if her father was seeing her, truly seeing her, for the first time in years.

More than anything, Harper wanted him to trust her. "Yes."

"You must keep it a secret."

Maurice's eyes were veiled in shadow. Harper tried to meet them anyway. "Even from Mom?" she asked, a terrible suspicion stealing over her. "You're not going to *leave* us—"

"No!" The horror in his voice was so palpable, Harper believed him instantly. "Nothing like that. It's simply that this is a dangerous thing. And I think you might understand it in a way the rest of our family can't, after... after everything you've been through."

Harper couldn't stop the hurt welling up inside of her. "Everything I've been through?" she whispered. "Just say it. I lost my hand. I don't have powers."

"And yet you're still fighting." Her father gently, almost lovingly, took her hand in his. "You're out in the woods in the middle of the night, training. But what if you had something to fight for? Somewhere to actually use your sword?"

"That's impossible." Harper tried to keep her voice steady. Tried not to feel even the smallest shred of hope. "I failed my ritual. You do that in this town and you're nothing—you said so yourself."

"I know. But there are other ways to be powerful."

Harper snorted. "Are you talking about putting me on patrol again? The Hawthornes would never allow that."

A strange smile stole over her father's face. "The sheriff and her family would never allow that, no," he said. "But what if the Hawthornes didn't have control of the town anymore?"

For Harper's entire life, her father had bent to the Hawthornes' will—Augusta's grandmother, her father, and now Augusta herself. He made their sentinels. He patrolled. He trained his children to serve them.

And when the Hawthornes had decided Harper was useless to them, he had followed their lead.

But in that moment, in her father's face, Harper saw that he was disillusioned with the Hawthornes, too. Just like her, Maurice Carlisle had a quiet, steady core of anger festering inside him.

"Are you talking about a rebellion?" she whispered.

"Rebellion's such a messy word," said Maurice, his smile widening. "I much prefer the term *coup*."

The thought sent a thrill down Harper's spine. There was just one problem. "Four Paths loves the Hawthornes."

A grim look stole over her father's face. "Not anymore. There was an incident last night. Deputy Anders was lost in the Gray."

She remembered Anders. He'd been a good man—one of the few people in the sheriff's office to even acknowledge her after her failed ritual.

And Harper had spent enough time wandering through that skeletal forest to know it was a horrible place to die.

She shuddered. "Not him, too."

Her father nodded solemnly. "I'm afraid so. And there will be more, soon. Things are getting more and more dangerous in Four Paths, and the Hawthornes have done nothing to stop it. So I'm taking matters into my own hands. That's where I've been tonight."

"Doing what, exactly?"

The moonlight shifted to the side of Maurice Carlisle's face. Yet again, Harper watched him deliberate.

"Dad," she said. "You promised to tell me."

"Isn't it enough to know that things are about to change?"

But it wasn't enough.

Harper had spent the last three years waiting, quietly, for things to change.

She no longer trusted anyone else to slay her demons

for her. And more importantly, if someone was going to take down the people who'd made her life a living hell, she wanted it to be her.

She had been ignored too many times.

"No," she said. "Whatever you're doing, I want in."

"Harper. You don't know what you're asking—"

"I know enough." Harper snatched her sword up and swung it in a fluid, perfect arc across her shoulder. Her father's eyes widened. "What more can this town really do to me?"

Maurice Carlisle sighed, shaking his head, and Harper felt a surge of triumph. "Very well. I suppose… it would be useful if you'd get close to the new Saunders girl. She could be a valuable ally to our cause."

Harper thought of the way Violet had looked at Justin back in the classroom. "The Hawthornes are already talking to her."

"I know," said Maurice. "But she knows nothing about her heritage. The Carlisles and the Saunderses were allies when I was a boy. She'll need help soon. She should get that help from you."

Warmth rushed through Harper's chest as she realized that he'd called her a Carlisle. But that made her think of her siblings—the ones with actual power. "Wouldn't Mitzi or Seth make a better ally?"

"Mitzi and Seth don't know what the Hawthornes are capable of the way you do. Show the girl that there's more to this town than that family."

There was such visceral hatred in the way he finished

his sentence, Harper didn't doubt it for a moment. She wondered how he had hidden it for so long.

She wasn't sure if she really could befriend Violet. But if it would help take the Hawthornes down, she was willing to try. "I'll do it."

Maurice nodded. "Consider this a test. If you pass, you can meet the others."

"Others?" said Harper. "How many of you are there?"

Her father's hand folded around the hilt of his knife. "Enough to change things."

Violet had been missing all night, but Juniper hadn't even noticed she was gone. She'd greeted her with nothing but a nod when Violet got out of a much-needed shower that morning, then shuffled off to her room.

Violet tried not to let that hurt sink in as she biked to school, her sore legs screaming with pain.

She didn't want to explain to her mother where she'd been, anyway. There was no way to talk about what she'd just seen without sounding like she was losing it. And she didn't trust Juniper not to treat her just like Daria if she told the truth.

Besides, there was a chance, even if it was a slim one, that it hadn't been real at all.

But that delusion was scuttled within seconds of her arrival in homeroom. Things seemed off from the moment she stepped through the doorway. Everyone was silent except for an occasional murmur, and Justin Hawthorne was missing. Isaac looked completely lost without him. He wasn't even reading a book, just staring blankly at his desk.

"Class, if I might have a moment." Mrs. Langham's nose and cheeks were slightly reddened, her voice hoarse. "As many of you already know, Deputy Frank Anders was taken from us last night in a tragic accident."

More murmurs, more nods. Violet fought down the urge to vomit again.

That body had to have been Frank Anders. She'd seen the badge on its chest.

Which meant she'd been in those woods with him— and with whoever, or whatever, had killed him.

"I must remind you all that the forest can be a dangerous place," continued Mrs. Langham, but Violet was no longer listening.

She lurched from her seat, her chair clattering to the floor behind her as she rushed out of homeroom. Her frantic footsteps reverberated through the empty hallways as she beelined for the front door. She'd never cut class in her life, had barely taken a sick day, but she could not sit in that room for one more second.

Violet stopped at the edge of the parking lot, leaving Four Paths High School behind her. A deep, impermeable wave of chestnut oaks rose far above her head, their shadows halting at the toes of her boots.

There was nowhere left to go but into the forest.

Violet blinked, and the trees were black and white. She blinked again, and Deputy Anders's sightless eyes were staring into hers.

She whimpered and shut her eyes, but Rosie's image was waiting behind them, half-transparent, branches curling toward them both.

"They're not real," she whispered. "They're not."

"What's not real?"

The voice was soft and feathery and came from behind her.

Violet whipped around, her defenses rising. Last night had left her jumpy.

But the white girl standing behind Violet clearly hadn't come to threaten her. She was small and finely sculpted, a porcelain doll with thick, winged eyeliner. Her left arm stopped at the elbow, and a tangle of dark, wiry curls hung down to her waist.

She had seen the girl in homeroom. Which meant, Violet realized, flushing slightly, she'd watched her meltdown. "Why did you follow me?"

The girl's eyes, dark and doe-like, stirred with something that might've been pity. "You ran," she said. "I think I know what you were running from."

Violet scowled. "Maybe I was just bored."

"Mrs. Langham told you someone had died, and it bored you?" The girl's smile should've been reassuring, but it only made Violet realize her skin was stretched a little too tightly across her skull. "Somehow I doubt you're that heartless."

Violet took a deep, shuddering breath. "So maybe I was upset. I don't like death, okay?"

"No one does," said the girl. "But you just moved here. You didn't even know him."

"And you did," said Violet, a trickle of unease rising in her stomach. "So why aren't you mourning him?"

The girl stared straight into the woods behind Violet's shoulder. The silhouettes of the trunks were reflected in her dark brown eyes.

"I *am* mourning him." There was something distant in her voice, something hollow. "I know exactly how he died, Violet. Bones sticking out of his sides. White eyes. Gray skin. It's just not the sort of thing I want to say out loud. Makes me sound like I'm losing it, you know?"

The palms of Violet's hands went clammy with sweat, her throat contracting until she could barely breathe.

Whoever this girl was, she had seen that body, too.

"How could you possibly know that?" she choked out.

The girl took a step forward, the shadows of the trees engulfing her tiny form. "The same way I can tell you do. I've been to the Gray."

Violet knew immediately what she was talking about. It was the perfect term to describe those colorless trees, that static sky.

"How do you know I've been to—that place?"

"Are you telling me you haven't?"

"No," she said, with a strange surge of relief. "I'm not. That forest. It's… here. In this town."

"Yes and no," said the girl, which did not help Violet at all. "It's certainly real. And it's certainly in Four Paths. But it's not here." She waved her hand dismissively in the direction of the trees. "Most people don't make it out, you know. You were lucky."

"Doesn't that mean you were lucky, too?"

The girl chuckled. "No, I wasn't." She stuck out her hand. Violet shook it. It was surprisingly callused. "Harper Carlisle."

"Should I bother to introduce myself?"

Harper smiled—a real smile this time. "Nope. Everyone here knows who you are."

Violet's mind was bursting with questions, but the first one that toppled from her mouth surprised her. "What kind of animal can kill someone like that?"

Harper turned to face the woods again, her voice distant and dreamy. The trees had stopped rustling, like they were listening, too. "It's not an animal."

"Then what is it?"

Harper was still facing away from her when she spoke next. "I think the word most people would use is *monster*."

A day ago, Violet would've rolled her eyes at this sentence and walked away.

But now she turned, so she could see Harper's expression, and chose her next question very carefully. "What word would you use?"

The unflappable veneer she'd first seen on Harper's face was gone. There was a raw pain etched into her features that Violet had only ever seen in her own mirror. "I'm not sure. I'm not in the business of naming things I've never seen for myself."

"Why did you follow me out here, really?" The answer suddenly seemed very important.

Harper met her eyes. "Because no one should run out of class and have no one to follow them."

But Violet could tell she was lying. "Try again."

Harper scowled. "Fine. Because… I saw Justin Hawthorne talking to you yesterday. The Hawthornes wouldn't be bothering with you unless they thought you were useful to them somehow. So I'm warning you now that everyone in this town is just a pawn to them. Nothing more. No matter how much they pretend otherwise."

Violet remembered how the rest of the school had looked at Justin. How those adults had stared at his mother.

Their adoration couldn't have been further from the cold fury in Harper's words. And Violet could tell that the girl at least believed what she was saying—whether it was true or not.

"What did they do to you?" said Violet softly.

The chestnut oaks rustled above their heads as Harper twined her shaking fingers in her hair. "Let's just say that when they were my friends, I still had a left hand."

And then she turned and rushed away.

SIX

WHEN VIOLET BIKED HOME that afternoon, she found Daria sitting on the front porch, knitting. Daria was always at her calmest in her ancient rocking chair, her crystal needles flashing away as she slowly unwound a ball of crimson yarn, usually with Orpheus the cat wrapping himself around her ankles. But this time, Juniper was sitting next to her in a chair dragged out from the kitchen, brandishing knitting needles of her own.

Violet paused for a moment at the base of the porch, just trying to take it in.

"Are you… learning to knit?" The words came out a little stilted. Violet hadn't really spoken to her mother since finding out about Stephen Saunders.

"Well, I'm trying to teach her," said Daria reproachfully. "She can't relax long enough to get any stitches in."

Juniper gave Daria the same frown Violet had always given Rosie when her sister was bossing her around. The expression looked wrong on her mother's face, too juvenile, too unpolished. "You always told me I never knew how to be patient." Juniper was still wearing heels and dress slacks, like she would have back in Ossining, but her blouse was wrinkled, her hair tucked carelessly behind her ears.

"You never learned how to wait, June," said Daria, although the words were more affectionate than biting. "There's still time, though. The stones haven't come for you just yet."

She patted her on the shoulder as Juniper stared hopelessly at the tangled mess of red yarn wound between her needles.

"Stones, coming for me. Whatever you say." She turned her gaze to Violet. "Can you keep an eye on her for a second? I need to shoot off a few e-mails."

Violet nodded. A moment later, Juniper was gone, the knotted yarn left in her place.

Daria eyed her. "Can you knit?"

Violet leaned her bike against the railing. "No."

"A pity," said Daria. "You have clever hands."

Violet flexed her fingers. "Piano."

"Yes. You remind me of Stephen." The ghost of a smile flitted across her face. "He was a musician, too."

Violet decided to try to push her luck, despite what Juniper had said about upsetting Daria. The stairs creaked beneath her boots as she climbed onto the porch. "You said he was a musician? What did he play?"

"The piano," Daria said immediately. "It was why Juniper and Marcus wanted you to play. To honor him."

Marcus Caulfield. Her father.

She hadn't heard his name said aloud in a long time, and the words conjured up a sudden flash of memory—dark hair and a loud, raucous laugh, muscular arms lifting her up from the ground and wrapping her in a hug.

It flickered through her mind in the space of a heartbeat, leaving her aching for both halves of her family. She had never felt further from the dad she'd never really gotten the chance to know—and even though they were now in her mother's hometown, she had never felt further from Juniper, either.

"I didn't know that was why they enrolled me in piano lessons," Violet said quietly.

Daria shrugged. "June's always had trouble explaining herself. But she wanted something of Stephen to live on, I think."

"What happened to Stephen?" Violet asked. "Did it have anything to do with the Gray?"

Daria froze mid-stitch. "Come here," she said, her voice creaking. Violet approached, slowly, her heart beating faster than was probably strictly necessary. Daria clasped her hand in hers. "Oh, Violet. You're going to die with a hat on."

Violet sighed, even as unease prickled in the back of her skull. She should've known the lucidity would only last for a moment—there were clearly no real answers here. "Well, then, I'll just avoid headgear at all costs."

Daria tugged her hand away. "You'll forget one day. Everyone in Four Paths does."

Violet stared darkly at her palm. A sudden breeze washed over them, a lovely break from the early September heat.

"Have you tried looking in the woods, little bone?" Daria's voice was barely audible. "That's the only part of this town that really matters."

Violet jerked her head back toward her. "What?"

But the door was swinging open now, and Juniper was back, phone in hand. "It's horrible out here."

Violet barely heard her.

Have you tried looking in the woods, little bone?

Violet turned toward the trees.

She thought of the way Harper had talked about the forest that morning. The pain on her face.

There was so much here that she was only beginning to understand. But pretending it wasn't happening would do nothing to help her figure it out.

"I'll be out back." Violet hurried back down the stairs and rounded the corner of the house to the backyard.

She pushed back thoughts of Rosie's ghost and Deputy Anders's corpse as she headed into the trees, the towering trunks the only witnesses to her meager act of bravery.

Everything looked utterly mundane: the chestnut trunks of the oak trees winding toward one another like old friends conversing, the birds chirping in the branches above them, the green-tinged sunlight. But unease still pulsed through Violet's stomach.

Daylight didn't mean bad things couldn't happen.

She heard the insects buzzing before she saw them,

a droning, heavy noise, like a whirring propeller. They hung in the air like a mushroom cloud over something limp and furry at the base of a tree, an unlucky raccoon or opossum.

Violet wrinkled her nose. She was turning away when she saw the bit of crimson yarn. It took a second for her head to process the scene, leaving her as stiff and still as the forest around her, unable to move forward, unable to look away.

What remained of Orpheus lay between two roots, baking slowly in the midafternoon sun. The animal's eyes were mercifully closed, his head bent at an unnatural angle. The blood on his neck glistened.

Violet's vision spun. She stumbled, braced a hand against the nearest trunk, and retched onto the grass. Nothing came up, but she was still shaking when she looked at the body again. Something flickered in her peripheral vision—had his tail twitched?

It seemed impossible, but she had to see if he was still alive. If there was any shot at saving him.

"I'm so sorry," she whispered, forcing herself toward Orpheus. Her fingers brushed against the cat's front leg as she fumbled for a pulse.

A feeling of sudden loss coursed through her. Violet felt drained, exhausted, as if she had run for miles. She snatched her hand away from the body.

He was dead. She didn't need to look at him any longer to know that.

She was about to turn back toward the house, already

wondering what she'd tell Juniper, when something soft brushed against a rip in her jeans.

Orpheus was head-butting her ankle, purring. Behind him, the insects dissipated into the foliage.

Violet let out a harsh, choked scream, stumbled backward on shaking legs. It couldn't be. But the place where Orpheus's body had been was empty.

She steeled herself. Then she knelt down, reached out a tentative hand, and waited for Orpheus to pad toward her again.

His fur was soft and gentle against her fingers as she stroked his head. He certainly felt real, albeit friendlier than usual. He nosed against her palm, purring, and the tension building in Violet's chest decreased a little. Maybe this had been a terrifying hallucination.

Just like Rosie.

Her brain was simply playing tricks on her, conflating Daria's warning with her strange night in the forest.

She was about to stand up when her fingers touched something sticky on the cat's neck. Violet pulled back her hand, staring at the blood coating the tips of her fingers.

"You're dead." Violet backed away from Orpheus. Her voice was toneless and shrill, a spurt of air being released from a balloon. Something spun between them—a sense of connection, a tether, as if, when she touched him, she'd left a piece of herself behind. "Holy shit. You're dead."

A familiar blond form appeared in her peripheral vision, standing at the end of the clearing, his face ashen.

"No," said Justin Hawthorne softly. "He was dead. He's not now. Thanks to you."

Violet staggered back another step, still light-headed. "I don't understand."

His brow furrowed. "Violet…"

And then the world behind him opened like a yawning mouth. Violet recoiled as stiff white clouds devoured the blue sky. Dread coursed through her, a heavy, leaden thing that weighted down her limbs. A high, tinny noise hissed through Violet's ears, a voice snarling out words she couldn't understand. But as soon as she had registered it, it was gone.

Her breath hitched in her lungs again as she realized she was back in that colorless, awful place Harper had called the Gray.

And this time, she had taken Justin Hawthorne with her.

Justin had spent most of the day trying to slip away from the Hawthorne house. His mother had put him and May to work assuaging the doubts of the townspeople. But when she left for the sheriff's office in the afternoon, Justin had seized his chance to take matters into his own hands.

He hadn't expected to find Violet using powers— powers that could bring something back from the dead, proving that Augusta's insistence that the Saunderses were an irrelevant bloodline was a blatant lie. And he certainly hadn't expected both of them to fall into the Gray.

May's reading had been accurate about one thing, at least: Something was seriously out of balance.

Not that it mattered to him anymore, because he was definitely about to die.

Terror clawed at his throat as the dense green forest melted away, replaced by the same lifeless woods he'd seen on his ritual day. He and Violet now stood at the start of a road with buildings stretching along either side. They were flimsy-looking structures made of brick and logs, all rendered in perfect grayscale. Some of the bricks sagged; a log roof had a clumsily patched hole in the center; smoke was frozen halfway out of a chimney.

"Why are we here?" Violet's voice was sharp and accusatory, echoing oddly through the dead space of the Gray. "Did you do this?"

"Of course not!" It felt odd to mouth the words, then hear them. Justin tried to keep his focus on everything he knew about the Gray.

But most of what he knew amounted to the simple fact that if you went in, you probably weren't coming out.

"Then why?" she whispered, her shoulders caving inward, her jaw tightening.

He spread his arms out wide. "I don't know."

"How do we get out?" Violet said, panic tightening across her face. Behind her, the gray-and-white brick of the nearest house went in and out of focus, like a choppy Wi-Fi signal.

Justin's limbs were tensed and ready to run, but there was nothing to run from. And nowhere to go. "I don't know that either," he said, trying to sound calm. "Most people who wind up in the Gray…"

"They die like Frank Anders, don't they?" Violet's voice was grim. She swiped her hair out of her face, leaving a smear of the cat's blood across her forehead.

Justin swallowed his surprise. She clearly knew far more than Augusta had claimed she did. "Yes."

A hollow, tinny noise rushed through his skull; a soft whistle that might've been a laugh. He whipped around on instinct, shuddering, but there was nothing there.

"Did you hear that, too?" Violet whispered.

He nodded.

"We need to get out of here." She gestured toward something at the edge of the trees; a place where the Gray was starting to shimmer.

As the shimmering began to shape itself into a vaguely humanoid form, Justin remembered the bodies.

The bleached eyes. The bite marks on their limbs. The agony on their bloated faces.

Terror thrummed through him, so tangible that he could almost reach out and touch it. This was it—the death he'd escaped after his ritual. It had finally come to claim him.

But the form that appeared at the edge of the trees was not the Beast.

It was Isaac, arms outstretched, hands shimmering with energy. There was a jagged rip in the Gray starting at his fingertips, a hole in the world. Behind him stretched the waving branches of Four Paths' chestnut oaks.

Justin had never been so grateful to see him.

"Are you both just going to stare?" Isaac called out. "I can't hold this for long." His sweaty curls were slicked against his forehead, shoulders heaving with the effort of keeping the Gray at bay.

Violet rushed toward the door Justin's friend had made. But as Justin started to follow her, the noise whistled through his head again; louder this time, insistent, demanding.

It was a voice.

A strange leadenness stole through Justin as he contemplated weaving his way through the trees, being hunted, being killed.

You disappointed your family. You're disappointing the town. Even Isaac would be glad to see you gone—one less thing to worry about.

"Shit," he muttered. This was what the Beast did—it got inside your head. It told you you were worthless, you were nothing. "You're wrong."

Am I? The voice sounded almost amused. *You've lied to everyone, Justin Hawthorne. But you can't lie to me. Not about her.*

And suddenly Justin was there again, by the lake, Harper behind him, his mother in front of him, her mastiffs growling at her sides. The panic on her face.

He had chosen his family that day, not Harper, because that was what Hawthornes did. They put one another first.

But no matter how hard Justin tried, he couldn't bury that guilt.

Yes, you betrayed her, said the Beast. *And you deserve to be punished for it.*

An arm snaked itself beneath his shoulders and yanked him to his feet.

It took Justin a moment to orient himself, to realize that he was still in the Gray, he was still alive, still standing. Violet hadn't left him after all.

"I need… your help," he panted, leaning on her bony shoulder. She was stronger than she looked.

"Hey!" called out Isaac. "What are you doing, admiring the scenery?"

There they were; the Five of Bones, the Eight of Branches, and the Three of Daggers, side by side. Just like May had said they would be.

Violet snorted. "Yeah, I noticed."

They staggered out of the Gray together, one agonizing step at a time, until they collapsed into the lush green embrace of Four Paths once more.

And Justin pushed down the voice, the guilt, and the sinking feeling, deep in his gut, that all the Beast had done was tell him the truth.

PART TWO

THE KNOTTED ROOT

SEVEN

THE BLOOD AND GRIME on Violet's body made a rust-colored swirl around the Hawthornes' shower drain. She'd done her best to scrub the horror of the past few hours off her skin, but even when the water ran clear, the truth could not be washed away.

She had raised the dead.

She had returned to the Gray.

And it was only through the efforts of a boy who'd shown her nothing but hostility that she had gotten back out.

Violet pulled on some ill-fitting white jeans, courtesy of Justin's sister—May, that was her name—and an oversize Four Paths track sweatshirt that reeked of campfire smoke and Axe. The smell made Violet's nose wrinkle. But her own clothes were soiled.

She couldn't stop thinking of that moment in the Gray when Justin had faltered.

She could have abandoned him, left him to fade into

those dark, ashen trees. Harper had told her not to trust the Hawthornes. But Violet had decided, when she pulled Justin out of the Gray, to make up her own mind about her allegiances.

Because there was one intoxicating thought that had been burning through her from the moment Orpheus began to walk again.

If Violet could bring back a cat, what was stopping her from bringing back Rosie?

She was not going to miss the opportunity to learn how to fix all her problems just because of a single warning. So she had let Justin and Isaac lead her back to the Hawthornes' house, and she had agreed to hear them out.

The Hawthorne siblings had told her to go to their reading room once she was done cleaning up. But when she pushed open the door, they weren't there. Violet took in the space—although it was called the reading room, she saw no books. Shelves along the walls were stacked with knickknacks, placed in such a way that she could tell they were valuable. A petrified branch sat beside an incredibly realistic sculpture of a rabbit. A broken dagger lay next to a dusty card that gleamed silver in the dim light, a dejected-looking jester etched on the front with two words engraved at the bottom: *the Fool*.

The only piece of furniture in the room was a scarred wooden table, right beneath the room's only window.

Violet was drawn to a calligraphic print hanging on the wall. Writing at the top identified it as the *Founders' Legacy*, whatever that meant.

She read the words like a poem.

> *Branches, they twine & grow about the forest;*
> *they will tell you where to plant your*
> *roots & prune those that disagree.*
>
> *Daggers, their allies, weakened in their*
> *Leader's absence; they raise their hands in the*
> *air & shatter the world & put it back together.*
>
> *Stones, stalwart & steady—do not discount*
> *the builders, for they can always break*
> *what they have made.*
>
> *& Bones, masters of all things,*
> *the Living & the Dead.*
>
> *Do not question these who have braved*
> *that which ye will never understand.*
>
> *Praise them instead & do not falter*
> *in the tasks they command.*
>
> *Only then may you reach salvation.*

The print stirred something inside of her that she wasn't sure how to explain. Like a flower unfurling for the first time.

Have you tried looking in the woods, little bone?

Like she was finally waking up.

"Snooping?"

The voice was low and acrid. Violet knew before she turned her head that it belonged to Isaac, but she wasn't prepared for the way he was looking at the print.

Like he wanted to rip it to shreds.

"I was told to come here." The words came out a shade more defensive than she wanted them to. "Not my fault Justin and May are late."

"They weren't expecting you to clean up so quickly." Isaac was taller than she remembered; broad-shouldered but lanky. His flannel shirt had been buttoned up to the collar, obscuring his throat. "The Gray isn't something people usually process in a few minutes."

Isaac studied Violet's face as she glared back. If he was looking for fear, he wasn't going to find it.

The Gray was scary, sure. But it was nothing compared to losing Rosie.

"It takes a lot to freak me out," she said. Thinking about the Gray reminded her of how she'd gotten out. Of Isaac, his arms outstretched like he was holding up the universe. "You can open the Gray, too. How?"

"I was wondering when you'd ask a real question." Isaac gestured toward the print. She'd noticed the medallions at his wrists but saw for the first time that while one was a perfect pane of red glass, the other was horribly cracked. "I'm a Sullivan. It's like it says in the creed—we raise our hands in the air, and we shatter the world."

Violet looked at the print again, a shudder running down her spine. *Branches, stones, daggers, bones—*

"So, what, you break things?"

"Bones, walls, supernatural barriers," said Isaac. "Also hearts. But I don't need magic to do that."

"Hilarious," drawled Violet, like he hadn't just said *magic* so casually, tossing the word out there like it wasn't the impossibility she'd believed it was a month ago. "So that's a creed? A creed for what?"

Isaac shook his head. "You really don't know anything. And yet Justin seems so convinced you're going to help us."

"What do you think?"

Isaac's eyes met hers. They looked like burned-out matches. "Honestly? I think you're trouble."

Violet bristled, but before she could respond, Justin and May appeared in the doorway. Violet saw immediately how they belonged to this room, and it belonged to them. They fit here the way Daria fit in her rocking chair. The way Violet had fit in her and Rosie's old art studio. It was the place where they were most themselves.

"Making friends, I see," said May, holding up a mug. Steam wafted across the room, and Violet caught a whiff of cinnamon and something else, something woodsy. Even though they were inside, she couldn't shake the impression that this room was somehow part of the forest. "Coffee?"

"Absolutely." Violet raised the mug to her lips and took a grateful sip, then followed Justin and May to the table by the window. Isaac joined them a moment later.

The only source of light was a chandelier with bronze arms sculpted in the shape of branches. It cast a dim yellow glow on Justin's and May's faces, accentuating their high cheekbones.

"We hope you're okay," said Justin. "What happened to you today... well, it shouldn't have happened at all."

"So things in Four Paths aren't... always like this?" Violet said cautiously, thinking of Frank Anders again.

Justin shook his head. "No. I'm not sure how much you know about this town, but our family is dedicated to keeping Four Paths safe."

"She obviously knows enough, if she can do what you said." The crimson pendant at May's neck gleamed in the dim light, and Violet realized it was the same red glass as Isaac's bracelets, as the sheriff's badge.

Across the table, Isaac nodded. "I'm with May. There's no way she resurrected something without a ritual."

"Ritual?" Violet was lost. "What ritual?"

May let out a sharp, disbelieving snort.

"Violet, I was looking for you because I thought you could help us," said Justin, giving May and Isaac a frown that looked a lot like a warning. "Now I think we might be able to help each other. The three of us know almost everything there is to know about this town. So why don't you tell us what you're curious about, and let us fill in the blanks?"

It was what Violet had wanted them to say.

So she told the Hawthornes and Isaac what she felt they needed to know. Violet didn't think she could

102

explain Rosie, or how she'd hallucinated her, without bursting into tears. She didn't see why she should tell them that her information had come from Harper, either, and her long-dead uncle was none of their business. But the Gray, and Orpheus, and her blackouts… all of that came spilling out.

"If I really brought Orpheus back…" Violet had reached the end. "What does that mean? What am I? How does that even work?" Her voice shook with the weight of the words—she couldn't help it. Saying it made it real. And if it was real, maybe, just maybe, she could save Rosie after all.

She couldn't stop thinking about her sister standing in front of her, only this time, Rosie would actually be there. Violet would be able to hug her.

And Rosie would tell her, with a loving smirk, to stop being so melodramatic, because everything was finally okay.

"I think I understand now." Shadows flickered on the wall above Justin's head, spiraling outward across the paneled stone like leaf-laden branches unfurling from behind his neck. "You've already figured out that Four Paths isn't just a town. Technically, it's a prison."

Frank Anders's bleach-white eyes swam to the front of Violet's mind. Her stomach jolted. "A prison? For that… that thing in the Gray? Then why are we here, too?"

"It's in our bloodlines," Justin said, which didn't exactly calm Violet's unease. "It might be easier if we show you."

Justin hurried over to the rows of shelves, returning a

moment later with a yellowing scroll of paper. It was only when he unrolled it across the table and began to weight the corners down with smooth red stones that Violet realized what she was looking at.

It was a map of Four Paths, clearly drawn by hand. The woods were everywhere, hundreds of tiny green-and-brown etchings bleeding onto the winding path of Main Street as it forked around the town square. Violet had noticed before that Four Paths was far more forest than town, but the overwhelming presence of the trees was even more prevalent from a bird's-eye view.

Her eyes traced the tiny columns of the town hall, pausing on a small, eerily lifelike drawing of what was clearly her new house. The words *Saunders Territory* were inked beneath the manor.

This was one of four such "territories" that had been marked on the map. As Violet glanced at the Carlisle family's rustic stone cottage to the east and the Hawthornes in the south, she realized she recognized the other names.

There was no house in the western part of town, just a blacked-out bit of map with the words *Sullivan Territory* beneath it. Violet could make out the outline of a house under the blotched ink, but someone had clearly gone to great pains to strike it from the picture.

Violet's eyes flickered to Isaac, whose face had gone perfectly still. "What happened there?"

May started to say something, but Isaac cut her off. "Nothing good."

"And nothing relevant to our current conversation,"

added May, her voice sharp and shrill. "What really matters is here." Her pale pink fingernail tapped the words written at the top: "The Founders' Map."

Violet's brain spun as she remembered what those women had called her back at the Saunders manor.

What Justin had said to her in the Diner.

How everyone at school had looked at him, and May, and Isaac.

"We're descended from the town founders, aren't we?" she asked, raising her gaze to meet Justin's. "That's why our names are on this map. That creed is about our families. And that's why I can't go anywhere without people staring at me."

The surprise on his face told her she'd been right. "I'm not sure how you don't know this," said Justin. "But yes. Four people started this town in the 1840s— Hetty Hawthorne. Lydia Saunders. Richard Sullivan. Thomas Carlisle."

The reverence in his voice didn't escape her. Neither did the fact that Harper was from a founder family, too.

"Why does everyone care about that so much?"

"Because the founders are more than just people to Four Paths," said May. "When this town first began, they were worshipped. People called them the Four Deities. Together, they represented the four paths to salvation— hence, our name."

So Violet hadn't imagined the way everyone had looked at them. It *was* like they were gods.

She wasn't sure why that thought sat so poorly with

her as she clutched her coffee mug. "What did they do, exactly, that made people worship them?"

The woodsy scent Violet had noticed before seemed stronger now. As the light outside the room faded, the shadows of the objects on the shelves had grown long and slender, spilling onto the wall behind the Hawthorne siblings.

May smiled. "They defeated a monster."

"You mean the thing that lives in the Gray?" said Violet. "Because it doesn't seem all that defeated to me."

This time, Isaac was the one who answered. "This monster has been in Four Paths for a long time," he said. "It was—is—a creature unlike anything you've ever seen before. Normal weapons couldn't harm it. It was smart enough to get inside your head, see your thoughts, even your future. It could destroy you with a single touch." His eyes met hers again, and Violet thought of what he'd said just moments ago, about breaking things. "And it was difficult—maybe even impossible—to kill."

Isaac's words held the low, effortless cadence of someone telling a story they had heard a thousand times before. Like a fable. Like a lullaby.

"So they couldn't kill it," said Violet. "What did they do instead?"

Justin traced a finger across the curve at the edge of the map, a gesture as intimate as a lover's caress. "They tricked it. Bargained away parts of themselves to the monster in exchange for some of its magic. Then they used those powers to bind the monster to the town itself.

Well, to a version of the town. That place you got sucked into is its prison—another Four Paths, laid over ours, frozen in the moment the founders bound the monster inside of it. The Gray."

Violet thought of the row of strange, old houses. Of that static sky, those awful, twisted trees.

"So they worshipped them... us... for that," she said slowly, trying to understand.

"Yes," said Justin. "The religion was called the Church of the Four Deities. It died out a long time ago, but... the remnants are still there. We still protect the town. And they still respect us for it."

"You're lucky, you know." May's voice sounded a little less pinched now. "Most people who wander into the Gray don't come out alive. Especially people who haven't done a ritual."

Violet wondered why, exactly, May's eyes had flicked toward Justin at the end of that sentence. "You mentioned a ritual before. What is that?"

Justin answered. "Each founder bound themselves to the monster in a different way. As Hetty Hawthorne's descendants, we must pass the same trial she did to earn our powers. Each family's ritual is different, at slightly different ages, although it's always somewhere between thirteen and sixteen."

"So you both did these rituals?" said Violet.

A look passed between them. It reminded her of the wordless conversations she and Rosie used to have, and witnessing it made her insides seize.

"Yes," Justin said after a slightly protracted pause. "You're a senior—you're seventeen, right?"

Violet nodded.

"So you're past the age you should've done your ritual by, and you're pretty vulnerable until you do. You've got powers, but you won't be able to fully control them until you go through the right steps. The Gray will hold you here until that happens."

"Hold me here?" Violet's thoughts spun with sudden panic. "But I can leave, right?"

"No," said May solemnly. "You can't."

Violet's breaths were coming in short, choppy gasps. Rosie was in Westchester. Not here. Nothing but death and these strange god-families and the Gray were here. But she didn't want to break down like this; not here, in front of strangers. "I thought you said this prison was for the monster."

"It is." She was pretty sure Justin was trying to sound soothing, which only made her panic worse. "But your family line is bound to that monster. Which means that until you do your ritual, you'll effectively be treated the same way."

"So you're saying, what, none of you could leave until you did your rituals?"

Justin shook his head. "Of course we could leave. I'm saying that if you *don't* do your ritual when you're supposed to, the town keeps you here until you either gain control of your powers... or, well..."

He trailed off uncomfortably.

Isaac finished his thought, the barest trace of a smile on his lips. "Or you die."

Violet had no time to dwell on this, because her mind chose that moment to put something together that she should've realized minutes ago.

"Wait. My mother and my aunt must've done this ritual." Her words rose on a wave of slow, cresting anger. "Juniper must know all of this. She must be lying about everything."

She choked back a pained laugh. Justin placed his hand over hers, but she jerked it away.

"Actually, I don't think your mother is lying," May said delicately. "Just because founders can leave Four Paths for good doesn't mean it's easy. Our powers don't even work outside the town."

Violet's heart sank further. She had the means to bring Rosie back, and yet retrieving her sister had once again become borderline impossible.

It was an irony so cruel, May's next words barely registered.

"It's our sworn duty to stay here, to honor our ancestors, to protect the town. The price of leaving could've been her knowledge of the town's true nature."

Beside her, Justin nodded in affirmation, his eyes skating over Violet's head.

"This place can do that?" Violet said dubiously. She was still grappling with what she'd just learned. "Wipe someone's memories?"

"You have no idea what Four Paths is really capable of," said May darkly.

"Okay," Violet said. "So assuming my mother doesn't know, and since my aunt isn't exactly a reliable source, tell me what my ritual is supposed to be. And then I'll do it, and then I'll be able to leave."

Justin frowned. "The Saunders family hasn't really been a presence in this town since our mom was in high school. We barely know what kind of powers you have."

A strange laugh bubbled in Violet's throat. "You don't know what my ritual is. So you brought me here to tell me I'm trapped? That's it? There's nothing you can do?"

"Just because we don't know what you need to do to gain control of your powers doesn't mean we can't help you figure it out," said Justin indignantly. "We've got resources. And we know how this town works."

Violet forced down her panic. This was not the time to get angry—this was the time to think. "So you said we could help each other. What's in it for you if you help me?"

The three of them exchanged a glance. "We're sure you've noticed," Justin said carefully, "that things are... tense in town right now. There are fewer founders than there have ever been, and our ranks are stretched thin trying to protect everyone. We need your help—especially with the equinox coming up."

"Equinox?" asked Violet.

"When summer changes to fall, and winter changes to spring, the Gray is at its strongest," said May. "Usually, we can keep it contained. But this year, things haven't been going so well. And the fall equinox is a week and a half away."

"You saw Frank Anders's body," Isaac said bluntly. "More founders patrolling means fewer deaths. We'll help you learn to control your powers, if you agree to use those powers to help us keep the town safe."

"It's a great honor, you know," added May. "You should be proud of your legacy."

But Violet wasn't sure that was true.

She'd always wanted to feel like she was part of a real family. Coming here had made her wonder if Juniper's walls were finally falling. But all she'd seen of her mother's legacy was pain and secrecy. And her father's family was still as much of a mystery as it had ever been.

Violet wanted to run back to Ossining.

Was she really trapped here? Or did the Hawthornes just want her to believe that?

"I need to know it's true before I say yes," she said, locking eyes with Justin. "That I'm really stuck in this town. That you were telling the truth. That I need to do my ritual to leave."

But it was May who responded. "I figured you might say that." She rose from her seat and grabbed a wooden box from one of the shelves, lowering it carefully onto the table. Burned into the center of the wood was a symbol Violet had seen before: a circle with four lines crossing through it, almost touching. May added, "And I know exactly how to answer your questions."

The woodsy smell Violet had noticed in the reading room seemed to grow even stronger as she stared at the box. She turned her eyes on May, whose face had gone ashen, almost wraithlike, in the fading sunlight, shadows pooling like dark pits beneath her eyes.

"What's in the box?" Violet said hoarsely.

May's smile widened, revealing canine teeth that seemed a bit too pointed for someone so outwardly polished. "A family heirloom."

She flipped the box open, revealing a deck of cards the size of Violet's palms. The outline of a bone-white eye was etched into the back of the top card.

"Are those tarots?" Violet could've sworn the portrait on the wall behind May frowned at her as she spoke, but when she gave it a closer look, it was perfectly still. She shuddered and returned her gaze to May, who let out a disdainful sigh.

"They are the Deck of Omens," she said, drawing the cards out of the box and shuffling them easily in her thin, bony hands. Beside her, Justin gazed at the cards reverentially, while Isaac shrank away, as if he could vanish into the shadows. "Created by Hetty Hawthorne, the first great Seer. She used tarot as a template." She jerked her head toward the shelf where the silver *Fool* lay. "But this deck is her own. There are four main suits. Branches, bones, daggers, and stones, each with nine number cards and two trumps, plus two wild cards."

"Wild cards?"

The shadows of the branches behind May's back seemed to draw a little closer to her as she smirked. "They show up when they feel like it. Now, my power is tied to the roots of this town. These cards use me as a conduit to answer any questions you might have. They can tell you anything—about your past, your present, your future."

"Okay, but if the cards said something you didn't like, couldn't you just lie to me?"

May chuckled mirthlessly. "No. I can't. It's a covenant you make with the deck—it will tell you the truth, but you're honor bound to pass that on. If you lie…" Her face darkened. "They stop talking."

"I didn't know that," said Isaac softly, from across the table. He was eyeing the deck like it would burn him if he touched it.

May shot him an acrid glare. "Maybe you would if you'd ever let me read your cards."

Justin frowned at them. "Both of you. Focus."

May cleared her throat. "Right, then. Violet, this is your chance. Ask a question."

Violet straightened up, her mind whirling with the possibilities. "Can I ask what my ritual is?"

"You have to ask a question that directly pertains to you," said May. "You didn't create the ritual, so no."

Violet frowned. There was still so little she knew, so much she wanted to know. This question had to be phrased right.

"Is it true that I can't really leave town?" Violet said slowly. "And how can I figure out how to do my ritual?"

"I said one question," grumbled May, but she was already shuffling.

To Violet's astonishment, the cards were vanishing between her hands, one by one.

There were only three cards left when May finished. She laid them out on the table and let out a somewhat huffy sigh.

"We have to hold hands now," she said, looking rather uncomfortable. "All our powers need skin-to-skin contact to work."

So Violet reluctantly slid her hands into May's clammy grasp and Isaac's fingers. Physical contact made Violet severely uncomfortable—she'd barely touched anyone since Rosie's death. Both their palms were strong and calloused, but May's grip felt perfunctory while Isaac's was surprisingly gentle.

But the sensation she felt a moment later was a hundred times worse than holding someone's hand: like fingers reaching *inside her skull*.

"What the hell?" she gasped, yanking her hands away. "What is that?"

"I probably should've warned you," May said. "It's a Hawthorne thing. We get inside your head."

"Yes, you should've warned me!" Violet glared at her. "I don't want you reading my mind."

"It's not mind reading," said May crossly, although she at least had the grace to look ashamed. "I don't really see anything important. It's how I connect you to the cards. They link together the things you've done and the most likely outcome of your question. It just feels a little strange, is all."

"A little strange?"

May shrugged. "Do you want answers or not?"

Violet scowled at her, but she'd come this far. So she grasped May's hand again and spent the next thirty seconds in agonized, shuddering silence.

"All right," May said at last. "That's enough."

Violet pulled her hands away and balled them up in her lap, sagging with relief. Her only consolation for what she'd just let May do was that the girl looked just as pleased as Violet was that they were no longer touching.

"All right," she said. "Here we go."

She turned over the Deck of Omens. Violet let out a startled sound as she saw the card in the center.

It was like peering into another world, a world she wished she didn't recognize. Swirls of paint rendered a person, mostly in shadow, standing in the center of a clearing ringed with thin gray trees. A single shaft of light shone onto the figure's hand, but instead of flesh and blood, the artist had chosen to paint only bones. An outline of a bone with the number five inside it was etched into the top right corner.

"I see you recognize your card." May rested the tip of her pale pink fingernail against the painted wood. "The Five of Bones."

"I'm not one of the trumps?" said Violet.

"You wouldn't want to be," May and Justin chorused.

"It's not unusual to have an avatar of yourself represented in a reading like this," May continued. "Now, on your right, we've got the Wolf." The art on this card depicted an animal with fur that looked black at first glance, but had a thousand tiny iridescent colors glimmering just beneath the surface. Whoever had painted the Deck of Omens had been ridiculously talented. Violet could've sworn the wild, searching eye of the creature was locked on hers. "The Wolf doesn't mean a literal wild animal. It represents an unpredictable source of power—yours. However, what gets interesting is when we take a look at your question in conjunction with this." May's hand moved across to the third card, the Eight of Bones. Two skulls were nestled nose to nose on a bed of loamy earth. One was polished and pristine, the other horribly disfigured, with cracks all down the head and a jawbone that had been snapped in two.

"There's a science to these cards," she said. "The four suits were created to represent each of the founding families of Four Paths. The branch suit represents us, the Hawthornes. The daggers are the Sullivans, the stones are the Carlisles..." May's voice grew more hesitant when she talked about the Carlisles, but she kept on speaking. "And the bones are, of course, you. So that's why this is so odd. This card must represent someone in your family, but it's answering your question. This is what's trapped you in this town, what's stopping you from completing your ritual. Or perhaps the reason why you're even stuck in this predicament at all. The answers you're looking for lie with them."

Violet's heart pressed painfully against her rib cage, her fingers sliding automatically over the rose at her wrist.

She couldn't speak, couldn't think, and all of them were watching her now, Isaac most of all.

"You know who this card is talking about," he said. It wasn't a question.

Violet flinched away from him, as if she had been struck—but no, that would hurt less. Because there were no words for this that weren't followed by tears, and she would not cry here, not in front of them. Let them think her cold or callous, let them think she was a liar, let them think that she was anything but weak.

"Shit," May said in her high, shrill voice from across the table. Violet yanked her gaze back toward her.

Redness bloomed in the corner of May's eye, spreading across her sclera. Violet watched, horrified, as she blinked, sending a crimson tear down her cheek.

"Are you all right?" she whispered.

"Don't look at me," May snarled at her, wiping the blood away with a shaking fist. "Look at the cards."

So Violet looked down.

At the fourth card that had appeared in the center of the table.

A crown with four spires had been painted onto a dark background. Each spire was made from the material of a suit: a mass of entwined branches, a bleached, whittled bone, a gleaming blade, and a jagged bit of stone. Each point of the crown was soaked in blood, and beneath it was a pair of cruel yellow eyes.

Written beneath them, in letters so splotched and shaky that Violet could barely read them, were two words: *the Beast*.

She knew without asking that this was the monster in

the Gray. And she realized then that she believed in it, believed unquestionably, to her core, that there was something horrible gazing out at her from inside that bit of wood. The skeletal outlines of trees swam in her mind as she stumbled back from the table, her coffee sloshing onto the floor.

Beside her, Isaac was already moving—toward Justin, who sat still, too still, mere inches away from the card. The expression on his face reminded her of how he'd looked in the Gray: like the light behind his eyes had flickered out.

Isaac clasped Justin's shoulder at the same time that May snatched the cards up from the table.

The moment May slammed the lid down on the box, it felt as if all the air had rushed back into the reading room. Isaac slowly withdrew his hand from Justin's shoulder. The concern on his face as he watched Justin was so palpable, so tender, that Violet had to avert her eyes. No one had ever looked at her like that.

"Okay," Violet said, wiping her coffee-stained hand off on her jeans. "Does someone want to explain what the fuck that was?"

May's bloody fingers were clenched around the box tightly enough to turn her knuckles white. Two more streaks of blood had joined the first on her face, crimson lines that marred the porcelain skin of her cheek. "Proof that you need to do your ritual," she said. "Because if you don't get your powers under control, you'll keep summoning *that*."

Violet's throat went dry. "You're saying that card showing up was my fault?"

"It was your reading," said May.

"You'll figure it out," Justin said hoarsely. His tan skin was still a bit washed out, sweat beaded across his temples. But he looked better than he had mere seconds ago. "We can help. And then we'll be able to make it so that monster can never kill anyone again."

"Well," Violet said, "I guess I don't have a choice."

Across the room, Isaac let out a deep, guttural chuckle. "Welcome to Four Paths," he said. "Nobody would ever stay here if they had a choice."

EIGHT

JUSTIN COULDN'T REMEMBER A time when he hadn't known the truth about Four Paths. Some of his first memories were of his grandfather, the sheriff before Augusta. He'd been a big man, big enough to rock both Justin and May to sleep as he sang the "Founders' Lullaby."

> *Little children, led astray,*
> *Wandered through the woods one day.*
> *Stumbled right into the Gray,*
> *Never to return.*
> *In that place where nightmares dwell,*
> *Only four have lived to tell.*
> *That is why we have to stay:*
> *Branches and stones, daggers and bones,*
> *They locked the Beast away.*

The familiar words of the song rang through Justin's head as he and May walked through the woods on their way to check in for that night's patrol.

Memories of Justin's grandfather reminded him of the man he would never become, even if he did remain in Four Paths. These were the woods where he had learned to run, where he'd learned to kiss—among other things— where he had sought shelter when his family was too much to handle. But while the woods were the same, Justin wasn't.

Now he could barely glance at each impossibly tall trunk without thinking of the Gray opening behind it. He did not belong in this moon-dappled forest, breathing in the good, clean smells of wood and earth. He should have died on his ritual day, beneath those clouds the color of dulled steel, lost forever in that endless expanse of bowed, ashen trees. If not for May, he would have.

"You look grim," said his sister, stuffing her hands in the pockets of her pink satin bomber jacket. Although it wasn't even mid-September, the air was starting to grow chillier. "I thought you'd be happy. You cracked the ice queen."

"Violet's not an ice queen," said Justin, wincing at the soreness in his calves from that evening's run. After talking to Violet, he had desperately needed to blow off some steam. "And I didn't crack her. The Gray did that."

Justin had been looking for an ally when he'd sought her out. Instead, he'd found a problem he wasn't sure he could solve.

"She doesn't actually care about protecting Four Paths," Isaac had said matter-of-factly a few hours ago, after

Violet had gone home. "She just wants to get the fuck out of here."

"So you don't think we should help her?" Justin had asked him.

Isaac twisted the cracked medallion on his wrist. "I didn't say that."

"She raises the dead," May said now. "Could be... interesting, seeing how she does on a patrol."

Justin nodded in agreement as the lights of the sheriff's station cut through the darkness, drawing them both toward the squat, ugly building at the edge of town like moths to a flame.

He was expecting the normal setup for patrol once they got inside—Augusta and a few deputies lined up, dividing routes, giving orders. But instead, their mother was waiting for them in the foyer, alone, her choppy blond hair glowing almost neon where it was silhouetted by the fluorescent lights.

Justin's first thought was that something terrible had happened, again.

"Is everything all right?" said May sharply, who had clearly had the same thought.

"Everything's fine," Augusta said quickly. "There's just something I need to discuss with your brother. May, you can go ahead to the conference room, where the deputies are planning the routes."

May vanished down the hallway, shooting Justin a confused look.

Justin had grown enough in the past few years that

they were about the same height, but Augusta still felt taller than him as she led him down the corridor and into her poorly lit office. The mastiffs were curled up on the floor in a pile, napping. Brutus's tail twitched as Justin sat down and patted his head.

"What's this about?" he asked. Augusta situated herself behind the desk as Justin racked his brain for what he could've done wrong. All he could think of was Violet—but if that were the case, she would've kept May around, too.

"I felt it was best we discussed this in person." Augusta fixed him with a look that made Justin feel like he'd been pinned to his seat. "I don't think you should go on patrol tonight."

Justin frowned. "Why? Does Mitzi or Seth want to trade?"

"No," Augusta said. "But I'm worried about your capabilities. Especially now that we're close to the equinox. It's for your own good, really—I'm just trying to keep you safe."

Justin had spent enough time on various athletic teams to know what she was really saying. "You're benching me?"

"I'm protecting you."

The words hit him like a dull thud in the chest.

"And what about the people who might die because I'm not patrolling?" he said. "Who's going to protect them?"

"I won't let you risk your life like that," Augusta said,

almost gently. "Everything is under control. I promise."

"Mitzi, Seth, Isaac, and May can't protect the town on their own. Maurice Carlisle doesn't patrol and—" Justin cut himself off before he could mention Violet.

Augusta narrowed her eyes. "And who? Please don't tell me you're about to bring up Harper Carlisle."

Justin swallowed, grateful for the easy lie. "You said her name. Not me."

Augusta Hawthorne did not appreciate anyone she couldn't control. Anyone who might be dangerous to Four Paths.

He'd learned that lesson when she'd forced him to betray Harper three years ago.

If he told her about Violet's blackouts, her powers, how she'd taken him into the Gray with her, Augusta would treat Violet as a threat instead of an ally. And another founder who could potentially keep the town in one piece would never even get the chance to help them.

Justin couldn't let that happen. Which meant he would need to lie to his mother, and so would May and Isaac.

He thought of the people who'd died that year— Vanessa Burke, who'd disappeared from a party one chilly February night; Carl Falahee, who'd been discovered right behind the high school. Hap Whitley. Deputy Anders.

Their bleach-white eyes. Their bloated, shiny skin. The bones protruding from their abdomens in a rippled, gruesome wave.

He had enough on his conscience already. He refused

to add Violet Saunders to the list of people he had failed.

"I know what happened with Harper upset you," said Augusta, folding her gloved hands across her desk. "But it wasn't as if you would have been allowed to be with her long-term, anyway—and you've certainly had no trouble finding young women to replace her."

"Mom!" Justin could feel his cheeks flushing. He would rather be back in the Gray than spend another second on this topic of conversation. "Can we please not talk about this?"

"Very well, then," said Augusta primly. "I'm just saying, this patrol business isn't nearly as bad as you're making it seem. It's only for a few weeks. You can use the time to work on your college applications."

"Yeah, great," muttered Justin. "I can write my common app essay about how my mom won't let me protect my town from an ancient evil."

His mother's face contorted into an expression he hadn't seen in ages. It took him a second to realize she was holding back a laugh. "Well, it would certainly stand out."

The hardest part about having a mother who could switch between unyielding and wryly self-deprecating at a moment's notice was that he could never tell whether he had amused or upset her. Sometimes a single offhand sarcastic comment was enough to send Augusta into a cold, vicious rage. But other times, she was the one making the joke.

Justin was tired of always having to brace himself

before they talked. Tired of wondering which version of his mother he'd get when they butted heads.

He had been lucky this time.

Probably because she knew she'd won.

"All right," Justin said dully, rising from his chair, suddenly exhausted from the enormous difference between who he was and who he wanted to be. "I'll go home."

Across the table, Augusta's face split into a smile, like a crack forming in a slab of concrete.

Violet barely slept that night. She spent hours going over everything she'd learned during the day, trying to separate the truths from the lies, trying to understand this new world she'd just been plunged into headfirst.

She couldn't shake the belief that there was more going on with the Hawthornes than what they'd told her. But they hadn't been lying about the monster. They hadn't been fazed by what she'd done to Orpheus.

And, most crucially, they had promised to help her find a way out.

She just wasn't sure what other strings were attached to it.

Juniper was fiddling with the coffeemaker when Violet came down the stairs for breakfast. Her ears were Bluetooth-free, but her phone sat on the kitchen island. Orpheus wound around the legs of the kitchen table, his yellow eyes glimmering in the shadows.

Violet tried not to think about what he'd looked like

the day before, the blood glimmering on his neck, his body sprawled beneath the trees.

He was okay now. That was what mattered.

"The local coffee stock is terrible here," Juniper said by way of greeting. Violet grunted in assent. "And do you know how much trouble I've had with ordering anything online? No one wants to deliver to this town."

Violet studied her mother, who was dressed like she was about to head off to her New York City office instead of spending six hours taking conference calls in her bedroom.

There was something else the Hawthornes had told her about the night before—something about Juniper.

"Mom," she said. "You lived in Four Paths for eighteen years, right?"

"We've covered this." Juniper fluffed her hair. It looked sleek and straight today, which meant she'd blow-dried it to within an inch of its life. "What is it? Are you going to ask more questions about… you know?"

So much had happened over the past day, Violet had legitimately forgotten about Stephen Saunders.

But now she thought about him again. Was the pain of losing her brother enough to make Juniper stay silent about Four Paths for all these years? Violet knew by now that Juniper had hidden a lot.

She'd hidden Stephen's entire existence, Daria's illness, her family's reputation. She hadn't let Violet and Rosie see their Caulfield cousins and grandparents for all those years, even when they'd asked. Violet hadn't even known how to invite them to the funeral; there were a million Caulfields on social media, and it had been a long time since they'd been in contact beyond occasional holiday cards. So Violet wouldn't put concealing a strange magical heritage past her. It was hardly the worst thing her mother had done.

"Not about your brother," Violet said, not missing the way Juniper's shoulders relaxed. "About Four Paths. Haven't you noticed how weird things can get here?"

"I dearly wish weird things happened in this town. It would be an improvement over all the nothing."

Violet could tell her mother wasn't lying by the way she'd deflated after Violet mentioned Stephen, like the worst thing she could've talked about had already been taken off the table.

But she still had to know for certain.

"It's okay," said Violet. "You can tell me the truth."

"The truth?" said Juniper. "Violet, what are you talking about?"

Her mother's phone blinked, and as Juniper reached toward it, frustration swelled in Violet's chest.

"You know what I'm talking about," Violet said.

Juniper tapped absently at the phone, her focus changing to the brightly lit screen. "I don't have time for this."

Her clear lack of understanding loosed the anger in Violet's chest. "About the founding families," she said. "About the Gray, about powers, about rituals. I mean, it's not like they had phones back when you were a kid, so you probably had to pay attention, right?"

But there was no recognition in her mother's gaze at all—only concern.

"I know you're suffering," Juniper said calmly, the phone still hovering beside her head. "But accusing me of hiding nonsensical things won't help. Maybe we can talk about finding a therapist here. Your grief counselor recommended we find someone new anyway."

The lump in Violet's throat swelled to bursting as she realized that for once, Juniper didn't sound disinterested. She sounded worried.

She darted out of the kitchen, her hunger gone. When she heard Juniper answer her phone, she sank down against the wall of the foyer, choking back tears as she gazed into the eyes of a stuffed falcon pinned to a wooden frame.

The Hawthornes had been right. Her mother was genuinely clueless.

A familiar flash of turquoise hair flickered in her peripheral vision. She whipped her head around, but the hallway was completely empty.

Something twinged in the back of her skull, a sensation that reminded her of the way May's power had felt when it had slid inside her head.

And before Violet could take another breath, move another muscle, her world went black.

Violet woke to something soft and cold nuzzling against her cheek. When her eyes fluttered open and met a pair of slitted yellow ones, she immediately thought of the cruel, intelligent eyes she'd seen on that card in the Hawthornes' reading room.

But then she saw Orpheus's ears twitch as he brushed his tail against her arm, and she let out a panicked breath that had yet to fully balloon inside her chest.

"Oh," she said hoarsely, reaching out to stroke Orpheus's neck. "It's you."

Violet knew the wooden ceiling stretching above her head. The row of boxes along the wall marked ROSIE.

She'd blacked out again. But at least this time, she'd woken up in her bedroom.

Orpheus let out a reproachful meow as she ran a finger down the divot in his neck where his spine had snapped. Although his body had stitched itself back together, a gap between his vertebrae still remained.

"I hope that doesn't hurt," she said softly.

He nuzzled against her palm, as if to reassure her, and she felt that tether between them again, a rush of energy that tied them together.

He looked like a cat. He felt like a cat.

But his body was far too cold. And when she cautiously petted his stomach, she felt no sign of a heartbeat. The fact that he let her touch his belly without scratching her *proved* that he was no longer an ordinary cat.

Not alive, not exactly. Yet he could still glare judgmentally at her as she sat up, bracing her hands against her comforter, a wave of nausea running through her.

Justin, May, and Isaac had told her that, until she did her ritual, her powers wouldn't be under her control. Were these blackouts a symptom of that? Or were they something else?

She could ask them. They had promised to help her.

But as the red yarn on Orpheus's ear shone in the light streaming through the window, Violet realized there was still someone in this house who could possibly answer her questions.

So Violet swung her feet from the bed and padded down the hallway, to Daria's room.

"Hello?" she called, knocking. "Aunt Daria? Are you in there?"

Violet's aunt often sequestered herself in strange corners of the Saunders manor, but her room seemed as good a place as any to start looking. When the door creaked open a few seconds later to reveal Daria, clad in another hand-knitted dress, Violet felt rather gratified that she had guessed correctly.

"I have a few questions," she said. "About our family. If you're in the mood to answer them."

Daria scratched absently at her graying hair. She was only a few years older than Juniper, but time had not been kind to her. Her face looked as if it had been crumpled into a ball and smoothed out again.

"Maybe," she said, sounding hesitant. But she opened the door wider and gestured for Violet to come in.

Violet had never been in Daria's room before, but it was more or less what she'd expected. Yarn, cat toys, and stacks of strange curios covered every surface. Dried flowers adorned the walls, and a large window looked out on the garden. Violet felt as if she were standing in the lair of a washed-up witch.

After what she'd learned these past few days, maybe she really was.

Violet perched uncomfortably on a purple velvet ottoman as Daria bustled about the room, grabbing strange objects, turning them over, and tossing them onto the floor.

"I've been talking to the Hawthornes," she said, trying to steer Daria back to earth. "They say we've got powers, but we don't get them until we do a ritual."

"The Hawthornes love to act like they're better than us." Daria lifted a block of amber containing a spider to her nose, sniffed it, and tossed it on the bed. "Their roots grow everywhere, twining around everyone's lives. They should let us grow on our own. That's what we always did."

"We? Do you mean the Saunders family?"

But Daria didn't even seem to hear her. "That Hawthorne boy. You should warn him. Tell him the Crusader's coming back here to die, at long last. He always does, you know. Everyone always comes back."

"Sure," said Violet slowly, trying to push back to when the conversation had made sense. "Do you know anything about us? What our ritual is?"

Daria stopped rifling through her items. "I used to know. I should know that." Her face went distant and frightened, almost childlike.

Violet's frustration turned immediately to concern. She had pushed her aunt too far. She could see that now.

"It's okay that you don't remember," she said quickly. "I'll figure it out."

Daria pinched a strand of the yarn woven into her dress and tugged, hard. "No, it's not," she said. "You should talk to the Carlisles."

Violet remembered their name on the map. Harper's warning. And risked another question. "Why?"

"Because we trusted one another," said Daria. "Go. And take the cat with you—the ungrateful little creature. He likes you better now, since you brought him back to life. Since you made him your companion."

Violet gaped at Daria. Orpheus mewled reproachfully from his seat beside the ottoman.

"You can tell he's... different?"

"I haven't forgotten everything," said Daria acridly. "We're the family of bones for a reason. Now let me knit in peace."

Daria shooed Violet out of the room and shut the door before she had the chance to get out any more questions.

Violet stood in the hallway for a moment, her mind whirling. And then her hand tightened around the phone in her pocket.

NINE

HARPER MET VIOLET AT the edge of the lake.
She was embarrassed by the way their last
conversation had ended, certain she'd looked strange for
rushing off like that. It was still hard for Harper to talk
about Justin. That night, she'd avoided her father, unwilling
to tell Maurice Carlisle that she had let him down, again.

But Violet had texted her the very next day, asking
to hang out. Which meant she hadn't ruined things
after all. She'd left Brett and Nora with Seth in order
to meet Violet solo—a risk, considering how irresponsible
her little brother was, but one she was willing to take
for this.

Harper waved Violet over when she caught sight of
her dark hair through the trees. Although the forest was
thick and fairly impassable along large stretches of the
water, no branches extended more than a few feet across
it—in fact, they twisted backward, some dramatically so,
in order to avoid it.

The Beast had come from the lake when the founders settled in Four Paths. The forest remembered that.

So did the Carlisles.

"I didn't realize the lake was this big," said Violet, when she reached Harper at last. A long-ago thunderstorm had felled a tree at the edge of the lake, creating a natural bench of scarred, knotted wood. "Do people swim here?"

"Never."

"Let me guess—there's a creepy reason why?"

"You really are learning about Four Paths," said Harper dryly.

Violet snorted and sat beside her on the log. She looked far more in control than the day before—and yet there was something hollow behind her perfectly applied makeup.

Harper noticed how she tapped her barely scuffed booties against the dirt.

How she picked at her crimson nail polish.

How she watched the trees around her, as if a threat lurked behind every branch.

She was trying so hard to keep herself together. But that only made it easier for Harper to see she was broken.

"Something's wrong," Harper said. It wasn't a question.

To her credit, Violet didn't treat it like one. "Yeah," she said flatly, something like a laugh in her voice. "You could say that."

"And you texted me because…"

"Because I think you might be able to help." Violet fixed her with a careful, shrewd look. "The Carlisles are a founding family, right?"

Harper nodded slowly, unsure where this was going. She'd assumed Violet knew something about her heritage. But news of the Saunders girl joining the patrol roster surely would've made its way through town by now, and it hadn't, not yet.

"So your family does rituals?"

Again, Harper nodded.

"Did you do one?"

Harper's eyes fell on the crumbled stone forms of ancient guardians on the other side of the lake, their bodies forever poised at the edge of the gently lapping tide. Behind them, she could just make out the walls and roof of her father's workshop. "I… don't have much experience with rituals."

"Because of your arm?" said Violet bluntly. "Because you're clearly perfectly capable—"

"Not my arm." It was oddly good to say the truth aloud, even though the words felt like a blade dragged across her tongue. "My ritual. I failed."

Violet ripped off a strip of crimson polish so viciously, Harper was surprised she didn't take the nail with it. "Wait. You can fail?"

"It happens." It only took two words to describe the worst day of Harper's life.

"Is that…" Violet hesitated, but Harper could already see where her eyes were focused: on the residual limb of her left hand.

"Yes," said Harper. "It's how I lost my hand."

Her family's ritual was simple: Descend to the bottom

of the lake and bring back a rock, the same way Thomas Carlisle had a hundred and fifty years ago. It had given Mitzi and Seth the power to turn their arms to stone. Given Maurice Carlisle his ability to craft the sentinels.

But when Harper had emerged from the lake, she had been in the Gray, not Four Paths. And her left hand, which had been clutching her precious handful of pebbles, had turned to reddish-brown stone from the elbow down—and immediately disintegrated.

In the months after she failed her ritual, she'd been terrified of the lake. Her dreams were filled with muddy water closing over her hand and feet, crushing her limbs to a pulp. But over the years, Harper's fear had faded. Now she felt only the slightest twinge of unease at the end of her left arm as she gazed down at the water lapping a few feet below her legs, another echo of phantom pain. In fact, she'd chosen to meet Violet by the lake in order to remind herself that she had already faced the worst this town had to offer. And as she finished relaying her story to Violet, she was proud of the fact that her voice had hardly faltered at all.

"Holy shit." Violet's eyes were wide not with pity, as Harper had feared, but rather with something that looked a lot like respect. "I'm so sorry that happened to you."

Harper shrugged. "Not your fault."

"Still." Violet paused. "I'm honored you told me all this, but why? You don't know me."

"The whole town knows what happened," said

Harper, thinking of the rumors she'd heard. If she wanted Violet to trust her, she needed to make sure her head wasn't filled with lies. "I'd rather you get the story from me. And besides, our families have traditionally been close."

Violet looked surprised to hear Harper bring it up. "So I've heard."

The traditional alliances had mattered a lot less since the Saunders family had faded out and the Sullivans had left. But the bones of them were still there. Harper's father would be happy to know that Violet thought so, too.

"If your family knew my family," Violet continued, "maybe there's something you can help me with. A question I don't know how to answer."

Harper remembered the promise her father had made her. Befriend Violet and earn a chance to take the Hawthornes down. This was it—her chance to make herself indispensable to Violet. "Go ahead. Ask me."

But there was something guarded in Violet's expression now. "What's in this for you? Really?"

Harper could tell Four Paths had already left its mark on Violet, had shown her that everyone in this town had an agenda of their own. That their help came with a cost. So Harper told her the only thing she had left in her arsenal: the truth. "It is the founding families' job to keep this town safe," she said. "A task I failed at the moment I didn't come out of the lake. Which means that most of the people here act as if I'm invisible."

Violet frowned. "Being invisible in a place where an

evil forest monster noticing you means an awful death doesn't seem like the worst thing in the world."

Harper bristled. Only a newcomer would sound so naive. "You wouldn't say that if you'd lived here your whole life. Being invisible when you used to be seen... it's like being dead, but no one mourns you. And you have to watch it." Harper didn't realize how close she was to crying until her voice cracked. "Helping you will force people to see me."

Violet rested her hand on the branch between them. A thick silver bracelet shimmered on her wrist. "I understand. Well, in that case, I need to know what my ritual is. Badly. It seems like no one in my family can tell me, but I thought maybe someone in your family would know."

Harper's heart sank.

Most of the family rituals were open secrets. There was a reason the Carlisles had built their house on the lake bed. The Hawthornes tried to keep theirs carefully guarded, but Harper knew their ridiculous tree was somehow involved. The Sullivan ritual was shrouded in horrible rumors since Isaac's had gone terribly wrong, driving his surviving family members out of town.

But the Saunders family had been hiding too long for even the rumors to survive.

"I don't know what your ritual is," Harper said. "But I'm still in. I'll help you figure it out. There must be some record of this in our archives—or at least a clue that can help us."

Violet's fingers curled around the bracelet. "Thank you." Her face hadn't moved, but her voice was hoarse enough to tell Harper that she was holding in whatever she was feeling. "The Hawthornes have promised to help me, too. I know you're not exactly their biggest fan, but... I was wondering if you'd be willing to work with them?"

There it was.

This had all been too good to be true.

Because if Violet trusted the Hawthornes, if she'd gone to them, if they'd offered to help her, then she was already a lost cause.

But Harper had one thing on her side that they didn't.

"I warned you about the Hawthornes," she said, meeting Violet's eyes. "You can work with them if you want. But I won't."

Violet's gaze was solemn. "Why? What happened?"

"Justin used to be my best friend." Harper had never told the story out loud like this. She wasn't sure she knew how to. "Until I failed my ritual, and then..."

Her throat was burning now. The phantom pain in her arm surged again, stronger this time, as if someone had stabbed a dagger through the palm of her left hand and twisted it.

Something had been waiting for her at the bottom of the lake. The Gray had opened for her, sucked her into its harsh, colorless embrace. Ripped her arm off below the elbow. Left her to wander among those trees for what had felt like mere minutes, but she would later learn had been days. She couldn't remember much about the Gray itself—the few memories she did have were of the Beast's voice hissing through her mind as she curled up on the ground and sobbed. She had no desire to reach deeper into those moments—she had gone through enough.

But Harper's suffering didn't end after she had returned to Four Paths, when she'd come home from the hospital. The Hawthornes had ignored her. Her family hadn't stood up for her.

She had been left all alone.

"I proved I was weak," Harper finished, aware as she said it that she must sound incredibly vulnerable. "So they started acting like I didn't exist. They still do."

Violet's long, pale fingers were pressed against her kneecaps. When she spoke, her voice quivered. "I'm sorry to hear that."

Harper swallowed down a lump of relief that Violet hadn't judged her, wasn't looking at her like she was broken. "It's all right."

"No, it's not. You said you were stuck in the Gray for days?"

Harper nodded.

Violet's dark eyes filled with a quiet, burning fury. "I could barely stand the Gray for a few minutes. So if you could endure that for days, then you're strong as hell, and anyone who says otherwise is full of shit."

The noise that emerged from Harper's throat hit the exact midpoint between relief and disbelief. She usually felt weak unless she was wielding a blade. All she had ever been able to focus on was what she'd failed to do, not what she'd achieved.

But now she saw a glimpse of what she might be—who she could've been, maybe, if things had gone differently.

"I don't need the Hawthornes and Isaac for this," said Violet, although she sounded a little uneasy about it. "I'm done. I can't support anyone who treated you that way."

She whipped her phone out of her pocket and began to type furiously.

Panic welled up in Harper's throat. "What are you doing?"

Violet tapped her phone, then looked up, a grim smile on her face. "Telling the Hawthornes their services are no longer needed."

Harper gulped.

She never would've been sure if Violet would believe her. She hadn't even dreamed that she would react like this.

"So, where do we start?" said Violet. "How can we find some potential leads?"

Harper thought about it. One clear answer came to mind. "The town hall is the easiest place to find information about the founders. It's basically a museum. All the interesting stuff about the powers isn't on public display, but there are still hints, I bet. It's worth looking."

"We could go today?"

Harper thought of Brett and Nora, and frowned. "I've got some babysitting to do. Tomorrow?"

"Fine with me." That grim smile was still fixed on her face, her expression frozen in place like a body in rigor mortis.

Harper tried to look strong and reassuring as Violet walked away. But even as her victory began to dawn on her, she knew it would not come without a cost.

She wasn't sure how yet, but she would pay for crossing the Hawthornes.

Violet walked down Main Street, her heeled boots clicking briskly across the cobblestones. The air felt soothing and balmy against her skin. Red-tinged trees bent across the quaint stone buildings, their chestnut trunks shining in the sunlight.

Four Paths had its charms, if you could ignore the fact that it was also a monster prison she apparently had some ancestral obligation to deal with.

"Worst magical destiny ever," she muttered as she stomped over the founders' symbol embedded in the square at the center of Main Street and climbed the steps to the town hall. Red-brown columns soared up on either side of her, stopping just beneath two stained-glass picture windows that depicted—what else?—a forest. The roof narrowed into a spire with a giant bell hanging in the center that reminded Violet of the spires at the top of the Saunders manor.

But she wasn't here to admire the architecture.

She was here for clues.

Violet had planned to do this with Harper after school,

but something had come up on Harper's end. She didn't really mind, though—she could handle a museum on her own.

She pushed open the door and stepped into an echoing stone hall. Dim light spilled in through the stained-glass windows above her head, casting everything in shifting browns and greens. Violet turned in a circle, her stomach tightening as she realized she was facing down a dozen portraits of stern-looking men and women with frizzy hair and clever eyes.

She knew, even before she peered at the first placard, that most of them shared her last name.

It was incredibly disarming to be faced with such unavoidable, permanent evidence of a heritage Violet had never known. A strange familiarity rose in her as she recognized the animals featured in a few portraits. The garter snake that was coiled around Helene Saunders's ghostly pale neck hung above the living room mantel, while the speckled falcon perched on Cal Saunders's dark brown hand graced the front hallway.

Companions. Like Orpheus.

They were mayoral portraits, as it turned out. The dates of their terms started in 1848, and they didn't stray from the Saunders family name until 1985, when Hiram Saunders was replaced by Geoff Sullivan.

The names traded off to different founders after that—a Carlisle, another Sullivan—until four years ago, when Mayor Storey had been sworn in.

"You're not going to find your ritual here." It wasn't

Harper's voice. "Just a lot of pictures of dead people. And people who wish they were dead."

"You're cheerful," Violet said as, behind her, the door to the town hall swung shut. "Did Justin ask you to follow me here?"

"I don't stalk people," said Isaac, joining her beside the portraits. His backpack hung carelessly off one shoulder. There was a beat-up book stuffed in the back pocket of his jeans. "Even if I'm asked nicely."

"So then what are you doing here?"

"Coming home."

Violet frowned at him. "You live in the town hall?"

Isaac tugged at his backpack strap. "It's a nice apartment."

"Yeah, but…" Violet remembered the blacked-out part of the map marked *Sullivan Territory*. The outline of a house she'd seen underneath it. "You live there by yourself?"

"Why do you care?" He shot her a grin. "Trying to get invited upstairs?"

Violet flushed. "I'm trying to do research. And you're getting in my way."

"There's much more to Four Paths than some old paintings of town mayors," Isaac said disdainfully. "Do you really think all the answers are just sitting out in the open? Our help means something. And you turned it down."

Violet stepped away from him, her fingers curling around the bracelet at her wrist. She didn't regret telling the Hawthornes to leave her alone. Harper's story had told her all she needed to know about them. There was no room in her life for disloyal, cowardly snakes—or anyone who chose to follow them.

"You didn't help me at all," she said.

"I got you out of the Gray, didn't I?"

"No, you got *Justin* out of the Gray." Violet had seen the bond between them. There was nobody left alive who cared about her like that. There was nobody left to save her. "I just happened to be there, too."

"You're alive, though, aren't you?"

"Is that your definition of *helped*?" Violet snapped. "Alive?"

Isaac's mouth twitched, and for a moment she felt uncomfortably seen. He was watching her like he'd watched her in the Diner, in homeroom, like he was waiting for her to lash out at him. Like he'd enjoy every moment of it if she did.

"Maybe I didn't help you, then." His voice bounced off the stone walls, echoing like the first roll of thunder before a storm. "But there are parts of the town hall that might actually have answers in them. They're just not accessible to the general public."

"Great," Violet drawled. "Thanks."

"I'm not done." He fumbled in his backpack for a moment and held up a ring of keys. "I am not the general public."

It was tempting. She had to admit it. But still, she hesitated.

Isaac huffed and shot her a look that Violet tried to

pretend was not pity. "Listen, if you run into trouble, and you don't come out, Justin will be inconsolable." He paused. "He's annoying when he's sad."

He was trying to be kind to her. Violet decided that if he could do that, she could try to let him help her.

So she nodded.

Isaac led Violet up a flight of stairs to a significantly less fancy door, protected by a brass deadbolt. Isaac unlocked it with his ring of keys.

"This floor is where the Four Paths archives are stored," he said, guiding her down a dingy, dimly lit hallway. "All the records of our town history are here. This is where Justin and May would've taken you if you didn't, you know, grievously insult them."

Violet would've been more concerned if he hadn't said it like he was amused instead of wounded. Although maybe those were the same thing with Isaac. "You don't seem that mad about it."

"It was kind of funny." Isaac shrugged. "People don't really say no to the Hawthornes. It's good for them to remember they're not invincible."

There were no pictures in this hallway, just wallpaper that smelled slightly of mildew and floorboards that creaked beneath Violet's boots. Violet couldn't quite believe they were still in the same building. She followed Isaac through another sagging wooden door, wincing as the mildew smell intensified.

Violet made out several dented metal filing cabinets and shelves piled high with books and papers, silhouetted by the light streaming in through the windows on the far wall. A strip of fluorescent lights flickered to life, casting the archive room in a sickly green glow.

Violet's eyes landed on a familiar face.

"Aunt Daria?" she whispered, then flushed, embarrassed, as she realized she was staring at a portrait on the wall, not a person. Although there was a distinct resemblance in the jut of their chins and the set of their eyes, this woman was not her aunt. She wore a high-necked dress that clearly wasn't from this century, a red medallion at her breast, and a live ermine draped around her shoulders.

Something about the painting looked a shade too alive—Violet almost expected her dark, heavy-lidded eyes to blink.

"These are the original founders," said Isaac dryly, from beside her. "They used to be downstairs, but people complained. Said they felt watched."

"Has anyone ever had a power that could do that?"

"No," said Isaac. "But the rest of the town doesn't know that."

"What does the town know about us, exactly?"

"They know we saved them," said Isaac. "They know we have powers. And they know about the monster."

Violet moved across the room, her eyes scanning the four paintings that hung on the wall.

On the left was Thomas Carlisle, a burly man with curls tied back in a ponytail and a wide, easy grin on his face. Laid across his upturned palms was a red-brown sword. Beside him was Hetty Hawthorne, sleek and blond and smug, a card held between two fingers, and on Hetty's right was Richard Sullivan.

Something about the man—slim and pale and looking off to the side, his hair streaked with gray—made her uneasy. Hetty Hawthorne had painted a dark smudge of something that might have been blood on the dagger he was tucking into his waistcoat.

But it was Lydia Saunders who primarily held Violet's attention.

This was the woman at the root of all her problems. She'd signed up her family for generations of strife and struggle, and for what? Powers that seemed to hurt just as much as they helped?

Violet's eyes drifted to the placards beneath the paintings, frowning as she noticed a distinct similarity between all four portraits.

"They died on the same day." She turned away from Lydia's slight, upturned smirk. "I'm guessing that's not a coincidence."

"Truly, your powers of deduction are remarkable," said Isaac. "The founders sacrificed themselves to create the Gray and bind the monster to Four Paths. Which is why we're all still so obsessed with them. Everybody loves a martyr—or four."

Violet swallowed, hard. "So they knew it would kill them?"

Isaac shrugged. "That's what the town believes."

She took a step toward him. "What about you? What do you believe?"

A shadow passed across his face. "I think our ancestors went looking for a monster. And I don't think they realized what the cost would be once they found it."

The weight of his words stayed with Violet as she began searching through the filing cabinets and rifling through the bookshelves, all under the watchful gaze of the founders' portraits.

When they'd first arrived, Violet had wondered why the archive room—a place that seemed important—had been left virtually abandoned. But after just a few minutes of sorting through dusty books and articles, she realized why.

Most of the information stored here was completely useless. Whoever had maintained these records had clearly believed in preserving everything they could find, from supply lists and order slips to ancient newspaper articles about people long dead.

Worst of all, there was no method of cataloging or organization that Violet could see. For a place that cared so much about its roots, the town was terrible at actually documenting them.

"Hey," said Violet, glancing at Isaac and noting the red spots on his cheeks. "Are you blushing?"

He jerked his head up from the stack of papers he'd been reading. "What? No. I just…" He cleared his throat. "Uh, I found some love letters. Between Helene Saunders and Malcolm Carlisle. Forbidden love, super sordid."

Violet frowned. "Forbidden? Why?"

"Founder descendants aren't supposed to pair off," said Isaac. "When two founders have kids, it cancels out their powers. Since only one branch of the family inherits powers anyway, competition is fierce, and no one wants to guarantee that their kids will be powerless."

"Oh," said Violet. She'd perched on a chair beside one of the bookshelves, building a nest of discarded materials on the floor beneath her. Her eyes scanned the picture of something called the Founders' Pageant—four grinning people wearing crowns and waving at an adoring crowd, like a warped version of homecoming.

"Does this Founders' Pageant thing still happen?"

"Every damn year, at the Founders' Day festival," said Isaac, who was sorting through a filing cabinet a few feet away. "Actually, as the only Saunders founder who's semi-functional, you'll probably have to participate."

Violet scowled at the back of his head. "Do I look like the kind of person who participates in things?"

Isaac shrugged. "You get to wear a crown. People clap. It's a morale booster."

"Clap for what?" said Violet. "Justin said three people have died this year alone."

"So you understand, then," Isaac said, "why it's so important to pretend everything is fine."

They fell silent for a few minutes after that.

She glanced up at the angles of Isaac's profile, his brow furrowed in concentration. Several buttons at the collar of his flannel shirt had come undone, exposing a line of crude discoloration that marred his throat. She was close enough to him to see the swollen, mottled flesh contract and expand as he breathed.

151

A scar.

Isaac caught her glance. An instant later, his hand was redoing the loose buttons with a kind of frenetic ease that told Violet he'd had a lot of practice.

"Don't ask," he said sharply.

"I wasn't going to," she said, and meant it. She could tell from the way his eyes widened that he believed her.

Everyone deserved the chance to tell their own story when they were ready, not when they were forced to.

She reached for the next thing on the bookshelf, realizing as she examined the binding that she recognized this kind of notebook. She'd used the same type of splotchy, black-and-white composition book in elementary school.

Violet flipped it open to the first page. The words were handwritten.

The Diary of Stephen Saunders,
January 1984——.

March 23, 1984

In nineteen days, my life is going to change.

I've decided to write in this journal because I want to be able to look back and see how things were when everything was just getting started. My life, I mean.

My name is Stephen Saunders, and if you're anyone else, you should stop reading this right now.

Yeah, sisters, that means you. June, I know about the

flask in your backpack. And, Daria, I know you caused that dent in Dad's car. Think very carefully about whether you want that information shared with our parents before you keep reading.

Not that you guys really care what I do enough to even find this journal. Honestly, in this family, no one really pays attention to you before you do your ritual.

Less than three weeks left until I turn sixteen. I can't wait.

"Hey," she said sharply. "I think I found something real."

And she began to read aloud.

TEN

CONSEQUENCES CAME MORE QUICKLY than Harper was expecting. A few hours after Violet had left her, Harper's phone buzzed in her skirt pocket.

She already knew on some level what would be waiting for her before she saw the screen.

It's me. Where are you? We need to talk—in person.

At first she was frightened. But that fear was quickly chased away by anger. So she ignored Justin's text for the rest of the night, contemplating her best course of action.

Only now was he paying her attention. Now that she was useful again. Now that she *mattered*.

She'd waited three years for him to reach out to her. He could wait a few hours for her to text him back.

When Harper woke up the next morning to start her training, she had made her decision. She and Justin Hawthorne did need to talk. But they would do it on her turf, on her terms, because for the first time in years, she finally had the upper hand.

After school, she told him. *At the lake's edge. Don't bother me before that.*

It felt good to tell him what to do. It felt better when he actually listened to her.

Yet when Justin's tall, agile form came into view at the edge of the water, Harper realized that all her mental preparation hadn't stopped her from wanting to throw up. Or turn invisible. Or melt.

Of course, she did none of these things.

Instead she rested her hand on the dormant German shepherd guardian beside her, for strength, and waited for him to come to her.

Harper had chosen the statue garden outside her father's workshop for a reason. She felt safer surrounded by the crumbling stone remnants of her ancestors' power: a reminder that the Carlisles mattered, too.

Besides, she knew the guardians tended to make people uneasy. And she wanted Justin Hawthorne on edge.

But as he drew closer, he didn't look rattled at all. Just tall and tan and annoyingly at home, even though he was in the middle of Carlisle territory.

Even though Harper had done her very best to look decidedly unwelcoming.

"I see you've convinced Violet that she needs your help more than she needs ours," Justin said, pausing between a half-crumbled raccoon and a crouching stone cougar, fangs bared. "I guess we deserve it."

Harper willed the cougar to come to life and sink its

teeth into Justin's throat. Unfortunately, nothing happened.

There was the slightest twinge of hurt in his voice. He was incredibly gifted at pretending to be wounded.

"Yes, you do." Harper was proud of how sharply the words came out. "Talk to her if you have questions. It was her call, not mine."

"Violet's new here. She doesn't understand how things work." Justin tugged at the neckline of his T-shirt. Harper's gaze, heedless of her attempts to keep it elsewhere, lingered on the part of his shoulder where fabric met skin.

"I know," she said, yanking her gaze up until it met his. "That's why I warned her about you."

Justin stepped forward. The branches behind him framed his head like a twisted crown. "You don't know what's at stake here, Harper."

Her name in his mouth was a knife in her gut. And Harper was sick of letting him wound her. "I didn't tell Violet not to trust you. I just told her the truth. It's not my fault what you did doesn't line up with how you want everyone to see you."

Justin fiddled with the medallion tied around his wrist, which shone crimson in the late afternoon sunlight. "I know that I'm not who Four Paths thinks I am. I can never be that person. But I never wanted to ignore you. It was the hardest thing I've ever had to do."

Justin was the perfect picture of guilt. Too perfect. The longer Harper looked at him, the less she believed it. And the more she wanted to rip the lie away from the corner of his downturned mouth.

Three years ago, after a week of the Hawthornes ignoring her, she'd shown up at their house. No one came when she rang the doorbell, not even when she saw Justin's face peering down from his bedroom window. She'd made eye contact with him for a moment—and then he'd pulled the curtains shut.

Harper had stumbled home in a haze of painkillers and tears, faced with the crippling knowledge that from then on, she could count on no one but herself.

That hurt welled up all over again as she watched Justin's head droop forward.

"Really?" she said. "Because you've seemed just fine these last three years."

"I'm trying to apologize—"

"No, you're not." Harper's voice had started to shake. She had listened to this for long enough. "Stop pretending to be sorry. You're only here because I took away something you wanted. But guess what? I couldn't do anything about it when you cut me out of your life. And you can't do anything about it if Violet doesn't want your help. You made your choice. Now she's making hers. Respect it."

Harper wanted him to protest. She was ready to argue. She would win—hell, she'd already won.

But instead, Justin's face slackened. His expression was devoid of false guilt now. It was devoid of everything. "You're right," he said numbly. "There's nothing I can do."

Harper swallowed her disappointment, sliding a hand down the dog's back. For a second something fluttered beneath her fingertips, a strange tingling that shot from her hand into the back of her skull. But the sensation was gone before she could take another breath. "You're not going to tell me to change Violet's mind?"

"What's the point?" said Justin, shaking his head. "You would never do it. But, Harper, if you're going to help her, you can't let the sheriff know what you're doing. We were keeping it a secret."

This, Harper hadn't been expecting.

Rebellion didn't come naturally to Justin and May. Back when they'd all been friends, Augusta had run her children's lives with the ferocity of a coach, the strictness of a headmistress, and the tyranny of a dictator.

For them to defy her... that took a spine Harper hadn't believed either Hawthorne child possessed.

"If your mother isn't letting you help Violet, why do you want to?"

This time, Harper knew in her gut that Justin was telling the truth. "Because I think our town's future depends on it," he said. "And because I'm tired of listening to my mother when she tells me to do things that will only lead to people getting hurt. It's why I stopped talking to you, you know—because of her."

And with that, Justin walked away, his wiry frame disappearing into the sinking sun.

Harper curled her fingers around the stone dog's ear, a rush of frustration coursing through her.

She'd had the conversation with him she'd daydreamed about for years. Told Justin what he'd done to her. And yet, somehow, he'd managed to make her feel guilty now that it was over.

They had been children when he'd left her all alone. Maybe that really had been Augusta Hawthorne's fault.

But it had still hurt her. And surely he had still known that it would hurt her.

Besides, Harper had done what her father asked. She had befriended Violet Saunders.

It was time to reap her reward.

The first few entries in Stephen Saunders's journal were boring. Violet was disappointed by her uncle's annoying teenage thoughts, which ranged from all the hot girls at school who would totally notice him after he did his ritual to talking about music and TV shows that she had never heard of and didn't care about. The one interesting part was whenever he talked about the piano.

But as his birthday approached, things became a bit more compelling.

April 4, 1984

Tonight Dad gave us this lecture at dinner about Saunders family responsibility. Grandma fell asleep at the table, and Daria left to "go check on the casserole" and didn't come back, but of course I had to stay. At the end of it, he fixed Juniper and me with this big stare.

Agatha made this cawing noise from her stand behind the table and flapped her wings. I swear, she was looking straight at me. Companions are creepy like that, like they know what their owners are thinking.

"Remember," Dad said. "The safety of Four Paths rests in your hands."

June says that Dad just lectures us a lot because he's mad that his brother became mayor, not him, but telling Dad that seems like a good way to get lectured until I die of boredom, so I won't.

My sisters did their rituals years ago. Daria sees people's deaths when she touches them. She won't tell anyone, though, so I don't really see how it actually helps. I mean, it's not like anybody has died since she got her power, so we don't even know if she's right. But sometimes she gets this look. Like she wants to throw up. She's never really had friends, but now she avoids everyone, even us.

I'm not sure if I would want to know what she knows.

No one will tell me what June can do. But I eavesdropped on Dad and Uncle Hiram talking about her once, going on about how "testing her powers" was going to be hard.

I guess she's something else. Something special. Figures—she's always been Dad's favorite.

Violet flipped to the next page. The entries got less carefree the closer Stephen came to his birthday. His original bravado was starting to falter, and in its place was more information about the town, gossip about the other families, and hints about his upcoming ritual.

"Do you think he'll talk about his ritual?" said Isaac. Violet frowned at Stephen's splotchy handwriting. "I hope so."

April 9, 1984

I turn sixteen in two days.

Daria won't even look at me, but June is worse—she keeps trying to hang out. This is the most I've seen her since she started spending all her time with Augusta Hawthorne. Augusta's bod is bodacious, but she's scary. Not even the biggest guys at school will talk to her.

"Okay, that's gross," said Isaac. "She's the sheriff. Also Justin's mom."

Violet's nose wrinkled with abject disgust. "I'm pretty sure I could live the rest of my life without ever seeing or hearing the word *bod* again."

I've been practicing piano more and more to avoid everyone, but it isn't working. So I walked through the woods for hours after school today, just to get out of the house. Maya Sullivan found me somehow—I guess I accidentally crossed into her family's part of the forest. Dad hates it when we go into Sullivan territory.

Isaac stiffened. Violet paused. "Your mother?"

He nodded, eyes fixed on her. "Go on."

But as Violet gazed down at the next few sentences,

she hesitated. "It's not exactly flattering. To you or the Hawthornes."

Isaac shrugged with carefully manufactured nonchalance. "I know what people say about my family."

So Violet continued.

He says their ritual is unnatural, their powers are wrong. June says it's just his old prejudices bubbling up—the Sullivans and the Hawthornes have always been allies, just like us and the Carlisles. So Dad associates them with one another.

He never misses an opportunity to tell us that the Hawthorne family wants what we have.

The mayor. The best house. The strongest powers.

Violet spared a glance toward Isaac's face, but it hadn't moved.

She wondered if that was still true. She didn't know.

Anyway, I don't care what Dad says. I like Maya. She gave me a scone she'd swiped from home and told me not to worry about my birthday.

"Your family wouldn't let you do it if they didn't think you were ready," she said.

"What if I don't think I'm ready?" I asked.

Maya has this way of smiling that makes her look like she's about to laugh or cry, she just can't decide which. I couldn't look at it, so I just stared down at the scone.

"No one ever does," she told me, the scars on her

shoulders tensing as she leaned back and stared up at the trees. "But we get through it."

I hope she's right.

April 12, 1984

I can't believe I was so nervous about my ritual! I'm not allowed to share the details here, because even though this journal is well hidden, Dad would disown me if he knew I'd written it down. Let's just say that it was sort of awesome.

I'm going on my first-ever patrol tonight! I don't know if I'm like him or Daria or June yet, but I feel stronger. I can't wait to find out what I can do.

"Are you kidding me?" Violet resisted the urge to fling the book across the room. There were no details about the ritual at all. How obnoxious. "I was so close..."

"You should keep reading," said Isaac softly.

So Violet sighed and flipped to the next page.

It was dated a few months later.

She could tell within a few sentences that things were changing. Stephen sounded older. He sounded tired.

September 5, 1984

It's been a long summer. The Gray usually quiets down after the spring equinox, but this year it's been stronger than usual. It seems like every few days, the border in our territory acts up, and Dad and Uncle Hiram go into the forest. Now I'm expected to go with them.

I know what I am now. I raise the dead, like they do. But I don't have a companion. Dad says not to rush it—it took him a month to find Agatha, who'd been hit by a car.

Easy for him to say. Companions are supposed to be a focal point for our power. Like flexing a muscle, working with them makes us grow stronger.

Except I can't get stronger. And it's all starting to get to me—Dad's disappointment, the way the Gray tugs at my mind when I watch it unfurl at the edge of town.

I've started sleepwalking; at least, I think that's what it is. I've woken up in the woods twice now.

Maybe that's why things have gotten so mixed up in my mind.

I've known since I was little that we'd bound ourselves to the Beast so we could lock it away. But sometimes, late at night, I feel something creeping up in the back of my mind. A strange sense that what we're doing is wrong.

Violet knew how that felt. Waking up in strange places, feeling strange things in the back of your skull.

"He was blacking out," she said hoarsely.

Isaac leaned toward her, a single dark curl falling across his forehead. Violet felt a strange urge to brush it away. "Didn't you say that was happening to you?"

She nodded, cleared her throat. Tried not to remember that, in less than a year from this entry, Stephen Saunders would be dead. "It happened again. Since we talked."

"It can't be a coincidence that he mentions it here."

"I agree," said Violet solemnly. "Let's see what else he has to say."

September 19, 1984

I feel it all the time now. Like there's something that lives inside my brain, peering into my thoughts. Sometimes I feel emotions that I know aren't mine—I'll be sitting in the kitchen and be struck with this intense, burning rage. I don't understand where it's coming from. All I know is that it's worse when I'm using my power, but Dad won't let me stop.

The woods are getting more dangerous. Last month, two men leaving the bar were lured into the Gray. We only found one of their bodies. It was awful—bloated, with bone-white eyes. I haven't been sleeping well since Dad forced me to look at it.

Uncle Hiram wants to take us kids out of the equinox patrol, but Sheriff Hawthorne insists that Four Paths needs all the help it can get.

September 22, 1984

The founding families weren't meant to run this town. I see that now.

Violet turned the page, her heart thudding in her throat,

but the rest of the journal was missing. Every remaining page had been torn out, leaving behind nothing but bits of yellow loose-leaf residue in its wake.

ELEVEN

VIOLET COULDN'T STOP THINKING about Stephen
Saunders's diary. She'd taken it home from the town
archives and perused it constantly over the past few days,
making notes and discussing potential theories with
Harper.

They were sitting on ancient lawn chairs in Violet's
backyard, the journal spread across Harper's lap. The
afternoon sun sent auburn highlights through her dark,
wiry curls as she inspected the torn-out edges at the end
of the notebook. Violet had reluctantly told her about
Isaac's role in finding the journal, expecting her to be
upset, but she'd just smiled.

"So even Justin's best friend is turning on him," she
said. "Perfect."

"You really hate him, don't you?" Orpheus stirred
gently from his seat in Violet's lap, butting his head against
her hand until she scratched him between the ears.

"I don't hate him," said Harper, lowering the

notebook into her lap. "I just want him to realize that everything his family stands for is complete garbage, and suffer accordingly."

"You can't judge someone by their family," said Violet, thinking of how little she and Juniper had to say to each other.

"You can when it's Justin Hawthorne," said Harper, sighing. "His family is everything to him. He genuinely thinks the Hawthornes are meant to be in charge, because that's what he's grown up hearing. And no matter how many people die, he'll always put his mom and sister first. He's always been like that. Even before the ritual."

The bitterness in Harper's voice was palpable. There was pain there that she had carried for years. Pain that seemed to stretch far beyond her ritual.

Violet understood pain. "Do you want to talk about it?" she asked.

Harper's dark eyes widened, and it was like a window opening—there was still misery in her gaze, but now there was hope there, too. "Are you sure you want to listen?"

Violet remembered herself and Rosie lying side by side on her bed, talking about all their worries, both the petty ones and the deeper wounds, the ones they were scared would never quite heal. It had never failed to make her feel better. Maybe it would work for Harper, too.

"Of course I don't mind," Violet told Harper. "It's the least I can do."

"Okay, then," Harper said quietly. "Look, you'll probably think this is pathetic. But Justin and I... What he did...

it felt like a breakup. Even though we weren't together."

"So you had a crush," said Violet. "That's not pathetic. Actually, it explains a lot."

It did. Violet was embarrassed that she hadn't noticed anything romantic about Justin and Harper's obvious baggage. She'd been too focused on her ritual and her blackouts to really care.

She was starting to care now, though. Even though it meant that she could feel Four Paths starting to grow on her, like roots burrowing into her heart.

Harper sighed. "Haven't you ever had feelings for someone, even though you knew it was a bad idea?"

There had been Gracie Coors, back in seventh grade, who Violet had thought was cute until Gracie said Violet was going to hell for having crushes on girls and boys. She'd cried to Rosie about that one for days. Connor something, who she'd met at the one Ossining party Rosie had managed to drag her to. They'd been making out in the basement when they were interrupted by his girlfriend. But neither of those seemed to qualify.

"Sort of," she said, stroking Orpheus's back. "I don't really date."

"Okay, well, have you ever had your heart broken?"

That was easier. Rosie's death had broken everything. "Yes."

"Then you know how badly it hurts," said Harper, looking at her. "But the thing is, it hurts more because I never should've expected anything else. Founder kids aren't supposed to date one another. And he never would've chosen me over his family. Even if my ritual had gone perfectly."

Violet stared down the slope of the hill, to the place where tangled weeds and uncut grass met the towering chestnut oaks of the forest. "Would you have chosen him?"

Harper lowered her head. The sun was sinking behind her, turning her into a silhouette, framed in gold.

"What do you think?" she whispered.

And Violet knew this was it. The root of all her anger. That she had expected more from Justin than he'd been capable of giving her.

"I think you shouldn't feel foolish for caring," she said softly, thinking about how much Harper had just poured out to her. How much worse she herself had felt since she'd stopped talking to Rosie about her problems. "My dad died when I was five. For a while, I thought, because I couldn't really remember him, it hadn't made that much of a difference. That I couldn't grieve for someone I didn't know. But when I lost him… I lost his family, too. I thought maybe coming here would help—but the Saunders family isn't what I was expecting. And all I can think about is that I'm not feeling any of the things I'm supposed to. Like there's just some part of me that's always going to be missing." A lump swelled in Violet's throat, and she realized that she was dangerously close to talking about Rosie—something she wasn't yet ready to do.

"Anyway," she said hastily, "what I'm trying to say is that I have the right to feel whatever I want. And so do you."

"I'm sorry about your dad," said Harper quietly. "But… thanks."

"For what?"

"For listening," said Harper, clearing her throat and gesturing toward the journal. "And now… don't we have some work to do?"

Violet and Harper had yet to make any progress on the connection between the blackouts and her ritual, or the location of the rest of the journal. But she felt better anyway after their conversation, even though everything was still a mess.

After Harper left, Violet walked automatically to the piano, the composition book clutched in her hand. Orpheus trailed behind her as she entered the music room. One thing Stephen's diary had made her feel better about was growing attached to the cat—getting closer to her companion could only mean that she was getting closer to understanding her magic. And she had to admit, undead or not, having Orpheus around made her feel a little calmer. A little safer.

She studied the piano from a distance at first, then approached it, laid a finger on the keys. Let a single note ring out through the air.

Violet had been on edge the past few days, but there had been no signs of turquoise hair. No waking up in strange places.

But that didn't mean it couldn't happen again.

"You haven't been practicing lately." It was Juniper,

fixing the clip at the back of her bun. Today she was more dressed down than usual—jeans and a blazer instead of a pantsuit. Violet figured that meant she didn't have any video conference calls.

"I didn't realize you paid that much attention to when I played," said Violet, sliding the notebook onto the piano bench—out of Juniper's line of sight. She didn't want to answer questions.

Juniper's smile was sad. "I was going to ask if you'd play for Daria. She requested it. But if you don't want to, it's all right."

Daria slid out from behind her, as if on cue. "Your mother says you're very good."

Violet eyed them both suspiciously. When she had seen them hanging out before, on the porch, she had assumed it was a fluke. Now she wondered if maybe it wasn't. If they were actually learning how to be sisters again.

The thought made her chest hurt.

But she missed the piano. And at least, if she blacked out while there were people watching her, they'd be able to stop her before she did anything dangerous.

"Fine," she said, sitting down and flipping her sheet music open to Chopin's Ballade no. 1 in G Minor, op. 23, her favorite piece of her old audition program. "But I'm going to make mistakes."

As promised, it was far from a perfect performance. She hadn't warmed up, and it had been weeks since she'd properly played. Once, auditioning for music school had felt like the biggest challenge she would ever face. Before

Rosie's death, before all of this, she'd even put together a list: the Eastman School of Music, Juilliard, the New England Conservatory, Curtis, Oberlin. But none of that would ever happen now.

Violet channeled that frustration into her playing. It flowed into every incorrect chord and fumbled fingering, and when she was done, she felt lighter somehow, as if she had exorcised some part of herself through the music.

When she lifted her hands from the keys, Daria clapped enthusiastically. But it was Juniper who made Violet pause.

Over the years, Rosie had made sure Violet went to her lessons, had kept her practicing, had held her hand and yanked her up the stairs at her first-ever recital, when she'd been scared she was going to throw up.

Juniper had barely seemed to notice any of it.

But today she was looking. And smiling. Like she was actually proud.

Violet remembered what Daria had said, about her parents being the ones who'd started her on the piano because Stephen had played it, too.

"Well done," Juniper said softly. But before she could say anything else, her phone began to buzz. She looked down at it, frowning, and hurried out of the room.

Violet swallowed down a twist of hurt.

"Anyway," Violet said, standing up and grabbing the notebook. "That's… yeah. That's it."

But Daria blocked her exit.

"That notebook," she said hoarsely, clutching Violet's hand. "Where did you find it?"

Violet swallowed, disarmed. "The town archives. It was Stephen's."

Daria's head inclined. "I know."

"Do you... do you know where the rest of it is?"

Daria's brow furrowed. Then she reached into a pocket of her dress and extracted a dark brown cylinder.

"I might be able to help," she said, her eyes shining, while Violet swallowed her disappointment. She'd been hoping for more pages. "After my brother died, my father wanted to get rid of the journal. But Mother hid it first. Half of it in the town archives. And the other half... she gave me this. Said it was the clue to finding it. Said to keep it safe. I keep it on me, mostly. But here." She pushed it into Violet's hands. "It's yours now."

Violet gaped at her, the weight of this gift settling in her chest. "Thank you," she said.

Daria smiled. "You're welcome, little bone."

"Daria? Violet?" called Juniper's voice from the other side of the house. Whatever had caught her attention before, it was clearly over with. "What are you two doing?"

"Better go," said Daria hoarsely. "She won't understand."

Violet nodded. She clutched the cylinder and Stephen's journal close to her chest and hurried back to her room.

When the door was safely shut and locked, she let herself inspect her aunt's strange present.

It was almost a foot long, and hollow, if the weight of it was any indication. There was a gap in the wood grain, close to the top. She twisted the edge of the cylinder, and it came off in her hands, revealing the roll of paper inside.

The lines and dots inked on the pages were incomprehensible. It took Violet a few seconds to realize what she was looking at, and when she did, she was even more confused.

It was the blueprints to the Saunders manor, hand-drawn in faded ink on yellowing paper. She spread the pages out on the floor of her room, weighted them with books, and looked them over, but as far as she could tell there was nothing interesting about them aside from how old they had to be.

She rolled them up again and sighed. She didn't understand why Daria had wanted her to have these.

Beside her, Orpheus mewled. He was batting around a yellowing piece of paper that sat beside the blueprint case. It must've been in there as well—she just hadn't noticed it before.

Violet snatched it away from his claws.

And then she gasped, because it wasn't a piece of paper at all—it was a photograph.

Three teenagers sat on the front porch of the Saunders house. The girl in the center had perfect posture and a poised, careful smile on her face, dark eyes fixed on the camera lens. On her right sat another girl with her head turned to the side, mouth wide open in a raucous laugh as her hands reached up to clutch the edges of her oversize windbreaker. Her dark, frizzy hair fell almost to her waist.

But it was the boy on their left that held her attention. Dark curls, a thin, handsome face, an easy grin.

She turned the picture over and read the caption:

The Saunders siblings (from left to right): Stephen, Daria, Juniper. 1984.

Violet flipped the picture over again.

The girl in the windbreaker was Juniper.

Laughing, wild, free. A version of Juniper unburdened by a dead brother, a dead husband, a dead daughter.

She was completely unrecognizable from the woman Violet had always known.

For the first time, Violet considered how much Juniper had been shaped by the people she loved being taken away from her. Losing Rosie had demolished Violet's world. To endure that three times was more than any one person should have to bear.

Were the past few months just the first step to her becoming as jaded and cynical as her mother?

Violet shuddered, wondering if, years from now, her own daughter would be thinking the same thing about her.

"That's not who I'm supposed to be," she whispered to the photo.

But maybe that wasn't true.

Maybe the thing no one had told her about growing up was that nobody ever really became the person they'd wanted to be.

Violet slid the picture carefully into the bottom compartment of her jewelry box, then crawled into bed, her fingers curled around Rosie's bracelet, Orpheus at her side.

Her heart was so heavy in her chest, she was surprised it could still beat.

Parties in Four Paths were small by necessity, because although inviting anyone meant inviting everyone, there weren't many kids to go around. But tonight, the shadowy interior of Suzette Langham's barn was packed, everyone yelling over the blasting music and posing for pictures under the out-of-season holiday lights strung up on the walls. A cloud of cigarette smoke drifted above Justin's head.

If Justin left Four Paths, he'd get to go to real nightclubs someday. Sit in real bars, flirt with girls he hadn't known since preschool, instead of dutifully avoiding eye contact with Seo-Jin and Britta and all the other girls he'd dated for a day, a week, a month. But if he didn't know them, they wouldn't know him. Before his ritual, Justin had relished the way any high school party's focus shifted where he walked. He could step into whatever conversation he wanted and know he was welcome there.

Any conversation, unless it included Harper Carlisle.

Years away from her, and still, within seconds of talking to her earlier that week, he'd wanted to tell her the truth. About what he'd really done to her. About what had truly happened the night she'd vanished into the Gray.

Harper had always been able to disarm him without trying, whether she was holding a sword or not. That hadn't changed. It had cost him Violet Saunders, which meant it had cost him everything. But he deserved it.

He hadn't told May and Isaac that he'd been desperate enough to confront Harper in person. Justin was drunk enough to enjoy the taste of the cheap beer someone's older sibling had bought, but he wasn't drunk enough to admit that he had failed. He wasn't sure he could ever be drunk enough to do that.

He wove through the barn, high-fiving Cal Gonzalez and tapping his red cup against Suzette and her girlfriend Lia's matching ones before tipping it up to his mouth.

But all socializing made him realize was how little he deserved to be treated this way. The way his classmates stared at him, with respect he hadn't earned… Fake. It was all fake.

Justin couldn't handle it anymore. He didn't care that it was a Saturday night, or that he had appearances to keep up. He did a shot of terrible vodka with Marissa Czechowicz, then chased it with the rest of his beer. The force of the alcohol hit him hard after that, and he gulped and staggered away, trying to forget how Marissa had laughed at him when he grimaced at the shot.

But there wasn't enough cheap liquor in the world to wash away the guilt Justin felt when he thought of what he'd done to Harper.

A flash of pastel pink appeared behind a hay bale, and Justin hurried over to May, the world spinning around him. His sister was usually alone at these parties—she liked it better that way.

But this time, she was talking to a boy.

A boy with dark, curly hair, a T-shirt that said PUBLIC

SAFETY HAZARD, and a half-smoked cigarette held lazily in his left hand.

Seth Carlisle.

Justin couldn't face a Carlisle right now. He was about to turn away when May caught his eye.

"Hey!" she called out. "You should go check on Isaac. He was matching Henrik Dougan on shots, and you know…" She trailed off, then hiccuped. Seth chuckled at her, raising the cigarette to his mouth. "You know how that ends."

Justin wondered, vaguely, if she was trying to get rid of him. He didn't like how closely she and Seth were standing. Or the way Seth was looking at her.

But May knew the rules about founder hookups. And May would die before she broke a rule. Also, she had a point.

Drunk Isaac had a tendency to disintegrate party decor he didn't agree with. It was getting to the point where Justin was considering texting hosts in advance and warning them to hide their books by Isaac's least favorite authors. Drunk Isaac would also sneak away with whoever caught his eye that night, girl or guy, which was partially why Justin had let him wander off in the first place. Isaac had only come out to him as bi a few months ago, and Justin wanted to be supportive—but knew how private his friend was about his love life. So he'd made a point of asking if Isaac needed a wingman, then backed off when Isaac had laughed and told him no.

But Isaac only hooked up with people when he was

179

in a good mood, and these past few weeks, he'd been nothing but preoccupied and grumpy. So, faced with the prospect of having to deal with a drunk, angry best friend, Justin left May and Seth and started across the barn.

It wasn't long before he caught sight of Henrik's bulky form among a crowd in the far corner. Justin moved past a few couples stealing furtive kisses, the noise growing as he approached. He found Isaac leaning against the slatted wooden wall, slurring and shimmering and short-circuiting, a semicircle of people forming around him.

"No, see, I can do it!" Isaac insisted as Justin pushed his way through the crowd, muttering *excuse mes* as he jostled shoulders and stepped on feet. Justin reached the front of the circle as the empty whiskey bottle in Isaac's hands disintegrated into ash. Henrik roared with approval and clapped Isaac on the shoulder. Isaac jolted forward, then stumbled, chuckling, back to the wall.

"Hey." Justin crossed the circle and stood between the other boys. Adrenaline cut through his intoxication—he had to take care of Isaac. That was more important than his self-pity. "You all right?"

"'Course I'm all right." Isaac frowned at him. "Best I've ever been."

"Want a swig?" boomed Henrik, holding up another bottle.

Justin shook his head, his stomach churning. The Dougans made their own whiskey. How, no one was quite sure, but everyone knew a few sips were strong enough to kill a goat. Judging by the way Isaac was swaying, he'd had at least enough to kill an elephant.

"Do it again!" called the crowd.

Henrik held out a bale of hay. "Think you can do that?"

Isaac snorted. "Easy." A second later, ash was dripping onto Henrik's size-fifteen shoes. But the crowd barely clapped this time. The looks on their faces were clear— they were no longer impressed.

Justin's mother had once warned him about showing off, back before his ritual day. *Our powers aren't cheap, silly tricks*, Augusta had said. *They are life and death. Never forget that.*

"That all you got?" said a kid who Justin vaguely recognized as someone's younger sibling. He couldn't have been older than fourteen, but he stood at the front of the crowd with a gap-toothed smirk. Writhing in his arms was a panicked barn cat, a scrawny orange thing doing its best to sink its claws into the boy's neck. "If you're really as powerful as people say, why don't you get rid of this?"

"Hey," said Justin, but Isaac had already taken a wobbling step toward the boy, distress leaking through the intoxicated expression on his face.

"I won't hurt something that doesn't deserve it. I'm... honorable."

The last word was barely decipherable. Justin was fairly certain this was the drunkest Isaac had ever been.

"Really?" said the boy. "'Cause that's not what they say about your family."

Isaac's hands began to tremble, the twin medallions on his wrists glowing dully in the dim light.

And Justin saw something he'd never seen before on the faces of the people watching them. Disgust.

He wondered if it was just the alcohol that had allowed them to be so bold. But no, this felt different. Like the alcohol was merely allowing them to show something that had been festering for a long time.

"Yeah!" called someone else. "Where's the Sullivan we've all heard so much about?"

"I bet you're not even that powerful. Your family probably made up all those rumors to scare us."

"Yeah, if you're so powerful, how come Hap Whitley's dead?"

"What about Vanessa? And Carl?"

"Aren't you supposed to be stopping shit like that from happening?"

Justin could feel the crowd swelling. He needed to do something.

"Enough," Justin said.

"Or what?" the boy said, still looking at Isaac. "You'll carve one of us up like your family carved up each other—"

"ENOUGH," Justin roared. One step put him in front of the kid's face. He swiped the barn cat out of his arms, handed it to Henrik, and yanked on the boy's collar until they were inches apart. "Get the hell out of this party."

"But it's not even your party," whimpered the kid.

Justin wasn't the type to threaten people. But he couldn't let this escalate any further.

182

"The Hawthornes don't forget an insult." He let the crowd hear the truth in every word, see it on his face. "Neither do the Sullivans. Do you really want to be on the founders' bad side?"

Justin released the boy. He ran off, and as the crowd around them dissipated, demoralized by the lack of a fight, Justin turned to Isaac.

"The cat," Isaac said, looking around frantically. "Is it okay?"

"It's fine," said Justin, glancing over his shoulder—the cat was snuggled against a drunk Henrik's chest, who was cooing soft endearments at it.

"Good," Isaac said weakly. "Fuck, I hate that you had to threaten them."

"Me too," said Justin. His mother and May relished the reaction their name got from the rest of the town, but the way Justin had used it tonight made him nauseous. So did the expressions on the faces in the crowd he'd seen just now. The Hawthornes were losing the town, they were losing everything, and it would only get worse once people realized he didn't have powers, either.

He'd already lost Violet's help. He'd been so colossally foolish to even try to get it.

The last place in the world he wanted to be was a crowded party. The barn swam around him, intoxication blurring his vision. The temporary clarity defending Isaac had given him was gone.

"C'mon, man." Justin swung Isaac's arm around his shoulders. "Let's get you out of here."

"It would've been so easy," said Isaac as they moved toward the barn door. "If I'd touched that boy, I could've made him just... go."

"Don't think about it."

"I could've."

"But you didn't."

They were almost at the door when Isaac looked at him, his eyes as lifeless as two snuffed-out candles. Justin had the sudden worry that Isaac could see the thoughts swimming in his brain, every gory detail of his insecurities and failures laid out for his perusal.

Isaac's hand, which had been hanging limply over Justin's shoulder, closed around his wrist.

"You always do that." Isaac's words didn't sound slurred anymore. "Show up when I need you. How do you do that?"

Isaac's jaw tensed, his face mottled and distorted by the Christmas lights, and Justin felt a rush of embarrassment he didn't quite understand. Isaac never wanted anyone to see him like this. It felt wrong to watch him with all his defenses down.

And then he caught a flash of pink again, and he shrugged off Isaac's arm, the moment gone, ready to tell May it was time to go home.

But May had a message for him, too.

"Thank goodness I found you," she said, holding up her phone. Her pale face was taut with worry. "Violet texted us, all of us. Something's wrong."

TWELVE

HARPER'S GUILT OVER HER conversation with Justin Hawthorne had lingered right up until the moment she told her father what she'd done.

She had barged into Maurice Carlisle's workshop to tell him about Violet. It was at the back of the statue garden, inside what had once been the barn. Over the past century and a half, Carlisles had used the workshop to create an entirely different sort of livestock—one made of animated stone.

Harper could tell her father was displeased from the furrows on his aging face when she opened the workshop doors. His workshop was almost always off-limits, even to the other Carlisles.

"Violet Saunders was recruited by the Hawthornes," she said. "But she left them—for us. I met with her by the lake." Harper felt a rush of satisfaction as the furrows in her father's face smoothed away, leaving a proud grin in their wake.

"I knew you were a fighter," said Maurice Carlisle, clapping her on the shoulder. His hand left fragments of crumbled stone on her shirt, but Harper didn't care. She was too busy blinking away tears at the raw pride in his voice.

Justin had deserved every bit of her ire. And she genuinely did want to help Violet.

There was no reason to feel guilty. None at all.

"Does this mean I get to meet the others?" she asked.

Maurice leaned against the door, those coarse brows knitting together across his forehead. Behind him, bells of all shapes and sizes hung from the ceiling, barely visible in the dim light of the workshop. Harper's father had always claimed he worked better in darkness. He said that stone sculpted better when it was felt instead of seen, so it could show him what it wanted to be.

"You know what?" he said. "You've earned it."

Which was how, a few days later, Harper found herself sneaking out of her bedroom after an evening spent helping her mother watch Brett and Nora. Mitzi and Seth were at some party she hadn't been invited to, so her mother had needed the help. Harper felt a pang of guilt for deceiving her as she made her way to the workshop, even though they weren't close.

But when her father smiled and presented her with a sleek silver dagger, the hilt ornately carved from red-brown stone, Harper found her regrets fading.

Maurice Carlisle hadn't let Seth or Mitzi in on this secret. He hadn't even told her mother.

But he was telling her. That meant something.

Harper knew the woods fairly well, although she'd stopped using them after dark when news of the deaths began to filter through Four Paths every couple of months. Most of the town had done the same.

The Beast had almost killed her three years ago. She didn't want it to come back for seconds.

But there was nothing amiss in the woods. The only noises Harper heard were the soft rustle of the leaves and the occasional chirping of sparrows in the trees. It was a perfect late-summer night in upstate New York, just cold enough for Harper's favorite light jacket, with the sleeve tied off at the elbow.

But she kept her hand on the hilt of her new dagger, just in case.

They stopped behind the row of buildings on Main Street, a few feet away from the back lot behind the library.

"Here," said Maurice, producing a rough burlap robe from somewhere within his coat. "Put this on."

The cloth had the same color and rough consistency as a potato sack. Harper wrinkled her nose, but she pulled it over her head, wincing at the whiff of mildew. She took an extra minute to tie the left sleeve in a knot just after the end of her arm.

Harper didn't mind that it drew others' attention to her missing hand. If she could live with half a left arm, other people could certainly handle looking at it.

"Why the robes?" she asked, careful to keep her voice

down. The sheriff's office was only a turn off Main Street away.

Maurice Carlisle finished pulling his own hood over his forehead. When he turned to her, she could no longer see his face—the darkness and the robe had left it utterly in shadow. "They're tradition," he said simply. "In these humble clothes, we are all equal: founder or not. Now come. We must be absolutely silent for this next part."

Harper had never heard of such a tradition, for any part of the town. But she trailed behind her father without protest as he walked across the empty lot, trying to make as little noise as possible.

If she questioned this, he could still make her go home. And she wanted so badly to know what was going on. To be on the inside, for once, after those years of lingering painfully outside of everything.

So she stayed silent when he drew a key out of his coat and deftly unlocked the library's back door. And she stayed silent when he pulled her inside into total darkness—until something was shoved over her head, and two hands yanked her upper arms behind her back.

"Dad!" Her panic was muffled by the fabric over her head. Whoever had grabbed her hadn't fumbled for a wrist that wasn't there—they'd known it was her. Phantom pain coursed through her left arm, making her shudder. "What is this?"

"No need to fret, Miss Carlisle," said a smooth voice she didn't recognize. "No one here means you harm. We merely want to make sure of where your loyalties lie before we allow you to glimpse our secrets."

"It's standard procedure, Harper," added her father's voice. The sound of it soothed her wildly ratcheting heartbeat, although it didn't entirely dispel her panic. She was led up what felt like a flight of stairs, then made to sit. They let her arms go free then, but she was too frightened to move. Harper could hear enough rustles and murmurs to know she was far from alone.

"Now, Miss Carlisle," said the first voice. "We understand you've been tasked by your father with befriending Violet Saunders."

Harper pushed down questions like *who are you* and *how dare you*. She trusted her father. She had to trust that this was all going to be fine. "Yes."

"A task he says you've completed beyond our expectations."

"Yes."

"Would you like to share with us how you've managed to win over a girl you barely know?"

Harper wasn't really sure how she'd managed to gain Violet's attention. But she didn't think that would go over so well right now. She scrambled for another answer, a real one. "We're not that different, really," she said, trying to keep her voice steady. "And I think she could tell that I was telling her the truth about wanting to help her. While the Hawthornes…" She hesitated.

It didn't feel safe to insult them so publicly, when she had no idea who she was talking to. Her feelings weren't popular ones.

"Do go on," said the voice. "And know that no one here will protest if you share some less than pleasant thoughts about your fellow founders."

"Right." Harper bit her lip, suddenly glad no one could see her face. "Well. The Hawthornes had already made her feel uneasy. She seemed to understand they weren't telling her everything."

"I see." Was that her imagination or did the voice sound impressed? "Close your eyes, Miss Carlisle."

Harper did. A moment later, the bag was lifted off her head. She filled her lungs with a deep, relieved breath of fresh air.

"Harper," said her dad, his hand suddenly squeezing hers. "You can look."

She opened her eyes.

She was sitting in the library's attic. Shelves of books that had been deemed either too boring, too scandalous, or too dangerous for public consumption filled every inch of available wall space. They'd put her in a circle of folding chairs with perhaps fifteen other people in coarse brown robes identical to hers. She recognized all of them, even with the hoods pulled over their faces—Pete and Theo and Ma Burnham from the Diner, Korrie Lee from the grocer's, even a few of her fellow classmates.

The only sources of light in the room were the moon, which streamed in through the skylight, and a flickering candelabra in the center of the circle. Harper's gaze darted nervously to the books. A stray ember from the flames, and there would be nothing left of this place but ashes.

"Welcome!"

Harper realized suddenly that the voice belonged to Mrs. Moore—the librarian. Of course. The woman appeared in her field of view a moment later, a smile on her face.

"Let us all welcome Harper Carlisle to the Church of the Four Deities."

As if on cue, everyone rose from their chairs except for Harper. Mrs. Moore joined the circle. And, before Harper could ask any questions, they began to sing.

At first, Harper thought it was the "Founders' Lullaby." But she realized quickly that it was something very different.

> *Sinners who were led astray,*
> *Wandered through the woods one day,*
> *Stumbled right into the Gray,*
> *Never to return.*
> *Hear the lies our gods will tell,*
> *The prison the Four wove so well,*
> *But listen to us when we say:*
> *Branches and stones, daggers and bones,*
> *Will meet their judgment day.*

When the song was done, they all sat down. No one clapped. No one fidgeted. The sight sent a chill down Harper's spine.

She didn't know much about the Church of the Four Deities. It was ancient history by Four Paths standards, a bunch of townspeople who'd worshipped the original four founders as gods. The religion had died out when the original founders did, and although most of the original practices had been lost, Harper knew enough to know this wasn't right.

Her father had said that he was involved in a plot to take the Hawthornes down. Worshipping them definitely didn't seem like a good way to do that.

As if anticipating her question, Mrs. Moore stepped back into the center of the circle again and cleared her throat. The flickering light of the candelabra reflected in her horn-rimmed glasses, making it look as if her eyes were balls of flame.

"As most of you know, our leader has more pressing matters to attend to tonight, so I will handle this explanation of our organization. The original purpose of the Church of the Four Deities when it was founded in 1847 was to find the path to salvation. We have taken on its mantle now to symbolize our intentions: Save our town. Save ourselves. The Hawthorne family has begun to lose their grip on the Gray, and we are paying for it with innocent lives."

The room fixed itself on Harper, fifteen expectant faces peering at hers.

She squirmed.

"We shouldn't suffer for the Hawthornes' mistakes," she said. Which seemed to be enough for Mrs. Moore to continue.

"Augusta Hawthorne holds this town in an iron grip. Our leader has come up with a plan that we believe will dislodge her—but it requires the help of a Saunders to work. That's why your connection to Violet is so important to us. Do you understand?"

Harper nodded. "What is this plan? I want to help."

Mrs. Moore's face froze slightly. When she continued, her words were far more careful. "As long as the Hawthornes hold power, they're a threat. So we have found a potential way to remove their abilities—for good. This will destabilize their hold on the town and allow more deserving families to take charge of the duties of keeping us all safe."

Harper shuddered.

It was exactly what they deserved, all of them. To know how she felt. To be powerless, and have nothing they could do about it.

There was just one question remaining. "How will we do it?"

Beside her, Maurice Carlisle squeezed her hand once more, and Harper felt a surge of vicious pride.

"One secret at a time, Miss Carlisle," said Mrs. Moore, a gentle laugh in her voice. "I'm afraid these plans are sensitive enough that even most of our own don't know every detail. For now, keep Violet Saunders close. Help her develop her powers. When the time is right, we will need her to use them."

"Can I tell her about this?"

This time, it was her own father who spoke. "I know you mean well, Harper, but this information simply cannot be shared with anyone unless we know they can be trusted. Hopefully, you can tell her soon."

Harper nodded, a twinge of unease rolling through her. "Understood."

"Excellent," said Mrs. Moore.

The sound of wind chimes rang through the room, urgent, insistent, and undeniably electronic. Someone's ringtone.

Harper realized, with a rush of horror, that it was *her* ringtone.

"Sorry!" she gasped, drawing her phone out of her sweatshirt pocket.

But the number on the screen was Violet's.

Maurice Carlisle glanced down at her phone. "It's the Saunders girl," he said, signaling to everyone else to stay quiet. "Take it."

Harper accepted the call, then held the phone up to her ear. Her mouth was dry with sudden nerves. "Hello?"

"Harper—please." Violet's voice was so ragged, so broken, Harper barely recognized it. "It's an emergency. Something's happened, something—" Her words were cut off by a choked sob. "Can you come over? Right now?"

Harper paused, her eyes frozen on her father.

"Go to her," hissed Maurice Carlisle. "We trust you, Harper."

"Of course," said Harper, even though something felt wrong about all this, something she was too stressed and overwhelmed to fully think about. "I'll be right there."

It wasn't the noise that woke Violet up. It was the ache in her head, a dizziness that spread through her dreams and yanked her back into reality.

She was nauseous. She was sore, as if she'd run a dozen miles. She felt like part of her mind was missing.

And she was standing. At the edge of the second-floor landing in the Saunders manor, the chandelier looming above her, the reddish stone stairs, cloaked in shadow, extending below her, starting just inches away from her bare feet.

Violet curled her fingers around the wrought-iron banister, shivering at the cool metal against her fingers. Moonlight danced across the feathers of a taxidermy falcon mounted on the landing wall. It lingered in the nooks and crannies of the chandelier, making the ivory carvings look as if they were actual bones.

Violet studied the stairs again, shuddering. Two more steps, and she would've tumbled down. She had never sleepwalked in her life, and now she was showing up in strange places in the middle of the night.

That couldn't be accidental. She'd have to text Harper about this in the morning.

Violet was about to turn around and head back to bed when she heard Orpheus meowing. The cat padded around the corner of the landing, yellow eyes glowing in the darkness.

"What is it?" Violet's voice echoed from the edge of

the landing, filling the wide emptiness of the house even though she'd tried to whisper. "Do undead cats still like to be let outside?"

Orpheus meowed again. He butted his head against her bare ankle, then descended gracefully onto the first stair. This time, his low, guttural mewls sounded oddly frantic. He leaped down two more stairs and turned, his tail waving from side to side.

Violet felt that tug at her insides again, the same one she'd felt back in her bedroom earlier that day. It reminded her of May's powers this time. Like there was something nosing at the edge of her skull.

Something telling her to look more closely at the bottom of the stairs.

Her eyes could make out something now; a figure standing in the foyer. Too broad in the shoulders to be Juniper. Too tall to be Daria.

Panic flooded through her chest. She reached, slowly and carefully, toward the light switch at the top of the stairs. "Who's there?"

The figure made for the door at the same time as her fingers flicked the switch. The chandelier flooded to life, reflecting off the crystals, sending refracting tendrils of light across the foyer.

Her eyes found the intruder.

Its face was mummified flesh clinging to a half-rotted skull, its body dressed in torn-up rags.

It didn't walk—it *shuffled*.

A sharp hiss of panic went through Violet's chest,

followed by a sudden tug of exhaustion, a sensation she recognized as her energy being sucked away.

It was a body.

And Violet understood in that moment that the nausea that had awoken her was the connection between them, like the one between her and Orpheus, but stronger.

Which meant it was a body she'd brought back to life. But when? And how? And *who*?

She started forward—but the front door was already slamming behind it.

And she could see, now that the lights were on, that it had left something in its wake.

There was a heap of crimson at the bottom of the stairs. A tangle of graying curls and red yarn, and more red, red everywhere, spreading slowly beneath Aunt Daria's motionless body, speckled across her lifeless, slack-jawed face.

Violet didn't remember descending the stairs.

All she remembered was pressing her fingers to Daria's neck and feeling the faintest possible thrumming of a pulse.

Her fingers smeared blood across her phone as she fumbled for 911, then dialed Harper's number, then—desperate—Justin's, and Isaac's, and May's.

And finally, hunched beside her aunt's motionless body, she allowed herself to cry.

THIRTEEN

THE SAUNDERS MANOR SHONE like a beacon from half a mile away. The lights flaring in the upstairs windows cut harshly through the forest, making it easy for Harper to keep the house in sight as she navigated the woods. Maurice Carlisle's words ran through her mind with every step: *Go to her. We trust you, Harper.*

It had been a long time since someone had shown any faith in her at all; and now, in the space of just a few days, she'd gained the respect of Violet Saunders—and her own father.

She was not about to let either of them down.

But as the bottom of the hill came into view, Harper froze. Parked in the center of the driveway were two police cars, their sirens casting red-and-blue shadows across the manor's front porch.

Standing next to the second car, her badge gleaming in the light that spilled through the windows, was Augusta Hawthorne.

The person Harper had sworn to take down at all costs.

The person who, if Justin was to be believed, had taken Harper's best friend away from her.

The person who Harper was more afraid of than the Gray. Than the Beast.

Her legs were heavy as stone, anchoring her to the forest floor. All her bravery had crumbled the moment she saw that shock of blond hair.

But if she bolted, she'd be disappointing everyone.

Worst of all, she'd be proving the Beast right the day it told her she was unworthy of her family birthright.

Harper patted the edge of the dagger she'd tucked into her pocket, then stepped carefully through the woods, circling the Saunders manor. If she could get in through the back door, there was still a chance she could talk to Violet.

But she'd barely gone a few feet when a series of rustles and curses came from the trees to her left.

Harper flattened her spine against the nearest tree trunk, struggling to calm her breathing. Someone was in the forest with her. Someone who, she realized as the stream of curses continued, was either very drunk, or very, very foolish.

"Are you fucking serious?" sighed the voice, apparently to itself. "I am the branch guy! It's, like, my whole thing! Don't you wanna be helpful, trees, instead of getting in my way?"

Harper groaned silently as the sea of branches parted

to her left, revealing a disheveled, visibly intoxicated Justin Hawthorne.

Very drunk *and* very foolish, then.

His gaze found her before she had time to duck behind the nearest tree.

"You!" Justin raised a finger and jabbed it in her direction. The gesture felt like an accusation. "Why in the founders' names are you here?"

Harper wondered if he would believe her if she told him she was a drunk hallucination.

"What are *you* doing here?" she asked, instead.

The question seemed to confuse him. "Violet asked for help," he said. "And Isaac was too drunk, so May had to take him home, so I came here."

Harper pushed down a surge of annoyance that Violet had reached out to the Hawthornes, too. At least Justin was in no condition to win back Violet's allegiance. If he was the soberest one in their little trio, Isaac had to be absolutely wasted.

"You should've gone home with May and Isaac," she said. "You're way too drunk to help her."

"I am not!"

A new chorus of voices rose behind them before Harper could respond.

"We've gotta check the forest," called one of the officers to another.

"She doesn't think it's the Beast?"

"You know what those bodies look like. Nah, this is a different kind of killer."

Harper's heart jolted in her chest.

Killer. That meant someone was dead.

And, more importantly, it meant that Harper could not be found nearby.

Yes, Violet needed her. But she would have to wait.

Harper was already halfway out of the clearing when she realized Justin hadn't moved. He was just standing in the middle of the trees, swaying back and forth, bewilderment spreading across his handsome face.

It would be so easy for Harper to leave him there. He'd get in a heap of trouble and distract the police for long enough to guarantee her escape.

But as the officers' footsteps crushed across the underbrush, Harper remembered what he'd said back at her house. The earnestness in his eyes as he'd talked about defying his mother, once and for all.

And, against every self-preservation instinct she possessed, she rushed back into the clearing.

"Come on, branch guy," Harper hissed, grabbing Justin's arm and yanking him after her into the woods. "Aren't you supposed to be good at running?"

"I am," said Justin indignantly, stumbling behind her as they wove through the trees. "I am the fastest." He knocked into her shoulder, nearly toppling her over, then overcorrected and slammed into a tree.

"You're a child." Harper ducked beneath a branch. The footsteps behind them were fainter now, but they weren't gone. She had no idea how the deputies hadn't noticed Justin's general idiocy. "And you're going to land

201

us both in your mother's office if you don't shut up and sober up, right now."

Justin chuckled. "Well, shit. I forgot how formal you get when you're angry."

"And I'm learning just how annoying you are when you drink."

But Justin must've finally processed her words, because he went silent for a moment and all Harper could hear was the sound of their footsteps in the underbrush. When he spoke again, his voice was slightly less slurred. "Doesn't make any sense for us to run. The officers'll just hear us. We should hide until they leave."

Harper was annoyed by how much she agreed with him. There was just one problem. "Hide? Where?"

"I know where," said Justin, with a confidence that Harper mightily hoped came from something other than whatever he'd had to drink. "Follow me."

He surged ahead, and she picked her way behind him. Twigs clutched at her sweatshirt and snagged in her hair; her sneakers stumbled across tree roots as she and Justin moved deeper into the woods. She had no idea how Justin was navigating, but a few minutes later, he paused in front of a thickly woven cluster of branches that looked identical to the rest of the forest and nodded.

"This is it," he said, gesturing toward the branches. "Go on."

Harper was skeptical, but the faint patter of footsteps and the distant glow of a flashlight beam to their right motivated her to pull the branches aside.

They bent easily beneath her hand, revealing a copse of trees that had grown so closely together, their roots and trunks were intertwined. A hollow of tightly woven branches knitted below her like an upturned hand.

Harper stepped inside the trees' embrace, sliding into one of the natural seats between two trees' bent trunks. Justin followed her a moment later, letting the branches spring into place after them as he sat down a few feet away from her. The hollow was barely big enough for both of them. Harper drew her knees against her chest, trying not to think about how easy it would be for their legs to brush.

"How did you know about this place?" she whispered, gaping at the patches of sky that shone above their cocoon of trees. The moon was nearly full. Its pale light, filtered through the canopy of leaves, gave everything a slight tint of green.

Justin shrugged. "Oh... you know. It's just someplace I go sometimes."

There was something cagey in his voice. She studied his face and realized there was a flush creeping up his cheeks, turned sallow by the moonlight.

He was embarrassed. Which meant either he'd never taken anyone here before, or... "Oh my god," said Harper. "This isn't where you take girls, is it?"

He ducked his head. It was all the answer she needed.

"Are you serious?" Harper scrambled to her feet, disgust roiling through her. "You took me to your weird forest sex den?"

She'd heard rumors about Justin's extracurricular

activities. She'd spent years trying to block them out. Now all she could think about was every other hand who'd pushed those branches aside. Every girl who'd sat where she was sitting.

Or maybe lain down where she was sitting. Which was not exactly a more comforting thought.

"It is not a sex den!" Justin stood up, still swaying, which made it even more obvious how little room there was in the hollow for two people. His arms were braced against the tree trunks mere inches from her splayed-out fingers; his face loomed above her, still flushed. "Look, I said I knew a place to hide, and I found one, okay?"

"I'd rather be at the police station than here." Harper's heart was hammering with equal parts humiliation and fury.

She never should've gone back for him. Justin wasn't hers anymore. Never had been. That had never been more painfully apparent than it was right now.

The next words she said came from somewhere different. Somewhere mean. "I don't even know why you were at the Saunders manor. Maybe Violet asked you to come help her. But you're in no condition to help anyone."

Justin let out a chuckle at that, but a painful one. An expression dawned on his face that Harper had seen back at her house.

Guilt.

"No, I'm not." There was something hoarse and awful in his voice. "But I wouldn't be able to help her sober, either."

He held up his hand, and Harper forgot how to breathe.

Dangling between his fingers was a rough stone pendant, identical to the one pressed against Harper's breastbone.

But founders didn't wear stone—they wore glass after they completed their ritual, to prove they were strong enough to stand against the Gray on their own.

"I don't understand," she said softly. "Why do you have that?"

The corners of his mouth turned up, but it wasn't a smile. The moonlight had turned him ashen around the edges, like something out of the Gray. "Because I need it. Just like you."

And Harper understood.

Why he'd seemed so set on recruiting Violet. Why Mitzi had come home with stories of May leading patrols instead of Justin. Why he would be willing to turn against his mother.

She let out a strangled, frustrated whimper. "You failed your ritual."

He released the pendant. It fell over the front of his T-shirt, a silent surrender. "I did."

She believed him. The Hawthornes were proud enough to lie to the whole town rather than admit they'd failed. "You're no better than I am," she snarled, trembling.

Justin bowed his head. She saw him as he was now, a king without a crown. A sad little boy playing at a future he couldn't have.

"I know," he said. "But now I get it, okay? I'm trying."

"No," she said coldly. "You don't get it."

Because he still had everything. And she still had nothing. And no ritual was enough to change that.

She closed her hand around the dagger's hilt in her pocket, fighting the urge to hold it to his throat.

There were other ways to hurt him. Better ways.

Harper closed the distance between them. "Look at me."

He tilted his head down. The branches around them were reflected in his hazel eyes.

She stood on her tiptoes until her face was alongside his, and still he did not move, even when the tip of her upturned nose brushed the side of his ear.

Mere moments ago, being this close to him would've left her dizzy. But now her shortness of breath was born of rage, not lust.

"It never stops hurting," Harper whispered. "And you know what? You deserve it."

Then she turned, pushed the branches aside, and walked back into the forest.

She tried to go back to the Saunders manor first, but the deputies were still swarming outside with no sign of a letup. So she texted Violet an apology and walked back to the Carlisle cottage, her fury growing with every step.

The Hawthornes had condemned her and forgiven him, because it was convenient for the town to believe that Justin was strong and she was weak.

And for that, they deserved to fall.

All her doubts were gone now.

In their place was the sharp, perfect certainty that she would have her revenge.

Violet didn't come to school on Monday.

Justin texted her a few times, but she never responded. Saturday night was a half-blurred mess inside his head that had left him and most of the senior class battling vicious hangovers.

He remembered the crowd's suppressed fury before he'd left the party.

He remembered Violet's frantic texts to him and May. And he remembered Harper.

Justin hadn't realized how close he was to cracking. All it had taken was alcohol and the latent guilt his classmates had stirred up to send his secrets spilling from his lips.

He could still feel the brush of her lips on his ear, the rush of warmth that had shot through him right before her words left him gutted and defenseless, alone in the forest with nothing but his guilt.

He did not remember going home, but somehow, he'd woken up in his own bed, a headache the size of a galaxy spiraling through his skull.

For the first time in his life, Justin Hawthorne wished he remembered less.

He had been a fool on all counts. Blowing his second chance with Violet by being so drunk. Making Harper hate him even more by telling her the truth. He'd wanted her to know she wasn't alone in her suffering. But Justin saw now that too much time had passed for him to heal things between them. All he had done was gouge open the scar of what they'd had before and let the wound fester.

May was furious with him, of course. But it was Isaac's reaction that caught Justin off guard. His cold, disdainful anger was a palpable presence the day after the party, leaving Justin confused and hurt in equal measure. What was it to Isaac if Justin saw fit to tell the truth about his ritual?

He was determined to find Harper and properly, soberly apologize. But over the past few years, she had made herself invisible. She didn't eat in the cafeteria or hang out in the courtyard at break times.

He had done this to her. Turned her cowed and small, a stranger in her own hometown.

He deserved her disdain, her disgust. He had walked away from her—she had earned the right to do the same to him.

But he couldn't spend the rest of the day chewing on his guilt.

So when classes let out, instead of heading to the locker room for track practice, he walked through the parking lot, avoiding the parking spot where May was fiddling with the keys to their shared truck.

Isaac caught up to him as he hit the main road, scratching absently at the dark stubble on his chin.

"You're going to see Violet," Isaac said as they turned onto the well-worn footpath beside the gravel.

"I am," said Justin, steeling himself for an argument. They'd learned earlier that morning that Daria Saunders was dead. It was why Violet hadn't come to school. Why she hadn't been answering his texts. She had reached out to Justin in her hour of need, and although he'd tried to help her, he'd failed. He knew her silence meant she was angry with him. But he wanted to apologize in person. Wanted to tell her that she didn't have to grieve alone. "How did you—"

"I'm coming with you."

"What?"

There were three things in the world Isaac cared about: his books, Justin, and May, in that order. Justin couldn't figure out how going with him to talk to Violet would benefit any of those things.

But then, there was a lot he couldn't figure out about Isaac lately. At least his anger at Justin seemed less present than it had that morning, even if there was something overly emphatic about the way he was walking, steel-toed work boots stamping out deep prints in the dirt.

"All founder kids grow up with baggage." The branches behind Isaac's head were crooked, reaching toward them like broken limbs that had healed wrong. Justin couldn't tell if it was an optical illusion, or if something had happened to this part of the forest. "Kind of hard not to when our ancestors gave us the lifetime gig of guarding a monster prison. But for some of us, there's a level of loss you just haven't experienced."

Justin held back a retort. He didn't want to get into a pissing contest with Isaac about which of them had been through worse.

Mostly because he knew he'd lose.

"And you're saying Violet has experienced this, now that she's lost her aunt?"

Isaac gave him a sharp look that seemed to suggest he was even less intelligent than he felt. "I did some googling. She had a sister. Rose Saunders, age eighteen, car accident, on her way back from prom-dress shopping. I saw her picture—they have the same glare."

"The one that makes you feel guilty for existing?"

Isaac nodded. "That's the one. So she's not just grieving her aunt."

It fit. Her weirdness at the reading. Her despair when told she couldn't leave town. The way she and Isaac had circled each other like two wolves searching for weak points, both wary, both haunted.

Justin refrained from commenting on the fact that Isaac had cared enough about Violet to look into the details. Anyone else, he'd tease him about. But there was no point mocking pain that recognized pain.

They reached the hill leading up to the Saunders manor, and Justin saw, with a flash of panic, that there was already a car in the driveway, idling beside the Porsche.

A silver pickup truck.

"Hey! Assholes!" May slammed the door of the car, then adjusted her headband, her pale cheeks flushed with annoyance. "You were going to talk to Violet without me?"

"I didn't think you'd want to." Justin hurried across the gravel, Isaac following close behind. "You haven't exactly been welcoming toward her—"

"Yeah, because I don't like lying to Mom," said May, jabbing a pointy pink fingernail at him. "Violet texted me, too. It doesn't matter that she blew us off before— something awful happened to her, and we owe her an apology."

"You were about to go without us," Isaac said mildly.

May frowned at him. "Not the point."

"Actually, it kind of undermines your point."

"Hey." Justin stepped between them. "We're all here now. Let's just go inside."

A moment later, they were standing in a solemn row on the front porch as Justin tugged on the brass door knocker.

Nothing happened. He was about to try again when a woman who looked oddly familiar opened the door. She cleared her throat, brushing back a lock of frizzy hair, and he realized why he knew her. There was an entire box of pictures and letters dedicated to her in the back of his mother's closet—he'd snooped years ago, not that he had ever told her.

Juniper Saunders.

Augusta's ex-girlfriend.

Justin didn't really want to think about his mom's love life more than was necessary. Augusta had explained to him and May a few years ago that she'd dated men and women, but after their dad, she'd lost interest in finding a partner.

"You two are what matters to me," she'd said matter-of-factly, in a tone that was the closest Augusta ever came to being vulnerable. "I don't need anyone else to be a family."

His father, Ezra Bishop, had left when Justin was eight and May was seven. They hadn't seen him since.

They didn't want to.

Augusta had gotten rid of all evidence of him, but Justin still saw his face sometimes, his cruel features imprinted behind his eyelids when Justin was trying to sleep.

Four Paths had lost one of its monsters the day he left town.

"Hello," he said to Juniper. "You must be Violet's mom."

"I am," she said, and his first thought—that there was nothing of Violet in this woman at all—changed immediately. So this was where Violet had learned to turn each word into a challenge, how she'd learned to stand a little too straight, like she had something to prove. "Are you three friends of hers?"

She sounded skeptical about it. And she seemed awfully put together for someone whose sister had just passed away.

"Yes." Justin knew full well that Violet would've vehemently protested this claim. "She wasn't at school today, so we picked up her homework. Can we give it to her?"

Juniper's eyes narrowed. "Violet already has a friend over. Can't you just e-mail her any homework?"

Beside him, May went still, while Isaac scowled at the ground.

Any other friend of Violet's had to be Harper. If Justin went upstairs, he'd have to face her.

But he'd come this far. And he'd already committed himself to apologizing. So he soldiered onward, turning on his last vestiges of persuasive charm. "It comes with instructions. From the teachers. We need to explain it in person."

"Hmm. Well. When she kicks you out, don't say I didn't warn you." She swung the door open. "Her bedroom's three doors to the right of the stairs."

The Saunders manor was a dank, forbidding place, halls lined with moth-eaten red-and-gold carpets and a taxidermy collection that would rival a museum. There was an area at the foot of the stairs blocked off by caution tape—Justin tried not to look too closely at the dark stains on the wooden floor.

He was pretty sure you weren't supposed to let people stay in a crime scene.

He was also pretty sure, having now met both Violet and her mother, that it would be very difficult to make them leave.

May gestured toward the chandelier as they headed up the stairs. "Do those remind you of bones?"

Justin inspected the swinging lamp. The ironwork did look kind of skeletal, especially in the dim, shifting light.

"I guess we're not the only ones who like to show off our family trademark," Justin said, keeping his voice low as Juniper disappeared into one of the downstairs rooms.

They reached the second-floor landing. A cat with a bit of red string tied around its ear prowled up to them.

Justin realized, his chest tightening, that this was the same animal he'd watched Violet resurrect days earlier.

It moved like a cat. It meowed like a cat.

But when he reached down to pet it, its body was far too cold for something living. He jerked his hand away, his heart thudding in his chest.

Here was evidence that what Violet could do was real, and powerful, and deeply, deeply strange.

Justin tried knocking on the bedroom door, but when there was no response, Isaac finally lost his patience and tugged the door open.

Violet's room was dark and shuttered, curtains pulled tightly across the windows, save for the light spilling in through the doorway. That slice of hallway light illuminated a pile of boxes on the far wall of Violet's room, each marked with the word ROSIE.

Harper's eyes widened as she took them in from her perch on the edge of the bed, but before she could open her mouth, Violet's voice rang out.

"Get out!" The covers stirred, then parted, revealing Violet's rumpled dark hair and her pale, indignant face. "Oh my god, you're all here? Who the fuck let you in?"

"Your mother," said Isaac. "Lovely woman. You inherited her charm."

"We're sorry to hear what happened to your aunt." Justin could tell from the pain blooming on her face that his words had been a mistake.

"I asked you to come here last night." Violet drew her comforter around her shoulders, like a cape. "None of you listened. So why the hell would I want you here now?"

"You let Harper in," said Isaac.

Harper glared at him. "Yeah, because I actually feel bad."

"You think we don't?" said May.

"Enough." Violet's voice was ragged and furious. "All of you. Leave. Even you, Harper. Go argue somewhere else."

Harper was visibly distressed, but she nodded, sliding off the bed. "I understand."

The look she shot Justin as she elbowed past him made him glad she wasn't saying whatever she was thinking.

It would probably be awful.

It would probably be true.

Justin took a hesitant step back as Harper slammed the door behind her. Isaac had been right: This type of pain was beyond him.

He did not know what to say. He did not know how to help her. And Justin suddenly wanted nothing more than to bolt, away from Harper, down the stairs, and out of that horrible, empty house.

But Isaac's hand landed on his shoulder before he could move.

"Hey," he said. "I got this one."

Before Justin could say anything in response, Isaac pushed open the door to Violet's bedroom and stepped inside.

FOURTEEN

VIOLET'S LIFE HAD BEEN a numb, quiet haze since the bottom of the stairs, since the resurrected body.

She could only remember it in flashes—Daria's body being loaded into the ambulance. The EMTs shaking their heads as they spoke to Juniper, her mother's face crumpling like a discarded piece of paper.

Daria's blood on her hands, dried into a coppery-brown residue.

Augusta Hawthorne's face slackening with relief when she saw Juniper standing by the staircase.

And finally, she and Juniper, the most alone they had ever been, sitting beside each other at the end of her bed. Orpheus was curled up at their feet, his yellow eyes staring mournfully at the door.

Her mother looked smaller than Violet had ever seen her, draped in a giant terry-cloth robe, feet shoved hastily into a pair of beat-up sneakers. Violet watched her twist a bit of red yarn around her fingers. She must've kept it after the ambulance took Daria away. Just like the bracelet clasped around Violet's wrist.

"You know," Juniper said, "I came back here because of you."

Violet looked at her mother's face. Without the makeup, she looked younger. More like the girl Violet had seen in the photograph. "Why?"

"Watching you... after everything... it reminded me how much losing Stephen hurt. It made me realize how much I'd regret it if I never got to see Daria again." She shook her head. "I couldn't live with that."

Violet flinched. "After everything? You mean after Rosie died, Mom. You can say it. I won't break."

"No, you won't," Juniper said softly. Her eyes were suddenly filled with the grief Violet had spent the past five months looking for. "But I might."

It wasn't nearly enough to fix things between them. But Violet was too frightened and tired to argue. So when Juniper reached for her hand, Violet let her take it, and they stayed like that for a long time.

The next morning, Juniper was already perfectly put together again. Already on her first conference call. As if the night before had never happened.

Violet knew that trying to discuss it would only cause them both more pain.

They would deal with this the only way they knew how: separately.

She had spent hours that morning inspecting the palms

of her hands, searching for any evidence that it had been her, not that body, who'd pushed Daria down the stairs.

And if it had been the body, and if Violet had resurrected it—didn't that leave her aunt's blood on her hands either way?

Those were not the kinds of thoughts that should be contemplated alone. Which was why she'd let Harper in.

She'd known the moment she saw Justin, May, and Isaac that it had been a mistake.

Violet didn't want to hear them fight about the ways they'd hurt one another. She already knew how it would end: They'd all insist they actually cared about her, when really, they just cared about proving their family was better.

She was done with their pettiness.

She could grieve without their help.

But now Isaac was standing in front of the ROSIE boxes, unbuttoning the top of his shirt.

"I told you to get out," Violet said, clutching her blankets close. "Not sure how you interpreted that as an invitation to strip."

"I used to have three brothers," Isaac said evenly, pulling his collar to the side and displaying his neck. "Two uncles. My mom, my aunt, my cousins. But they're all gone now, and the ones who are dead hurt me less than the ones who left."

"And the scar?" asked Violet. It shone gray and silvery in the dim light, like an extra shadow snaking across his throat.

"I got this the day it happened."

"How?"

She was waiting for him to stop talking. But he stepped closer instead.

"Some Sullivans can break things. Some can put them back together. But there was no one left who wanted to fix me."

Violet lowered her blankets to her waist. She was mildly aware of the fact that she hadn't bothered to look like a person today. But her baggy T-shirt and bare face didn't seem to matter right now.

"What were their names?" she said softly. "Your brothers?"

Isaac curled a hand around her bedpost. "Caleb. Isaiah." He hesitated. "Gabriel."

"Gabriel's the one who left, isn't he?"

A quick, curt nod. "How did you know?"

"You said the ones who left hurt you more. That name hurt you the most."

She had shoved the covers off now, her hands resting on her leggings as she met Isaac's eyes.

"I'm sorry about Daria," he said softly. "And I'm sorry about your sister."

"You knew?"

"I googled you."

"You could've just asked," Violet muttered, although something like relief fluttered in her chest. Someone had seen that she was hurting and found an answer. Isaac knew that there had once been her and Rosie, that she was all alone now. "But if you're going to talk about her, you should call her Rosie."

Isaac nodded. "If that's what you want."

"I'm sorry about your family. About everything. It's just—it's not fair." Violet's voice broke on the last word. The tears collecting in the back of her throat were impossible to hold back now, and she realized to her horror that they were beginning to spill down her cheeks.

She was crying now. In front of a boy she barely knew.

A boy who had just told her about the worst moments of his life, for no reason other than to show her that she was not alone after all.

A boy who was looking at her right now, not with pity or alarm, but with understanding.

"You're right," he said, reaching a tentative hand forward and wiping the tears from her cheek. "It's not fair. But you can't bring them back."

"You don't understand," said Violet hoarsely, remembering the body, the tether she'd felt between them. "I'm pretty sure I could."

He jerked his hand away. "With your powers?"

There was the alarm. The concern.

Violet snorted and swiped at her tears herself. "Look, it's my power, okay? Resurrecting things. So I thought that if I could get Rosie here, I could bring her back. But I wouldn't do it. Not now. They aren't alive like they once were, and I wouldn't want her to be... to be anything like..."

"Like your cat?" asked Isaac, while Orpheus, as if on cue, padded out from beneath the bed.

Violet hesitated. But she had held so much inside her for so long.

She was ready to talk now.

"Tell the others they can stop eavesdropping—which I'm sure they are doing—and come back in," she said. "Actually, wait. I want to see the Hawthornes first."

Isaac swung open the door, where Justin, May, and Harper were still standing, all doing a poor job of pretending they had not been listening.

"You wanted to talk to us?" said Justin eagerly.

Violet sighed. "It's not a compliment. I have some questions for both of you."

She waved Isaac out, and Justin and May in, feeling strangely powerful.

May flicked on the light switch as she passed it. "No offense," she said. "It was just super depressing in here."

Violet raked a hand through her tangled hair. "That was kind of the point?"

May shrugged. "Whenever Isaac gets too angsty, we show up and make him go outside. We'll do the same for you if we have to."

Violet choked back a badly suppressed laugh.

"Harper happened to mention, before you guys showed up, that you failed your ritual," she said, looking at Justin. "Explain."

"I did," said Justin quietly. "I'm sorry."

The truth was, Violet didn't really care that Justin didn't have powers. She understood why he would want to keep such a thing under wraps.

But she could also see who this information was really hurting.

"I don't think I'm the one you owe an apology."

If Justin had looked annoyed beforehand, he looked alarmed now. "I know. It's just... with Harper... it's complicated."

Beside him, May picked at her nail polish, her coral-colored lips pursed with disapproval. "It's a giant mess."

Violet wasn't sure she wanted to wade into whatever star-crossed bullshit Harper and Justin were clearly going through, but she needed to know if she could trust the Hawthornes or not. "She said you both ignored her when she failed her ritual. Is that true?"

Justin had been nothing but kind to her since she'd arrived in Four Paths. It was hard to match that image with the boy who'd given up on Harper the second she proved she wasn't powerful, and harder still now that she knew Justin had no powers, either.

"Our mother made us," Justin said, his voice raw and hoarse. "She said there was no use in wasting our time on someone who couldn't help protect the town. We were so young, and I thought she knew everything, and I was scared."

"Scared of what?"

May looked up from her nails, her blue eyes deadly serious. "You've never seen Augusta when she's angry."

"My ritual wasn't until last year," added Justin. "So I didn't know I was powerless for a long time. Most people still have no idea."

222

Violet listened as he went on. May shifted uncomfortably beside her when Justin told her about how he was being asked to leave Four Paths, about his desperate wish to stay.

She knew the bitterness in his voice like it was her own. How it felt to have a parent who was so far away from you, you had no idea who they really were. Who put themselves before their children, no matter how much they hurt their kids to by doing so.

Violet swallowed, hard. "So you've stopped trusting her."

Justin nodded. "I always thought she was right, but the older I get, the more I realize that my mom doesn't always make the right call. I can't fix what I did to Harper. But I hope I can help you."

"We both do," said May quietly.

Violet believed the earnestness she saw on both of their faces.

"Thank you," she said, surprised by how much she meant it. "Okay. Now I'm actually ready to talk to all of you."

Violet did her best to look intimidating as they filed into the room. "You can only stay if you promise to refrain from murdering one another while I talk."

"I'll do my best." Harper sighed, plopping onto the bed beside her.

"Yeah, all right," muttered Justin.

Violet looked around at them—May examining her nails, Isaac leaning against the wall, Harper and Justin trying very hard to pretend they weren't watching each other—and realized that she hadn't felt this way since Rosie's death.

There were people who would show up for her, then stay, even when she was angry. Even when it was hard.

"I think I did something," she said. "Something terrible."

And then she told them. About the body she'd felt that strange connection with. What had happened to Daria. How powerless she felt. How scared.

But when she was done, they didn't just stare at her. And they didn't leave.

They started talking, all at once, their voices overlapping, yet all bursting with the same caring intensity.

"I want to see this journal," said May, tugging on the medallion around her neck. "You're sure you have no idea where the other half of it is?"

"You should tell us if you black out again," said Harper softly, squeezing her hand as Orpheus pressed next to Violet's other side, his yellow eyes glinting.

"Or if you see any more signs of this resurrected body," added Isaac, frowning. "Justin, do you think there's anything about that in the patrol records?"

"A body would be tough to find in Four Paths," said Justin, and Violet remembered the mausoleum. Of course a town where people could raise the dead would have a way of dealing with that. "If there's anything in the records about this, we'll find it."

"We'll figure this out," said Harper, leaning against her shoulder.

And Violet, despite everything, smiled back.

★

Justin's next cross-country meet, the Friday before the equinox, dawned cloudy and hazy. Justin felt hazy himself as he walked to the starting line of his race, surrounded by a crowd of chattering runners. Tendrils of mist obscured the tops of the trees behind the athletic field, and for a moment the sight made him tense, reminded him of the Gray.

The past few days had been quiet and routine, but Justin knew it was an illusory calm. A thousand different troubles were suspended in the air around him, like juggling pins falling in slow motion.

They didn't just need to find Violet's ritual anymore. They needed to figure out what was going on with the body she had resurrected. There was a chance Augusta knew the truth, but Justin wasn't sure how to ask her without giving away the fact that he was working with Violet.

Then there was Harper. Who had spent the past few days doing a great job of acting like he didn't exist.

As if he didn't have enough to worry about, tomorrow was Founders' Day—and the equinox. One of the most dangerous nights of the year. He paced back and forth on the starting line of the track, trying not to think about how there was nothing he could do to help the town when the Gray was at its strongest.

This meet was local, a rarity, and there were scouts attending again. They tried to talk to Justin beforehand, and he smiled and nodded at them until they left. They weren't running a course through the woods today. The school had deemed it too dangerous.

"It's an opportunity," she'd said. "Do you know how many people would kill to get out of this town?"

It was still sitting on his night table.

If he performed well today, it could make the difference between him getting a scholarship or not. A scholarship he still wasn't sure he wanted.

"Runners, line up!"

The rest of the athletes shifted aside automatically as Justin approached the starting line, letting him through, buzzing in his wake. He was a Hawthorne, after all, and that meant running well, and keeping his head down, and pretending everything was absolutely fine.

He sighed and shifted his focus onto the track. Which was when a pink blur darted out from the crowd of spectators and sank her perfectly manicured fingernails into his arm.

"Justin!" said May, pulling him away from the mass of people.

"What?" Justin gaped at her. Behind them, the other runners buzzed with confusion.

"Justin," she said again. The hand on his arm was shaking. He reached forward with his own fingers, grasped her wrist, tried to steady her. "It's Isaac."

She tugged him away from the track, onto the grass, toward the waiting embrace of the trees.

Behind her, Justin saw the flash of a starting gun being raised in the air. He could stay here, and maybe earn his ticket out of town. Or go help Isaac.

It wasn't a choice at all.

He turned away from the track as the sound of the starting gun fired into the air, away from the runners that burst past them, away from Coach Lowell's startled, accusatory gaze.

This was his town. His birthright. His best friend. And he was not leaving—he was not going anywhere. "What happened?"

"He lost control at work. Someone's already called Mom. You have to calm him down before she gets there."

A cluster of taut, anxious faces was gathered outside the Diner. Justin heard their panicked murmurs rising above the growl of the engine as May pulled the silver pickup truck into the parking lot, skidding across two spots in her haste to park. Justin had the door open before she'd even shifted the truck out of drive.

He forced himself to even out his pace as he walked up to the crowd, to turn his expression into something neutral and mildly concerned. Half of fixing this was making it seem like an inconvenience. If he acted annoyed instead of panicked, people would follow his example.

Justin tried to catch a glimpse inside the Diner, but the interior of the restaurant was dark, its plate-glass windows spiderwebbed with cracks.

"I was expecting the sheriff." Blood trickled from a laceration on Ma Burnham's cheek, and her round face was ashen. But none of that scared him as much as the anger in her voice, or the distaste in her eyes.

She was looking at him the way Harper did. Like he'd failed her, and there was nothing he could do to fix it.

"My mother will be here soon." A sprinkle of rain dotted Justin's shoulders, his neck, but he hardly noticed. He had to make this right. "Tell me what happened." He swallowed. "Please."

"As if your family cares about us." The voice belonged to one of the people who'd collected around Ma Burnham. The crowd parted, and Justin swore, internally, as the boy who'd baited Isaac the night before stepped forward.

Justin still couldn't remember his name, but there was something familiar about the gap in his teeth, the way his hair fell across his bushy eyebrows.

"Of course I care about you," he said. "I'm here because I want to keep you safe."

"My brother died on your family's watch," said the kid. Justin's heart sank as he realized where he recognized those features from: Hap Whitley's pictures in the *Four Paths Gazette*. "And I know you're not here because you're worried about us. You're worried about him."

He jerked a thumb at the shattered windows, and around him, the crowd murmured with agreement. Justin had always loved the way he could command a group's attention. But for the first time in his life, he didn't want it.

Because Hap Whitley's brother was right. The reason he'd missed a track meet to come here wasn't because he was scared for the town. It was because he was scared for Isaac.

Justin stepped back from the crowd, his heart thudding in his chest.

And realized that May had stepped forward to stand beside him.

"Of course we're concerned for Isaac," she said, addressing not just the kid, but the entire crowd. "He's our friend. But we don't take our family name lightly. You're Brian, right? Brian Whitley?"

The kid nodded.

"I'm sorry about your brother." May's voice was a shade too polished and formal, like she'd been practicing for a presentation, and her hands were braced on either side of her corduroy skirt. But she sounded more confident as she spoke, and the crowd, Justin realized, was listening to every word. "I promise you, we grieve for every person we lose. But if you don't let Ma Burnham explain what's going on in there, more people could get hurt. Do you want that?"

Brian hesitated. "I guess not."

"Thank you," said May, almost gently, and then she turned to Ma Burnham. "Tell us everything."

"It was Brian," said Ma Burnham, stabbing a finger in the boy's direction. "He said something or other about the Sullivans, I can't recall what, exactly, but it sent Isaac into a terrible rage, and then there was just glass everywhere and people screaming."

"I see," said Justin. He'd known it would be something about Isaac's family. It always came back to his family. "Is everyone out?"

Mrs. Burnham shook her head, blood leaking onto her chin. Justin bit back a curse.

"My boys won't leave," she said. "I tried to warn them, but they said he had to answer for what he did."

"Your boys should've listened to you," he said, hoping desperately that they still had all their limbs, turning back to give the crowd a reassuring smile.

"Sorry for the inconvenience, everyone," added May. "But I promise, this will all be fine."

Justin didn't understand how it was possible to be simultaneously proud of May, relieved she'd known what to say, and jealous that he hadn't.

But he was.

The only power Justin had left in this town was charm and respect. And now May had shown that she could wield those tools, too.

This was his chance to prove he still mattered.

"I'm going in," he said, ignoring his instincts to run as he pushed open the darkened doorway and stepped into the restaurant.

The cozy booths and dim lighting that Justin knew so well were gone. In their place was a dim, cavernous space, littered with yellow foam lining and overturned chairs. Two figures stood beneath the blacked-out neon sign, and in front of them was Isaac, his back pressed against the wall, his limbs folded inward like a crumpled piece of paper.

★

The rituals were not designed to be easy. Justin had always known that the price of a hawthorn tree that did not bow would likely be his life.

But Richard Sullivan had taken a different path to power. The town loved to whisper about the Sullivans' large, messy family history, marred by disappearances and accidents. Yet Justin had paid the stories no mind until three years ago, when he'd jolted awake in the middle of the night with the taste of blood in his throat and the unshakable feeling that Isaac was in trouble.

He'd followed his gut through the forest.

What he found left him forever changed.

"Isaac?" Justin's sneakers crunched across broken plates as he stepped gingerly toward the back of the room. "Are you okay?"

Isaac didn't move.

"Hey!" said one of the figures hovering beside him. "Get up!"

"Yeah, get the fuck up!" said the other one, but there was no real strength behind the brothers' words. They were a pair of scavengers, nipping at a wounded tiger.

"Guys," said Justin, his voice low and steady. He had to get Isaac out of here before Augusta showed up. Before she took care of him, the way she'd taken care of Harper, or the way she'd take care of Violet if she learned what the girl could really do. "You should leave."

"Oh, great, the fucking cavalry's here," said the one on the right, crossing his arms. The light filtering in through the window glinted off his bald head, and Justin recognized Pete. "Prince Charming, running in to save the day."

"Except you're too late," added Theo as he flexed his biceps. The brothers looked nearly identical, but where Pete chose to keep his head shaved, glowing white and ghostly in the half-light coming in through the window, Theo let his dull brown hair grow long enough to tie back in a greasy ponytail. "He ruined our restaurant. Now he's gotta pay."

"Listen," said Justin, trying to adopt their slouching mannerisms, their deep drawl. "You sure it's even worth it? He's just sitting there."

"He made Ma cry," said Pete, scowling. "Nobody makes Ma cry."

"Damn straight!" bellowed Theo. "We give him a job and this is how he repays us? You can't just treat this town like trash because you're founders. You don't get to walk all over us anymore."

"You know the founders are here to protect you," said Justin, trying to keep his voice even.

"Really?" said Theo. "Well, look what your boy here did. Maybe it's you we need protection from."

"Maybe it's time to defend ourselves," said Pete, lumbering forward and kicking Isaac lightly in the side of the leg. Justin tensed, but Isaac stayed still.

"Stop," Justin said.

They didn't listen.

Now they were braver. Justin called out another protest

as Theo moved in. "You little. Piece. Of. Shit." Each word was punctuated by another kick, each one a little heavier than the last. Each time, Justin's anger boiled a little higher, but Isaac's body remained as limp as a rag doll.

When Justin had found Isaac in the woods that night, he'd been unconscious, his hands and feet shackled to the earth. He'd stepped across charred bits of bone and ash and knelt down beside Isaac, sobs catching in his throat. Soot-streaked blood pooled in the hollows of Isaac's neck, and Justin thought he was too late, that he was already gone. But when he placed a hand on the boy's shoulder, Isaac stirred.

His mother found them eventually—some of the nearby houses had heard screams—and she took them both away. By then, Justin's fingers had been scraped raw from trying to break Isaac's shackles.

Later, Augusta had told him that the Sullivans' ritual was a bloodletting, a test of strength and fortitude that proved they deserved their powers. But something had gone wrong during Isaac's ritual. Four Sullivans, including two of Isaac's brothers, were dead. Their bodies had been disintegrated to ashes and charred bone—nothing else was left. And his mother was in a coma.

Within weeks, the remaining Sullivans were gone. They left Isaac behind, signed over to Augusta.

Justin accepted the truth his mother had told him, and yet there was another truth, too, in the scar on Isaac's neck, in the evidence he had seen that horrible night.

The other Sullivans had scars on their shoulders, on their chests, on their backs.

You did not draw a knife across someone's throat as a test of fortitude.

"Get away from him," Justin said, stepping between Pete and Theo.

Isaac sagged on the ground beside them. Justin had a brief flash of concern that he might be unconscious.

"If you're supposed to protect us," said Pete venomously, "why does it seem like he's all you care about?"

And then his fist was swinging toward Justin's face, and Justin realized, too late, that being a founder wasn't going to protect him this time.

That being a founder made him a target.

The punch connected with Justin's jaw, jerking his head backward, sending a splash of spots before his eyes as he reeled from the impact. And it was only then, as Justin stumbled into the wall, that Isaac's eyes snapped open.

Isaac grinned. "Bad move."

Pete's and Theo's eyes widened as Isaac unfolded, his arms and legs spreading toward the ceiling like bits of ink spilling across a canvas. He was still wearing his apron.

"Run," Justin said to them.

Yet the brothers just stood there as the air around Isaac's hands began to shimmer. Within moments, the entire Diner was glowing; a maelstrom of reds and blues and purples bouncing off broken plates in violent, fragmented patterns.

Isaac stepped in front of Justin, his outstretched arms shielding his friend. Pete and Theo exchanged confused glances, their eyes shifting uneasily between the boy in front of them and the door behind them.

"Didn't you hear me?" Justin bellowed. "Run!"

But he was too late. Isaac's hands clamped around the brothers' wrists. The screaming started a second later, as first Pete, then Theo, fell to their knees, howling.

Justin stared, horrified.

Words would not help him here. And all he could think of was what Theo had said: *Maybe it's you we need protection from.*

He could not let this happen.

He sidestepped Isaac's arms, wincing at the sight of Pete's and Theo's skin flaking away from their hands, and stepped into the center of the shimmering air.

"What the hell are you doing?" snarled Isaac, his voice barely audible over the screams.

Justin reached forward and closed his hand around Isaac's exposed forearm.

The heat felt good at first, like basking in the sun. But quickly, the warmth became unbearable on his nose and cheeks. Yet Justin did not flinch. He did not move. He kept his eyes locked on Isaac's until his friend's gaze flickered away, and the room around them snapped abruptly back to darkness.

Isaac would die before he hurt him. Justin knew that the way he knew his own name, the way he knew how to breathe.

Pete and Theo collapsed to the ground, wailing at the stripes of raw flesh on their wrists, but a quick glance in their direction told Justin that their injuries were just surface wounds. Isaac hadn't reached muscle.

Justin was still holding Isaac's arm. He let go, stepped back. Isaac's eyes flickered down to their broken grip, then back up to him, his expression strangely disappointed.

"Get out," Isaac told Pete and Theo roughly. They scrambled to their feet and bolted, urine dribbling down Theo's leg.

Justin and Isaac were left alone in the ruins of the Diner, staring at each other.

"He called you Prince Charming," Isaac said finally, when the silence between them had gone on for far too long.

"What?"

"Pete. Prince Charming. You. Isn't it interesting that they think you're the one who always saves everybody?"

Justin kicked at a bit of broken glass. "Well. Don't I?"

Isaac tugged the ever-present book out of his back pocket, shaking his head at the singed pages.

"I'm not some charity case with a tragic past that you have to keep out of trouble," he said, brandishing the novel like a weapon.

"And I'm not some weak kid you have to babysit."

"I never said—"

"Neither did I."

This was how it was between them now, how it had

been since Justin had failed his ritual. A constant struggle for who was the saved and who was the savior, reversal after reversal. Each time their roles flipped, Justin could feel himself trying a little less hard to pull Isaac back from the brink.

"So." Isaac stuck the book back in his pocket and yanked off his apron. "I'm fired, right?"

"Oh, absolutely," said Justin, shaking his thoughts away. "And probably banned for life."

They left through the back door, and as they stepped out into the parking lot, the sound of their footsteps muted by a sudden deluge of rain, Isaac spoke again.

"I don't know why you haven't given up on me yet," he said. "Wouldn't that be easier?"

Justin turned to look at him, at the rain that dripped from Isaac's dark hair down to the bridge of his nose.

"I'll give up when you do," he said.

Isaac's mouth did something funny at the corners that made Justin wonder if he'd forgotten how to smile.

He and Isaac tried so desperately to prop each other up because it made them feel stronger. Because part of Justin wanted Isaac to lose it so he could calm him down. So he could be needed. And he knew that part of Isaac was glad Justin had failed his ritual so that Isaac himself had someone to protect.

He hated that part of Isaac almost as much as he hated the corresponding part of himself.

Isaac's shoulder pressed against his for a second, almost leaning, almost not, and then they walked into the parking lot, into the rain, waiting for Augusta's deputies to find them.

Founders' Day dawned bright and sunny, yesterday's rain clouds long gone, but Justin was in no position to appreciate any of that. Instead, he was stuck inside, staring his mother down from across the polished wooden table in the center of her office at the police station.

He'd been dreading this conversation from the moment Augusta found him and Isaac behind the Diner. His mother had been too busy between damage control and Founders' Day prep to corner him the night before, but Justin wasn't naive enough to think that this would be a pleasant talk just because she'd slept on it first. Augusta's anger was worse the longer she let it simmer.

"I'm interested in what you have to say for Isaac this time," she said. "Every property damage complaint we get, every furious mother, makes me less convinced he should be allowed to run around unchecked."

Justin hadn't been lying when he told Violet that his mother's lack of faith in him had made him begin to doubt her leadership. But the truth was that the erosion of that trust had started years before. What she'd done to Harper had left him perpetually concerned that she would do the same thing to Isaac. She'd been kind to him at first, taking him in, letting him stay in the town hall apartment. But Justin knew it was only to obtain Isaac's loyalty: People only mattered to Augusta as long as they were useful.

238

And Isaac was starting to tip the scales between useful and dangerous.

"He's the only Sullivan left in Four Paths," Justin said.

"The others will come back," Augusta said calmly. "Eventually. They always come back."

"And how long will it take for you to earn their trust, once they do?" said Justin. "Isaac owes you everything. I'm not saying he's not at fault here. But he's never hurt an innocent, and he never will."

"The Burnham brothers would beg to disagree."

"They goaded him into it," said Justin. "The things they said to him, to me—"

"Did not warrant what Isaac put them through."

"Mother," said Justin. "They're fine."

Theo and Pete were actually a lot better than fine. They were as good as healed after a few bandages at the clinic. On his way to the sheriff's station, Justin had seen them recounting their version of events to every girl they could find. They'd even tried it on Violet, and immediately looked so remorseful, Justin had to smile.

But Isaac had still hurt them. And that mattered.

"They're considering pressing charges," Augusta said, leaning across the table. "Vandalism, aggravated assault."

"That's ridiculous! It was provoked."

Augusta spread her fingers across the desk.

"You're not seeing the bigger picture here," she said. "The town is upset with us. They need a scapegoat. And Isaac is an easy target."

Justin bit back the urge to tell her that he'd noticed just

how upset the town was—no need to make her angry.

"So convince the Burnhams not to press charges," he said, trying to stay calm. "You've protected people before. I've seen it."

"And what will I do the next time?"

"There won't be a next time."

"You said that after the grocery store incident."

Justin knew he had to play this like a deal—a deal she'd be foolish not to take. With Augusta Hawthorne, everything was about bargaining.

"There won't be a next time," he repeated. "Because if this ever happens again, you can use your power on him."

It took a lot to surprise his mother, but Justin had done it. He could see it wash over her like a brisk breeze, her body stiffening, then relaxing as the idea sank in.

"Fine," she said at last. "Tell him he can participate in the Founders' Day Pageant today, but he's staying in tonight. An unstable patrolman out on the night of the equinox could be deadly."

"But we're already stretched thin!" Justin leaned forward. "It's not safe."

"I know," said Augusta, meeting his eyes. "Which is why I'm putting you back on the roster. Consider it my way of seeing if pulling you off patrol was a mistake or not."

"Oh." Justin tried not to feel proud, and then tried not to feel guilty about it. "Thank you. I won't let you down."

"I'm sure," said Augusta. "And, Justin?"

"Yes, Mother?"

"I hope you understand that what you've just agreed to means no regrets. Not like with Harper Carlisle."

Justin forced himself to smile at her.

"I understand," he said, and then a deputy came to lead him to the holding cell Isaac was in.

Isaac looked better than Justin had expected him to, considering. They'd treated the wounds the Burnham brothers had given him at the station clinic.

"You here to spring me from the pokey?" he said dryly, sprawled out on the bench in the back of Four Paths' one and only holding cell.

"Nah," said Justin. "Just came by to make fun of the prisoners."

"And you didn't even bring any fruit to throw at me? Shameful."

The deputy started to punch in the code on the keypad at the other side of the cell. Isaac rose, yawning and making a show of stretching his arms above his head.

"You know they don't even let us read in here?" he said as the reddish stone bars of the prison slid upward. "How inhumane is that?"

"You're supposed to meditate on your wrongdoing." Justin barely recognized this deputy—his mother was clearly hurting for staff after Anders's death.

"Do I look like I meditate?" said Isaac, stepping through the bars.

Justin gestured toward the exit as the deputy's light brown forehead furrowed with annoyance. "Let's go. Before they lock you up again."

FIFTEEN

OUTSIDE THE POLICE STATION, the sun shone brightly down on Main Street. People were everywhere, perusing stalls set up by local businesses who'd turned out to sell their wares at Founders' Day and chatting on the sidewalk. But Justin sensed an undercurrent of unease beneath the bustling town. Tonight was one of the most dangerous nights of the year in Four Paths. The night when the lines between the town and the Gray began to blur.

Which was why it was the perfect time for the Founders' Day festival. It was a way to boost morale for the town and remind the people of their trust in the founders—even when the founding families were at their weakest.

It was a smart idea. Justin was willing to bet a Hawthorne had come up with it.

The crux of the celebration was the Founders' Pageant, an event that was meant to symbolize the contributions the founding families had made to the town. One representative from each of the founding families would be "crowned" by the mayor, then sent to place a token of their family's esteem on the town seal.

For the past three years, Justin had been the Hawthorne to do the ceremony, joining a disinterested Daria Saunders, Isaac, and one of the Carlisle children in the town square.

But Daria Saunders was dead, and this was Justin's first festival since failing his ritual. The thought of wearing a crown and grinning at the crowd felt different now.

All the things that had once been easy for Justin were slowly becoming impossible. He didn't like it.

"She took me off patrol, didn't she?" said Isaac as they strode past the booth where Old Man Moore sold pigs— pigs that families desperately returned a few days later.

"She did," said Justin. "Said there wasn't any room in her equinox plans for unpredictable threats."

"So she's saying I'm a danger to myself and others?"

"Yep."

"How'd it take her so long to notice?"

Justin snorted, sidestepping a few kids trying their hand at an old wooden ring-toss game. "You still have to do the pageant."

"Seriously?" Isaac scowled. "I just destroyed the Diner. Does your mother really think the ceremony will make everyone less angry?"

"I think you should focus on making *my mother* less angry right now."

Isaac rolled his eyes, but he followed Justin to the front of the town hall, where a crowd was already beginning to form at the edge of the giant founders' symbol embedded in the square.

"Took your time getting here, didn't you?" said May. Nestled carefully between her hands was the wooden Hawthorne crown, a delicate thing made of intricately woven branches that had been made by Justin's great-grandmother, Millie Hawthorne, nearly eighty years ago. Their family had done a good job of preserving the wood, but Justin worried about it breaking as he took it from May and wedged it in his blond hair.

His sister looked at him, her normally expressionless face colored with longing as her eyes lifted to the crown upon his head. Justin felt a rush of guilt.

"Did you ask Mom if you could do it this year?" The words were out before Justin could stop them.

The way her face hardened around the edges told him she had. "Maybe next year," she said, each word a bit too carefully formed. "When you're at college."

"Ah."

"Yes."

The tense moment was broken by Isaac sidling up to them, the steel, pointed Sullivan crown nestled in his dark curls. He must've gone back inside the town hall to fetch it. "Excited to show everyone how pretty you look?"

"Oh, shut it, Sullivan."

Isaac grinned, but it was a bit ragged around the edges.

Justin could tell he was worried about how the crowd would react to him.

Truth be told, he was worried, too. He wasn't sure the Founders' Pageant was the smartest thing to do today, but it would look weirder if the founders didn't have it at all.

"Welcome, everyone!" called out Mayor Storey from the steps of the town hall, a microphone in his hand. His dark-skinned face was creased into a careful smile. After the Sullivans left town, Augusta had quietly dissuaded all potential founder candidates from running for mayor as a show of support for the rest of the town. Mayor Storey was a popular choice—a former principal of Four Paths High School and a well-respected member of the community. "Thank you so much for coming to this year's Founders' Day festival."

A half-hearted round of cheering greeted the mayor's announcement. Justin watched the crowd, noting uncomfortably that there was a neutral, unimpressed face for every smiling one.

A few deputies were strewn around the edge of the crowd, while Augusta herself stood at the foot of the town hall stairs, watching everyone carefully. So his mother hadn't just been talking about the town's changing morale to prove a point, then—she'd noticed it, too.

"As you know," Mayor Storey continued, undaunted by the lukewarm reception, "Four Paths' founding families have a special relationship with our town. For the last century and a half, they have dedicated themselves to keeping this town safe, healthy, and prosperous. We are honored to have all of you here today to watch this year's Founders' Pageant. Now, please join me in a round of applause for this year's volunteers!"

Across the circle, Justin's mother gave him a look, and he remembered with a start that he was supposed to go first.

He walked across the circle, kneeling on the southernmost line slicing through the founders' symbol and placing his crown on the seal. In past years, this had felt like a victory lap—winking at girls and waving to the crowd as he walked out.

But this year, the applause was polite, nothing more.

He watched Mitzi Carlisle saunter out in a crown of red-brown stone that had been set across her auburn hair. She smiled at him as she knelt on the eastern line and placed her crown on the seal.

He faked a smile back.

Violet was next, a thicket of twisted ivory spires rising from her jet-black hair. Her mouth twitched with annoyance as she knelt on the northern line. She'd texted him that morning asking if she really had to do the pageant. Justin was impressed she'd actually shown up.

Isaac was last.

Justin held his breath as he strode out into the circle.

And just as he'd feared, the applause from the audience faded from polite claps to dead silence.

Justin didn't know what he would've done, but he was proud of the way Isaac's face didn't change. He just kept walking, slow and steady, his footsteps ringing out across the silent courtyard, and he dropped to his knees on the western line of the founders' symbol.

He removed his steel crown and, with a flourish, set it on the seal.

Justin could see his friend's hands trembling. And he saw in that moment that this was hurting Isaac more than he'd told anyone, being put on display like this, being publicly humiliated.

A single round of applause rang out across the courtyard. Isaac's head jerked toward Justin—but it wasn't him who was applauding.

It was Violet. She was still kneeling on the seal, clapping her hands together, the look on her face daring the crowd to protest.

A moment later, Justin joined her, and then the mayor was clapping, and so was May, and his mother, and at least half the crowd standing around the square. Isaac looked around at all of them, visibly stunned.

Justin was weak with relief as Mayor Storey reached for his microphone again. He caught his mother's eyes across the circle—she was furious.

"Thank you, all," the mayor said hastily. "As you know, in 1847, a group seeking a new life in upstate New York decided to end their pilgrimage here. On this day, we celebrate the leaders of that group—Thomas Carlisle, Lydia Saunders, Richard Sullivan, and Hetty Hawthorne.

"Today, their descendants strive to keep this town healthy and safe, and to help it grow in the same way their ancestors did. These representatives of each family are a symbol of Four Paths' legacy and its enduring future. The crowns they have laid at their ancestors' feet symbolize their dedication to serving the town."

Justin heard a murmur sweep through the crowd. On his left, Cal Gonzales leaned over to whisper something to Suzette Langham, annoyance apparent on both of their faces.

"The Founders' Pageant is complete," Mayor Storey said, his dark brown hand clutching the microphone perhaps a bit too tightly. "Now go enjoy your day."

As Justin stood up, it struck him how fake all of this was. All his lies clustered within him, the secrets that were his and the ones that weren't, and suddenly he wanted to scream the truth at all of them, to tell them that he was just like the rest of the town. That he couldn't protect them.

As the crowd dispersed, Justin's eyes fell on the field beside the square. Some of the children had missed the ceremony, instead choosing to play on the stretch of grass in front of the town mausoleum. There were even a few kids squabbling over a bucket of play swords, whacking at one another with cheap wooden blades. He recognized two of them, one much taller than the other, laughing as they played at a sword fight.

Justin watched the sun tease its way through Harper's curls. Nostalgia plucked at the inside of his chest like a harp string as she dodged each of her little sister's attempts to stab her.

And although the thought of walking over there was scarier than walking into the Diner had been the day before, he shoved the Hawthorne crown into May's hands and headed straight toward the field.

Harper hated the Founders' Pageant. It was a display of all the worst parts of Four Paths—Augusta Hawthorne's arrogance, Mitzi preening over a crown, and the town collectively swooning over Justin.

She wanted no part of it, and so when Nora demanded they play instead of going to watch, she was happy to oblige her sister. She needed to think, anyway.

Daria Saunders's death had changed everything, again. The Hawthornes were back in Violet's corner, which meant Harper had to pretend to like them—right after Justin had proven that he was even less trustworthy than she'd originally thought.

Harper had reported everything she could back to the Church of the Four Deities, concerned they'd be upset that she was spending so much time with the Hawthornes, but they'd just told her to keep Violet close.

It concerned her that she had yet to meet their mysterious leader, or discover any more than she'd already known about their plans. Her father remained tight-lipped about the entire situation, only promising that Harper would get more information when the time was right.

Harper wanted to trust her father. But it seemed like, after all she'd done, he still didn't trust her.

"I'm gonna be a warrior!" Nora said, brandishing a

wooden sword at Harper's knees as if they had personally wronged her. "I'm gonna hit Brett when he's mean, and then he won't be mean anymore."

"I'm not sure if hitting him will help that," said Harper, shaking her thoughts away.

Nora pouted. "Can I practice on you?"

Harper stared at the crate of swords. It didn't matter that the blades were wooden—she still itched to grab one. Besides, Nora was only six, and half the size of the other kids clustered around the play area who she could wind up play fighting with. Wooden swords were blunt, sure, but they could bruise if wielded with enough force. And she was not about to let her baby sister get hurt.

She smiled. "Let's teach you how to be a warrior."

Harper selected her own blade from the crate, one with a washed-out blue hilt, and knelt in the grass. At first, she tried to explain the basics of fencing to Nora, but her sister had no interest whatsoever in what a parry or a riposte was. She just wanted to jump around while waving her sword and yelling battle cries. So Harper let her, barely paying attention as she batted Nora's blade away, occasionally letting her sister tap the blunted edge of the sword against her arm or knee or shoulder and yell, "I WIN!"

Things could've gone on like this indefinitely if Justin Hawthorne hadn't appeared beside her.

"Mind if I cut in?" The sunlight blazing out from behind him turned him into an imposing backlit shape, blocking out the rest of Harper's world.

Harper froze, completely unsure what she was supposed to say to him. Nora, however, had fewer qualms about responding to this new potential victim.

"I'm going to beat you!" she yelled.

Justin laughed as she whacked at his knees until he obligingly toppled backward onto the grass.

"You got me," he told her, blond hair spilling across his forehead. The dimple in his cheek appeared as his lips widened into a grin. "I'm the deadest dead person on this field."

"Dead people don't talk," Nora informed him, unimpressed.

"So?" said Justin, turning his head.

Heat kindled in Harper's chest as the power of that carefree smile hit her. She tried to pretend it was rage. "What are you doing here?"

The smile disappeared. Justin propped himself up on the grass, the fabric of his gray T-shirt straining against his broad shoulders. "Apologizing to you. If you'll let me."

Harper had wanted an apology for years. Yet she could feel in her bones that his words wouldn't be enough. When he spoke, he drew her back in. She couldn't trust herself to hold out against him, even now, knowing that he was a lying hypocrite. Even as her hatred stirred to life beneath her skin, sending a shiver of fury through her.

Her hand tightened around the hilt of her blade—and, with the sudden rush of an idea, Harper lifted it up and pointed it straight at Justin's chest.

"Go get a sword," she said coolly.

His hazel eyes went wide. "What?"

"You heard me," she said. "You want to apologize? Well, I want to fight."

Justin sucked in a breath. But he didn't protest, just got up, walked over to the crate, and grabbed the last remaining sword inside. It was dark yellow with stains that looked a lot like vomit, which gave Harper a petty rush of satisfaction.

"I guess I deserve this," he said.

"Don't you dare go easy on me," she said, and they began.

It was clear in seconds that her secret midnight practices had paid off. It didn't matter that Justin had a foot of height and half an arm on her. Her muscles knew what to do. She swatted his blade away and darted forward, nearly grazing his left arm. He stepped back just in time and met her sword with his.

Awareness dawned in his eyes. "You've been training."

Harper's skirt swished around her knees as she stepped forward, extending the point of her blade until it was a hair away from his chest. She had a sudden, fervent wish for it to be made of steel, not wood. "Stop talking."

When they dove back into sparring this time, she could tell Justin was no longer holding back. They parried and wove around each other, Harper easing into the pattern of the fight. Somewhere in the past three years, Justin's gangly frame had filled out, and that new strength showed in each of his lunges. His muscular arms batted away her blade with the easy confidence of someone who was used to winning.

They had trained together as children, and it did not take Harper long to catch on to the familiar rhythms of Justin's moves. He'd grown up but his technique hadn't, and so she knew every feint, every weak point. But the way Harper fought had changed since her ritual. Her missing arm had altered her balance and footwork, forcing her to develop different attacks, different defenses.

He didn't know who she was anymore. Which was why she would win, and he would lose.

Justin's easy confidence was dissipating, a thin sheen of sweat collecting at his temples as his chest rose and fell in small, shallow breaths. Harper could feel her own body starting to tire, her muscles straining with the effort of outmaneuvering Justin's larger frame. It was too easy for him to get close to her; a well-timed parry left their torsos only inches apart. Harper jerked away from him, but not before his scent filled her nostrils, a familiar mixture of soap and woodsmoke.

She steadied herself and lunged, whacking the hilt of Justin's blade hard enough to send it flying out of his hand.

Harper stepped forward, her muscles burning, and tipped her sword up to his throat. "You lose."

Justin's eyes met hers. There was something unsettled in his gaze. "I'm sorry."

"Stop it."

His voice was husky and low. "Harper, if you'd just let me explain—"

"Like you let me explain after I failed my ritual?" She extended her arm up, pressed the tip of the blade against the skin above his Adam's apple. "You never gave me a chance. Now you know how it feels."

Justin's eyes widened, his hands raising above his head. A clear surrender. "If it's any consolation," he said quietly, "it feels like shit."

Harper realized, dimly, that her hand was beginning to shake, the edge of her sword trembling against Justin's throat.

She wanted him to hurt like she was hurting. Was tempted to try to run Justin through with a wooden blade, for the past three years of her life, for the things he'd done to her, the damage he had caused.

Yet she was still overly aware of the proximity of their bodies. It would only take a half step for those muscular arms to close around her, for her forehead to nestle against the planes of his chest.

All this, and she still wanted Justin Hawthorne to touch her.

Harper lowered her blade, disgusted with herself.

"Just go," she said. "Please. Just go."

For once, Justin listened to her. Harper watched his slumped shoulders as he loped back toward the fair, the sword he'd left behind discarded in the grass.

Violet watched the clouds gather from her bedroom window, tendrils of gray that reached toward the trees below them like claws.

It annoyed her that her mother knew nothing of the Saunderses' heritage—except for the Founders' Pageant. Violet had woken up that morning to find a crown on her dressing table and a text telling her that the sheriff had asked her to participate, and wouldn't it be good for Violet to go hang out with her new friends?

Violet was pretty sure the crown was actually made of bone. She'd wanted to examine it more closely, but Augusta Hawthorne had taken it away after the pageant, claiming it needed to be stored in the town hall.

There was something different in the air tonight. She'd been able to feel it back at the Founders' Day festival, a slight charge in her fingertips like a static shock. That strange pulsating energy she'd felt when she was near Orpheus bubbled within her now, and she could tell it wasn't just because the cat was nearby, mauling a toy mouse from his perch atop her pillow. This was more than the tether she'd felt between them, stronger, even, than the tether she'd felt between her and that resurrected body.

It was power. Her power. And it was everywhere, fizzing through her blood, frightening and exhilarating in equal measure.

The Hawthornes had already told her that the fall and spring equinoxes were the days of the year when the prison was at its weakest, and the Beast inside it was strongest, but Justin had made a point to remind her again today. He'd warned her to pull down her storm shutters and stay inside until dawn. But Violet didn't feel scared—

she felt strong. Stronger than she had since she'd arrived in town. And she could not shake the feeling that there was something more she could be doing.

Violet stared down at the sheet music binder in her lap, at the phrases that were so basic, so flat, and sighed. She could feel the way she wanted the notes to change just by looking at them.

On a whim, she leaned forward and penciled in an extra flourish in the margins of Abegg Variations op. 1. She wondered what it would be like to start from nothing, to improvise on an empty page. To create music the way Rosie had created art on a blank canvas.

But Juniper appeared in her doorway, and in an instant, those thoughts were gone.

Daria hung between them, a conversational albatross that had weighed on them since the night she'd died. Alongside Juniper, Violet had watched Daria's ashes slotted beside her younger brother's in the Saunders section of the town mausoleum earlier that week. A funeral of two.

Violet wanted to talk to her—about Daria and Rosie and Stephen. About her father. But she didn't even know where to start.

The journal had made her uncle real to her. She'd read it over multiple times since she'd found it in the archives, and each time, she had felt more and more as if she was grieving this boy she'd never known alongside his older sister.

"There's a storm coming," her mother said.

"I noticed." Violet jerked a thumb toward her window.

The clouds behind them had blotted out the setting sun, and a thin white fog was beginning to collect at the edge of the trees, sending a shudder of residual panic through Violet's chest.

Juniper's lips pursed. "Hail. Wind. Rain. Don't leave the house."

"Do I ever go anywhere unless you make me? Like that ridiculous pageant?"

Juniper sighed. "Just help me with the storm shutters."

They cranked down the safety blinds in front of every window, ancient metal things that groaned as they were unfurled. All the things Violet wasn't saying churned in her mind the longer she stood next to her mother. But she stayed silent.

Because what good would it do?

Because when had they ever really talked about how they felt?

The wind began to kick up, a harsh, high whisper against the metal blinds that sounded like a whimpering child. Violet pulled the final storm shutter into place, jumping back as it began to rattle and shake against the living room window.

And maybe the unsteady storm shutters had dislodged something in her, too. Because she turned to Juniper, the words waiting in her throat.

The words she'd wanted to say for the last five months.

"Do you even miss them?"

Juniper's face went still. "Miss who?"

"All the people you've lost. Because I don't understand

how you can just keep going. Don't you realize they're gone?"

The lamps on the mantelpiece provided the only remaining light in the room, casting a dull glow across the edges of Juniper's frizzy hair.

It was hard to look at her. Because Violet could see the resemblance between them. In her posture. In the twitching of her long, elegant fingers. And, most of all, in the grief etched into her face.

"You don't think I miss them?" said Juniper softly. "There isn't a day where I don't miss my brother and sister, or your father. And there isn't a second where I don't miss Rosie." She let out a badly concealed sob. "But you need a parent who doesn't fall apart. So I won't."

Violet had a sudden rush of understanding that this was where she'd learned to pull her feelings inside. How to put a tough, neutral façade over pain. Not because she wasn't hurting, but because if she let herself feel it, it would overwhelm her.

But Violet had started opening up these past few weeks. And it hadn't made her pain worse—it had made it better. Showed her that she wasn't alone.

"But you did fall apart." Suddenly, Violet wasn't just sad anymore. She was angry. "You were never there for us, after Dad died. You never told me and Rosie anything about your family. And you kept us from Dad's side of the family, too, even though we asked to see them. You cut me off from a whole bunch of people who could have loved me. That's not holding it together, Mom—that's running away."

Juniper's face crumpled. "I have been the best parent to you that I know how to be. And I was there for you and Rosie when your father died."

But that couldn't be right. Violet had been there, same as Juniper. "You're lying."

She whirled around and rushed back to her room, where she lay on her bed, shuffling through her audition program. But her mind wasn't on her sheet music anymore.

She stared up at the ceiling and thought about her father, her few cloudy memories of him, his wide smile, his kind eyes.

And then Violet let herself remember how painful it had been, after he'd died. The hands that had pulled up the covers on her back and smoothed her hair until she fell asleep. That gave her a perfectly packed lunch each morning. That hovered over her as she practiced the piano, flipping through the pages.

They had always been Rosie's hands to her—but Rosie had been only six when their father died, and she was startled to remember that these hands were lean and elegant, much like hers.

The memory of her first recital unspooled back into her mind again, but this time, it wasn't Rosie tugging her up to the piano.

It was Juniper.

I was there for you and Rosie when your father died.

Violet choked back a sob.

Her mother had made mistakes, that much was true. She had hurt Violet and Rosie. She had kept them away from their family, kept secrets, told lies.

Yet Violet had lied to herself, too.

She wanted Rosie to be the perfect sister. She wanted Juniper to be a shitty parent. Because it was easy to make someone perfect when they were gone. And it was so much harder to work through all the complicated messiness of a mother who had cared for her, but imperfectly. Who had been selfish, but not irredeemably so.

People could hurt each other without being monsters. And they could love each other without being saints.

She would have to learn how to handle that.

Violet rolled over on the bed, clutching her comforter, listening to the beating of the rain against the storm shutters.

And realized, her heart jumping into her throat, that it wasn't just the storm she was hearing. Something was tapping against the metal blinds across her bedroom window.

SIXTEEN

VIOLET ROSE FROM THE bed, gazing at her window.
The shutters kept rattling.

Based on the past two weeks, whatever was out there
probably wanted her dead.

But there was Orpheus, curled up at the edge of the
bed, his yellow eyes fixed on the window. Violet watched
as he raised his head, his tail twitching—and then yawned.

Whatever was out there, it didn't bother her companion.
And some deep, instinctual part of her trusted his
judgment.

The sound rang out from her window again, and now
Violet heard another, lower noise accompanying it, too
deep to be the wind. A voice.

She swung her feet to the floor and walked to the
window, listening. A gust of wind set the storm shutters
rattling, carrying the voice through the glass as it spat out
a series of curses.

Violet knew that voice. She cranked open the storm

shutters, and sure enough, there was Isaac Sullivan, crouching beside her window. The planes of his face were shadowed and angular beneath the hood of his rain jacket. Hail dotted his broad shoulders as he gestured toward the glass.

The sight of him sent something sparking in her, a pleasant, heady rush of surprise Violet wasn't sure how to process. She unlatched the window and slid it up, wincing at the gust of wind that tumbled into her bedroom as Isaac maneuvered his way through the opening with catlike grace.

He straightened up and tugged down his jacket hood as she slammed the window shut.

"What are you doing here?" said Violet, once she'd cranked down the storm shutters again. "Shouldn't you be on patrol?"

There were bits of hail in Isaac's hair. Violet watched them melt into his dark curls, leaving behind droplets of moisture that glimmered weakly in the dim light.

"Didn't you hear about my little mishap yesterday?" he said bitterly.

Violet had heard. It had been hard to miss the broken glass in the front window of the Diner at the Founders' Day festival, and harder still to miss the town's pointed lack of applause when he'd participated in the pageant. She nodded.

"Figured you had. Yeah, so the sheriff benched me from the equinox patrol."

Equinox patrol. Of course that would be a thing.

Violet was glad she'd clapped for him. "That sucks. But it doesn't explain why you're here."

Isaac sighed. "Right. Well, Justin figured it was probably a bad idea for you to wait out the equinox alone because, in his words, you're a disaster magnet and he's not sure how you get to school every morning without something trying to kill you."

Violet's newfound fondness for Isaac evaporated in an instant. She should've known he'd only come here because Justin wanted him to. She couldn't mistake one guilt-induced visit to her house for actual care. "I do not need a babysitter."

Isaac shrugged off his jacket. He'd tied a thin strip of leather across his neck to hide his scar. Three crimson beads were strung across the center, hanging in the hollow of his throat like drops of blood. They matched the medallions at his wrists.

"Ah, yes, you are perfectly self-sufficient," he drawled. "You haven't done your ritual, you keep winding up in the Gray, and you don't remember raising someone from the dead."

"And yet I still managed to avoid vandalism and assault."

Violet knew the moment the words left her mouth that they had been a mistake. Isaac's torso caved inward, and his eyes winked out like candle flames flickering in the wind.

"I'm sorry." Violet halved the distance between them. She didn't try to hide the shame in her voice. "That was a terrible thing to say."

Isaac worked his jaw back and forth. The veins in his

left forearm tensed as his fingers dug into his palm, the cracked red medallion straining against his wrist.

"It's all right," he said, in a tone that indicated just the opposite. "I've been called a lot worse."

"By the Burnhams?"

Isaac's mouth curved into a smile that could've sliced through concrete. He leaned toward her, and Violet's body responded, repositioning itself to mirror his. "No. By my brother."

"The one who left?" Violet said.

Isaac nodded, and Violet realized his clenched fist was trembling. "My neck—what happened—that was Gabriel. A souvenir, I guess."

She remembered his fingers on her cheek, how he had looked at her with tenderness when she was at her worst.

She could give him that, too. Not pity or empty words of affirmation, but understanding. He had been hurt and so had she; it did not matter that she didn't know the details. His pain was bone-deep. So was hers.

Violet reached for his hand. His fingers uncurled the moment she touched him, and she wrapped both of her hands around his, her thumbs making gentle circles across his palm until the shaking stopped.

"He can't hurt you," she said fiercely, suddenly certain that if anyone ever tried, she would be the first to stop them. "Not anymore."

His lips parted slightly, his eyes swimming with something that was no longer fury, yet was somehow far more frightening.

Which was when the noise rang out, a thump so loud Violet actually jumped, her hands falling away from Isaac's.

"What's that?" she hissed. "Did you come with reinforcements?"

But Isaac shook his head, looking just as spooked as she was.

The thumping continued—it was coming from downstairs. Violet started toward the front door. The tension of their conversation still hung between them, but it was lessening now, overtaken by this new potential threat.

"You shouldn't answer doors on a night like this," Isaac called after her.

That was quite enough for Violet, who had been told what to do far too many times that evening.

"I opened the window, didn't I?" she said, darting down the hallway before Isaac could protest further. She worried briefly about Juniper finding them, until she saw that there was no light coming from beneath her mother's bedroom door. Isaac trailed after her as she padded down the stairs, grumbling about her refusal to listen to him, which Violet found pretty rich coming from someone who'd showed up uninvited at her bedroom window.

The noises were definitely coming from her front door. As Isaac raised his hands, his palms shimmering, Violet unlocked the deadbolts and pulled it open. A bundle of dark curls tumbled into the house and sprawled out on the floor, accompanied by a furious rush of wind and hail. Violet didn't have a chance to see beyond the darkness before Isaac slammed the door shut.

"Harper!" Violet said, kneeling beside her as Isaac swung the deadbolts back into place. "Are you okay?"

Harper sat up slowly. Her hair was mostly unraveled from a braid, her baggy jeans pockmarked with melting hail. There was a reddish-brown blade clutched in her remaining hand.

"I need help," she said hoarsely, raising the blade into her lap. Violet felt a slight twinge of unease at the way she cradled the sword, like she was rocking a baby.

"What's wrong?" she asked.

"It's Nora," said Harper. "I can't find her, and Brett says she went out in the storm—said another kid dared her to go to the town hall. She's only six, she doesn't understand—" she coughed, spat out a piece of hair— "how dangerous... You have to help me find her."

And Violet saw, beneath the sweater, beneath the sword, that Harper was shaking.

"Of course I will," she said without thinking, because there was nothing to think about. Nora was Harper's sister. That was a loss Violet would never wish on anyone else.

"Thank you," said Harper, her dark eyes glowing. "I knew you'd help me."

Then she swiveled around, her eyebrows furrowing.

"Why is Isaac Sullivan in your house?" she said.

"Because Justin thinks I need a bodyguard," Violet said, giving Isaac, who was hovering behind them, a sarcastic little wave. "Doesn't he know that if I needed to be protected, I'd ask someone myself?"

"You're way too stubborn for that," Harper rasped. Behind her, Isaac chuckled.

"I'm going to ignore that," Violet grumbled. "Okay, so if we're going to go out in this weather, we probably need raincoats."

"Actually—" said Isaac. Violet glanced up at him.

"Let me guess," she said, trying not to think about their hands intertwined. She wasn't sure what that moment had been—but it was done now. "You're going to tell me I can't go outside? Because you're starting to make me wish I'd pushed you off the roof instead of letting you in."

"Curb your violent impulses for a second and think," said Isaac. "Neither of you should be outside right now. Harper's deadweight, and you're worse. I can look for Nora."

"She's my sister," said Harper, rising to her feet. Violet stood up with her, surprised by her volume. "And I'm not deadweight."

"No, she's definitely not," said Violet, eyeing the sword Harper was now brandishing in Isaac's general direction. "And I'm not letting my friend out on the equinox without me. Come with us if you want, but we're going either way."

Isaac groaned and pressed his palm to his forehead.

"Apparently running straight to our probable deaths is contagious," he mumbled into his wrist. "But if you must go, it makes more sense to drive than walk."

"Drive?" said Violet, her heartbeat accelerating in her chest. "What about visibility?"

"There'll be no other cars on the roads, and the town hall's a few miles away," said Isaac. "It'll be easy. And much safer than walking."

"Okay," said Violet. "So you drive."

"I can't, actually," said Isaac, dipping his head.

"Harper?"

"I don't have a permit yet," said Harper flatly.

Violet stared at Juniper's car keys, dangling from the coat rack beside the doorway like a broken promise. Isaac and Harper were looking at her expectantly now, and as much as she wanted to bolt up to her room and go fetal beneath her covers, Violet knew she couldn't run from this anymore.

"I'll drive, then," she said, reaching over and grabbing the key ring. It felt smooth and cold against her suddenly sweaty hand, and all Violet could see was Rosie behind the steering wheel, her turquoise hair wild, her eyes wide with fear as the semitruck barreled toward her.

But Nora's life was at stake. And Harper—her friend—had come to her for help. So she pushed down her fears and strode toward the door, her heart ramming against her rib cage like a hummingbird trapped in a net.

The fifteen minutes Harper spent in the backseat of the Saunderses' Porsche were among the most harrowing of her life. Harper could feel Violet's fear in each jerky, hesitant motion of the car as hail battered the windshield.

It was the kind of deep-seated terror that felt tangible enough for her to close her fingers around it, the kind that sent Harper's heartbeat ratcheting into her ears.

Nora was lost in the woods. Alone. On one of the most dangerous nights of the year.

And her father and siblings were already out on patrol, leaving any hope of a rescue up to Harper herself.

When they finally pulled into the parking lot beside the town hall, Harper was running her fingers up and down the flat of the sword to keep herself from screaming. Violet had been kind enough to give her a giant raincoat that hid her from the worst of the elements, but the storm still hit Harper hard when she pushed open the car door. They checked the town hall for all signs of Nora, but it was locked, and she was nowhere nearby.

"Don't you have keys?" Violet asked Isaac.

"I do," said Isaac. "But there weren't any kids in this building when I left, and she couldn't have gotten in without them."

So they headed into the trees. Each step was an effort against the hail that seemed to be coming down at every angle, bouncing painfully off her shoulders.

Four Paths looked like the Gray tonight, full of skeletal trees that bent and twisted against the force of the wind. The trees around Harper flickered ashen for a second, the weak light of a white sky shining through them, and she shuddered, pressing closer to Violet as Isaac set his jaw and forged ahead.

A flash of lightning jolted through the forest, sending

the world around them into harsh illumination—and Harper froze.

For a brief second, she could've sworn she'd seen the forms of two hooded figures only a few feet away.

But no. That couldn't be right. The Church of the Four Deities would have no business going into the forest on a night like this.

She stared into the trees, but as far as she could tell, the figures were gone.

A moment later, Isaac's yell echoed through the wind. Harper whirled around to find him kneeling only a few feet away, beside a tiny figure curled up against a tree trunk.

Only a few feet away—and yet, in this storm, Harper easily could've walked right past her.

"Nora?" Harper rushed toward her, fresh panic engulfing her as she realized how still her sister was, the roots of the tree curled around her like grasping fingers. But her sister stirred immediately at the sound of her voice.

"Harper!" she cried out, opening her arms. Harper dropped the sword on the ground and knelt, Nora's tiny body shivering against Harper's raincoat as they embraced.

"Are you okay?" she whispered, planting a kiss on the crown of Nora's auburn hair.

Nora nodded, burying her face in Harper's shoulder. "They said you'd come find me, but you took longer than they thought. I was scared."

Harper drew back, unease coiling through her. A twinge

of phantom pain surged through her left arm. "They? Who said that?"

"Dad did." Nora's words turned Harper's stomach. She searched her sister's freckled face for some sign that she was lying, but Nora's cheeks were blotchy with fear, not deceit. "He told me to go to the town hall and wait, but I got lost in the woods."

Harper did her best to keep her voice even, not panicked. "And what, exactly, did he say?"

"That he needed me to sit still until you and the new Saunders girl came to get me. He said he knew you'd get her, and they needed her to come out into the woods tonight." She hiccuped, then added, "Harper, can we go home now?"

"Of course we can," said Harper absently, gathering Nora close to her, her eyes scanning the ground for her sword.

She hadn't imagined those hooded figures after all.

Maurice Carlisle had used his own daughter as bait for Violet.

Which meant they were all in danger—because if her father couldn't be trusted to protect Nora, he certainly couldn't be trusted to have any of their best interests in mind.

"Violet?" called Harper, rising to her feet, Nora's body curled against her arm. "We need to get out of here."

The forest was overwhelming, but not because of the weather.

Violet had felt herself growing stronger from the moment she'd stepped outside. And the feeling had only increased the longer they'd spent in the woods; making her fingertips crackle like lightning bolts, her skin supercharged with energy.

It was hard to focus on anything but how *good* it felt.

This was strength.

This was power.

Violet watched Harper embracing her sister as if from a great distance. Her heart was skipping in her chest. Her hands were shaking.

She leaned against the nearest tree trunk to regain her balance.

"Hey." Isaac appeared in her field of vision, the concern clear on his face. "Are you okay?" he asked, at the same time that Harper called, "We need to get out of here."

A surge of power washed through her as another bolt of lightning split the sky. Violet opened her mouth to answer, but nothing came out.

She tried to move an arm, a leg, a finger, panic welling up inside her as she realized that her body wasn't responding.

She couldn't call for help or move or scream. Pain shot through her skull as her head swiveled itself toward the clouds that hung above the trees, flickering between the blackness of night and the pale, static clouds of the Gray, and her lips tugged themselves outward into a smile.

"Yes," said something that was not her at all. "Let's go."

And then Violet's mind went blank.

The forest was surprisingly quiet. Justin had started his patrol expecting the worst, considering the events of the past few weeks. But although the wind and hail were annoying, they were all his group had encountered.

Justin looked around at the rest of his group, pushing down the thought that Augusta had deliberately given them the safest route in the entire forest. Mitzi Carlisle had actually pulled out her phone to text, scowling as raindrops dotted her screen, while her brother Seth was absently tugging at the strings on his hoodie.

"This is boring," Seth said.

Mitzi nodded in agreement.

"That's a good thing," said Justin, even though he wasn't so sure he believed that. "Mitzi, can you please take this seriously?"

"I'll take it seriously when I have something to fight," she said, but she slid her phone back in her pocket.

If Isaac had been there, he would've said something about Mitzi's priorities, or perhaps suggested she fight him instead. But he wasn't. So their patrol group moved toward the heart of the storm in silence.

As the wind around them grew fiercer, hail raining down on their heads, Mitzi and Seth readied themselves for battle, their flesh stretching and morphing into stone from the shoulder down. They grinned and bumped reddish-brown fists, wiggling their stone fingers at one another in a silly but endearing handshake.

Being around them took Justin back to earlier that afternoon.

To Harper.

The memory had to be handled carefully. Justin knew it would leave him raw and blistered if he let it kindle inside him for too long, and yet he couldn't stop replaying that moment over and over again. He would forget his own name before he forgot the feeling of her blade pressed against his throat, the fury in her eyes.

She didn't want him near her anymore, that much was clear. And yet Justin could no longer deny that despite what his mother had done to Harper, despite the years he'd spent trying to pretend otherwise, his feelings for her hadn't gone away.

There was no good way for him to talk about this, not with Isaac, not with May. Yet keeping it inside left him with a hot, sick feeling brewing in his stomach, like he'd sat in the sun for too long.

"That's not normal, is it?" Mitzi asked Seth, and Justin was pulled back to the world around him. Seth shook his head, his fists returning to flesh and blood.

"What's going on?" Seth asked Justin, who realized only then why the Carlisle siblings looked so concerned.

The hail was starting to slow around them, the wind moving from almost a gale to a light, whispering breeze in the span of a few seconds. The forest loomed out of the darkness, each tree trunk sharply defined against the night.

Unease stirred in Justin's gut. There was something expectant about this sudden stop, like water receding from a stretch of sand in the moments before a tsunami crashed in.

"I don't know," said Justin, shining his flashlight at the woods around them. But there was no sign of the Gray. The world had gone completely still.

Which was when a series of loud, piercing screams rang out up ahead.

Justin's throat closed in on itself as he recognized the high, shrill wail of a child.

It could be some kind of trick. But he was not going to leave a defenseless kid in the forest on one of the most dangerous nights of the year.

"Go!" he snapped, and they sprinted toward the sound, crashing through the underbrush. In their haste to reach whoever was screaming, they made more noise than a herd of stampeding elephants, but Justin didn't care. They burst out into a clearing near the meadow and then froze.

A few feet away from him stood Isaac and Harper, who was clutching a crying Nora to her chest. Isaac stood in front of Harper and Nora, his hands outstretched, his palms shimmering. Violet stood at the other side of the clearing, her arms spread wide. The trees behind her flickered between Four Paths and the Gray, moving from dark green to white and skeletal in the space of a single breath.

Justin was pretty sure he caught a glimpse of a shadowy

figure or two standing behind Violet, but when he blinked, they were gone.

"Harper?" gasped Mitzi, hurrying over to her sister. Seth followed suit. "What are you doing out here?"

"Run," Harper said, turning toward all of them. Her face was white with fear. "You have to go, now."

"Oh, I'm sorry," said Violet. "Am I bad company?"

And Justin knew in that moment that something was terribly wrong.

Her voice was still Violet's voice, raspy and a little sweet, but there was something off about the way she was enunciating. It was too crisp, too formal. And the way her arms were spread apart in the air... the flashes of Gray were opening up with every flicker of her fingertips.

"Justin," said Isaac, his voice low and measured. "Use your team to get Harper and her sister out of here. I can handle this."

"What's happening?" said Justin. "Why is she acting like this?"

Across the clearing, Violet yawned.

"Little Hawthorne boy, charging straight into trouble," she said. There was nothing playful in these words—just cold, calculated malice. "It was foolish, letting her out of the house on an equinox. But then, you've always been foolish."

It hit him then. That this was not Violet at all. There was something else inside her. Something that wanted to get out.

"You're... *it*, aren't you?" he said hoarsely.

"It's been so long since I had access to a living, breathing human," said the Beast, stretching out a hand and wiggling each finger with mechanical precision. Justin could see in the beam of his flashlight that each digit was slowly losing its color, the fingernails turning from crimson to gray. "These are strong. I suppose a lifetime of piano will do that to you."

It flicked Violet's fingers to the side, and the Gray ripped through the forest, an opening that gaped behind her like a wide, gruesome mouth.

Justin couldn't help it: He felt the call of the trees behind him. Felt an unmistakable desire to give himself to the Gray, let it claim him...

Which was when Isaac charged straight for it, his hands shimmering, engulfing Violet with his kaleidoscopic light as they clamped around her wrists.

The thing inside her let out a horrific snarl, arched Violet's spine as it bucked away from the attack. But Isaac didn't flinch. His power burned bright and steady, a beacon against the line of ridged, sunken trees that were splayed out behind Violet's body.

Justin watched, his heart rattling in his throat, as the Gray shrank away, dissolving at the edges. The moment it winked out of existence, Violet crumpled toward the ground, unconscious.

Isaac fell with her, still gripping one wrist, the other arm reaching deftly around her before she hit the dirt. His arms shook as he lowered her the rest of the way to the ground.

Isaac was strong but not invincible. Justin could see the exhaustion setting in as he rested Violet's head on the dirt.

And then something else flared in Isaac's gaze—panic, his chin jutting toward something behind Justin's shoulder.

Isaac always seemed to notice things a second before Justin did. So he turned.

The first thing he saw was May, unruffled by the hail, her pale face nearly translucent with horror. But his eyes only lingered there a second. Because standing beside her was his mother, her face a mask of cold, twisted fury.

There was a swathe of light shining in Violet's eyes. She blinked them open and realized that she'd fallen asleep on her side, her head tilting directly toward the sunlight streaming in through her window.

But there were safety blinds on her window.

And this was not her room. No, this was a sterile white space that reminded her of a hospital, and she was lying on a cot, still wearing the clothes she'd had on the night before. She could remember that much, at least. Isaac had been in her room, and then Harper had asked them for help. There had been trees and hail and the sense that she was strong, so strong...

"What happened?" she whispered.

"Isn't it obvious?" said a voice from the other side of the room. "You blacked out again."

Violet scrambled back on the cot, as if that would somehow dispel the turquoise-haired figure standing on the other side of the room. A rush of light-headedness coursed through her as she took in her sister's ripped jeans, her paint-splattered tank top, her sardonic smile.

"You're a concussion symptom," she said, struggling to keep the hysteria out of her voice as Rosie moved closer. "Just a hallucination my brain made up, because it has a terrible sense of humor."

"Are you sure?" Rosie's shadow trailed across the floor behind her like a cape, the ends writhing and twisting. "Maybe you're finally starting to get what you want."

A noise rang out from behind the door, not a knock but a thump, as if something had been slammed against it. Violet realized, dimly, that there were voices emanating from the hallway outside.

"I'll see you soon," said Rosie, glancing from the door to Violet, who was still huddled on the cot. Her tone was almost soothing, but there was a calculated undertone to it that sent Violet's stomach sparking with unease. "Don't be frightened, little sis. Don't you miss me?"

She vanished, and now Violet could hear the voices more distinctly, as if they'd been muffled before.

"Don't," someone was yelling. "I swear, I can explain—"

"I don't want to hear it." This voice was low and cool. "You're staying outside."

The door was open and shut in a single second, and then there was only Augusta Hawthorne, the silver shield on her turtleneck gleaming in the morning sunlight.

Violet could put it together now: She was in the police station. She just didn't know why.

"Hello again, Violet," she said calmly. "How are you?"

Violet frowned at her. "Fine, I guess. What happened?"

Augusta's lips tugged up into something that would've been a smile on anyone else. On her it just looked like a fissure in a statue, like a sculptor's hand had slipped.

"You got lost in the storm," she said, striding toward the cot. "But don't worry about it. You're going to feel much better very soon."

As the sheriff reached out to her, Violet realized, in a moment of horrible, piercing clarity, that it was the only time she'd ever seen Augusta Hawthorne without her gloves on.

It was the last thought she had time for before the sheriff's hand caught her wrist, and then her mind was not her own anymore. Fingers peeled back her skull— harsh, cold, unwelcome, stabbing into her brain like knives as they rummaged through her thoughts.

Memories flashed across her eyes like images on a projector screen: She and Rosie lying on the floor in their art studio, laughing. The flat white clouds of the Gray. Isaac smiling at her, hail melting in his hair. And then the ground fell out from under her, and she was falling, her mind slipping out of her grasp as the world around her faded into blackness.

PART THREE

THE SKELETON

SEVENTEEN

WHEN JUSTIN'S GRANDFATHER WAS still alive, his study had been a warm, welcoming room, with a fireplace and earth-toned rugs and windows that were always flung wide open. But when Augusta Hawthorne moved her things into the room, she bricked up the fireplace and kept the storm shutters permanently pulled over the windows. The plush leather chairs were replaced by stiff, hard-backed wooden seats that forced Justin to sit perfectly straight as he stared at the dour-faced photographs hanging behind his mother's desk.

The Hawthornes were a gorgeous, dutiful, miserable bunch, even in black and white. Although their skin tones ranged from pale to dark brown, their hairstyles and outfits encompassing a dozen different trends, their faces all said the same thing: *We know best.* Justin wondered if his picture would be up on that wall someday, staring imperiously down at his descendants.

The way things were going, his mother was more likely to burn a picture of him than hang it anywhere.

It was the day after the equinox. Augusta had left Justin and May in her study while she finished conducting business at the sheriff's station. Justin knew they were being forced to wait as punishment, yet he didn't move from his seat.

"How could you tell her?" he asked May, who was sitting ramrod-straight in the chair beside him.

"How could you not?" she said. "The Beast was inside her, Justin. It opened up the Gray. It made her bring someone back from the dead. Something had to be done."

The other patrol had converged on Violet for the same reason Justin's had: They'd heard the screams. But after they'd figured out what they were looking at, May had cracked, confessing to their mother the second they returned to the sheriff's station. Justin had been too shocked by her betrayal to do much more than feebly protest as she told her the whole story of the past few weeks, emphasizing that she'd been against deceiving their mother from the very beginning.

Justin tried not to think about that voice coming out of Violet's body. The color leaching away from her fingers. "You knew what Mom would do to her."

"What?" said May. "Fix her?"

An ugly chuckle bubbled up in Justin's throat, but he choked it back. "Our mother doesn't fix things," he said. "She just takes away the parts of people's lives that are inconvenient for her. You know that."

Augusta hadn't let him anywhere near Violet after she'd been taken to the station clinic. But Justin had seen his mother in action enough times by now to know what would happen next. Violet would wake up in a few hours with no memory of Four Paths as anything but a normal town. Her brain would fill in the gaps on its own.

She would forget she'd ever had powers—just like Harper had.

"Give it a few weeks," said May, pressing a pale hand against his knee. "This will all matter a lot less, I promise you."

"The Beast is still out there. The town is still turning on us." Justin wondered why she couldn't understand what she'd done. "What about that person Violet resurrected?"

"The only proof you have that they even exist is something Violet said. She probably lied about what she saw."

Justin had always known his sister was good at ignoring the more unsavory parts of their world. But it hurt more than he'd thought possible to see her face turn sharp and dismissive.

"They killed Daria Saunders."

"Or she had an accident." May's voice dripped with cold, patronizing disdain.

"You're doing what Mom does. Pretending problems don't exist."

"At least I'm not trying to solve problems I can't do anything about. Has it ever occurred to you that we've all made sacrifices to be where we are? That maybe, if it's this hard for you, Four Paths doesn't need your help?"

Justin saw in that moment that everything he'd done since he failed his ritual had been a useless, futile stand against the inevitable. He'd lost his family's respect the day the hawthorn tree did not bow for him, and there was nothing he could do that would ever be enough to fix it.

He pressed the face of his red medallion against the arm of the chair. "I know I can help this town. And you know I can, too. You saw it in the Deck of Omens."

He'd expected sympathy at this reminder, some surge of emotion. But May's face barely changed. He had never seen May like this before, clear as glass and hard as steel.

"No, you can't," she said, each word clipped and precise. "And it's time you stopped pretending otherwise. Because when you collect damaged people to feel better about yourself, all of you end up getting hurt."

"I don't know what the hell you're talking about."

Her fingers strangled the arms of the chair as she bent toward him. "You loved fixing Harper's messes before Mom got to her, because you were her hero. You get off on Isaac treating you like you pull the sun up every morning. And you're not upset about Violet because you care what Mom did to her—you just want a reason to be here, and Mom took it away from you."

There was something wrong with the walls in the study. They were bending inward, getting smaller. There was a sharp pain in Justin's chest, as if someone had placed a hand inside his rib cage and pushed the bones against his skin.

Barks rang through the house, signaling his mother's arrival. Justin sat, shell-shocked and silent, all his failures laid out in front of him like the deck of cards he'd never be able to read.

Augusta entered her study with the chill and vigor of a gale-force wind. May shrank back in her seat, but Justin forced himself not to react as she swept behind her desk. He knew deference was exactly what Augusta wanted.

"I never believed the stereotypes about children who felt the need to deceive their parents." Augusta's gloved hands steepled together beneath her chin. "Rebellious teenagers belong in towns where the biggest danger is a drunk driver. But you were raised to understand the stakes we deal with every day. Which means you know how badly you owe me an apology."

"I'm sorry, Mother," said May immediately, inclining her head. Her hair slid in front of her face, baring the blond, wispy tufts at the nape of her neck. "I should've told you about Violet immediately."

"Stop," said Augusta sharply. May winced. "I said apologize, not lie at my feet and beg like my dogs. No one will ever respect you if you don't take responsibility for your actions."

"I'm sorry!" May said frantically. "I'll do that, too. It was my fault, I know it now, just don't—" She broke off.

Augusta looked at her askance. "Don't what?"

May twisted her hands together in her lap. "Don't take Isaac's memories away."

Justin's insides spiked with surprise. This didn't excuse any of the things May had said to him, which were still rattling about in the ruins of his chest. But he realized now that she was terrified. Isaac was one of the few people who didn't just tolerate May, but liked her.

"I'm not going to punish Isaac Sullivan," said Augusta gently. "At least, not for this."

May nearly flopped over the desk with relief. "Thank you."

Justin and May were immune to their mother's powers. They were blood, and so her touch didn't work on them the way it did on the rest of the town. Only they knew how she kept herself in the sheriff's office. Only they knew how many people were walking around with gaps inside their heads.

"Enough," said Augusta, looking slightly pained. "Now, Justin? What do you have to say for yourself?"

The easy thing to do would be to copy May. To beg. But the words wouldn't come.

This wasn't just about Violet anymore.

His mother had never apologized for Harper. For threatening Isaac. For pushing Justin away after he'd failed his ritual. He didn't see why he should be expected to show her the respect she'd never given him.

"I'm not sorry."

Augusta's marbled features twisted into an ugly smile.

"I thought you might say that. May, you can leave. It's time your brother and I had a talk."

May scurried out of the room, a blond mouse. There was a miniature founders' symbol carved into the arm of Justin's chair. He scratched at it with his fingernail as Augusta began to speak.

"So, you don't think you owe me an apology," she said. Justin shook his head.

"Do you need me to list what you did wrong?"

"I didn't do anything wrong."

"Oh, Justin," said Augusta. "You put this town in incredible danger for a girl you've known less than a month. And you lied to me. I know you love to act like some sort of local hero, but surely even you can't think this was justified."

"I'd do it again," Justin said softly. "To keep her safe from you."

Augusta groaned, pressed two gloved fingers to her temple.

"I don't use my ability lightly, you know this. It's a last resort. But the town is safer if she doesn't have access to her powers. Not when they are so clearly a direct pipeline to the Beast."

Justin wondered, deep inside, if the words she was saying were true. Maybe Harper, Isaac, and Violet really were too dangerous to be let loose on the general public. Maybe it would be better to make them live their lives without powers.

It would be easy to grovel like May had, until the

whole town moved on like none of this had ever happened.

But there were already so few founder descendants remaining. The town had noticed. The town was turning. It would make so much more sense to nurture founder children instead of snuffing them out. And all Justin could see when he opened his mouth was the rage in Harper's eyes as she pressed her blade to his throat. Rage she didn't even properly understand, because she didn't know what Augusta had taken away. The powers she couldn't use.

For so long, Justin had dwelled on all the things he couldn't have. But at least he knew what he was missing.

Harper believed she was powerless. So did Violet. And there was nothing he could do to save them.

But he knew what they would've done if they'd been the ones sitting across from Augusta Hawthorne.

They would've fought back.

And he owed it to them to prove he'd learned something from what they had lost.

"You didn't take Harper's and Violet's memories away because they were dangerous to the town," he said, rising to his feet. Their rage was his rage, filling in the places May had collapsed, bolstering him until he understood what he needed to say. "This town desperately needs strong founders. They threatened your authority, so you made them forget. Isaac's done more damage than they ever did, but you keep him around because he listens to us. But you couldn't control Harper and Violet, so you got rid of them. And you're trying to get rid of me, too."

For once, Augusta was silent, her pale face tinged with just a touch of pink, her gloved hands frozen at her temples. They stared at each other, mother and son, as Justin backed away from the desk.

When Augusta spoke again, it was in a quiet, hateful whisper. "Being a founder is all about sacrifice. If you cannot learn to put others' safety above your own emotions, then it's a good thing you failed your ritual. Because you are unfit to serve this town."

Justin didn't say anything more. Didn't blink, didn't breathe. Just fumbled for the doorknob, rushed down the hallway, and sprinted out of the house.

He ran farther than he ever had before, until the world was wide and blurred and strange around him and his body was ablaze with pain. And when his feet came to a stop, hours or days or years later, he stood at the door to Isaac's apartment.

"I can't go home," he said, and then he yelled it, banging his palm against the cracked, peeling wood, as if that would somehow make the words hurt less. When the door creaked open, he was trembling and weary, ready to collapse.

"I can't go home," Justin told him again, and Isaac's mouth did that same thing it had done back at the Diner, that almost-sad almost-smile he couldn't read.

"So don't," Isaac said gruffly, pulling the door open wide enough for Justin to stumble inside.

He was used to Isaac trailing behind him, but tonight, it felt right to be the one following Isaac's broad shoulders and dark curls as he led him to the couch. Where he could finally, mercifully, rest.

Harper hated how easily she could be left behind. Mitzi and Seth had taken her home after the sheriff showed up in the clearing. She tried to talk to her father about what had happened to Nora, but he reassured her time and again that it had been an accident.

She did not believe him, but she had no proof otherwise.

The next few days passed quietly.

Justin, Isaac, May, and Violet were all out of school. Violet didn't answer her phone, and Harper couldn't bring herself to contact Justin. So when she walked into homeroom a few days later and saw Violet sitting in her usual seat, looking well rested and peaceful, she was confused, to say the least.

Harper sat down across the room and watched as Justin and Isaac slid into the back row. She waited for something to happen, some acknowledgment of the things they'd all seen, the monster inside Violet. But nothing happened at all. Violet didn't speak to anyone, just stared at Mrs. Langham with a vague half smile on her face.

The same thing happened in history and biology, so when Harper saw Violet fumbling with her locker before lunch, she swallowed her nerves and marched up to her. After all, Violet had called Harper a friend on the equinox. Maybe she was processing the events of the previous few days.

"Do you need help with your lock?" Harper said.

"I should know the combo, but I can't remember it."
Violet scowled. "Pretty embarrassing, right?"

"I've been here my whole life, and I still mess it up
sometimes," said Harper.

Violet chuckled. "Thanks for making me feel more
adequate. What's your name?"

Harper's stomach sank through her shoes and into the
floor. "What? Violet, that's not funny."

"I'm sorry, have we met?" Violet's face was still fixed
in that odd half smile. "You do look familiar. Is it Hailey?
Holly?"

Harper couldn't stand the way Violet was looking at
her. It was the same look Justin had given her three years
ago, vague and apathetic. And although she knew
something else had to be going on, that Violet wouldn't
just *forget* her, she could not stop the panic rising
inside her.

"I have to go." Harper fled to the music practice room
where she usually ate her lunch and tucked her knees
up to her chest.

Something was wrong with Violet. Either that, or she
had chosen to ignore Harper on purpose.

But no. That was too cruel. She wouldn't do that, not
after Harper had told her what Justin had done to her.
Violet knew, she had to know, that Harper could not
handle that again.

Her father had stranded Nora in the woods. And
Violet, the only person she wanted to talk to about it,
was no longer an option.

She was lost and scared and sad and more alone than ever.

A surge of phantom pain from her left arm jolted through her. Harper shuddered and clutched her residual limb in her right hand.

Three years ago, she had let her panic win. She'd bent to the Hawthornes' will, become the person they'd told her she was, small and scared and forgotten. But Harper knew, now, that she was so much more.

She tucked her hair behind her ears and wiped her eyes, and as her heartbeat began to decrease, the pain in her arm fading away, someone knocked on the practice room door.

"Sorry," she called out. "This one's occupied."

"Harper? Is that you?"

Harper lifted her head, adrenaline coursing through her. "Justin?"

"Can I come in?"

She wanted to say no.

But if she was going to figure out what had happened to Violet, she'd need help. And she wasn't really in a position to be picky about it.

So she swallowed down the remains of her tears, stood up, and pulled open the door.

Justin looked even more unraveled than he had on the night he'd confessed his lack of abilities to her. There was something gaunt in his expression now, a raw, unveiled part of his gaze that hadn't been there on the equinox.

"I know you told me to leave you alone," he said. "But

do you mind if I join you? I'm not sure I can face the whole school today."

She was too surprised to do more than nod her head, watching with abject disbelief as he balanced his backpack on a music stand and plopped down in a chair. The door swung shut behind him. Harper retreated to her own chair, conscious of how little space there was in the practice room.

Even with their backs pressed against opposite walls, their knees were almost touching.

"Where's Isaac?" she asked.

Justin pulled a hand through his thatch of blond hair. An image sprang up in her mind: her hand on the back of his neck, strands of hair shining like spun gold between her fingers.

She forced it down, but not before her fingers twitched.

"Sitting with May," he said. "Trying to keep the pretend peace."

"Pretend peace? I don't understand."

"I was kicked out of the house," said Justin. "Well, kind of. I ran away. But I think I would've been formally kicked out if I didn't."

"What? Why?"

"I couldn't do it anymore. My mother told me it was a good thing that I failed my ritual. And I'm starting to think she's right. Because it's forced me to look at the damage my family does to this town." He let out a deep, shuddering breath. "No one deserves to be treated the way I treated you."

Harper had wanted to hear him say those words for so long. But as they echoed through the practice room, through her skull, she didn't feel relief. She just felt empty.

"There's a point when it doesn't matter," she said slowly, unaware at first that she was even speaking out loud. But she didn't want to stop. "You don't get to absolve three years of guilt with this. And you don't get to crawl back to me when it feels convenient."

"I know. There's no taking back how cruel I was, or how I hurt you. I just wanted you to know that I see now. I should've stood up to my family. I should've helped you. And everything I've done for Isaac and Violet is because of what I couldn't do for you."

Harper didn't know if the words he was saying were real or not—but, oh, she wanted them to be.

She choked back a sob. "I don't forgive you."

"I know."

"I can't forgive you."

"I don't care."

Harper's heart tightened, because this was the Justin she had known. Kind, honest, loyal to a fault.

The night before her ritual, they'd snuck out to the lake, watched the dark, lapping waves eroding the muddy bank at the water's edge.

"What if I don't come out?" she'd asked him, and he had twined his fingers through hers and given her a grin of utmost confidence.

There had been a promise in that smile, in the way he held her hand. "You will."

And Harper had loved the boy Justin had been, so she'd believed him.

Maybe she loved him still.

But she was pretty sure love was supposed to feel like growing stronger, not rotting from the inside out. Whatever remained between them was a knot of lust and anger and regret that had festered inside of her for so long, she wasn't sure who she was without it.

She couldn't shake the knowledge that Justin had been content to ignore her when he still believed he was powerful. He'd taken full advantage of the opportunities being a Hawthorne provided him: girls, friends, unquestioned respect.

Only when he was broken had he come back to her. Because she was broken, too.

Harper would not mistake his desperation for affection. So when she opened her mouth to speak again, it wasn't to give Justin hope for reconciliation. It was to get answers.

"Something's wrong with Violet," she said.

Justin didn't even try to look surprised.

"I know," he said. "My mother got to her."

"Got to her? What do you mean?"

"That's what my mother does," said Justin. "Takes people's memories away when she thinks they're too dangerous. They can't access their powers anymore, because they don't remember that they have them."

Perhaps the news should've shocked Harper, but it immediately made sense. Of course the Hawthornes had leverage they weren't sharing.

More secrets. More lies.

Tears built in Harper's throat again as the full implications of this surged through her. Violet couldn't remember her. Which meant the girl she'd known, the girl who'd actually cared about her, was gone.

"Her memories?" she said. "Can she ever get them back?"

Justin's voice was thick and raspy when he said, "I don't think so."

Violet had really mattered to him, if he'd truly fought with Augusta over this, if he'd really left home.

"I guess..." Justin continued. "I'm here to tell you that I think something bad is coming for us. My family probably deserves it. But the rest of this town doesn't. So stay out of the woods, okay?"

And suddenly, Harper saw a path forward.

For years, she'd seen her life as a certain kind of story. The tale of a girl who'd wanted nothing more than love and power and family. The test of valor she'd failed. The wicked, villainous Hawthornes who'd sentenced her to a lonely, miserable existence, using their charm to cover the ugliness beneath.

Her father had offered her an easy ending to that story. One that made them both heroes.

But as Harper looked at Justin Hawthorne, she knew in her gut that none of it was true.

She thought about heroes, and villains, and legends, and monsters. And decided that whoever told the story was more powerful than all of them.

Harper would never let someone else tell her story again.

Maybe Violet couldn't remember what had been done to her. But Harper still wanted to save her.

"I'm not sure your family are the only ones in this town who are up to no good," she said slowly, hardly able to believe the words were coming out of her mouth. "Justin... there's something I have to tell you."

EIGHTEEN

V IOLET STARED DOWN AT the piano keys below her outstretched hands and sighed. All day, she had felt off. She'd thought practicing would snap her back into focus, but dread bloomed in her stomach each time her hands touched the keys. Something about the instrument just felt wrong.

It didn't help that Orpheus was pacing behind her, mewling piteously, the noise ringing through the house like a revving motor. Violet was pretty sure the cat missed his owner. But Aunt Daria was gone now.

Orpheus mewled again, and another noise rose behind her now, the steady, careful thrum of footsteps.

Violet turned around, confused. Her mother wasn't home.

But it wasn't Juniper. Instead, there was a tall blond girl with sleek, straight hair and unnervingly symmetrical features standing in the center of the music room.

There was something hard at the edges of her pleasant

smile, something gaunt and hollow in her cheeks, that sent unease stirring in Violet's chest. She was looking at her the way Harper had that morning—like they shared a secret, even though Violet had never met her.

A name surfaced within her, although she wasn't sure how she knew it.

"You're May, aren't you?" she said. The girl nodded. "What are you doing here?"

May shrugged, her shoulders draped in a flowy, cream-colored top. "You invited me. I knocked first. The door was unlocked, so I let myself in." She gestured toward the piano. "You're very good."

"Not as good as I used to be." Violet frowned. "I don't remember inviting you over."

Although there was a lot she couldn't remember. Her life after Rosie had descended into a blurred fog, and things only got murkier when she struggled to recall her first few weeks in Four Paths.

Thankfully, May looked utterly unfazed by her disorientation. "We're doing a local-history project together," she said, pulling out a wooden box from her shoulder bag. "You told me to come over after school. So we could finish our research?"

Violet did have a hazy recollection of doing research on the town. Of a room with dented metal filing cabinets, with portraits on the walls. It seemed like it had been important.

"Of course," said Violet. "Right. We're researching, uh..."

"These, actually." May opened the box and withdrew an oversize deck of cards. "The Deck of Omens. They're local folklore. A tarot variant created in this town." Her lips quirked up into that hard-edged smile again. "I'm here to read your cards. For the project. What is with you today?"

Again, Violet felt a rush of unease. "I don't know. Just having an off day, I guess."

"Well, we can always do this later this week, if you don't feel up to it."

But May was already here, and Violet couldn't think of a good reason to say no. "It's fine," she said. "Let's just get this over with."

May insisted they both sit on the floor. Violet had always considered herself the sort of person who didn't follow others without asking questions first, but she was too tired to protest. The strangeness she had felt all day had intensified the moment she'd seen May; when she blinked, she swore she saw tendrils of something moving behind her eyes, almost like unfurling branches.

The way they were sitting, the image of May's fingers effortlessly shuffling the Deck of Omens, seemed oddly familiar. She wondered, dully, if they had done this before, but she surely would've remembered *that*.

There was some kind of optical illusion happening with the cards. Violet knew May was just cleverly shuffling them, but she could've sworn the deck was getting smaller.

That the slim bits of wood were disappearing, one by one.

When there were only a few cards left—where had the rest gone?—May raised her eyes to Violet's.

"We're supposed to hold hands now," said May, the edge of her lip curling. "Weird, I know. But it's an old superstition."

Again, Violet had the sense that they had done this before. "I'm not sure—"

But May's hands were already wrapped around hers. Her palms were cold and clammy, her fingers surprisingly strong, and as Violet struggled against her grip, something cracked open in the back of her brain.

It was as if roots were burrowing into her skull, small, deliberate tendrils that changed everything they touched, making each memory brighter and clearer. Like restoring the colors in a faded landscape painting. Violet gasped from the force of it, the truth unfurling, May's mind snapping every tether that had been placed on hers. She jerked back involuntarily, breaking away from May's grasp, as the events of the past few weeks rushed back into her mind.

For a moment, it was all she could do to stare at the girl across from her, shuddering. But soon her racing thoughts crystallized into a harsh, furious truth.

"Your mother," she hissed, the words echoing through the music room.

May nodded, her pale face dead serious. "So you can remember?"

"Yes."

"You're angry."

"Of course I'm angry. What the hell did you expect?"

This was why the Hawthornes had lied to their mother. Why the town seemed so transfixed by them— because they never knew when their golden family had messed up.

No wonder Juniper couldn't remember anything about Four Paths. No wonder Harper's history with the Hawthornes was so muddled.

It was Augusta. It was all Augusta.

How many others had suffered the way she had? How much had the town forgotten?

"So she's been taking people's memories away," Violet said, her voice pulsating with fury. "But you can give them back. And you haven't."

The shadows pooling in the hollow of May's throat deepened as she ducked her head. "I only did my ritual six months ago," she said softly. "I wasn't even sure this would work. You're the first one I've ever tried this on."

"Well, now you know it does work," said Violet. "So you should just—"

"No!" It was the loudest Violet had ever heard May speak. Her entire body radiated panic. Her eyes were wide, one hand extended toward Violet, imploring, pleading. "I can't. And if you tell anyone what I did, I'll deny it."

"Why?" Violet said softly. She was still angry, but May Hawthorne, despite her fear, despite everything, had just saved her from forgetting. And Violet didn't want to spook her now.

May gulped. "My mother will be furious if she finds out I've helped you. She'd never forgive me."

"Then why did you help me?"

Violet waited impatiently as May fidgeted, her eyes flicking back and forth. The girl raised a hand to her head, letting a ray of late afternoon sunlight dance across her skin. Her small gold earring was a tiny leaf.

"I don't know," she said finally. Violet heard the truth in her voice as surely as she saw it on her face. "It just wasn't right. What Mom did to you." Tears pooled in the corners of her eyes, but May rose to her feet before Violet could be sure she hadn't imagined them. May cleared her throat.

"I should go," she said, clutching the Deck of Omens to her chest. "I can't stop you, but please. Don't tell anyone."

And then she was hurrying toward the door, her sandals clicking softly against the wooden floorboards.

Violet scrambled to her feet. "Wait!"

She was certain May wasn't going to listen. But she did, coming to a halt a hairbreadth before the exit.

Violet wasn't sure if she was angry with May or not. If there even was a right thing to say.

She settled for a hoarse "Thank you."

May's head inclined swiftly into a birdlike nod. The front door of the Saunders manor slammed shut a few moments later, leaving Violet standing, shell-shocked, in the golden remnants of the afternoon sunlight.

She wasn't sure what to do next. She wanted to call Justin and Isaac and yell at them for lying to her. But May had been so scared.

She didn't want to betray her trust. But she needed answers. Which meant she'd just have to find them herself.

There had to be something she had missed, about the blackouts, about her ritual.

She hurried to her room and spent the next few minutes in a frenzy of activity, collecting all the evidence she could find. The photo of Stephen, Daria, and Juniper. The pictures on her phone of the poem she'd seen in the Hawthornes' study. And finally, Stephen Saunders's journal—the half she'd been able to find, anyway.

As Violet gazed down at her hoard of clues, wondering how she could tie them all together, something soft and furry rubbed against her ankles.

"I guess you count as evidence, too," she said, stroking Orpheus between the ears. The cat let out his chainsaw mewl and bumped his head against something half-buried beneath a cardigan on the floor.

Violet's heartbeat quickened as she recognized the smooth brown cylinder Daria had shoved into her hands.

"Maybe someone killed her because she knew something after all," she said softly, tugging the cylinder out from beneath the cardigan and rising to her feet. She unscrewed the top, but before she could pull out the blueprints, her eyes caught on the wood grain on the side of the case.

The dark wood was uneven, faded. Violet held it up to the nearest lamp and squinted, grinning as her eyes made out a barely visible circle carved into the wood. A circle with four lines cutting through the edges, a slice of wood that was just the tiniest bit raised above the rest of the cylinder.

She pressed her thumb into the center of the founders' symbol, and it moved inward with a slight click. What she'd thought was one cylinder was actually two.

Violet upended the case and dumped the smaller cylinder out into her hand. There was a lone sheet of paper rolled up inside the outer layer of wood.

It was another page of blueprints: this one depicting a single room. The founders' symbol was scrawled in one corner of the page in blotched, faded ink, and beneath it was one word: *spire*.

"Of course there's a creepy attic," Violet said to Orpheus as she gazed up at the thin square of stone embedded in the ceiling above her head. "Because our family couldn't just keep their secrets in a closet or something, like normal people."

There were three spires on the roof of the Saunders manor, but Violet had known immediately which one the blueprints were referring to.

It was the one in the center of the house, directly above the foyer. The one she'd seen slicing through the trees when she'd been trapped in the horrific embrace of the Gray—the only spire that had been part of the house a hundred and fifty years ago.

And sure enough, here it was: a bit of reddish-brown stone that didn't fit the rest of the ceiling.

A trapdoor.

Violet stood on a chair to investigate it further. Juniper had claimed she was going to the nearest coffee shop to work, so Violet had no qualms about making noise as she tried to figure out how to open the door. It seemed to be spring-loaded somehow—she could feel a mechanism behind it, but it was jammed. Violet wedged her fingers into the edge of the stone and pushed until it gave way, groaning on rusted metal hinges as it slid to the side.

In its place was a bit of slatted metal that Violet realized was the underside of a ladder, meant to be folded out. But it was secured to the ceiling by a combination lock. Violet tugged on the lock, frowning. It looked dirty, but it didn't look centuries old. She recognized the brand from her gym locker in middle school.

While the padlock itself was secure, the bolt it had been fastened around was almost rusted through. She yanked on the edge of the lock again, but it didn't give. So she fetched the hammer from the ancient tool kit inside the hall closet and slammed it down as hard as she could until the oxidized metal gave way.

The combination lock crashed to the floor, sending orange residue fluttering across her black jeans, but the trapdoor was hers to open. Violet tucked the hammer into the back pocket of her pants, in case she needed to hit something else. She wedged her fingers beneath the metal corners of the ladder and tugged.

The ladder unfolded with a squeal that made Violet wish she could cover her ears. She unfolded it as far down as it would go, coughing on the rush of musty air that had come with it.

She tried to gaze up into the spire, but whatever awaited her was cloaked in a deep, impenetrable blackness. Violet turned on her phone flashlight and raised a cautious hand up into the attic. But there was nothing menacing on the sloped stone ceilings, and the opening was too narrow to see much of the walls. So in the end, she tucked her phone away and climbed the ladder, her heart pounding a little too quickly in her chest.

She had never been more conscious of the fact that, if something went wrong, there would be nobody coming to save her. Justin, Isaac, and Harper thought her memories were gone. May had told her to keep her secret. Her mother couldn't remember anything. And Rosie... Rosie was dead.

The inside of the spire was bigger than Violet thought it would be, larger than her walk-in closet back in Ossining, with perfectly circular walls and a ceiling that tapered upward into a point. Black velvet curtains disguised most of the wall. Violet caught a glimpse of a frame behind them, a window. She strode toward it, but before she could draw the curtain away, a dark shape sank its teeth into her ankle.

Violet stumbled back, yelping with surprise. But it was only Orpheus. As Violet gazed down at his hissing form, she saw that a panel of stone had been ripped out of the floor, replaced by a perfect circle of wood lined with white paint.

Violet tried to step around Orpheus's furry body, but he darted in front of her once more. Her companion's tail rose into the air, the tip twitching as his glowing yellow eyes met hers.

Violet had seen enough horror movies to know that when an animal tried to tell you something, it was probably wise to listen. Besides, she could feel something pulsing deep inside of her as she gazed at the dusty bit of wood—the same thing she'd felt on the equinox.

"Don't go inside the circle." Violet stepped away from the line of white paint. "Got it."

There wasn't much in the rest of the room, just a single shelving unit full of odd bits and pieces: the dull edge of a stone sword; a small, chipped bell; an empty, ornate wooden box that reminded her of the one May had kept her cards in.

She'd started to surrender her hopes of finding anything useful when something on the bottom shelf caught her eye.

A sheaf of college-lined pages sticking out of the top of a leather-bound book.

Violet pulled the book off the shelf and flipped it open. The papers had been crammed hastily inside a book of poetry.

She knew from the moment she saw the handwriting what she had found.

"Jackpot," Violet whispered.

Here, at last, were the missing pages of Stephen Saunders's journal.

The Carlisle lake stretched before Harper like an open mouth.

Justin, standing next to her, looked slightly ill. He had been visibly uneasy about their plan since Harper had proposed it to him, but she wouldn't let that stop her. Nothing would stop her now.

"It looks like it's sucking in the daylight," he said quietly, gazing down at the silt-clogged water.

Harper looked from the lake into his ashen face. It was true that the sunlight seemed dimmer here, cloaking the stone animals behind them in shadow.

It had barely been two weeks since the last time they'd talked here, and yet everything was different.

He'd lied to her about his powers.

She'd lied to him about the Church.

But back in the music room, she had told him the truth. That she was part of a new faction of the Church of the Four Deities that was actively plotting to take his family down. That she was pretty sure they'd had something to do with what had happened to Violet.

That she needed his help.

Justin had taken it very well—almost too well, but Harper didn't have time to worry about why he'd reacted with understanding instead of anger.

At least everything was out in the open, now that

they'd both confessed. The power balance between them finally felt equal.

And the plan they'd made had led them here after school, ready to get some answers. Ready to figure out what was truly going on in this town.

Harper stared at the shed behind the statue garden and readied herself for what she had promised to do.

Mitzi and Seth were out of the house. Harper's mother had taken baby Olly for the day, visiting her sister a few towns over, while Justin had agreed to babysit Brett and Nora, claiming he was amazing with children.

An opportunity to catch Harper's father alone like this wouldn't come again for a long time.

"I'm ready," she told Justin.

When he looked at her, she remembered them standing at the edge of the lake bed three years ago. His hand twined in hers. His smile. His faith.

He didn't smile this time. Didn't touch her. But there wasn't a single shred of doubt in his voice. "I know."

Harper was grateful for that as she approached her father's workshop.

This was her battle to fight.

NINETEEN

THE FIRST WORDS ON the page were dated the day after the journal entries had stopped.

But although they were unmistakably in Stephen's scrawled handwriting, they weren't a journal entry.

The Revised Creed of the Church of the Four Deities, September 23, 1984.

The Church of the Four Deities.

Violet had heard that before. It was the name of that religion Justin had talked about. The one that had worshipped the founders.

She wasn't sure what they had to do with all of this. But she read on anyway.

I swear to reveal to no one but the most loyal of my followers the contents of this Creed. I swear it on my family, my honor, and my immortal soul.

A hundred and forty years ago, the Church of the Four Deities was created by the people of Four Paths as a way to show their appreciation for their founders, who they believed had protected them from a monster.

But I know now that what they believed was wrong. The founders did not seek to protect anyone—they sought to abuse an innocent creature and take its power for themselves, then murder it in cold blood to hide the evidence.

They did not succeed in their plans. The creature endures in a hellish containment, and the town worships its tormentors, unaware that they have brought their suffering upon themselves through arrogance and greed.

The Church of the Four Deities was conceived of as a path to salvation. And so I have taken up that mantle, and that sentiment, and I will apply to it the truth. I know what this town has done, and I have been shown a path to redeem us from it.

I will take these false founders down.

I will fulfill my destiny. And I will be rewarded most handsomely for it.

Branches and stones, daggers and bones, will meet their judgment day.

The stretch of grass outside the workshop was littered with sculptures. Harper's father dutifully provided Augusta Hawthorne with sentinels for the town border, and the town with sentinels to hang above their doors, but he made other things, too, strange, twisted creatures carved from the stone he excavated from the bottom of the lake.

Harper knew he was trying to make guardians of his

own. But his statues were only getting stranger, not stronger. A fox with a tail that was a cluster of eyes; a squat, hideous frog with a human arm sprouting from its mouth in place of a tongue; and other things that were not recognizable as animals or people at all, disparate parts that somehow melded together.

The dull partial sentience of the statues made Harper uneasy. They couldn't move—but they could stare. She tried not to flinch as all those misshapen eyes locked onto her, tracking her movements as she entered the shed.

Maurice Carlisle was seated at his workbench, humming tunelessly as he chipped away at a block of clay. Three steel blades hung on the wall behind him. Statues and bells peered out from shadowy corners, hung from the ceiling, crowded at the edges of the shelves. An audience.

"Harper," he said, not even bothering to glance up from his work. His brow was furrowed with mild annoyance. "What is it? Do you need something?"

"I have a question." Harper wasn't sure how this was going to go. But if Justin Hawthorne could find it in himself to tell her the truth, surely her own father could do the same. "Dad—what does the Church of the Four Deities really want?"

Her father's head raised from the block of stone. "To remove the Hawthornes from power, Harper. We told you ourselves."

But it was more than that. Harper knew it was more than that.

She'd seen the Beast inside Violet's skin. The fear in

Nora's eyes. And she knew there was something wrong with the way she'd been asked to win over Violet without understanding why.

She was running out of excuses for her father.

"Maybe you're trying to protect me," she said. "But I'm your daughter. Please, just trust that I can handle this."

"There's nothing to handle," said Maurice Carlisle, his wrinkled forehead furrowing with false concern. "Has your arm been bothering you again? There's no need for such dramatics; we can take you to the hospital if it's that bad."

Her arm. That was a low blow, designed to make her stop asking questions. Designed to make her feel small.

"I know when you're lying, Dad," Harper said softly. "Why are you lying?"

Maurice Carlisle's face tightened. "Harper, please," he said, rising from his seat, a slight note of panic in his voice. "Don't push me on this."

"You took me to a meeting," said Harper. "You got me to take Violet out on the equinox—"

"I promise you," he said tersely, "that if you just stay quiet and do as you're told, you'll be perfectly safe."

It occurred to Harper, then, that she was being used.

Just like she'd warned Violet the Hawthornes would use her.

All this time, and she still hadn't learned that there was no one she could trust.

"Is that all you think I care about?" she asked.

"Following instructions? Staying safe? Do you really think I'd go along with whatever this is for long without a real explanation?"

Her father met her eyes. "You've done a great job of only hearing the answers you want so far. I'm not lying about the Hawthornes. Look at how Augusta treats you. How she treats everyone who isn't powerful."

"But, Dad, you have powers!"

"Not enough," he said bitterly, widening his arms and gesturing at the rest of his workshop. "Our family is weak, Harper. And no matter how hard I work, these sentinels will never match my mother's guardians."

His eyes met hers, and there was something feverish in them, something that made her stomach churn. "Our family made a horrible mistake when they imprisoned the Beast. They've put us through generations of strife and turmoil. And I am going to set it right."

From then on, every entry ended with that same line. Violet's stomach clenched more tightly every time she saw it.

November 20, 1984

The first meeting went wonderfully. Some were skeptical at first, but when I laid out our plan, they were swayed. All who attended have been sworn to secrecy. If they break their vows, they will be punished accordingly. I'll make sure of that.

317

My father is grateful that the woods have been calm. I wish I could tell him it's because of me, so that the Beast can gather strength, but he cannot know. Not yet.

Only four months remain until the spring equinox. There is much preparation ahead of us, but I know the end will be worthwhile. I have full confidence in the might of the Church.

Branches and stones, daggers and bones, will meet their judgment day.

"Dad," Harper said slowly. "What do you mean, you're going to set things right?"

Her father hesitated. "The leader won't allow us to say."

Harper realized that if she wanted to get any real answers here, she would need to lie. So she drew on the rage that was always bubbling beneath her skin, and she let it show.

"You recruited me because I'm a fighter," she said. "I want to fight for the Church. The real Church. But I can't do that if you won't tell me what you're really doing."

The words came out perhaps a bit more emphatically than Harper had wanted them to. But they seemed to work. The fear in her father's eyes was gone now, replaced entirely by that feverish glee.

"Are you sure?" he said softly, starting toward her, gripping her remaining hand in both of his. "Because, Harper, if I tell you this, there is no turning back from the Church. Our mission is of the utmost importance."

Harper swallowed, hard. She thought of Justin, waiting for her with her siblings. Of Nora, terrified in the woods. Of Violet's lost memories. Of Daria Saunders.

"I understand," she said. "Now tell me about the Church's mission."

The dim light of the workshop spread the shadows of his smile across her father's face. "It's very simple, really," he said. "The founders imprisoned the Beast because they wanted its power. So we're going to set it free."

It took everything Harper had not to react to her father's words.

The Beast still killed people. The founders had imprisoned it because it was dangerous, and it had cost them their lives. Everyone knew that. So to hear her own father, a founder, a Carlisle, insist that their ancestors' sacrifice had been wrong—it was horrifying. It was *blasphemous*.

"Set the Beast free," Harper echoed. "I see. And how exactly are you planning to do that?"

But she wasn't lying as well as she'd been lying before. There was a wobble in her voice.

Suspicion stole across her father's face. His grip tightened on Harper's hand, and for the first time, true fright stirred in her.

She sized him up, not as her father, but as an opponent. One who had an arm and at least eighty pounds on her.

He'd believed in the Church of the Four Deities enough to strand Nora in the woods.

She didn't know what he was capable of. She didn't know him at all.

"Harper," he said, a tinge of something ugly creeping into his voice, "do you doubt our mission?"

She shook her head. "No, I'm just… I'm just trying to understand…"

"But if you really believed that the founders were wrong," he said slowly, "you would understand."

"Well, I do," she said quickly. "But this is all so new to me. Surely, you had doubts at first? There are so many questions I still have."

"Of course you do," he said. "Please. Allow me to dismiss your doubts."

Harper's throat went dry. She had to make him see what he was doing led nowhere good. "What will you accomplish, Dad?" she said. "After the Beast is freed—what are you hoping to gain?"

His eyes went slightly glassy. "It has told our leader that it will reward us," he whispered. "With power—real power, beyond the founders' wildest dreams. Don't you want that, Harper?"

Harper felt a rush of relief. His suspicion was ebbing away.

And it all might have been fine—if Isaac Sullivan's loud, angry voice hadn't drifted through the workshop door at that very moment.

"You need backup," he said. "You can't just keep running off without me—" His voice abruptly dropped in volume, but it was too late.

"You didn't come here to pledge your loyalty," her father breathed, his eyes glimmering with fury. His grip on her fingers tightened until it hurt. "You've betrayed us." One of his hands slipped away from hers, and Harper realized a moment before she saw the familiar glint of steel what he was reaching for.

His dagger.

"Dad," she said, her voice breaking with panic as she struggled to pull her hand away. "Dad, what are you doing?"

"I've told you too much," he hissed, panting softly. The point of his dagger glittered wickedly; his hand trembled, but still, he pointed it toward her. "The Hawthornes—they can't know. Not when we're so close."

The change in his behavior was terrifying, as if something else had shrugged on her father's skin.

But this wasn't like what had happened to Violet.

Harper recognized her father's posture, his body language, the way he carried himself.

This was her father. And he was going to hurt her, maybe kill her.

Harper broke out of Maurice Carlisle's grasp a second before he lunged for her. She reacted purely on instinct, bolting for the wall behind her, yanking down one of the swords, and whirling toward her father.

The length of shining steel in her hand was enough to keep his weapon at bay—at least, for now.

"Harper, think about what you're doing," said her father. "That's not a toy."

Harper's hand was shaking, anger and fear rushing through her in equal measure. Pain surged through her left arm. "Neither is your dagger."

This didn't feel real, none of it: the shadowy interior of the shed, the watching eyes of the sentinels, the ugly rage spreading across her father's face.

"Please," Harper whispered. "Don't come any closer."

He cocked his head to the side. "Are you really threatening me?"

And then he lunged for her, for real this time.

Harper's training kicked in. She ducked beneath his outstretched arm, pivoted, and swung her blade around in a perfect strike, knocking the dagger from his hand.

It skittered across the floor in a flash of silver.

Harper swung her sword up to her father's chest as he made to dive after it, the tip of the blade quivering at the edge of his shirt. A torn strip of fabric peeled away from the tip of her blade, revealing his bare chest.

She was so close to hurting him, really hurting him.

Harper took a deep, shuddering breath. She wanted to throw up.

"What the hell is this?" her father hissed, touching the torn fabric of his shirt with quiet disbelief. "You have no idea what you're doing."

"I'm protecting myself." Harper's voice was shaking. Tears glimmered in her eyes, blurring the fury on her father's face. "I'm saving my friend. I'm saving our town. And if you try to hurt me, I'll use this again, I swear I will. So tell me how the Church is going to set the Beast free."

★

The journal entries from December onward were monotonous and vague. The lack of detail was incredibly frustrating, but Violet kept reading anyway, searching for clues, trying desperately to understand what Stephen had been planning.

March 1, 1985

Juniper talked to me today. She said I've been acting differently lately, that I'm not the brother she knows. I told her I'm growing up. I'm stronger. She told me this was good. We need strong founders to fight.

I wish I could give the Beast what it needs on my own, but I do not even have a companion. I am not Juniper. She is the strong one.

Branches and stones, daggers and bones, will meet their judgment day.

March 18, 1985

Two days until the world is made right.

I didn't want to do it at first, but the Beast has shown me Juniper is the proper choice. When it joins with her in blessed unity, the world will bend before them.

I have prepared the circle of bone.

It is almost time.

Branches and stones, daggers and bones, will meet their judgment day.

★

"The Beast's body is bound to the Gray," said Harper's father, his back against the wall of the shed. "But there is a way to let it out—by giving its consciousness a new body."

Harper was still shaking. She tried not to think about what her life would look like after this. The lines her father had crossed by attacking her. The lines she'd crossed by defending herself.

"Like Violet?" she asked, thinking of the way her friend's fingers had changed to gray.

Maurice Carlisle shrugged dismissively. "The girl is a temporary measure. She's not strong enough to hold it for long. No, there is a perfect vessel, one the Beast has wanted for decades."

"Who is it?" said Harper.

Her father bared his teeth in a poor facsimile of a smile. "Juniper Saunders, of course. Because Juniper Saunders can't be killed."

He lunged forward, kicking her in the knee, and Harper toppled to the floor.

Violet turned the last torn-out page over, her heart hammering against her chest, but the back side of the loose leaf was blank.

There were no more entries in the journal.

What had happened to her mother on the night of the spring equinox? Was that when Stephen had died? He'd wanted her for something. And whatever blessed unity with the Beast was, it didn't sound good.

Frustrated, she lowered the journal to her lap. Turquoise flashed into her peripheral vision, and she whipped her head around as Rosie materialized on the floor beside her, sitting in the middle of that circle of white paint.

This time, Violet saw the flatness in her dark eyes.

And it all fell into place.

The Beast had gotten inside Violet's head, the same way it had gotten into Stephen's.

She wondered how it was possible that she'd never seen it before. That it had taken her this long to link together why she had been pulled into this.

She'd allowed the Beast—and the Church—to pick up where they'd left off.

"You're not my sister," she said hoarsely.

Not-Rosie's mouth creased into a cruel smile. "But I gave you the power to bring her back," said the thing beside Violet. It was still using her sister's voice. "Isn't that what you wanted?"

Harper's father was crushing her. They rolled around on the wooden planks of the workshop, scrambling for control of the blade between them. A lock of Harper's hair swung to the side, sliced off by the sword's edge, and then the blade bit into her shoulder, drawing blood, as her father struggled to rip it out of her hand.

He was not a particularly big man, but he was so much stronger than her, and she only had one hand. Soon he was kneeling above her, pinning her to the ground. He kicked the sword across the floor behind him. Harper's breath rose in her throat, sharp and panicky, as she stared up at his face. Ropes of hair were caught in his gnarled hands.

There was a deep sadness in his eyes as he closed his hands around her neck.

"I never wanted this," he said, digging his fingers into her throat. "Believe me, Harper, if there was any other way… But the Beast demands that we put secrecy first. No matter what we sacrifice to do it."

Harper sank her nails into his arm, but it did no good. She wanted to cry for help, but she couldn't get the words out. Her lungs felt like they were filling with dark, muddy water; her body was cold and limp, as if it were sinking beneath the surface of the lake. Her eyes fixed on the sentinels that hung from the ceiling as her vision began to blur.

The door to the workshop slammed against the wall.

"Get the hell away from her!" yelled Justin, and then her father's hands were wrenched away from her neck and she was gasping and sputtering for air.

She rolled over, groaning, her eyes barely taking in Justin's blurry form as he knelt beside her.

"Harper." The planes of his face were stark with fear. "Shit, Harper, please be okay. Tell me you're okay."

She coughed, braced her hand against the floor. The crushed residue of red-brown stone pressed beneath her palm as she sat up.

"I'm okay," she rasped.

They were close enough for her to see the sprinkling

of freckles across the bridge of his nose. To hear each thin, ragged breath.

He reached for her. Harper was too stunned to even consider stopping him as his fingers traced the tender skin of her neck.

"Was he…" He worked the muscles in his jaw as he tried again. "Was he trying to kill you?"

It seemed right, that he should be touching the part of her that hurt the most.

Harper tried to feel some semblance of sorrow, of disgust, of regret. But there was nothing. She was blank inside, scooped-out and hollow. "I think so."

Justin's fingers were cool and gentle against her neck. But when her eyes met his, he pulled his hand away.

Behind Justin's shoulder, Isaac was calmly and methodically tying her father to his workbench.

"Now, don't struggle," he said. "You know what I can do. It won't be fun for either of us if you try and lash out."

"You didn't go watch Brett and Nora," Harper said blankly. "You were waiting outside. In case."

It wasn't a question. She should've been upset that Justin thought she couldn't handle this. But he'd been right.

And she wasn't angry, wasn't scared, wasn't grateful, wasn't anything anymore. She wasn't even sure she was human.

Harper rose to her feet, her eyes fixed on the man sitting at his workbench.

He was still the man who had raised her. But he was not her father, not anymore.

He'd tried to strangle her. He'd almost succeeded.

The knowledge of that sent a dull, sick feeling through her, weighing down her limbs.

There was no place in this town for someone like her, betrayed and betrayer, no one's daughter, no one's friend.

"You know," said Isaac, "what he just did is assault."

Harper knew Isaac Sullivan didn't like her. She could see it even now, in his body language. He'd helped her, but only because she'd been in mortal danger. He was only here because he'd been worried about Justin.

But there was a strange kind of understanding in his gaze now.

Broken things called to broken things.

Isaac was right about what her father had done. But Four Paths only had one real law: Founders handled their own problems, and everyone else pretended not to see the ugliness that lurked within the families who supposedly protected them.

She'd see no justice here unless she delivered it herself.

"I don't care," she wheezed. "I just want him to finish telling us what the Church is going to do."

"Harper." Justin took her hand and tugged her to her feet. The concern on his face had only deepened. "Are you sure?"

She forced her bruised throat to swallow so the words would come out clear. "I'm sure."

She was Harper Carlisle. She'd survived the loss of an

328

arm, her reputation, her friends, and, now, attempted filicide. She'd spent her entire life silencing the dark thing that lay coiled in her chest. The rage that swam beneath her skin.

Now she wondered why she'd tried so hard to ignore herself.

Why she'd decided, all those years ago, that being angry when people hurt her was a dark thing at all.

"Tell me what you're planning," she said, locking eyes with her father. Maurice Carlisle looked shell-shocked, clearly unsure how he'd ended up tied to a bench by three teenagers. "Tell me why you want Juniper. Why the Beast needed Violet."

And when he answered, it was almost monotonous, mechanical. "We needed her to resurrect our leader."

"Your leader?" said Harper. "Who is that?"

"Stephen Saunders," said her father. "Juniper's brother."

Not-Rosie stood before her—flat-eyed, unsmiling, dead. Always dead. Even though Violet knew she wasn't real, seeing her sister still reminded her how much easier it had been to deal with their fragmented family when Rosie was around. They had been a family of two; no matter what, they belonged with each other.

Rosie was the only other person who would have understood Violet's fight with Juniper. And now Violet was being taunted with her, a cruel reminder that she could never have her sister back, that she would accept this warped version of her because she couldn't let go of her for good.

"But I can't bring you—her—back," Violet hissed, clutching the journal close to her chest. "And I don't want this. If you've been in my head, you know I never would've wanted this."

"So ungrateful." Frustration rasped beneath Not-Rosie's calm, high voice. "You came into this town with your mind wide open, full of vast, untapped potential, and I have sculpted you into something magnificent."

"You used me." Violet lunged toward it, but Not-Rosie chuckled and reappeared on her other side.

"You let yourself be used," it said. "You led yourself through every step. All I had to do was show you what you wanted to see."

Violet thought of every moment she'd spent wishing that Rosie was back again. How she'd craved her sister's company. How she'd felt when Rosie was standing in front of her—so light-headed, almost dizzy with joy. It hadn't occurred to her that she was being weakened.

She had played right into the Beast's hands, and now the whole town would pay for it.

Beside her, Orpheus hissed at the thing that had taken her sister's face, her sister's voice.

Not-Rosie rolled her flat eyes. "Oh, stop whining," she said to the cat. "I'm the only reason you even exist." She turned to Violet. "Did you know your powers wouldn't work properly without a companion? I made that mistake with Stephen."

Bile rose in Violet's throat as she remembered the way Orpheus had been laid out for her. Like a present.

It had killed him so she would use her powers. So she would grow.

"Get the fuck out of my mind," she said.

There had to be a way to fix this. A way to fight it off.

Not-Rosie tilted her head to the side. "Too late."

Orpheus hissed. Violet looked down.

Her hand had crossed the white line of the circle.

The last things she saw before the room went black were Not-Rosie's dark, flat eyes.

TWENTY

VIOLET CAME TO SLOWLY, her thoughts sluggish and aimless, like a leaf bobbing on the surface of a pond.

Her skull felt like it had been split in two. She tried to move her head, but it hurt too much.

Her arms were bound behind her back, which rested against something rough, but she sat on soft, loamy ground. Her eyes opened, blinking blearily as she tried to make sense of where she was.

She'd been in the woods, trying to get Nora home.

No, that wasn't right. She'd been with May, getting her memories back.

No, that was wrong, too. She was in the attic, reading Stephen's journal.

But no. She was missing something, because she had no idea how she'd gotten here. Wherever *here* was—somewhere suffocatingly, oppressively dark.

She shuddered, realizing why everything looked so uniform, why the world smelled faintly of mildew and body odor. Some kind of bag had been shoved over her head.

Terror rushed through her, but at least it was her terror. At least that *thing*, the Beast, was out of her head—for now.

She shuddered, thinking of what it could've made her do. What she had already done.

"She's awake."

A chorus of murmurs approached her as Violet squirmed uncomfortably in her seat.

"Should we take the hood off?"

"Not until the ceremony starts."

"But what if she can't breathe?"

"Then she can't annoy us."

"Surely she's too smart to talk."

"She went to the Hawthornes. She's already talked too much."

Violet knew there had to be a way out of this, if only she could concentrate. But her skull ached, her hands throbbed, and she couldn't shake the panic roaming through her rib cage.

Her aunt's prediction rushed back to her: *You're going to die with a hat on.* Did a hood count?

"Enough." This new voice was soft and syrupy, like an adorable southern grandma holding a glass of alcoholic iced tea. Violet knew her brain was getting loopy, possibly from the Beast, possibly from air loss. The hood was yanked off her head, and as she gasped for air, Mrs. Moore, the town librarian, came into her field of view.

"There you are, honey," she said, smiling in a way that seemed far more at home at a picnic than a kidnapping. "Isn't that better?"

Violet took in the world around her. They were deep in the woods, branches laced above her head like the bars of a cage. It seemed unfair that the sky was a perfect velvety black, speckled with stars.

Bells hung in the trees before her, like the ones she'd seen hanging from the eaves of the houses on her first day, like the one she'd seen in the tower above the town hall. But the robed figures that bustled about were untying them, removing them from the trees.

"You're the Church of the Four Deities," Violet whispered. "Aren't you?"

Mrs. Moore smiled. "In the flesh."

Violet screamed.

Mrs. Moore's face crinkled with disappointment. "Oh, sweetie. Now we'll have to gag you."

A roll of duct tape shone in her manicured hand. She tore off a strip and slapped it across Violet's protesting mouth.

Unable to speak, Violet scanned the Church member's faces instead, trying to commit them to memory. Although they were mostly adults, she recognized a few people from homeroom. Apparently, the Church of the Four Deities had been recruiting fresh blood.

"He approaches!" called out a deep male voice. Robed figures scurried around in disarray as the same figure she'd seen standing over Daria at the foot of the stairs emerged from between two shadowy trees.

The hooded robes and the gloves it wore hid most of its form, but they couldn't hide the sickly-sweet, rotten smell as it passed through the clearing.

The other figures parted around it automatically, from respect or fear, Violet couldn't tell. She pressed her back against the tree trunk, gagging, as it shuffled toward her.

"That's right," said a robed figure who was walking beside it, like an aide. "We've acquired the girl."

It stopped only a few feet away from her, then slowly, deliberately, its hands lurched to its hood. And pulled it back.

The eye sockets were rotted away, the forehead half-demolished; the hair clung on to the scalp in patchy bits of frizzy, dark curls.

It didn't matter.

Violet recognized the face immediately.

He was a funhouse-mirror version of the boy in the photograph. The boy behind the journals. The boy who'd died with the Beast inside his head.

Stephen Saunders.

The corpse was disturbingly young, the slender build and half-rotted face of a boy forever frozen at sixteen.

Bits of preserved flesh flaked off him as he leaned toward her. As he tugged off a glove.

Violet whimpered behind the gag as he reached out a skeletal finger and raked it down her cheek. The smell of decay assaulted her nostrils. Bile rose in her throat; every instinct begged her to flee.

The tether between them snapped into place, like the one she'd sensed with Orpheus. But while the energy that tethered Violet to her companion was a thin, warm strand of effort, this felt different. Something was being forcibly extracted from her chest, leaving her breathless and dizzy.

She tried to pull back against it, to break it. But Violet's already-sore limbs were going numb. The branches around her blurred. Her vision had begun darkening around the edges when Stephen jerked his hand away, then rose slowly to his feet, leaving her lolling against the tree in relief.

When her vision cleared enough to watch the Church members again, she noticed they seemed somewhat confused. Several whispered among themselves, until finally one member approached Mrs. Moore. She caught snatches of the conversation.

"…late?"

"Supposed to…"

"Start without…?"

"We can't hold off any longer." Mrs. Moore's voice made the other robed figures turn their heads. "It's time to begin."

The bells were gone from the trees by now, a discarded row at the edge of the clearing. The Church members assembled in a circle. Violet caught a flash of the founders' symbol on the ground, made of bones that glowed white against the dirt. They were too small to be human, a minuscule consolation. It hadn't been there before—the Church members must have made it, a gruesome tribute to her family's Deck of Omens suit.

Two robed figures stepped out from between the trees. Juniper's limp body sagged between them.

The sight of her mother, so helpless, was far more frightening than Stephen's undead body. Violet cried out, but the duct tape muffled her screams. None of the robed figures even flinched.

They dragged Juniper into the center of the circle and laid her diagonally between the lines of bone. A second later, her brother joined her. He raised his hands toward the sky, and the singing began.

"Sinners who've been led astray,
Wandered through the woods one day…"

They were an unnerving sight, their dark hoods pulled back to reveal the reverence on their faces. They were calling on a monster. Calling for it to take Violet's mother away. The air crackled around them as the line between Four Paths and the Gray began to blur.

She was going to die. So was Juniper.

Her tears grew thicker as she realized that she'd never get to tell her mother she was sorry.

The Gray began to spill open before her, harsh white clouds seeping through a tiny sliver of the night sky. The trees around them turned squat and dark, the ridges on their trunks pulsing to the rhythm of the Church's song.

Which was when the ropes around her body went slack, pooling at her waist. Violet wriggled her fingers cautiously, her eyes darting to the side.

A familiar head of blond hair peered out from behind a neighboring tree. A moment later, a flash of dark curls and concerned, furrowed eyebrows joined him.

The tears on her cheeks were relieved ones now.

Isaac and Justin had come to help her. Which almost made up for them lying about Augusta Hawthorne.

"Don't move your hands," said Isaac. "Pretend you're still tied up."

"And don't freak out," Justin added. "We're your friends. I'm not sure what you remember."

Violet ignored Isaac and ripped the duct tape off her mouth. Half the skin on her lips came off with the adhesive, but she didn't care.

"What did I just say—" hissed Isaac.

"I know who you are." Blood pooled into Violet's mouth from her ruined lips. She would keep May's secret. But she couldn't pretend she didn't know what was going on, not when her mother's life might depend on it. "I got my memories back."

Isaac's face slackened with such undisguised happiness, Violet had to wrestle down a grin.

There would be time later to discuss how they'd deceived her. Right now, she had other things to worry about.

"My mother's in there." Violet jerked her head toward the circle, where the singing was reaching a feverish pitch.

"We know," said Justin. "We planned for it."

"You're both getting out of here alive." Isaac locked eyes with Violet. "Your mom's going to be okay. I promise."

Violet believed him, or at least the rush of warmth in her chest did.

But they were three on fifteen. She didn't know how that was possible.

And then, on the other side of the clearing, a flash of silver emerged from beneath a hooded figure's robe.

A sword.

A moment later, the Church member closest to the figure was howling in pain, stumbling back into the woods.

The figure's hood fell back, revealing a tangled mane of dark curls and a face filled with murderous rage.

Violet grinned.

Harper.

It didn't matter that they couldn't stand one another. They'd teamed up—to rescue *her*.

And if she was worth enough to these people for May to defy her family and return her memories, for Harper and Justin and Isaac to put aside years of hurt to come to her aid, then she wasn't alone. Not anymore.

The circle shifted uneasily, the chant weakening. Isaac took advantage of the moment to charge forward, his hands already beginning to glow.

"Hey, assholes!" he called out. "Come and get me!"

Violet shoved the ropes away from her torso. "The Beast wants something with my mom," she murmured to Justin.

"I know." Justin helped her to her feet. She could barely feel her limbs. "It wants to possess her permanently so it can escape the Gray."

The thought was horrifying. "Like it's been possessing me?"

Justin nodded. "So you figured it out."

"Yes."

Behind them, a scream rang out through the air—Isaac's distraction had done its job. Harper's silver sword flashed on the other side of the clearing, and two robed figures fell back, yelling with pain.

The singing was completely gone now; everything was chaos and screams. But the circle of bone was still intact, Stephen and Juniper at its center.

That was all that mattered now.

Violet caught sight of a flash of steel behind Justin's shoulder. "Look out!"

Justin dodged the blow and jumped backward as a figure emerged in front of them, a knife in his hand. It was a boy Violet didn't recognize, but Justin clearly did.

"Justin Hawthorne," the boy said viciously. "I was hoping you'd show."

Justin's voice was clouded with resignation. "Brian Whitley. This won't get you the revenge you want."

Violet didn't know how they knew each other, but as the boy brandished his knife, the defeat on Justin's face was palpable.

"Leave them alone!" called out a voice from the other side of the fray. Brian Whitley charged toward the trees as Harper Carlisle appeared beside them, her sword gleaming in the moonlight.

340

"Traitor!" Brian cried at Harper as he fled into the forest.

"Traitor?" said Violet.

Harper and Justin exchanged a loaded glance.

"I'll explain later," Harper said softly. "You need to get to your mom."

Violet's eyes sought out the circle. Stephen was on his knees, his corpse crouching over her mother's body. Every part of her was flooded with panic; but she would not let it overwhelm her. She could cry later. Now was the time to act.

But beside her, Justin nudged her elbow. "You might not have to."

He gestured at Isaac, who was running toward the circle of bone. Violet shuddered with relief as he began to step over the line—but something sparked upward, like a firework, and he stumbled back.

"I can't get in!" he called, panic lacing his voice.

Stephen Saunders's hand slid into his robe. It emerged clutching a knife made of bleached, whittled bone.

Violet's entire world narrowed to the blade as Stephen lowered it to her mother's neck.

The Gray wasn't letting anyone in. Which meant there was no way to stop Stephen.

No way, of course, unless your mind was somehow bound to the monster that lived inside it.

She bolted toward the circle, shoving away a figure who came at her with a knife. Maybe Justin was yelling in protest, and maybe Isaac was yelling, too. She didn't care.

Because Juniper was her mother. And she would do anything, anything, to save her.

She leaped over the line of bone. And just as she'd known in her gut, just as she'd feared, it let her pass.

Violet landed in the Gray.

Bent-back trees with pulsing, ashen trunks. Dull, unmoving sky. A feeling like static in her chest. Already she felt like she couldn't breathe. The Church and her friends were gone.

Juniper lay on the ground, still surrounded by bones. Stephen Saunders hovered above her. The ivory blade in his hand was as menacing and colorless as the world that stretched around her.

Violet lunged for the blade, wresting it from her uncle with no real resistance at all. She shuddered at the feeling of his dead hands on hers as she knelt beside Juniper, pressing two fingers to her neck. The thin, erratic pulse of Juniper's heartbeat against Violet's fingers was the sweetest thing Violet had ever felt.

She tipped her head up to Stephen, extending the knife he'd held just moments ago.

"Get away from us." Violet shuddered as the words echoed through the dim landscape a second too late. The bond between them tugged at her again, but she ignored it as she gathered her mother into her arms. She half carried, half dragged her toward the edge of the circle.

Stephen didn't try to attack her. He didn't even move.

"It won't work." Her sister's voice floated through the circle.

The Beast gnawed at the edge of her mind, coating her skull like a second skin.

Violet froze, her boots crunching bone.

Where would she go? This was the Beast's prison. In here, they were at its mercy.

"You won't get her out like that." Not-Rosie's voice was languid, almost lazy. She appeared a moment later. Her body was no longer transparent, and her shadow crept across the circle, the edges twisting and winding like the branches behind her head.

Almost real, except for the utter lack of empathy on her face.

Violet clutched Juniper like a lifeline. At least her mother didn't have to be awake for this. "I'm not letting you take my mom away from me."

Juniper wasn't perfect. But she was the only family Violet had left.

She couldn't let the last memories they had of each other be a fight. She couldn't let it end like this.

"She won't be gone," said the Beast dispassionately. "She'll just be dead. And I…" Not-Rosie's mouth stretched into a wide, mad grin that did not belong to her sister at all. "I'll be free, and your ancestors' greed will have been their own undoing."

"Greed?" The question spilled out of Violet's throat.

"Oh, child," said the Beast. "Do you really think I was bound here out of altruism? They wanted my power, and they achieved it. But they can only keep it where I'm trapped, so they stay forever in this miserable little place. You should be glad to set me free. The founders have never understood my view of things. But I knew Stephen was different from the moment he let me into his mind."

Those words triggered something in Violet, a realization that had been working in the back of her head since before the equinox.

She knew why her mind had gone blank. Why the Beast had burrowed into her head, why Stephen had been such an easy target for it. The Saunders family had to prove they could handle their powers. And what better way to show their worth than to let the Beast inside their heads—and drive it out again?

It would solidify that tether between them.

It would show that they were stronger than the monster they were bound to.

It had to be her family ritual. Which meant there was a chance she could still fix this.

Violet laid out her mother on the ground and rose, trembling, to her feet.

"How about this?" she asked as the Beast cocked Not-Rosie's head to the side. "How about you take me instead? I know you love hanging out inside my head."

"You're not nearly strong enough," said the Beast disdainfully.

"But I'm willing," said Violet. "Was Stephen willing? Because I think you brainwashed him into doing this. I don't think he wanted you in there at all."

"Stephen was weak." The word hung in the air between them, echoing back from the trees that wound around them. "So are you. Weakened by grief and love and sadness. You called to me from the moment you entered the town, from the moment you sat down at that piano. Your mother's power is the only one strong enough to hold me."

"I thought you might say that." Violet steeled herself for what she was about to do. It was a bad plan. But it was the only one she had. "I guess expecting you to cooperate was unrealistic."

She charged toward Not-Rosie and closed her hands around her sister's wrists.

They were real because she needed them to be real, and as she stood nose to nose with her sister's image, something flickered in those dark eyes. Something hungry.

"Stop that," hissed the Beast.

Her sister's form shimmered in the air.

"Stop it," whined the Beast. "Stop it and I'll let you bring her back. For real. That's what you want, isn't it?"

And suddenly Rosie looked even more solid than before. Her skin glowed with life and health; her hair shone turquoise in the Gray's weak imitation of sunlight.

Her mouth opened in a grin. "You know you can do it," said her voice. "You brought back Orpheus. Why not me?"

Violet saw it in her mind then.

Saw herself letting go. Letting the Beast take hold of Juniper, then granting her powers that would let her leave the town, that would be strong enough not just to reanimate Rosie's body, but to heal her.

Trading a mother for a sister. A life for a life.

"I'm all you'll ever have," her sister's form whispered. "I'm the only person who's ever loved you. Are you really ready to let me go?"

It was the hardest thing Violet had ever done—but she looked away from her sister's face.

To Juniper, lying in the dirt, looking both older and younger than Violet had ever seen her before.

"Do you really think," she said, moving her eyes back to the Beast—because no matter what it looked like, that was what it was—"that I would ever consent to you murdering my mother? You're the monster here, not me."

Not-Rosie hissed with displeasure. "Then you've doomed me," she snapped, and suddenly her skin was shriveling across her skull, her eyes blackening with rot, her hands withering in Violet's until Violet was clutching flaking skin across yellow bones.

Maggots writhed behind her sister's empty eye sockets as her withered mouth cracked open into a grin—or perhaps it was just a silent scream.

"You're not real," Violet whimpered, shutting her eyes, but she could *feel* Rosie's dead hands in hers.

Smell the sweet, musky scent of decay.

Violet gagged and gripped harder. Knives seared at the back of her skull as the Beast's voice—its real voice— echoed through her, hissing in an unfamiliar language.

It went against her every instinct to pull the Beast into her mind. But she pushed her panic away, tugging its presence toward her and forcing herself not to retreat. Cold hands grasped her mind, and Violet let out an involuntary shudder as her toes, her feet, her ankles went numb.

Tears forced her eyes open, dripping in viscous lines down her cheeks that were too thick to be water. Gray ran up the inside of her wrists, racing toward her shoulders, her chest, her heart. Violet felt as if she were sinking into a treacly black lake. She was holding her breath, but soon, she'd have to open her mouth and take in a lungful of molasses.

It was inside her. Wrestling control away from her body the way it had on the equinox.

Violet couldn't remember why she'd thought she could beat it. Why she'd let it in. But it didn't matter anymore, none of it did.

All that was left was to surrender. It would be so easy to surrender.

And as Violet stared out at the bleak, colorless world of the Gray, the last vestiges of her consciousness slipping away, she saw Rosie.

At first, she thought this was another cruel trick of the Beast's. But Rosie's eyes were brown and glowing, with gold liner at their corners. And she wasn't wearing the clothes she'd had on the night she died. Instead, she wore the dress she'd bought for prom, a flowing black thing that struck the perfect balance between edgy and classy, with a chunky gold statement necklace.

She'd never gotten to show it off anywhere besides a dressing room.

"Damn straight I'd choose to spend eternity in this." Rosie frowned at her. "I can feel your judgment. Figures you'd lose control of your motor functions before you surrender your attitude."

"Rosie?" Violet wasn't sure if she was talking or thinking. But this wasn't the Not-Rosie the Beast had shown her. This Rosie felt like her sister the same way her paintings did. "Are you real?"

Even the Gray began to flicker as the Beast burrowed into her mind. The edges of her vision were blurring black.

"Real or not, you know what I'd say," said Rosie. "I love you, but I don't want any company. Not for a long time."

"I love you, too," Violet whispered.

Rosie gave her a grin that was tinged with sadness. "I'm sorry I left you."

And then she was gone, and there was only blackness. Something inside Violet had cracked the day Rosie died. There was an abscess in her chest, a gaping hole in the back of her skull.

A place for evil things to slip right in.

Her grief had let the Beast inside her head. But Violet's grief was also her anchor to herself.

And she could use that grief to drive out the Beast.

Violet let the months of pain and sorrow rush through

her as she clawed back her mind. This was hurt it would never understand. This was hurt made from love. And as she immersed herself in grief, embraced it, the parts of her that had been so lost and broken, so long her enemy, were now her savior.

"You're not coming back," she said, to Rosie, and to herself, the girl she'd been before. She was different now, broken and remade. There would always be sorrow buried within her. But that was okay—that was part of who she was. And as the Beast's grip over her mind snapped like a bone breaking in two, Violet knew it would never leave her head, either. Not completely.

That was the price the Saunders family had paid for power.

Violet opened her eyes.

The Gray was gone, and she was back in the clearing, surrounded by woods, noise rushing through the circle of bones.

Color spread back across her skin, chasing the Gray past her wrists, past her fingertips—which were curled, unconsciously, around her sister's silver bracelet.

Stephen Saunders still stood at the edge of the circle. It might've been her imagination, but his rotted eye sockets seemed to gleam with fear.

She breathed in deep. The cool night air filled her lungs with the smell of earth, the smell of the woods.

Then she strode across the circle, her feet crunching across animal bones, until she and Stephen were inches apart, nose to skull.

The tether she'd felt earlier spun between them, a horrible, queasy thing.

Violet remembered the boy in the journals. He hadn't deserved to end up like this, a heap of ruined clothes and eroding bones, held together by her magic.

He deserved peace.

She reached her hand up, mimicking his movements from before, and touched a bloodstained finger to his rotting cheek.

"We both know you're not supposed to be here," she whispered. "I hope it's not so bad, where you're going. Maybe I'll see you there one day."

She harnessed the same part of herself that had clawed her mind back from the Beast's hold. Power surged within her, wild and wonderful and, at last, truly hers.

Something on that decayed face twitched with what might've been relief. And as the tether between them snapped, Stephen Saunders collapsed beneath her hand.

She stepped away from him, shuddering, and wiped her fingers off on her jeans.

To her surprise, far more than three figures were now dealing with the Church members. They were older and better trained, which meant only one thing: The sheriff had arrived.

Violet dragged Juniper across the barrier, bones crunching beneath her boots with every step. Then she knelt down beside her, smoothing a lock of frizzy hair away from Juniper's slack-jawed face.

"Wake up," she said softly. "Come on, Mom. It's over."

A figure knelt down beside her, a blond, angular slab of marble. "Is she all right?" asked Augusta Hawthorne, her words raw with panic.

Violet recoiled. "Don't try anything."

Augusta held up her gloved hands. "I won't."

Violet was surprised by how the fear in the sheriff's voice matched the fear that pulsed through her as she stared at Juniper's limp form. Behind her, figures in brown robes were being handcuffed and led to squad cars, while other officers squatted beside the circle of bones, putting fragments into plastic evidence bags.

"Violet?"

She turned at the sound of her name. Justin and Isaac trotted out of the fray, Harper trailing behind them. And if her eyes stung a little at the sound of Justin's familiar voice, well, it was dark, and no one noticed, so it didn't count.

"Your face," said Isaac softly. "There's blood…"

"I'm fine," said Violet. "Juniper's the one who needs help."

"She should see a doctor," Augusta said. "She could be concussed. Or drugged. There's a clinic at the station."

"Only if I get to stay with her the whole time," said Violet firmly. "And only if those gloves stay on."

Augusta hesitated, her face still creased with concern. "You remember."

Violet smiled. "Yeah. I do. And I *will* find some way to set an undead army on you if you lay a finger on either of us again."

Augusta raised an eyebrow at the threat, but it must've worked, because she backed away.

As Juniper was lifted up onto a stretcher, Violet realized that Justin, Harper, and Isaac were flanking her.

"You didn't have to do this," she muttered. Her gaze darted from Justin's dirt-streaked hair to the bloody paperback sticking out of Isaac's pocket to the sword gleaming in Harper's hand.

"Do what?" said Justin.

"Come on. You know what."

"I want to hear you say it."

Violet raised her arms to the sky in protest, Rosie's bracelet jangling on her wrist.

"Save me." It was a struggle to spit the words out, because she really meant them. "But you did. So thank you."

Harper ducked her head and swung her sword up onto her shoulder. The corners of Isaac's mouth twitched as he wiped a smudge of dirt off his nose.

"I'd give that a four out of ten," he drawled.

"I'll be sure to consider your judgment the next time I'm trapped in an alternate-dimension prison with a monster that has possessed me."

His eyes crinkled with mirth, and suddenly it was a little harder for Violet to stand straight.

"Are you going to be okay?" said Justin.

"I think so," Violet said. "I figured out my ritual."

Justin let his smile loose. His white teeth glowed like a beacon against the night.

She didn't know how he could still look so happy, but she was grateful for it. She was grateful for all of them. And she could tell they knew it. She could see it on their faces. There was a sense of mutual relief humming among all four of them. They were alive, and they were safe.

"How did you know where to find me?" she asked Harper as they headed toward the edge of the clearing. The trees around them were bathed in red and blue light from the sirens flashing at the edge of the forest.

"My father," said Harper hesitantly. "Violet... there are some things you should know. Now that your memories are back." The beam of a police flashlight caught Harper's neck, illuminating the bruises on her throat. Bruises that were shaped a lot like fingers.

Violet remembered, with a rush, that Harper had been wearing one of those robes, too. "What happened?"

Harper cast a careful glance at Augusta Hawthorne. "I'll explain later."

Her voice sounded different. Smoother. Stronger.

Violet had questions for all of them, but right now, her priority was getting to the squad car that held her mother. She had earned herself a second chance with Juniper, and she would not waste it. It was time she started learning to move on.

TWENTY-ONE

T HE FOUR PATHS SHERIFF'S station was cold and sterile. Justin suspected Augusta Hawthorne had tried as hard as possible to provide an alternative to the sea of chestnut oaks outside. He'd spent the past hour since Violet and her mother had arrived at the clinic in the waiting area, staring at the white tiles and fluorescent lights.

When they'd first come in, the clinic staff insisted on treating Violet for weeks' worth of minor injuries. Justin had watched the nurse practitioner bustle her away, her latex-coated hand wrapped firmly around Violet's upper arm like she was a child prone to running off.

Violet looked back at him when they got her to the doorway, blood and grime smeared across her face, and shot him a tiny, wicked grin. They were actually friends now. He could tell that was new to her.

Honestly, wanting to be just friends with a girl who wasn't related to him was new for Justin, too.

He had no idea how she'd gotten her memories back.

Part of him was scared to ask, because that meant there was a solution. A cure. Another way in which he'd failed Harper.

Justin thought back to that night at the lake. How Harper had screamed as his mother advanced, flanked by her mastiffs.

He hadn't been able to stop himself from touching her back in Maurice Carlisle's workshop. It had taken everything he had not to slide his fingers from her neck up to her cheek.

He'd wanted to kiss her. But Justin knew he couldn't. They were both founders, powers or not.

And she'd lied to him. He'd lied to her.

But they weren't even.

Everything she thought of him now was a consequence of not knowing what had really happened to her. It was selfish to get close to her when she didn't know the truth.

Justin either needed to let her go, or find some way to show her what had really happened the night she'd lost her arm.

He shook the memories away to find May standing in front of him.

Her ruffled white blouse was tied in a neat bow at her neck, her skirt billowing out in perfect pleats. But Justin had learned a long time ago to read May's small signs of disarray. Her red-rimmed eyes. The chewed-off bits of her nail polish.

She was upset.

Good.

"Mom wants to see you." Her fingers twisted together

in front of her paisley skirt like pale, grasping roots. "But she says you don't have to if you don't want to."

"Isn't that generous of her?"

May fixed her clear blue eyes on the scratched linoleum floor. "I'm sorry. The things I said were unwarranted and cruel."

In that moment, Justin saw that May's powers had hurt her, not helped her. She'd gotten everything she'd ever wanted—which meant she had no reason to question why Augusta ran Four Paths the way she did.

He'd expected to feel angry the next time they spoke, but all he felt was pity. He had been May's most ardent defender during the years when Augusta had anointed him as the favorite child. But May had shredded the bond between them now that she was the one in power. And for the first time in his life, he had no interest in mending something shattered.

"You didn't care that you were being cruel," Justin said. "You wanted to hurt me."

An unreadable expression flashed across her face. "That's not true."

"Really?" said Justin. "Violet could've died. I hope you're happy."

He turned away, starting toward his mother's office. Justin heard her footsteps behind him, but he didn't look back.

A few officers were clustered around Augusta's desk, but when Justin pushed open the door, she waved them out with a flick of her hand.

"Justin." Augusta's voice was soft and feathered around the edges, like she was sculpting each word with utmost care. "So you've decided to join me."

"I decided to hear you out." Justin shut the door before May could follow him in. This was between him and his mother. "I'm not like you. I don't decide people are worthless before they get a chance to apologize."

Augusta's broad shoulders twitched. "I know I was harsh with you. I should've taken your concerns about the town potentially planning a power grab into account."

"What about Violet?" asked Justin. "Are you going to apologize for what you did to her?"

He knew it was a lost cause to ask about Harper, or any of the other people whose lives Augusta had casually rearranged.

Yet he couldn't bear to walk out the door.

The thing was, Justin had never been very good at giving up on lost causes. Especially when they needed him.

"I did what I thought was necessary with the evidence provided," said Augusta. "Perhaps, if you had pleaded your case to me earlier, I would've been more understanding. But you didn't trust me enough to tell me the truth."

"Can you blame me?" said Justin.

The corners of his mother's mouth drooped. "No. But I have something for you that might help us move forward. May suggested it."

She withdrew a sheaf of papers from her desk, then offered it to Justin.

He took it.

She'd printed out the applications for the liberal arts schools within a thirty-minute drive of Four Paths, along with the information for the local community college. Justin swallowed hard. "You want me to stay."

Augusta locked eyes with him. "I think you've proven by now that you are useful to Four Paths in ways I hadn't anticipated. Perhaps my determination to make you leave town was unwarranted. So, yes, I want you to stay."

It was everything Justin had ever wanted.

But her version of his decision to remain would mean ignoring the truth of his family legacy.

It would mean surrender.

He thought of the cards May had laid out before him. *This* was his chance to change things.

Failing his ritual had put him in a unique position. No powers, but a life spent with the founders. He might be the only person who truly understood both sides of the problems in Four Paths. It wasn't the future he'd planned on. But it was a future spent where he belonged: at home.

Justin laid the papers back down on the desk. Then he untied the medallion at his wrist, dropping the thin glass disc into his palm.

"*If* I stay in Four Paths," he said, "I won't hide who I am anymore. I'm telling the town the truth about my powers. And I won't let you erase it."

Augusta's face had gone alabaster white. "You will lose their respect."

"Maybe. But at least I won't be lying anymore." He

released the medallion, let it fall onto his mother's desk. The red glass glimmered like a dying sun. "One more thing. I want you to promise you'll stop using your powers on people."

Augusta chuckled. "Absolutely not."

But Justin had prepared himself for this. "Then I'll cut off your access to Isaac Sullivan. After what you've done to her, Violet Saunders will never answer to you—you know that. Which means you'll barely have any founders on patrol."

Augusta's nostrils flared slightly. Justin could tell he'd struck a nerve.

"My powers are an essential part of keeping this town safe," she said. "Right now, we have fourteen members of the Church of the Four Deities in custody. Would you rather I sent them a county over and let them be tried for attempted murder, or erased their involvement and allowed them to live in peace? Removing their memories neutralizes them as threats. It's effective. It's humane."

Justin paused. As much as he hated to admit it, Augusta did have a point. But surely there was some way to find a balance between people like Violet and the members of the Church of the Four Deities.

"Give them a choice," he said at last. "Ask them if they'd rather go to jail or have their memories taken away. And promise me you'll never touch a founder kid again."

The office was silent for a second as Augusta's face went still, considering. Then she extended a gloved hand.

"You'll come home?" she said, a quiet sort of respect ringing out in her voice.

It was worth surrendering for this. For the possibility of change. For a town where the Hawthorne name meant something more than fear.

He clasped Augusta's gloved hand and shook.

The nurses at the clinic gave Violet a hideous paper gown and forced her to sit still as they re-bandaged every scratch and wound. The only thing she managed to cling to was Rosie's bracelet, which sat on her lap in a plastic bag, the silver scrubbed clean, as she watched the staff swarm around her mother, who lay unconscious on the next pallet over.

From what she could gather, the Church members had drugged Juniper. She was unharmed aside from that, but the sight of her mother's limp body still hurt whenever Violet looked at her.

Violet was arguing with a nursing trainee about getting her phone back when Augusta Hawthorne burst through the door. She didn't even acknowledge Violet, just made her way straight to Juniper's side while volleying questions at the nurse practitioner.

"She'll be fine," the nurse practitioner said. "Yes, it has to flush itself from her system. No, there won't be lasting damage."

"But it's been hours." Augusta's forehead creased. "She should be awake by now."

"She will wake up, Sheriff Hawthorne." The nurse hesitantly patted her on the arm. "Give her time."

"What's the deal?" Violet's voice was sharp and loud. "Are you here to take her memories when she wakes up, just in case?"

Augusta turned away from Juniper, her arms folding across her chest. Violet felt exposed in her flimsy hospital gown, but she refused to flinch beneath the other woman's gaze.

"I know what you did," Violet said. "When she tried to leave town, you took her memories of Four Paths away. The real Four Paths. For all I know, you took Daria's memories away, too."

"I never laid a finger on Daria," said Augusta quietly. "As for what happened with your mother—well, that's complicated."

Violet curled her fingers around the edge of the cot. "I know about Stephen. He tried to kill my mother thirty years ago, but he failed, and suddenly your family was in charge of Four Paths, not mine. So what really happened? What are you hiding?"

The clinic staff had fallen silent, their eyes flicking back and forth between Augusta and Violet like they were watching a tennis match.

"I think you should go," Augusta told them. "Miss Saunders and I need to have a conversation."

The nurse practitioner gulped. "We should stay with the patient."

"You just said she'd wake up eventually," said Augusta. "You're not doing anything important here. Now get out."

The clinic staff scuttled off, although Violet was pretty

sure they'd spend the next few minutes doing their best to eavesdrop.

"Does that mean you're going to answer my questions?" Nerves thrummed through her—she had control of her powers now, but raising the dead wouldn't help her if Augusta attacked. "Or are you here to take my memories again, too?"

But Augusta didn't even move toward taking off her gloves. "You did your ritual. You're no longer a threat to Four Paths, so I will not be attempting to neutralize you. Although I am interested to know how you restored your memories."

Violet tried to mask her relief. "As if I would ever tell you that."

"Perhaps we can trade?" said Augusta icily. "I'll fill in the blanks of the spring equinox of 1985, if you tell me how you retrieved your memories."

Violet considered it. Augusta Hawthorne was her best shot at knowing the truth. But the thought of selling out May to a woman who had nearly gotten Violet killed made her nauseous.

"Oh, please," she said. "You would never tell me the real reason why you took my mother's memories away."

A new voice rose up from the cot beside Violet, precise and coiled, like a viper waiting to pounce.

"That's an easy one to answer, actually," said Juniper Saunders. "She took away my memories because I asked her to."

Augusta whirled back toward the cot, while Violet hopped off her own, not caring what her flimsy hospital gown was showing off as she rushed over to her mother's makeshift hospital bed. Juniper was still lying down, but her eyes were wide open.

"Mom?" she said, but her mother wasn't looking at her. She was looking at the sheriff.

The room was suddenly thick with tension. There was something in their body language that spoke of truth. Of pain. Of history.

"August?" said Violet's mother.

"June?" said Augusta. "Is that—are you..."

Juniper nodded, and then Augusta swept her up in an embrace, heedless of Juniper's hospital gown. Her mother looked so small like that, almost doll-like against Augusta's larger frame.

Juniper had called them best friends. But Violet saw the truth between them, the tenderness that spoke to something very different from friendship.

They were looking at each other the same way Justin and Harper did.

And Violet realized that, for all she and her mother had learned about one another, there was still so much uncharted territory between them. But for the first time, she truly wanted to bridge that gap.

It wouldn't be easy. But she thought of her new friends, who had risked their lives to save her family, and promised herself that she would try.

"How?" the sheriff whispered, once Juniper had pulled

away and settled herself on the cot, her brown hair frizzing out in all directions.

"I was part of Violet's ritual," said Juniper. "I suppose it makes sense that it could be a cleansing, too, especially when ours is so cerebral. Violet…" Her mother's smile, unpolished and real, showed off her incisors. "Thank you. I'm so sorry you had to figure this out on your own."

"So you know?" Tears welled up in Violet's throat. "About our family? Our powers?"

Juniper nodded. "It all came back."

Violet swallowed hard. "Can you tell me what happened to Stephen?"

Juniper's face tightened. She raised a hesitant hand to her frizzy hair, pushed it behind her ear.

"You don't have to do this right now," Augusta said, her voice still soft and wobbly.

"No, August," said Juniper. "She's waited long enough. And she deserves to hear it from me."

Violet felt a pang of recognition in her chest at the determination on her mother's face.

Juniper knotted her hands together in her lap and began. "Stephen was the baby of the family. Daria and I completed our rituals by the time he turned fourteen." Her eyes flickered toward the sheriff. "I'm going to talk about our ritual now. August, you know the rules."

The sheriff sighed but nodded, moving away as Juniper beckoned toward Violet to lean in close.

"It's slightly ridiculous," she whispered in Violet's ear. "But we do keep the particulars of the rituals a secret from one another. On a Saunders's sixteenth birthday, we go into the ritual room hidden in the spire, enter the founders' symbol painted on the floor, and let the Beast inside our heads. We travel into the Gray and best it there. To understand death, you must be intimately close to it. When you traveled into the Gray and forced the Beast out of your head, you completed the ritual, too—albeit under far more dangerous circumstances.

"Unfortunately, Stephen's ritual went awry. The Beast took up residence inside his mind, as it normally does, but he hadn't gained control over it before he came back out. It changed him over time, altering thoughts, moods, and eventually his actions. But Stephen had always been a little unpredictable, and the Beast used that to keep the reformation of the Church—frankly it was a bastardization of the Church—a secret."

"So you really didn't know the Beast was in his head?" Violet asked.

Juniper's lips tightened into a rueful smile as she pulled away from Violet. "I had no idea."

Augusta turned around. "I trust you're done with the family secrets?"

Juniper smiled. "You were never good at hiding your annoyance."

Augusta huffed but stayed silent as she made her way back over to them.

"As I was saying," Juniper continued, "I didn't know what had happened to my brother. Not until the equinox, anyway. Stephen dragged me out of bed and into the woods at knife-point. He was going to let the Beast take control of me so it would have a physical form, which would break its bonds to the prison. He would have given it his own body, but he wasn't strong enough. My powers were… uniquely suited to the Beast's needs. But he didn't…" Her hand jerked up toward her face, then stopped, trembling, by her shoulder. "He didn't know," she whispered.

And then her mother was crying. She hadn't cried for her husband, she hadn't cried for Daria, she hadn't cried for Rosie. But here she was, tears nestling at the rims of her eyelids, ready to splatter across her cheeks.

"June," said Augusta again. "You don't have to tell her."

"I do," Juniper said, her voice wobbling. "Stephen didn't know what my power was. We'd kept it a secret because it was a difficult thing to prove. But every Saunders family deals with death somehow. Daria saw it. Stephen raised it." Juniper's hand steadied itself, then lowered, methodically, back to her lap. "I suppose you could say I've mastered it."

Violet gaped at her. "Mastered it? What, you mean you can't die?"

"Oh, no, I'm not immortal," Juniper said, which made Augusta tense up for some reason. "I still age. I can be drugged, as you've seen. But I am impervious to most things—I fell off the roof of the manor a few weeks after my ritual, and I walked away without a scratch. I don't get ill. And when someone hurts me, whatever they were trying to inflict on me is done to them. That's why the

Beast wanted me. In my body, it would have been almost impossible to destroy, at least for some time."

Violet shuddered at the thought. "So you were its perfect host."

Juniper nodded. "Exactly. But when Stephen tried to stab me…"

She didn't have to finish. Violet understood with a rush of nausea exactly what would've happened next.

And she understood now why the Church had needed Stephen to be resurrected. Because an undead boy would be unaffected by Juniper's abilities.

Juniper grabbed a tissue from the stand beside her cot and dabbed briskly at her eyes. "After Stephen died, his body went missing. His vault in our mausoleum is empty. But the Saunders family kept the entire tragedy a secret, and all of that guilt, that shame, eventually became too much. So I asked Augusta to take it away. I thought if I couldn't remember my grief, it would be easier to get on with my life. But it was a weak thing to do. My family fell apart after I ran away. And while I'm so grateful I met your father and had you and Rosie." She gave Violet a teary smile. "That's not the life I was supposed to live. I've always felt like I was running from something. It found me in the end. It always does, I guess."

Violet choked back tears of her own.

For the first time in her life, she understood her mother. Juniper wasn't insensitive or clueless. She had weathered incredible loss, greater than even Violet had ever known.

She also hadn't been strong enough to handle it on her own. It had made her hurt people, even the ones she loved. Violet understood that feeling, too.

"I'm sorry," she told Juniper. "For what I said, about you, about Rosie."

Juniper reached forward, clutched Violet's hand in hers. "I'm sorry, too. I can't imagine how terrifying it must have been, dealing with all of this alone. There is so much I want to show you now. So much I can teach you."

"About Four Paths?" said Violet.

Juniper smiled. "Four Paths, yes," she said. "But what you said about your father's family... you were right. You deserve to know them, and they deserve to know you, if that's what you want. No more secrets. No more lies."

When she leaned in for an embrace, Violet let her.

The front hallway of the Hawthorne House was unchanged. He ran his hand along the stone wall, the familiar touch of the foyer's cool, oppressive air pushing against his skin. A twisted branch of the hawthorn tree was splayed against the window like a hand beckoning him inside.

The truth about his failed ritual was already spreading through town. But wearing a stone pendant to school instead of his medallion was the easy part. The hard part was just beginning: The whispers in the hallways. The dirty looks in class. People's faces closing up as he walked past them on Main Street, when they'd once been friendly and open.

It hurt, oh, it hurt.

But it was a good kind of hurt, like sore muscles after a long run.

"Thanks for taking me in," he told Isaac, who lingered behind him in the front hallway.

Isaac slid his index finger along the edge of an ornate picture frame. His face was clouded; he seemed preoccupied. Justin knew he'd been working to clean up the Diner, even though Augusta had already paid for the damages.

It seemed like that had happened years ago, but it had barely been a week. So much change in such a short time.

Isaac looked at him, and every strange thing Justin had noticed about his behavior in the past few weeks reared its head. He was standing in a battle stance, his shoulders jutting forward like he was about to face down an enemy.

But he and Justin were the only people in the hallway.

"Now that you're home, there's something I have to say." His voice was guarded, careful. "Justin, I'm done."

Justin wondered if he'd misheard. "What do you mean, done?"

Isaac's eyes fixed firmly on something above Justin's head. "Have you ever noticed how I'm always there? You ask me to be your backup. Help Violet. Help Harper."

He spat Harper's name out of his mouth with obvious revulsion.

"I always say yes. But I can't do that anymore."

Justin thought he'd faced down his greatest fear when he'd failed his ritual. But the feeling building in his chest now was somehow worse than that. "I don't get it. Are you angry with me?"

Isaac's face twisted with anguish. "I'm never angry with you. That's the problem." There was something strange in his voice. A tenderness that didn't match the hurt on his face.

It hit Justin all at once, a heady, unpleasant wave of realization, like cold water dumped over his scalp.

Isaac's hand closing over his wrist at the barn party. Isaac rising from the ashes of the Diner, not to save himself, but to defend Justin. Isaac's visible dislike of Harper. That half smile that Isaac always gave him, only him, the one that Justin had never been able to figure out.

Justin had known Isaac was bi. That this was, technically, an option.

"So," he said hoarsely. "It's like that."

Isaac's hand curled into a fist, but there was no spark, no shimmer, just him. "Yeah. It's like that."

"How long has it been like that?"

Isaac's mouth twitched. "How long do you think?"

Justin's stomach hollowed out with quiet understanding. "I guess I should've seen it."

He'd just refused to let himself believe it. Because it was impossible for him to feel the same way, and Isaac knew that, too.

"I don't think you wanted to. And I thought maybe it would go away, and we'd never have to talk about it." Isaac paused, worked his jaw. "I know you aren't—I never expected anything. Fuck, I didn't want to make this weird, but I don't think I have a choice."

"It's not weird." But the words sounded unconvincing, even to him.

Justin forced himself to meet his friend's eyes, but the hurt he'd been afraid of wasn't there. The resignation he saw instead was somehow worse.

It was hopelessly, cruelly unfair.

"You've never lied to me before," Isaac said.

"So it's a little weird." Justin's voice was hoarse with desperation. "But that doesn't mean we have to be done."

"Yes, it does." Isaac bristled with conviction. "You own me, Justin, even if you never realized it. I'll do whatever you want because your happiness trumps my misery. So we can't be friends right now. I have to do this for myself. And after everything I've done for you, you don't get to try and stop me."

Isaac had been there when Justin's family turned on him. His unflinching loyalty had given Justin the courage to stand up to Augusta, to tell Four Paths the truth.

He needed Isaac—but for the first time, that wasn't enough to make him stay.

Thinking about how much this would hurt Justin churned his stomach; made him raw with fury. But it would be incredibly selfish to protest further.

Isaac had made up his mind. Justin owed it to him to listen. So he didn't speak as his best friend walked, each footstep careful and measured, out the door.

TWENTY-TWO

T HE PIECE OF MUSIC above the piano was a long way
from perfect. Violet had struck through half the
handwritten notes. Potential alternate phrasings were
scribbled everywhere. Violet played slowly through the
piece, pausing to scribble down new notes, new possibilities.

It was scary, beginning to compose. The blank sheet
of music had daunted Violet when she first sat down to
start, her mind blank. But once she'd pushed past that
initial wave of doubt, it had been hard to stop. She would
play other pieces, of course. But there was a special thrill
that came with creating something new.

The song Violet had written was simple and clunky.
She couldn't get the countermelodies to properly weave
together. But maybe one day, she'd be able to write
something other people would want to play.

She wasn't doing it for Rosie. But she knew Rosie
would've been proud of her, all the same.

Juniper had started opening up. Not just about Four

Paths, but about Violet's father's side of the family, too. Violet had narrowly avoided bursting into tears when her mother gave her the contact info for her Caulfield cousins. They'd all added each other on social media, but she was still working up the courage to say hello.

A lot of her conversations with her mother had come out wrong, fumbled words and awkward moments. But it was a start. Violet could feel them learning how to pull together, like two knitting needles tangled in a ball of crimson yarn.

Violet's phone buzzed, jolting her from her thoughts. She glanced at it, smiled, and bundled her composition away. Orpheus trailed behind her as she went to get the door.

Justin was waiting for her, hands stuffed in the pockets of his bomber jacket. Fall had come to Four Paths in a sudden rush of orange leaves and chilly air.

"You wanted to see me?" he asked her.

Violet knew he was surprised that she'd invited him alone. But she didn't want an audience for this.

"I have questions," she said delicately as he stepped into the foyer.

"Questions?"

"About Harper."

Suddenly, the light streaming into the sun-soaked foyer was too bright, the air around them oppressively stuffy and warm. Justin's hand froze on his coat zipper.

"That's not your story."

Violet met his eyes. "You're not a bad person. In fact,

all I've ever seen you do is advocate for people who probably don't deserve it. Me included. So what the hell made you give up on Harper Carlisle?"

Harper had told her about the Church of the Four Deities. Violet had decided, as she spoke, that Harper had been through enough with her father. There was no sense in being angry.

It was easy to forgive someone who'd made the right choice before it was too late.

"It's none of your business," Justin said now.

"No, it is my business," said Violet. "Because if I'm going to trust you, I need to understand why you would betray someone like that."

Justin's neck inclined slowly and stiffly, like a robot in need of joint repair.

"Fine." The carefree ease that had been there when she opened the door was completely gone. "I'll tell you."

They ended up in her room. Violet couldn't help but think of Isaac perched beside her window. She would have much preferred him slouching on her bed instead of Justin, still wearing his jacket, uncomfortably stiff.

"The truth is…" He paused. "The truth is, Harper's the most powerful person in Four Paths."

Violet jolted with shock. "What?" She'd suspected Augusta had taken Harper's memories away. But she had never thought this was the reason why. "So she didn't fail her ritual."

"No. You've probably noticed by now that people's powers work by touch. Your touch raises the dead.

Augusta's touch takes people's memories away. It's why she wears the gloves—to avoid accidents."

Violet nodded. "So what does Harper's touch do?"

The expression on Justin's face was pain and desire in equal measure. "Harper's touch turns you to stone. And it lets her control you."

Violet remembered the statues littered outside the Carlisle house. The bells, the swords, the sentinels.

"Control you?" she whispered.

"The Carlisle founder petrified things, then commanded them, like a stone army," said Justin, his brow furrowing. "The town called them guardians."

"And she could do that, too."

Justin nodded.

"Holy shit," Violet breathed. "That's terrifying."

"That's what my mother said," said Justin dully. "The Carlisles do their rituals alone, and return to their families once they've figured out what their powers are. They don't know this, but my mother's been supervising every Carlisle who comes of age for as long as I can remember, to make sure their powers aren't a threat. My mother was there the night of Harper's ritual. When she walked into the lake. When she came out." He paused. "I know, because I followed her."

"I imagine that didn't go so well."

"It didn't," said Justin. "When my mother realized I'd followed her, she forced me to stand alongside her, said that if I was going to be the Hawthorne heir, I would have to make tough choices. So we met Harper at the edge of the water and Augusta demanded a demonstration of her new powers."

"Harper was so scared. My mother had her cornered. And when Harper gets scared, she panics. So she grabbed Augusta's arm. And I saw——" He shook his head. "I saw it start to turn to stone. And I knew she'd been pushed too far. She wouldn't stop."

"What did you do?"

Justin's voice had gone so low, so ashamed, Violet could barely hear him. "I couldn't let her kill my mother, so I pushed her away. Into the lake. I thought she'd be fine, I just wanted her to stop, but I didn't…" He broke off.

"What happened?" said Violet softly.

Justin shook his head, staring out at the branches that waved beside her window. Violet pretended she didn't see him rub clumsily at his eyes before he spoke again.

"The Gray took her. She was lost in there for days, and when she came out, half her arm was missing. Augusta removed her memories in the hospital, before her family could ever find out the truth."

It was rare that Violet opened her mouth and found there weren't words waiting to spill out. But Justin's guilt over Harper was justified. He'd made a mistake he couldn't fix.

"Now do you understand?" Justin said. "She doesn't remember I betrayed her. She doesn't remember she was dangerous."

And then Violet realized that she *did* know what to do. What to say. "Would you give her those memories back?" she said. "If you could?"

Justin turned his head away from the window. His face was ashen. "Absolutely."

Violet had seen the feelings for Harper that lingered beneath the story he'd just told her. The ones he may as well have confessed to aloud.

She could try to handle this on her own. But after all Justin had done to help her, all the guilt he carried with him, he deserved the chance to make this right. And if he didn't take this chance—well, then she would help Harper herself. And she would know that what Harper had said about the Hawthornes was true: They would always put themselves first.

Violet didn't tell him the truth about May. But she told him enough.

After Justin left, Violet walked all the way to the edge of town, until she stood before the WELCOME TO FOUR PATHS sign.

A month ago, she and Juniper had driven into town. Now her boots crunched across the gravel of the road as she stepped beneath the sign. She expected to feel something, a rush of power leaving her, the harsh embrace of the Gray even, but there was nothing.

The sign swung behind her.

She was gone. She was out.

Violet turned her back on Four Paths, stared at the road snaking away from town. She was back in a world without rituals, without founders, without power.

She turned around.

She thought of Harper and Justin and Isaac and May. She'd given them so much trouble, yet each of them somehow decided she was worth fighting for.

It was time to fight for them, too. All of them.

Violet stepped back into the leafy embrace of the great chestnut oaks teeming at the side of the road, reaching out to her in welcome, in recognition. Determination rushed through her, thrumming in her chest like a second heartbeat as the WELCOME TO FOUR PATHS sign swung above her head.

She was going to make things right in this town, once and for all. And she knew where she wanted to start.

The inside of the Diner looked like a battleground. The fluorescent lights were shattered, their plastic casing mixing with ceramic and glass on the shadowy floor. Violet had expected resistance when she tried to walk inside, but the restaurant was gutted, empty.

Empty except for Isaac, who swept debris into a great pile in the corner. Justin had told her that despite the termination of Isaac's employment, he'd insisted on helping. The overturned booths around him looked like the discarded playthings of a giant, the OPEN sign above his head a cruel mockery of the restaurant's current state.

Violet took a second to watch the light streaming in through the cracked plate-glass windows at the front of the Diner, casting fragmented shadows across Isaac's neck and shoulders. He wasn't even trying to hide the scar anymore. She'd noticed it at school, too. She was proud of how little he'd reacted to the stares.

The light hit his face when he turned, casting a perfect diagonal line from his left eyebrow, across his lips, and into the planes of his neck.

"What are you doing here?" Isaac asked.

"Looking for you."

He frowned. "How did you...?"

Violet shrugged. "You're the kind of person who likes cleaning up their messes."

Isaac's lips curved into a wry smile. "Well. I've had a lot of practice."

Behind him, a row of black garbage bags were stacked neatly against the wall. Evidence of many hours spent like this one, making amends.

Violet didn't know the details of Isaac's ritual. But she'd gleaned enough to understand that something horrible had happened to him.

The Beast had broken him the same way it had broken her family. The same way it had broken Harper.

"I've been thinking," she said. "About what we're all really doing here. Why the founders actually locked the Beast up."

"They locked it up because it's dangerous." Isaac's response was rote, automatic.

But Violet could not shake what the Beast had told her in the Gray, the words it had spat out of Rosie's mouth.

Do you really think I was bound here out of altruism? They wanted my power, and they achieved it.

"But, Isaac," she said. "Look at us. We're dangerous, too."

It was the first time she'd ever said his name aloud. She liked the way it sounded in her throat. She liked the way his eyes widened a little bit, like he'd noticed.

Like he'd been listening.

She swallowed, forged onward. "Being new here means I don't know a lot. That ignorance almost got me killed. But it also means that I can look at this from the perspective of an outsider. The holidays, the ceremonies, the patrols. I can see how much this town has hurt us. Our ancestors bound our bloodlines to something awful, and they trapped us here with it. Is that really the life you want?"

Isaac's body had gone very still. "You can leave now, can't you? You're not trapped anymore."

"That doesn't answer my question."

His gaze flickered to the broom in his hand, the overturned booths. "No. That's not what I want."

Violet exhaled slowly. "Good. Because I'm going to find a way to kill that thing in the Gray. The thing inside my head. I could try and do it alone, but I need someone who knows what the Beast is really capable of. That's you."

Again, he dodged her question. "Why not ask Harper?"

Violet smiled ruefully. "Her memories are gone. Justin told me. And I need a second before I can face her again, knowing what I know." She paused. "He loves her, doesn't he?"

The words rang out through the husk of the restaurant, louder than she'd intended. Something awful passed across Isaac's face, and Violet knew she'd been right.

But his expression told her something else, too. Knit together all the things she'd noticed about the way he'd treated Justin. And the knowledge of what he felt, who he felt it for, sent a rush of disappointment roiling through her stomach.

Violet gave herself a moment to acknowledge why she would be upset at all. She let her own unsaid truth bloom, like a budding flower—and then she pushed it away.

She would not let this bother her. She would not consider how much those feelings had informed her decision to approach Isaac at all.

"You want to kill the Beast?" Isaac said hoarsely. "I'm in."

Violet nodded. But the rush of victory she should've felt was muted.

She left the Diner and started down Main Street, following the gravel road until it was just her, gazing up at the reddish-gold leaves hanging above her head.

Harper didn't know where the piece of paper had come from. It tumbled out of her pocket as she shrugged her jacket off in her living room. She knelt down to inspect it as it fluttered down to the floor, like a bird that had left the nest too soon.

When she unfolded it, the words scrawled across it made no sense.

It was a cruel joke. It had to be.

But as Harper moved through the rest of her evening, the words wouldn't leave her head.

They beat through her brain as she tucked Nora into bed and arranged each of her stuffed animals in the perfect position. As she nodded goodnight to a father who she couldn't look in the eye anymore, who didn't remember what he had done to her.

It was only when she stood silently in the bathroom, draped in her lace nightgown, that she allowed herself to mentally unfold that paper.

Do your ritual again.

Harper stared into the mirror. Bandages swathed her neck like a premature Halloween costume. She remembered a story she had read as a child, about a girl who wore a red ribbon around her neck that kept her head in place, and shuddered.

Violet and her mother had told Harper she could stay at the Saunders manor if she wanted, for as long as she liked, but Harper hadn't made up her mind yet.

The Carlisle cottage had always been her home, and she didn't want to leave Brett and Nora to face it alone.

Yet she could not deny that she no longer felt safe there.

She tugged the bandages off and stared at the purpled finger marks that crisscrossed her neck.

Three years ago, she had failed her ritual. The lake had deemed her too weak. The Gray had devoured her whole.

There was no changing that.

Do your ritual again.

An uncontrollable urge rose up in her throat, to shout, to sing, to swing a blade.

Do your ritual again.

Harper opened the bathroom door and padded down the hallway. She hesitated at the doorway to her room, at Mitzi's slack-jawed face illuminated by the moonlight streaming through their window, but the words didn't feel like a joke anymore.

They felt right.

A moment later, she was at the back door.

Harper traversed the slope of shadowy grass in her backyard, her white nightgown shining as she entered the forest. The nights were growing colder, but the rush of chilled air against her skin didn't bother Harper—it just made her feel more alive. Her bare feet made no sound on the fallen leaves, and although she kept her gaze trained on the well-worn path ahead, she could have closed her eyes and walked there just the same.

At the edge of the lake, she stared down at the darkened water, watching as it sucked in the moonlight instead of reflecting it. It wanted to suck her in, too. She could feel the pull of the lapping waves like a lodestone in her heart.

Harper remembered the muddy water closing over her head. Her reddish-brown arm, lost at the bottom of the lake.

She stepped into the water.

Her bare toes sank into silt as wetness spread across the bottom of the nightgown. Crumbled bits of stone scraped the soles of her feet, but she didn't stop, didn't waver. The water was like crushed velvet against her skin, cool and welcoming. Soon the lake had reached her chin. Her hair floated around her head like strands of seaweed.

Harper tilted her head back. Stars circled the moon, bright freckles orbiting a half-shut eye.

She breathed in, closed her eyes, and submerged herself in the water.

There was no light beneath the surface of the lake. The world around Harper felt like a womb, a dark embrace that urged her, improbably, to sink. She pulled her residual limb across her knees and let the current take her, driving her to the bottom of the lake.

Stone scraped across her shoulder, and she tumbled out of her little ball. Her body splayed across the lake's heart as she breathed out in a rush, air bubbles winding invisibly back to the surface.

Her hand reached forward, fingers scrabbling in the earth, until they closed around a single stone.

Her feet embedded themselves in the lake bed. She unwound upward, bit by bit, until she stood at the bottom of the lake. Her hair streamed around her shoulders and her waist, tangling with the lace of her nightgown. For the first time in years, Harper was utterly, completely calm.

She was waiting.

Something loosened in the back of her mind as the lake water rushed and roared around her, pushing open a door she hadn't realized was there.

And Harper remembered. She remembered everything.

Her grip tightened around the stone as she kicked her

legs back through the water. She hit the surface seconds later, sending rippling waves back toward the shore as she gulped a lungful of air.

Harper tilted her head back to the winking moon and sang a long, low note of rage.

A copper crown of leaves was nestled in Justin's hair. Now that the trees had begun to change color, he couldn't seem to return from an early morning run without taking a bit of the forest home with him. He picked them out of his hair as May's voice rang through his bedroom door.

"Come out," she said. "Justin, please. I need to show you something important."

He ignored her. Yes, he'd come home. But it would be a long time before the things she'd said stopped resonating within him.

He wondered if there would ever be a day when he didn't believe them, just a little bit.

There was a twinge of panic in May's voice now. "Our mother's already seen this. You need to look—now."

Justin was curious, despite himself.

But he was tired of protecting May when she'd shown, very clearly, that she didn't care at all about protecting him. He had stopped being that person the moment he turned in his founders' medallion.

May's voice had turned shriller than he'd heard in months; shriller even than it had been in their mother's office. "At least open your window."

Against his better judgment, Justin slid the pane of

frosted glass upward, sending the dark, sprawling form of the hawthorn tree into sharp focus.

And gasped.

Because the hawthorn tree, from root to tip, had turned to red-brown stone.

Petrified branches spiraled from a lifeless trunk. Confused birds perched among frozen leaves that would never float softly to the ground, chirping in low, panicked voices.

And as he stared at the evidence that Harper had gotten his note, that she'd believed him, that she'd listened, Justin couldn't stop himself from grinning.

EPILOGUE

ISAAC SULLIVAN REACHED THE edge of the ruins just before dawn.

They were easy to find. All he had to do was let his muscle memory take over as he left the main road behind, winding through the trees, until he reached the remnants of what had once been his home.

Isaac paused at the place where the grass gave way to a crater of scorched earth. Three years ago, the Sullivan mansion had stood here, tall and proud and full of life.

All that was left now was a crude foundation of charred brick and timber.

As far as Isaac was concerned, it was an improvement.

He took a moment to admire his handiwork, pushing down the impulse to mentally overlay the ruins with the house that had once been there—the stained-glass window above the doorway, the great stone pillars that held up the gables like a pair of hunched shoulders.

Every time he came here, he left remembering less of

the house it had once been and more of the pile of rubble it was now.

It was why Isaac visited so often. It was why he'd destroyed the Sullivan mansion in the first place.

He wanted to forget it.

And because this was where he came to forget things, it was the right place—the perfect place—to get rid of everything that reminded him of Justin Hawthorne.

He had brought the three most important traces of their friendship: *This Side of Paradise*, the only novel he and Justin both enjoyed; a pair of running sneakers Justin had given him, which he'd barely used; and a tiny silver figurine shaped like a tree, which Justin had stolen from the sheriff in a moment of anger and stashed in his apartment.

Isaac destroyed the figurine first; his mind narrowing with concentration until the silver had smoldered into ash. Then he disintegrated the shoes.

He hesitated over the book. Isaac didn't like to hurt books. But when he flipped open the cover and saw Justin's name written inside in his familiar chicken-scratch handwriting, the hurt coursing through him was enough to make his palms turn hot.

His loyalty to Justin had deepened into an inability to put himself first. To say no. For a long time, he'd thought that was love.

He'd been wrong.

But knowing that didn't make it hurt any less.

He raised his hands in the air and let the remnants of

388

the novel trickle to the ground, then dusted them clean.

Through the cloud of soot he'd left behind in the air, a figure stirred on the other side of the crater.

Isaac took in the figure's large hands, made for closing into fists, the tattoos that ran from his wrists to his shoulders, and a face that had only grown sharper and crueler in the years since he had seen it last.

The scar on Isaac's neck began to pulse in time with his heartbeat as Gabriel Sullivan met his eyes.

"Miss me, little brother?" he asked, the words echoing across the ruins, and Isaac knew, for the first time since his fourteenth birthday, what it was to be afraid.

ACKNOWLEDGMENTS

I HAD THE IDEA FOR this book when I was a college student abroad. I'd traveled to Europe hoping to find inspiration, only to realize that I needed to write about the upstate New York woods I'd left behind. I didn't know then that it would change my life. I didn't even know if I could write it. I just knew that I had fallen in love with Violet, Harper, Justin, Isaac, and May, and I had to tell their story.

I'm so glad I did.

But no book is ever created alone, and without all of the following people, *The Devouring Gray* would not be what it is today. To my agent, Kelly Sonnack, thank you for your tireless guidance and wisdom, your thoughtfulness, and your impeccable editorial insight. From the very beginning, you've understood *The Devouring Gray* on a level I'd only dreamed of—and you've understood me, too. I'm so lucky to have you in my corner, and so grateful for all you've done for me and my woods book.

To my editors, Hannah Allaman and Emily Meehan—

thank you for reading my book an uncountable number of times, and for understanding my vision for this duology from the very beginning. You are a total dream team, and I'll forever be honored that you chose to go into the Gray with me. Hannah—thank you for loving these characters just as much as I do, for the Hamilton references, the mutual lack of chill, and the impressively fast e-mail responses.

Thank you as well to the entire team at Hyperion, who've been so supportive through this whole process, especially Mary Ann Naples, Dina Sherman, Holly Nagel, Elke Villa, Andrew Sansone, Guy Cunningham, Patrice Caldwell, Cassie McGinty, Jody Corbett, Meredith Jones, and Tyler Nevins.

Amanda Foody—you came into my life when I was ready to give up on this book and showed me how to save it. You're my first line of defense, the other half of my brain, my greatest champion, and my most honest critic, and sometimes I truly believe you can read my mind. Thank you for always knowing exactly how to help me, for being one of the few people this introvert never needs a break from, for countless late-night epiphanies and brainstorming sessions and eternal inside jokes. I'm in awe of your talent, your work ethic, and your impeccable sense of style, and there's no one else I'd rather have by my side during every step of my publication journey. I don't have words for how much you mean to me, so "best friend" will have to do.

I wouldn't be writing these acknowledgments at all without my incredible critique group, whose feedback, encouragement, and friendship mean the world to me.

Thank you to Kat Cho, Katy Rose Pool, Claribel Ortega, and Joan He, 2019 debuts extraordinaire—I'm honored to have my first book releasing the same year as all of yours. Thank you to Amanda Haas for being the world's best listener and my honorary big sister, Ella Dyson, Janella Angeles, and Erin Bay for your early beta reads, Meg Kohlmann for demanding more romance, Mara Fitzgerald, my dead sea buddy, Axie Oh, Akshaya Raman, Tara Sim, Melody Simpson, Maddy Colis, Ashley Burdin, and Alexis Castellanos. I've learned so much from every single one of you, and I'm so proud to be in the presence of all your collective talent. Best. Cult. Ever.

Rory Power, my tree sister, thanks for the groundbreaking realization that publishing is just Dance Moms for grown-ups. Emily Duncan, my goth queen, thanks for the hours-long character talks and sequel solidarity. Thank you both for letting me burst into your lives like the Kool-Aid Man, for writing two of my favorite books, for seeing the best and worst of me and loving me anyway, for embracing my sharp edges even when I couldn't, and, of course, for dealing with all the possum GIFs. Your writing has changed me for the better—and so has your friendship.

Thank you to Claire Wenzel, undisputed empress of graphic design and out-of-context-quote humor, to Swati Teerdhala and Isabel Sterling, debut sisters and givers of excellent advice, to Deeba Zargarpur and the 6:00 a.m. bus ride that changed my life, to Paige Cober, my fellow murder girl, and to Nicole Deal—your art never fails to make my day. Thank you to Claire Legrand for being a friend and a role model, and never judging me for long, emotional texts. Kati Gardner, I am so grateful for your insight and feedback.

Laura Lashley, Anna Birch, Emily Neal, and Rachel Griffin, thank you for being my lifelines from Pitch Wars 2016 onward. Thank you to Sierra Elmore for all the midnight cat pictures, and for reminding me no book is complete without accompanying memes.

Shelby, Ian, and Sam, thanks for being the kind of friends who are worth coming out of my writer cave for.

Brigid, you're the Kelly to my Holly, and don't you forget it. Thank you for understanding me both on and off the page.

Thank you to my parents, who encouraged me to be a storyteller, who moved all forty boxes of my childhood books around the world for eighteen years. I am so grateful for all of your support. Thank you, Grandma Barbara and Grandpa Mark, who always listened to my stories. Thank you, Nanny and Poppy, who let me write most of the second draft of this book in your dining room while feeding me world-class Italian food.

Nova, you are a cat and therefore you cannot read (as far as I know), but I'm putting you in my acknowledgments anyway. Thanks for walking across my keyboard, biting my toes at 4:00 a.m., and keeping me humble.

Lastly, Trevor—thank you for loving me exactly as I am, for reading many years of first drafts, and for listening to me talk about fictional teenagers for hours on end. You are far too good of a person to ever become one of my book characters.

ABOUT THE AUTHOR

BORN IN NEW YORK CITY but raised in Japan and Hong Kong, Christine Lynn Herman subscribes to the firm philosophy that home is where her books are. She returned to the United States for college, where she traded a subtropical climate for harsh, snowy winters and a degree at the University of Rochester. She resides in Brooklyn, where she works in publishing by day and writes novels by night.